PLAYING *Deep*

BETH BOLDEN

CHAPTER ONE

The beer was warm, generic, and served by a bartender who looked like he moonlighted fighting gators in the swamp.

It might not be the only beer available in Central Florida, but it was the closest bar to the tiny university the Miami Piranhas took over for training camp, and since he technically was not supposed to be off campus, *or* drinking beer the night before their first practice, Kenyon decided it was a good idea not to press his luck with the brand-new coach.

He still didn't know what to make of Asa Dawson—but the man was notorious for not taking anyone's shit.

It seemed prudent not to piss him off on the very first day.

Of course, that hadn't stopped Kenyon from going out.

He'd intended to stay in, and to attempt something resembling good behavior, but that itch had started up under his collar, and even after he'd pulled his shirt off, it had continued.

So he'd snuck out of the dormitory, hopped the fence surrounding the campus, and found this sad little bar tucked down a side street only a few blocks away.

"Imagine finding a guy like you in a place like this."

Kenyon glanced up, sure he'd just been caught.

His face wasn't unknown. He'd been a Heisman finalist his senior year at Stanford, and had been the highest-drafted running back when he'd gone pro the next year. For the last eight years, he'd played in the NFL, the last three for the Piranhas.

He wasn't in the mood for autographs or excited exultations about the upcoming season, but he glanced over anyway.

Glanced over, and then kept looking, because he couldn't look away.

The guy was blond—the kind of blond that couldn't be natural, because a thousand shades of molten gold like that didn't exist in real life, and it was all feathered in a messy bedhead that had to be styled within an inch of its life—with piercing blue-gray eyes that seemed to look right through Kenyon.

He wore jeans, a striped polo shirt, and honest-to-God loafers without socks, all of which made him look like he belonged at a country club, tossing a golf club to a nearby caddy or pushing off from the dock, wind blowing through that ridiculous head of hair.

Kenyon typically had no patience with an entitled jerk like this. He'd seen his share of them during his life, the cocky tilt to his grin screaming that he was better than anybody else, and he'd prove it to you, and you'd enjoy it the whole goddamn time.

Watch out, a voice in the back of Kenyon's head warned, while the itch under his collar, not even remotely satisfied by the mild rebellion of sneaking out and drinking this gross, warm beer, ignored it entirely.

"Uh, hey," Kenyon said. Forgetting entirely what the guy had said.

Not sure it really meant anything, anyway.

The words weren't important.

What was important was that the guy was sliding onto the barstool next to him, that grin growing impossibly cockier.

God, Kenyon wanted to hate him.

But that itch was quickly morphing into an itch of an entirely different kind, the longer he looked into those piercing eyes.

Maybe this guy was a smug asshole, but he was a *hot* smug asshole.

"The point remains," the guy said. "What *are* you doing here?" He glanced around. Kenyon didn't need to follow his eyes to take in the rest of the inhabitants of this sad little bar late on Wednesday night: blue-collar guys wearing worn-out t-shirts, staring mindlessly into their drinks and at the TV screens.

Kenyon picked up his warm beer. Tipped it towards the guy before he took a sip. "I was thirsty," he said.

The guy hadn't flirted. Not explicitly. There was an undeniable glint in those insane eyes, but Kenyon had learned to be careful.

A lot of people—both girls and guys—were interested in making him a notch on their belts. Kenyon, however, was not usually into being a notch. Except for this guy. He'd be a notch for him. Several notches, maybe.

Maybe he'd approached Kenyon because he recognized him, and knew that his sexual preferences weren't exactly a secret.

Or maybe . . .

"What a coincidence," the guy said. "Me too. Especially after I walked in and saw that guy, looking like a real snack." He waved in the general direction of the TV, where LeBron James was trying to sell cell phones. "He's got a real Daddy energy, don't you think?"

"Uh," Kenyon mumbled. He'd actually *met* LeBron, and this guy wasn't entirely wrong, now that he considered the question. "I can see that, actually."

The guy leaned forward, this time waving at the bartender. "I'll have whatever he's having."

"You sure?" Kenyon asked dryly. "I don't want you to be overwhelmed by the awesomeness of this completely mediocre beverage."

The calculated shine of his grin shifted, until it felt a little more real. "If I do, I'm sure you'll save me." The bartender deposited the beer on a stained coaster with a grunt, and took off, probably to lean against the far end of the bar and stare at the Marlins highlights—or lowlights, since it was the Marlins.

The guy took a sip of his beer, and then made a face. "Well, you weren't kidding."

"I try not to do that," Kenyon said. Which was actually true. Now, sarcasm, that was another thing entirely.

"I'm Julian," the guy said. He even had a smug asshole name. Kenyon wasn't the tiniest bit surprised.

"Ellis," Kenyon said.

Julian cocked his head, like he was puzzling something out, but didn't challenge Kenyon's name.

Giving his last name and not his first worked better than he'd ever imagined it would. He'd started doing it right out of college, and it did its job about ninety percent of the time.

Maybe in the morning, Julian would google him, and discover why it was that he'd looked so familiar, but by then Kenyon would be long gone.

"So, you never answered the question," Julian said. "I wasn't expecting to find a guy with a smile like yours in a place like this."

Kenyon shot him a look, not trying very hard to ignore the sparks lighting up his spine. "I didn't smile," he said.

"But," Julian said, "you're smiling now."

He probably was.

"It's kind of a shithole," Kenyon agreed. But the real miracle was that Julian was here. He was a shiny gold doubloon in the midst of a bunch of dirty, grimy pennies.

The thing about it though, was whether it was doubloons or pennies, the money spent the same once you got your hands on it.

And Kenyon intended to get his hands on Julian.

"I'm new in town," Julian said. "Just passing through, really. This was the first bar I saw, so this is the bar I walked into. It's a habit of mine, trying the first thing that I come across."

"Lucky for me." He was also passing through, but Kenyon had no intention of telling Julian who he was or what he was doing here, in this small town. He leaned a little closer. "What about me? Am I the first guy you saw in here?"

"The first guy in here I didn't think would give me rabies." Julian's smile, more real now, was infectious and undeniably charming.

"Thanks, I think?" Kenyon found himself grinning, too.

He'd seen right through the ploy about LeBron—he'd done the same thing a handful of times. Making sure that he wouldn't get punched in the face for flirting with a guy. Julian had been feeling him out.

Though, how Julian hadn't been one hundred and ten percent sure he was interested after Kenyon had been so busy checking him out he'd nearly fallen off his barstool . . . that was a mystery.

"You *should* be grateful," Julian said. There was that ego speaking again. But was it ego if he was right?

Kenyon *was* fucking grateful.

So grateful he'd happily drop to his knees.

"Believe me," Kenyon said, dropping his voice, and using the excuse to lean a bit closer, "I'd be happy to show you just how grateful I am."

Julian's eyes swept up and down him in one agonizing, cock-hardening glance. No man should have eyes or lashes like that—they should be illegal—and what he was doing with them was a real fucking crime.

Of course he knew the effect he was having.

But somehow that didn't ruin the effect, not in the least.

"Right now?" Julian raised an eyebrow.

Kenyon shrugged. They could spend the next hour flirting, and then go to the bathroom. Or they could just do it now. Cut through the red tape. Cut right to the chase.

"Direct." Julian considered this, tilting his head. "I think I like it."

"Oh honey," Kenyon said, "I *know* you do."

"Well, since I don't have anything else to do tonight . . ." Julian picked up his beer and tipped the rest of it down his throat. "Might as well be you."

Kenyon slapped a twenty on the bar.

He'd nearly pulled a hundred out of his wallet, but that would've given him away.

He was supposed to be Ellis tonight. Anonymous, completely touchable Ellis.

"Come on," Kenyon said, sliding off his barstool.

Julian's hips were slender under his jeans—designer, Kenyon recognized as they walked towards the bathrooms in the back—and he wasn't surprised at all to see Julian push open the door of the women's bathroom, not the men's.

There wasn't a single woman at the bar, they wouldn't be needing this bathroom, and besides, as Kenyon's fingers found what he was looking for and flipped it, women's bathrooms usually had this . . . a *lock*.

He leaned against the now locked door and looked at Julian, who was somehow just as hot under the ugly fluorescent lighting as he'd been under the dim, smoky light out in the bar.

Julian acted like he did this all the time, like it was totally normal to pick up a random guy in a bar and fuck him in the bathroom, but when his hand reached out, flipped up his shirt and pressed his palm against Kenyon's chest, he could've sworn his fingers were trembling as they drifted down the bare skin of his stomach.

"When I walked into the bar, I thought you were a mirage," Julian said in a low, sexy growl. "So fucking hot."

"I look real good like this," Kenyon said, and he reached out, took ahold of Julian's wrist, and in a quick movement, reversed their position. Pressed Julian's slim hips against the worn and pitted wood of the door. Let him feel his undeniably hard erection under his shorts. "But I think I look even better now."

He sank to his knees.

Julian groaned, his fingers brushed against Kenyon's scalp, shaved close, and he could feel them still trembling as he reached for Julian's belt. It was worn brown leather, incongruous compared to the rest of the guy's wardrobe, but then it was opening under his touch, and . . . *fuck*, if this cocky hot asshole wasn't wearing anything under his jeans.

His cock was just as gorgeous as the rest of him, slim and perfect and leaking at the tip. And shockingly, the downy hair, trimmed low, around the base of his cock?

It was the exact same blond as on his head. The same blond that he'd been sure had to come from a bottle. But didn't.

Kenyon couldn't help himself, he leaned in and licked.

Above him, Julian shuddered, the back of his head falling against the door, and wasn't he something like this? Kenyon thought he could look at him for a hundred years, but he was only going to get tonight, so he kept his eyes glued to Julian's face as he explored more of that perfect dick with his tongue.

Giving blowjobs always turned him on—there was something gloriously dirty and forbidden about it, something he couldn't get enough of—but nothing had ever turned him on the way blowing Julian did.

Was it because this was even dirtier than normal? Not just because he was on this ugly bar's undeniably gross floor? In the women's bathroom with only a wimpy-ass lock between them and anyone who wanted to come in? Was it because they hadn't even kissed, and he had Julian's cock halfway down his throat and he was groaning about how good it was, and begging for more?

Kenyon slid more of Julian's dick into his mouth, sucking him hard, and felt him tremble with the force of the pleasure.

He could already feel the shadow of Julian's long elegant fingers wrapped around his own dick, giving it to him hard and rough, not giving him a chance to breathe or cry or groan. The antici-patory edge made him breathless, made him suck Julian harder, made him push through the burn in his throat and take his cock even deeper.

"I knew it," Julian moaned as his whole body shuddered, "I just knew you'd be good at this."

It was so goddamned smug. Knowing and smug and maybe Kenyon should've hated it, but it made him impossibly hotter.

He wanted to reduce this man to nothing but come on his tongue, and down his throat.

Slipping a hand between Julian's thighs, he stroked his balls, then worked further back, Julian gasping as he pushed a thumb against his hole.

It wasn't going to happen; all they were going to get were dirty blowjobs in a dirty bathroom, but he thought it anyway. *What if I fucked you here? What if I prepped you so good you cried for it? What if I pinned you down, pinned your hands, wouldn't let you touch yourself until you were begging for it, begging to come? And then you did anyway, because you couldn't help it anymore, because my dick felt too good inside you?*

Kenyon found himself growing harder at just the thought, then with one last hard suck, Julian's eyes grew wide, and his hips stuttered against Kenyon's grip, and then he was coming down his throat, expression incredulous, like he'd been shocked in the best possible way.

Kenyon couldn't remember the last time he'd been this aroused.

He stood slowly, knees creaking, and palmed his dick through his shorts, nearly gasping at the feel of some kind of touch after so long without.

But then Julian was pushing his hand aside, crowding close to him, and reaching down, and *God,* there it was. That grip he'd fantasized about. The way he worked him without mercy. The way he stared right into his eyes, that blue ice cold and never wavering as he wrung every bit of Kenyon's orgasm out of him.

It was the hottest sex Kenyon had ever had.

And he'd had some sex in his life.

It shouldn't have made sense, because nothing about it was special, they hadn't even kissed, for God's sake, but he knew even as they cleaned up that he wouldn't forget this night anytime soon.

Kenyon threw the paper towel in the trash and eyed the door as Julian went to unlock it. "Thanks," he said, his hair still as fucking perfect as it had been ten minutes earlier.

Kenyon resisted the urge to mess it up before they left the bathroom. It was going to be obvious enough what they'd been doing, even if he didn't do that.

But in the little hallway outside the bathroom, Julian put a hand on his arm.

We barely touched each other, Kenyon thought, almost disappointed. *I had his cock in my mouth but I wanted to touch him all over.*

He nearly said so. He nearly decided to hell with everything and offered to sneak Julian onto the college campus. Or to go to wherever Julian was staying.

But then before he could, Julian said, "Well, that was great. Thanks."

It was a dismissal.

Kenyon knew it. Kenyon didn't like it.

But he respected it.

"Alright, yeah," he said. "Guess we got lucky."

There was a glimmer of that real smile again, on Julian's face. "Yeah," he said. "Real lucky."

And then he was gone, heading out the hallway, and by the time Kenyon was back in the bar, the front door was swinging closed against the humid night.

The bartender shot him a lazy look, full of semi-annoyance. Not outrage, just … frustration that he had to bother himself with anything. "You want anything else?" he asked as Kenyon hesitated by the empty row of barstools.

No. He didn't want anything else. He shook his head and headed for the door.

By the time he got outside, he knew what he'd find.

Nothing.

Julian was gone. If he'd ever actually existed. Maybe he'd been a mirage that he'd invented in his own head.

But the itch was gone, scratched fully and completely, and Kenyon told himself as he headed back towards the campus that this was better. That it was good that they hadn't exchanged info, or histories, or preferences or even kisses.

Julian would be so much easier to forget this way.

Except Kenyon had a feeling that wasn't going to be true at all.

You, Julian Anderson told himself as he headed towards the field the Miami Piranhas were currently practicing on, *are in over your head.*

It wouldn't be the first time. Or probably the last time.

He was ambitious, and people who were ambitious generally got themselves into situations where they might definitely sink a bit.

But Julian didn't sink. He always swam.

You're gonna swim today.

Sure, he didn't know much about this team he was now suddenly covering, as of twenty-four hours ago, but he'd learn. And sure, he was new in town. And sure, he was still kinda thinking about that guy from last night, with his formidable biceps and his sweet, dirty smile, but he'd move on.

Julian always learned. And he always moved on.

He'd discovered, the hardest way possible, that these were the two things he was best at.

The small college that the Piranhas took over for every summer's training camp was exactly as described: as in, it was *small.* His boss, Nikki, had mentioned that, but he was unprepared for how close everything was. The bar from last night was only a few blocks from the campus, which was only a block away from his hotel.

It also meant that when Julian walked down the stairs towards the practice field, ready to observe the first day of practice, he was close enough to see a number of players.

Didn't recognize any of them, but that wasn't a surprise.

He'd only had twenty-four hours' notice. No time to memorize the roster, yet.

Before six AM yesterday, he'd been planning to spend the year as the assistant to the local reporter for the San Francisco 49ers. He'd been settled into the Bay Area, and now, the pathetically miniscule contents of his apartment were currently being packed up at his boss' expense, so he could be here for opening day.

"Walter is being annoying," Nikki had informed him. "He thinks the Piranhas are insane, so he's decided this is as good a year as any to quit-slash-retire. But let's be honest. He's fucking quitting."

"Because they hired Asa Dawson? The man's won multiple national championships." Julian might not have planned to cover the Piranhas this year, but he wasn't stupid. Ambitious men listened. And Miami hiring Dawson had been major news—but that had been months ago. Surely Walter wasn't just now deciding that Dawson was going to go down in a fiery ball of failure.

"You didn't hear, then." Nikki sounded satisfied. She wasn't a bad boss, but she always liked to be the first to hear everything, and Julian rarely bothered to pretend cluelessness as a sop to her ego.

Probably because he had a healthy ego of his own.

"Dawson hired Davis Abernathy as the new quarterbacks coach," Nikki continued. "How's that for a fucking bombshell?"

Personally, Julian didn't think it was all that bombshell-worthy. It was just smart business. Davis Abernathy was a good quarterback who'd been steamrolled out of Charleston, but still had plenty to offer.

"And that's what has Walter's panties in a twist? *Really*?"

"You know Walter," Nikki had said. And he *did*. "He's an ancient white misogynist. He probably thinks Tom Taylor's innocent."

"Probably." Julian didn't bother to hide his disgust. Everyone knew Tom Taylor was guilty as fucking sin.

"Anyway, he quit in a big show of . . . I don't know what, even. Assholery? Solidarity for abusers everywhere? Flaming, fucking stupidity? But it doesn't matter why," Nikki had said, tone turning from annoyed to businesslike in a second. "Because now you gotta get your cute ass to Florida."

He hadn't quite been able to believe Nikki had given him the Piranhas job, but he saw it for what it was: a test.

Nikki was shrewd. It made a hell of a lot of sense to replace the mothballed Walter with young blood. She knew he'd work hard. Harder than anyone else, because nobody had more to prove than Julian.

Maybe he should have resented that Nikki had no issue using both the chip on his shoulder *and* his ambition to hire the hardest worker in the room. But he didn't, because it had still gotten him this job—and a much-needed raise, too.

There were a few sets of old rickety bleachers from when the college here had still had a football team, and they were full of fans. But there was a newer, smaller set, still shiny metal, behind a fence, a sign attached to the chain link that proclaimed "Media."

He sauntered over, pulling his credentials from his back pocket.

Not every practice was open to the media and to the Piranhas' fan base, but this was the first one, and clearly nobody wanted to miss out, because it was packed.

Julian took a seat in the front row, at the end, because he'd been *that guy* in school, and nothing had changed.

He slung his backpack down by his feet and pulled out his tablet, setting it up on his knees.

"Hey."

Julian glanced up. A guy, mid-to-late forties maybe, with a comb-over and a slight beer belly, but a nice smile, was staring right at him.

"You're new," he said.

"Correct," Julian said. He wasn't here to make friends, and nearly turned back to his tablet—but then he rethought his cold shoulder. He *was* new here and he could use all the help he could get.

"Name's Ed," the guy said, and he stuck his hand out. Julian shook it quickly. He had a good, firm grip, which Julian matched instinctively.

"Julian," he said.

"You're not local, either," Ed observed.

"Nope. From all over, really, but I work for the national side of CBS Sports."

"I'm from one of the Miami papers, but I've been covering this team for twenty years," Ed said. "Never seen so much press here, not even after O'Connor came out."

He said it so matter-of-factly Julian relaxed another fraction. This wasn't going to be another Walter.

"Assuming the big draw must be Dawson," Julian said.

Ed shaded his eyes as Asa Dawson jogged onto the field, followed closely by his son, Beau. "Partly, yeah. He's shaking things up."

Julian had spent yesterday's flight to Jacksonville trying to read everything he could get his hands on about Dawson—both the elder and the younger—and it was clear that he wasn't going to be the typical NFL head coach.

Which was either going to go really fucking great, or it was going to be, as Nikki would put it, a hot garbage mess.

Julian didn't think there was much room in the middle for this particular experiment.

"You think things could use some shaking up?"

"After O'Connor retired and they won two games last season?" Ed raised a mostly gray eyebrow. "Better than the alternative. Rudy wants a team that makes money. That means a team that wins at least half their games, and goes to the playoffs. He's going to spend some money to get there." Ed shot him a sideways glance. "What do you think about Dawson not trading Kelly?"

It was a test.

Julian had been facing them—and passing them—long enough to recognize Ed's question for what it really was.

"Paxton Kelly?" He was the quarterback the Piranhas had drafted the year before to replace Colin O'Connor after he'd retired. And while yeah, the Piranhas had only won two games with him under center, everything Julian had seen and read had left him with one impression: it wasn't Paxton's fault.

"I think Pax is gonna get to repeat his rookie year with a coaching staff that actually gives a shit about his development," Julian said.

Ed nodded slowly. "You think Abernathy can teach Pax to be a decent QB?"

"Why not?" Julian retorted. "Why not him?"

"Huh. I thought I was only one of a few who thought Abernathy wasn't trash."

Julian knew people thought it. He'd heard it plenty even in San Francisco.

"Here they come," Ed said, and began snapping some photos with his camera.

Julian glanced out at the field, and nearly dropped his phone, which he was trying to set up to get a good video with.

Because right there, less than twenty feet away, was the guy from last night. And he was wearing a jersey and carrying a helmet, and *wow*, Julian rarely felt stupid but he felt stupid right now because he recognized that name. Hadn't recognized the face—or the rest of him—but the name was familiar.

Kenyon Ellis.

He was the Piranhas' starting running back.

Fucking hell.

"Ellis looks good," Ed said, clicking away, and that was when Julian *did* drop his phone, because hadn't he had that exact same thought, half a dozen times last night and a dozen more this morning?

Of course, Ed was thinking about Kenyon looking good in an entirely different context than Julian had.

Than Julian *did*.

Because he was just as hot today, with the mid-morning sun shining on him, his white practice jersey stretched across his chest, his name emblazoned on the back.

The jerk had said his name was *Ellis*.

Julian supposed, at the very least, he hadn't lied to him.

His name *was* Ellis.

It just wasn't his first name.

Really, did it matter? So they'd hooked up. And maybe Julian had thought about it this morning. Maybe he'd had trouble *not* thinking about it, but it was still just a hookup.

It wasn't like he hadn't had plenty of those.

Kenyon too. They'd been on the exact same goddamned page.

Julian was just reassuring himself of that very fact, ducking his head down to retrieve his phone, when Ed said, with a wry chuckle, "Thought you said you were new here, Julian."

"I am," Julian said, scrambling in a very unprofessional way to find where his phone had gone.

"Funny, Kenyon's looking over here like he knows you."

"Funny," Julian echoed, panic streaking through him. His fingers finally closed over the offending item, and he lifted it up, reminding himself of one thing: *nobody ever rattles you, you aren't a cage that shakes that easily.*

"Maybe I remind him of someone else."

Ed glanced at him dubiously. "Son, I sincerely doubt that's true."

Okay, it wasn't like Julian didn't know he was memorable looking. He knew. He looked in the mirror every day, didn't he? And he'd been told more times than he could count, that it would be so much easier for him to make it to TV because he was good looking.

That shouldn't have mattered, but of course it did.

Julian risked a glance in Kenyon's direction. Yep, he was definitely looking his way. Not just looking but *glaring*.

Well, Julian couldn't say he was all that surprised.

The sports media wasn't supposed to be the enemy, but somehow that was always what they got painted as. No doubt Kenyon now believed that he'd approached him because he'd recognized him, and suggested the hookup as a way to weasel some supersecret info out of him.

What could Julian say?

Sorry?

I didn't recognize you because I'm so new here, I didn't even know I'd be covering you when I went to bed the night before?

Would that even fix it? He didn't know. Not with the way Kenyon was currently glaring at him.

"He looks mighty pissed," Ed observed. "What on earth did you do to piss off Ellis?"

"Existed," Julian said flatly.

He didn't flinch, even when it felt like Kenyon's glare might actually melt a strip off his face.

He'd done absolutely nothing wrong, though there was little chance of Kenyon believing that. Still, he wasn't going to apologize, because what the fuck would he even apologize for? Not recognizing Kenyon on sight? The guy hadn't even given Julian his real name. So *no*. He was not going to be cowed or shamed or forced into an apology he didn't mean, all because he just hadn't known who Kenyon was.

Finally, Kenyon turned away and joined where the rest of the team was clustered around Coach Dawson, but Julian wasn't stupid enough to think that whatever had passed between them was over. There'd been an undeniable promise in those dark eyes; a vow that at some point, no matter how much Julian tried to avoid him, they'd be having a real reckoning over what had happened.

Wasn't that going to be a fucking joy?

At least, Julian thought, trying to find the silver lining, he'd gotten a really good orgasm out of it.

Chapter Two

Kenyon didn't have much of a temper.

Not that he couldn't get into a good snit, he *could*. He just usually didn't.

But he was pissed as hell right now.

Because sitting right there, on the bleachers conspicuously labeled "Media" with a goddamned press badge around his neck, was Julian.

There was zero chance he could possibly mistake him for anyone else. Julian was just way too distinctive, that blond hair waving in the breeze like he was carrying a freaking wind machine around with him. And those blue eyes, which had seemed hot and wild the night before, looked like ice-cold chips in his handsome face.

Even though he didn't employ the glare often, people usually quailed when confronted with it. Kenyon knew it could sting. But Julian? He just shrugged it off and stared right back, totally unconcerned. Totally unapologetic.

That not only pissed Kenyon off even more, it convinced him that Julian must've known who he was.

Why else approach?

Why else seem so unembarrassed by the entire thing?

Kenyon ground his teeth together.

"You look pissy," Logan said, squirting Gatorade down his throat.

"It's a thousand fucking degrees out here, with humidity levels that rival the sun," Kenyon said. It *was* hot. There was no denying that.

"Yeah," Logan said sympathetically. "I saw Rob trot over about an hour ago and barf on the sideline."

"That's disgusting," Kenyon said.

Not really surprising, but absolutely disgusting.

"Not the first or last time someone's gonna chuck on a football field," Logan said cheerily, patting his stomach. "But me? I'm solid, man. I'm in the best shape of my life."

He looked it too, like a surprisingly agile mountain.

Kenyon had met Logan for the first time this morning, but even with only a handful of sentences exchanged, he already liked the guy. Which was the one positive so far today, because it was definitely in his best interest to get on the offensive line's good side; he'd learned *that* the hard way. His rookie season, right after he'd been drafted by Atlanta, he'd made a stupidly snide comment in a press conference about the line's blocking ability, and for the rest of the season they'd given him the cold shoulder.

He'd learned that year that there was nothing more precious in football than loyalty.

You could only earn it, you couldn't buy it.

Which, Kenyon thought, glancing over at where Julian was still sitting on the media bleachers, was something *he* would find out about real quick.

Practice ended, and after Pax called him over so they could work on a few extra reps, making sure their handoff was looking strong, was as seamless as it could be, and then when Pax finally said he was done for the day, Kenyon picked up his water bottle and headed in the direction he'd been dying to go all morning.

Not because he was still thinking of Julian laid out against the dirty bathroom door last night, the rapture on his face, the sound of his groan as he'd tipped over into orgasm, the way he'd trembled, just a little, like the only time he was vulnerable was at that single moment. Nope, he wasn't thinking about that at all.

Or the way that Julian's hair was even brighter in the sun, or his eyes even colder.

Nope, no way.

The guy was an asshole, just as much of an asshole as Kenyon had assumed from the beginning he might be, and nothing much was going to change his mind on that.

"Hey," he called over, as Julian packed up his bag. The rest of the players were over on the other side of the field, signing autographs, tossing over practice jerseys, kissing babies, the usual fan bullshit, but Kenyon, he could do that anytime.

This couldn't wait.

Julian stood slowly, and didn't flinch when he looked up at Kenyon.

Like he'd known he was coming and he was completely immune to Kenyon's anger.

Maybe he was.

He wasn't immune to you last night.

Kenyon pushed that thought far, far away.

"What the hell," Kenyon said in a low, furious voice.

Julian barely blinked as he picked up his bag and started walking towards the exit. "What?" he said. Like he had no idea why Kenyon might be angry.

"What?" Kenyon barked, following him. "*What*? Are you really gonna pretend that you didn't come up to me last night because you knew who I was?"

But Julian just shrugged, and kept walking. They were almost to the stairs now. "You're gonna believe what you want to believe, so I don't understand why it matters what I say."

"Of course it matters," Kenyon felt his temper ratcheting up another few degrees. "You picked me up last night *on purpose*."

Julian shot him an incredulous look and kept on walking.

Kenyon didn't even think about what it looked like that he kept chasing him.

"I wasn't the one trying to obscure who he was, *Ellis*," Julian said reproachfully.

"Yeah, I can't imagine why I don't tell people the truth," Kenyon said, pushing away the spike of guilt he felt. Because he *had* given Julian the wrong name—well, sort of the wrong name—and he hadn't told him who he was. That was the problem with being a rich and famous person. Everyone always wanted a piece of you, and sometimes, *sometimes*, Kenyon wasn't interested in giving those away.

They were almost at the top of the stairs now. Kenyon was resolutely ignoring the interested looks the clusters of fans they passed kept shooting them. He was used to it, because he was still in his jersey, and even if they didn't recognize him by sight, they could easily read the name on the back.

But deep down, he knew the truth: everyone was looking at Julian because he looked like Julian.

"Come on," Kenyon said abruptly.

"What? Why?"

"Because I don't want to have this conversation with everyone watching us," Kenyon said between clenched teeth.

"A conversation? Is that what we were doing? I thought you were just yelling at me," Julian said mildly.

Kenyon rolled his eyes. "You got something to say, too? Then, come on," he said, this time more insistently.

Surely they could find an empty room with a door that would lock.

Not because they were about to repeat what had happened the night before. *Nope.* Only because he needed Julian to stop walking away from him, and just *listen*.

Julian hesitated, but then, sure enough, he followed when Kenyon gestured towards one of the buildings that he was pretty sure would be empty right now.

It didn't take them more than a minute to reach it, and another for Kenyon to find a dark classroom and duck in, locking the door behind them.

"This is more for me than for you," Kenyon said, gesturing at the locked door.

"Oh?"

Kenyon rolled his eyes. "The last thing I want to have to explain to my brand-new coach is that I somehow ended up hooking up with a reporter last night. Now, *you*, you might actually get promoted."

"Actually, I did get promoted," Julian said steadily, hopping up on the bare desk at the front of the room. "And not for letting you give me a blowjob."

"You're really going to say you didn't know who I was?" Kenyon challenged. "You came up to *me*. Knew I'd be interested."

Julian shrugged. "Did you see the other guys in that bar? I'd get punched or worse."

He probably would have, because Kenyon *had* seen those other guys in the bar.

That begged another question: *Did that ever happen to Julian before this? Did he ever hit on the wrong guy? Almost get punched? Actually get punched?*

Kenyon felt a flare of temper that had nothing to do with Julian possibly tricking or trapping him, and everything to do with all the homophobic assholes in the world.

The biggest problem with that was now he wasn't angry *at* Julian but on his behalf, the red clearing from his brain, like cold water had just been dashed all over it, he saw right through Julian's nonchalance. Right through all his many defense mechanisms.

He walked up the aisle between the empty desks and stopped right in front of Julian's swinging legs. All he wanted was the truth. Not to argue. Not to fight. Just the truth. However it shook out.

"You really didn't know who I was, did you?"

Julian shot him a look. "I *told* you, you're going to believe what you want to believe."

"I want to believe," Kenyon said, his voice a little unsteady, "whatever the truth is. That's all. I promise."

"What if the truth isn't what you want to hear?" Julian angled his head, licked his lips. He was trying to be flirty again. Tough. Put those walls back up between them. Kenyon could see his technique now, easy as breathing.

The thing was, Kenyon could never hate Julian flirting with him. Even if it was because he was trying to deflect from the truth.

He pressed a palm right into Julian's chest, felt the firmness of his pectoral muscles. He was slim, but he was strong. What would he look like naked?

Gorgeous, that's what he'd look like.

Kenyon kept trying not to think about it, but instead, it was all he could think about, the possibilities fogging up his brain, obscuring every bit of good sense he had.

"Fine," Julian said with a resigned sigh. Like he was finally giving in. "Fine. Okay. I didn't know who you were."

Kenyon curled his fingers into the cotton of Julian's polo. This one was baby blue with a tiny white and red stripe through it. The man looked like the hottest goddamn American flag that he'd ever seen.

It *should* have been such an asshole move, like he was the guy who mounted a flag on the back of his giant truck, or hung one from the tallest mast of his fucking sailboat, and Kenyon should've been desperate to steer clear. But that wasn't Julian. He knew it wasn't. He could see just a flash, just a glimpse of the guy behind the polo. Behind the act. So, instead, he took another step closer. Until he felt the warmth of Julian's thighs through the thin fabric of his shorts.

"Thank you," Kenyon said. "I think we both deserved the truth, didn't we? It was . . ." He hesitated.

There was another crack in Julian's armor. A genuine smile, flashed quickly, Kenyon barely getting the impact of it before it was gone. "The best thing that could've happened and also the worst?"

"I think," Kenyon said, dipping his head, so tempted to just end this ridiculous standoff by kissing Julian so thoroughly he always smiled at him that way, "we should just focus on the best part."

Julian shot him an unimpressed look, clearly trying to pretend he wasn't affected by Kenyon's nearness, but Kenyon could feel the faintest tremor in his chest, just like he'd trembled last night and there was no denying it now. Kenyon wanted him to give in. Wanted to feel him shake when all that self-possession and self-control fell and the orgasm overtook him.

"It would be a terrible idea to do it again," Julian said. There was a look in his eyes, though, that said he wouldn't exactly mind it.

Kenyon knew it was a bad idea to repeat their initial mistake. But they'd done it last night, hadn't they, and the world hadn't stopped revolving. Coach hadn't found out. Julian's boss hadn't discovered any deep, dark, dirty secrets about him.

"You know what I think?" Kenyon asked.

"What?" He was still pretending. Kenyon could feel it, and wanted nothing more than to strip Julian down to the bare essentials, so he could see the real man behind the act.

"I think you want me." He stripped off the practice jersey. Tossed it on the floor. Then reached over and tugged Julian's polo out of his jeans.

Julian didn't stop him. Just kept looking at him with those inscrutable eyes.

Like they could see right through him, see down to every single thing he kept close, every single thing he hid from the world.

It was all laid bare before Julian.

"I think you," Julian said in a soft, damning voice, "want *me*."

Before Kenyon could correct him—or stop him—he'd jumped down from the desk to the floor in front of him, and he was tugging his shorts down.

For a split second, Kenyon froze. He'd just *practiced*, for God's sake, shouldn't he stop him? Apologize, maybe? But then, *fuck*, Julian nuzzled right next to his undeniably hard cock, and Kenyon's pulse throbbed. And *fuck*, he liked it.

"I've been thinking of the way you smelled, all night and all morning," Julian murmured. Then he was licking up his dick, like it was his favorite kind of lollipop, and Kenyon stumbled back, bracing himself against the edge of the desk, shocked at the sudden wet heat of Julian's mouth as he enveloped him.

It shouldn't have surprised Kenyon, but the man knew how to suck a cock.

It didn't even piss him off, as Julian took him down expertly, circling the head with his tongue, making Kenyon's entire brain stutter. He was just ridiculously grateful for however he'd learned how to do it like this.

He'd definitely been thinking about this too, because the moment the anger had evaporated out of him, leaving just heat and adrenaline behind. He was already on the edge. Or maybe it was the insanely good suction of Julian's mouth. The way he kept leaning into it like he couldn't wait to take more.

"Wait," Kenyon said, his mouth still trying to catch up with his thoughts. "I don't . . ."

Julian pulled off, *his* mouth red and wet and swollen, and *goddamn*, it was a privilege to see him like this. Kenyon almost regretted stopping him—*almost.*

His eyes were hotter now, an unspoken question in them.

"I don't want you to do this unless you want to," Kenyon said stupidly. "Not just . . . 'cause you want to prove yourself or something. I want you . . . I want you to want it, too."

It had suddenly seemed terrible if he was just doing it—giving Kenyon this crazy, insane, unbelievable blowjob just to be right . . . or wrong . . . or something.

There was no denying it. Julian's eyes softened. Shining with the emotion Kenyon wanted to see more than anything else.

"Don't worry about me," Julian said, shifting in place, and then Kenyon realized he was hard as a rock in his jeans, and then Julian tucked his hand under his waistband, the bliss on his face unmistakable. Doing this turned him on. Just as much as it had turned Kenyon on last night.

Now he was the one trembling. Insatiable and trembling.

"Okay, I won't," he muttered, his words trailing off in a groan as Julian sucked him down again, keeping up that expert suction as his hand reached up and cupped his balls.

Kenyon liked to pride himself on his self-control, but it was only thirty seconds later that he was coming down Julian's throat as it swallowed convulsively around him, sucking the last bit of come out of him.

"Goddamn," Kenyon ground out as Julian fell back on his heels, shoving his hand down his pants, face a mask of rapture as he shuddered through his own orgasm.

For a minute, Julian didn't utter a single word. Just stared at him.

Don't say what I think you're going to say.

They hadn't even kissed, which normally was fine with Kenyon. Kissing was . . . well, he hadn't ever thought it was particularly convoluted, but everything with Julian was both as easy as pie, and also complicated as hell.

"That was unexpected," Julian said. He got to his feet. Unsteady, still, but he took the tissues that Kenyon had found in a drawer, and shoved in his hand, cleaning up as best he could. He hesitated. And Kenyon realized he had more he wanted to say, but wasn't sure he should. "I wanted it to happen again," he added, in such a soft voice, Kenyon wasn't quite sure he'd meant him to hear. "Just didn't know how it *could*."

"Me too," Kenyon admitted.

"I really didn't know who you were," Julian said, straight out. It was clearly the truth. Kenyon could see the honesty shining in his eyes, his walls, for once, transparent. "I got promoted like . . . what, forty-eight hours ago? The guy before me left because he thinks your new coach is fucking crazy, so I got sent here."

"He is a little fucking crazy," Kenyon admitted.

Julian laughed. A real laugh. He could recognize them now, and he *loved* them.

"This is really inconvenient," Kenyon said. They'd had sex twice in less than twenty-four hours. It seemed impossible to think it wouldn't happen again, especially if they spent an entire season in close proximity to each other.

He knew himself well enough to know the lengths he'd go to make sure that it did, and maybe in an actual bed next time. He wanted to hear if Julian cried out when he bent him over and fucked him. He wanted to see what he looked like when Kenyon pinned him down and rode him hard.

"Oh, a little, but . . . we could figure it out," Julian said. "It could be . . . just sex, right? And if we're just fucking, it's not like I'm gonna uncover any of your deep, dark secrets. If I'm gonna use you, it's gonna be in bed."

"You're saying you just want to fuck," Kenyon said. "That's all you want."

He wasn't sure that was all either of them wanted, but what else could they have?

Every other option seemed worse.

Julian shot him another one of those unimpressed looks, and damn, if that wasn't almost as much of a turn-on as how good his mouth had felt on his cock.

"That is exactly what I'm saying, *Ellis,*" Julian said. Teasing. A look in his eyes that would've normally gotten Kenyon hard in a moment, but how could he when Julian had already given him such a fucking amazing orgasm less than five minutes before?

"You can call me Kenyon, you know," Kenyon pointed out dryly. He was also totally, one hundred percent capable of being a pain in the ass, too. Julian didn't have that market exclusively cornered.

"But I like calling you Ellis," Julian said. He tossed the wad of tissues into the trash, and picked up his bag.

It wasn't like Kenyon didn't have a few hookups he called up when he wanted sex.

He did.

But none of them had ever felt as . . . *easy,* as it did with Julian.

He was the last person who should have felt easy, but it was undeniable that it did.

Was that weird?

Did he even like that?

He wasn't sure, but he had a feeling this was what Julian was offering because this was the only option available.

"You've got this apprehensive look on your face, like you're worried I'm gonna get all damsel in distress and cry about you someday," Julian said, and it was surprising, that Julian could be kind, but he *was*. He could be generous, and it shouldn't have taken Kenyon by surprise, but it did.

He reached up and smoothed out the frown between his brows. "Don't worry," he continued, "that's not gonna happen. I'm painfully pragmatic. I'm also here to do a job. Sex with you is just an extra bonus, some good stress relief, you know? I'm sure you've got people you call for that, during the season."

He did.

He definitely shouldn't have been annoyed that Julian had him pegged like that.

But he was.

Julian pulled his phone out of his bag and handed it to him. "Put your number in," he said, and then made a face when Kenyon hesitated. "For *hookups*," he clarified with a roll of his eyes. "Just for hookups, alright. Unless you want to try to deploy smoke signals across Miami, for God's sake."

"Right, right," Kenyon said. He should be better at this. It wasn't like he hadn't done this before. He *had*.

He put his number in and labeled it Ellis. Not that that would probably fool anyone, but it couldn't hurt, right?

Plus, maybe it would make Julian smile like that every time he saw it.

That couldn't hurt, either.

Chapter Three

November

Julian's phone beeped again. The sound was impersonal. It couldn't possibly seem insistent, but he heard noise's perseverance, anyway. Even if nobody else could. But he couldn't look at the notification, no matter how much he wanted to, because his arm was currently holding his boss up.

He wasn't precisely sober either, but he was definitely a hell of a lot more sober than she was.

"It's so good to have you back here, where you belong," Nikki half said, half slurred, her arm slung around him as they walked down the sidewalk towards Julian's hotel. They'd agreed she'd catch an Uber there, to take her home.

"Oh, this is where I belong, huh?" Julian teased. But he didn't really believe it. Not anymore.

It had been fun, for sure to take advantage of the Piranhas' bye week, to come back to California, to visit the office in person, to hang out with Nikki, but if he was being completely totally honest with himself—something he actively tried not to do when he was sober—there was some things he missed about Miami already.

Okay. *Someone* he missed in Miami.

Not the person, really, because of course he couldn't miss Kenyon. They weren't dating. They weren't involved. They weren't crazy, madly in love. Nothing like that. They were just . . . well, they spent a lot of time together now.

In bed, yes. But also in supply closets and the back seat of cars, and once, memorably in a whirlpool tub in Kenyon's hotel room the night before a game.

The sex was so good. That was definitely what he was missing.

Not the man.

No way.

But then, if Nikki would freaking stop leaning on him so much, maybe he could check his phone and see if it was really Kenyon who was texting him.

Maybe he was feeling it too.

Julian hoped so.

Normally, he'd cut that thought off hard and fast, because he knew it wasn't like that between them, it was just sex.

But he'd had more than a few drinks tonight, and he felt loose and exposed and it was a hell of a lot tougher to lie to himself right now.

"You think you belong anywhere else?" Nikki sounded surprised. "I thought you kinda hated Miami."

He'd bitched, sure, when he'd first been sent there, but mostly because he thought Nikki expected it. But he hadn't hated it, not during that first whirlwind of trying to figure out his new job and then there was the absolutely fantastic sex he kept having with Kenyon.

Really, Miami wasn't so bad. Not really. Especially once the Piranhas had started winning. And then there was Kenyon.

Wasn't that the frustrating punctuation to that thought: *and then there was Kenyon.*

"Oh, Miami's fine," Julian said. He didn't say why, because he wasn't stupid.

Was it still sneaking around if you were still doing it five months later? If you were doing it all the time? Julian wasn't sure.

Rather, *sober* Julian wasn't sure.

Tipsy Julian felt like he was moments away from just propping Nikki up against the next convenient vertical surface and yanking his phone out of his pocket.

But he didn't, because Nikki wasn't nearly drunk enough to forget being ditched, and she was still his boss.

She could still move him around, make him go someplace else, even though she'd just told him tonight, her effusiveness bolstered by several vodka cranberries, how good of work he was doing.

"Are we at your hotel yet?" Nikki complained. "My feet are killing me."

"Don't you dare take your shoes off, that's gross," Julian retorted. He dragged her a little closer and pulled her along faster.

The sooner they got to the hotel, the sooner he could shove her into an Uber and look at his goddamn phone.

Just as he thought it, it chimed again.

Julian lost the fight with himself. He pushed her lightly against a light pole. "Here," he said, "hold that up for a minute."

"Why?" Nikki looked at him, utterly confused, but did it anyway.

Julian yanked his phone out of his pocket.

You around? was the first text from Kenyon.

Of course you aren't, the second one read, sent less than a minute after the first, **you went to LA.**

Which sucks, the third read. **By the way. I'm horny.**

And, the fourth said, **I bet you are too. You're insatiable. I love it.**

I miss you too, Julian thought before he could yank the thought back.

His fingers shook as he typed out. **Give me ten minutes.**

But Kenyon didn't answer in words.

Instead, he sent a picture.

Kenyon naked was a fucking work of art. All those rippling golden-brown muscles. Julian was intimately familiar now with how they flexed and how they tensed and how he trembled when Julian pulled an orgasm out of him a tantalizing little bit at a time.

In the picture, Kenyon had a hand around his dick, and it was hard, and the most infuriating smirk on his face that said one thing: *I have what you want, and I can't wait to give it to you.*

And *oh God,* Julian wanted it.

He wanted him.

"What are you grinning at your phone about?" Nikki demanded, dashing cold water all over his head.

What would she do if she found out who it was making him smile like this? Making him want like this?

She would kill him. Slowly. But first, she'd force him to sell Kenyon out, to stab him so badly in the back Kenyon would never forgive him.

Julian wouldn't do it.

He just wouldn't.

He hoped it would never come to that.

"Nothing," Julian said, shoving his phone back into his pocket. "Come on, let's get you home, okay?"

"Okay," she said, pouting, sticking her tongue out at him as he collected her from the lamppost.

It took only a few minutes before they blessedly entered the hotel lobby. He set her down on the little couch in the lobby, pulled her phone out of her purse, got her an Uber, and five minutes later, Julian was in the elevator heading up to his room.

Trembling, he knew, with anticipation and excitement.

Sure, they'd fucked plenty of times in person.

Enough times, really, that he shouldn't be so excited about the possibility of having phone sex with Kenyon, but it was *Kenyon*, and everything about him excited Julian.

It was a blessing, and also, most definitely, a curse.

He dropped his key card three times before finally managing to successfully shove it in the lock, and tossed it on the dresser as he passed by on the way to the bed. First he pulled out his phone. Propped it up on a pillow, and set it to record.

Took a nice slow video of him peeling every layer of clothing off.

It was meant to turn Kenyon on. He knew what he liked. Knew that he liked the teasing more than he'd admit to. But it ended up working a little too well on *him*, and by the time he was naked, he was breathless and struggling really hard not to just close a fist around his dick and send himself into the stratosphere.

But Pre-Kenyon Julian was used to not indulging in every whim and want he had, and had notoriously rock-solid self-control, so he managed to hit send. Then he lay down to wait. Sure enough, as predicted, less than a minute later, Kenyon called him.

"You're a fucking tease," Kenyon said, after Julian fumbled to put him on speaker. "You know that?"

"I know it." Julian knew how smug he sounded. So *sure*. "You know what else I know? You freaking love it."

Kenyon made a rumbling sound of approval. Something between a groan and an agreement.

He'd heard that sound a hundred times by now, but hearing it never got old.

"What else do I love?" Kenyon asked.

Julian's heart stuttered.

Me, it screamed, before Julian shut that thought down hard.

They didn't love each other. *They didn't love each other.*

He'd been the one to make this choice, and it was the right call. He'd known it then, back this summer, and he knew it now.

The booze was just making the line extra super-duper blurred right now.

He knew where it was. Normally, anyway.

"I know you love it when I suck your cock," Julian crooned seductively, and he heard Kenyon's breath catch in the back of his throat. "You touching yourself?"

"Can't stop." Kenyon's voice was a rasp along the line. Julian could close his eyes and imagine him bending down low, murmuring in his ear. "Not when I think about you."

Julian trailed a hand down his chest, and finally let his fingertips brush the back of his cock, hissing as the pleasure spiked through him.

"I can't stop either," Julian murmured, in a low voice. Heard the vulnerability in it. Because he knew it would be better to stop.

They were toeing the line. He could feel it. But they kept going, anyway. Because they *couldn't* stop.

He couldn't stop now, either.

He leaned into the bed, listening to his own groans mingle with Kenyon's.

"God," he choked out, as he stroked himself, "I wish you were here."

"If I was, what would I be doing?" Kenyon's voice got sterner. And oh *God*, that was hot. Julian shuddered. "Tell me. Use your words."

"You'd be fucking me. With your fingers first." Julian gasped as he twisted his wrist adding a hint of pain to the pleasure. "Slow. Then fast, hard, until I can't handle it any longer." Julian's voice cracked. "Until I'm begging you for your dick."

This time it wasn't just Julian who groaned but Kenyon, too, like the idea of pleasuring Julian, of making him feel good, was enough to push him over the edge.

"God, I wanna give it to you." Julian hadn't ever heard Kenyon's voice so deep. So desperate. "Touch yourself."

"Trust me," Julian half laughed, half sobbed, "I *am*."

"No, no. Wet your fingers. Slide them in your mouth. Real slow for me."

Julian couldn't help but obey. He moaned around them. Imagined they were thicker. Harder. Tasted just like Kenyon.

"They real wet for me?" Kenyon crooned.

Julian made a garbled noise. It felt like coherent words were way beyond his capabilities right now.

"Alright," he soothed. "Just slide one in. Just a little. I want you to feel it, okay? Feel every little bit of it."

This was why he couldn't quit Kenyon. He burned him up from the inside out.

Touched something inside of him that felt like it had been cold forever. Something nobody else had ever touched. A place Julian had kept separate from every other hookup.

Kenyon wasn't here to see what he was doing, but he wanted to be good for him, it was something he *always* wanted, so he went slow, even though it nearly killed him to do it.

Felt every inch of his finger as it slid in, just as Kenyon had ordered.

Shuddered around it, feeling so close to the edge of orgasm, but never quite toppling over it.

"God, please, *please*," Julian begged.

He wasn't the kind of person who normally begged in bed, but with Kenyon it felt . . . easier. Like they were totally comfortable with each other now. Having sex for over five months would do that, but it was more than that, Julian knew it was. It was trust.

His sober brain would've shied away from that idea, because he'd gotten this far in life by not trusting anyone but himself, but how could they be doing this for all these months and he *not* trust Kenyon?

"You want it? You want to come all over my fingers?"

"*Yes*," Julian exhaled hard.

"Touch your cock. Jerk it real slow for me, okay?" Kenyon said. "Close your eyes. Think about me moving in you. All over you . . ."

Suddenly, Kenyon's voice fractured, and he was groaning through what Julian knew was his own orgasm.

Tipsy Julian couldn't help but think, *it was because he was all over you. It's you, you made him come.*

But, sober Julian argued, *you do that anyway. All the goddamn time. It doesn't mean anything. I swear. I promise. Just let me have this.*

He did. He pushed the thought away, far out of reach, and focused on how it felt, to slowly twist his cock in his fist, to finger himself with the other hand. He let the pleasure overwhelm him and then overtake him as Kenyon babbled a rush of compliments. How sexy he was. How much he loved fucking him. How good it was when they were together.

It was maybe a little more intimate than they usually were, but it was the phone, Julian reasoned, when his orgasm finally let up, and he lay panting, listening to Kenyon breathe on the other end of the line.

Even the way he sounded after sex was familiar and both comfortable and not comfortable at all. Exciting. Invigorating. Julian felt the rest of the buzz begin to start to fade away, leaving him sleepy.

"That was . . ." Kenyon's voice trailed off.

"Yeah," Julian said.

"You're gonna be back in a few days?" Kenyon asked, hopeful, and Julian felt the impact of it right in his chest. Because he was hopeful too.

I missed you. He almost said it but he'd sobered up just enough he knew it was a bad idea.

Knew saying it crossed a line they'd somewhat carefully preserved up until this point.

"Yeah," Julian repeated.

"Good." Kenyon sounded satisfied by that.

But Julian couldn't quite help it. Couldn't help himself. "I'll text you when I land."

"Oh?" He could nearly see Kenyon's eyebrow raise. His surprise.

But how was this different from not being able to wait until they were even out of the Piranhas' practice facility? It wasn't.

It was just . . . *convenient*, Julian told himself.

"Unless you don't want to," Julian said slyly.

"Oh I do," Kenyon retorted, chuckling. "I really do."

Julian hesitated.

At first, he couldn't deny they'd both tried very hard to stick to the line. They'd even tried to avoid conversation, but over time, desire overcame reluctance, because Julian *enjoyed* talking to him, too—and was fairly sure that was a mutual problem—and so they usually chatted a bit before getting down and dirty. Sometimes they even chatted after.

Not about football. Not about anything that Julian could ever use, if he'd decided to stab Kenyon in the back like that, even though he'd never. *He'd never.*

But not like this.

They never just sat here on the phone with each other and listened to the other person's breathing.

"Well," Julian finally said, hearing the reluctance in his own voice. "I'd better get going. Get to bed."

"Yeah," Kenyon said. Was that regret he heard? Maybe it was. But Julian *knew* this worked because of how they'd set it up.

And, Julian reminded himself, *you're not in a position to date. You're definitely not in a position to date a player.*

"See you in a few days."

"Good night, Julian," Kenyon said.

The warmth in his voice, the care in it, stuck with Julian for longer than he wanted it to.

Even as he lay in bed later and tried to fall asleep, he thought about it.

Because the truth was, it wasn't what they were supposed to be doing, and the other, much more unpleasant truth was, he didn't hate it at all.

Chapter Four

December

Julian expected to hear Kenyon's knock.

He'd been hearing a version of it for the last six months.

But tonight, there was an unexpected urgency in it.

He stood up, stretching his back, aching from hunching over the desk, working on this story for too long, and headed towards the door.

After he pulled the door open and Kenyon walked in, panic written clearly across his features, Julian wondered if he'd ever get used to the animal charisma of this man.

From the first moment he'd spotted him in that shitty bar, he'd felt drawn to him.

You're sexually attracted to him, and that makes total sense, because you're fucking.

But Julian had never been stupid, and he still wasn't, even if he kept lying to himself.

"Hey," Julian said as Kenyon shed his hoodie and tossed it on the chair he'd been sitting in only a few moments before. "What's wrong?"

The problem with only fucking was that it wasn't ever *only* fucking.

"I just got caught on the stairs," Kenyon said. He began pacing in front of the bed.

Maybe it had been ego, thinking they could fuck literally under the nose of all of Kenyon's team and all his coaches, and never get caught. This weekend, Nikki was even here, two hotel rooms down from Julian. But he'd not hesitated to text Kenyon this afternoon: **usual time, usual place?**

"By?" Julian asked, settling on the edge of the bed. He wasn't wearing a shirt, only a pair of ratty old gym shorts.

And nothing under them either, if Kenyon could focus on what was really important—which was his cock.

Usually, they didn't have a problem with that, but Kenyon looked unusually agitated.

That was another blow to the carefully constructed lie that Julian had begun building in his mind, all those months ago. The idea that they could only have sex, and it wouldn't bleed into anything else . . . that had been a little insane. Because even sex, if you did it as often as they did, meant that you got to know each other at least a little bit.

If Julian was being really honest, he knew Kenyon a lot better than just a little bit.

"Dawson."

"Well, shit," Julian said. "The elder, I assume?"

"Yeah," Kenyon said. He shoved his hands into his pockets. "But . . ." He hesitated.

"But?"

Kenyon shot him a look. The kind of look that kept Julian from asking one of these nights, *what are we really doing?* The kind of look that kept any thought of just leaning in and kissing Kenyon far, far from his imagination.

He trusted Kenyon. He was pretty sure Kenyon trusted him too, but it was difficult because when Kenyon stood at the podium and he sat in the press room, they weren't on the same side. Not really.

Every once in a while, they got a hard reminder of the realities of this situation.

Why it was better it was just sex between them.

"You're not gonna tell anyone this, right?"

Julian kept his temper in check. Didn't slap Kenyon upside the head, even though he *dearly* wanted to. It was good news for Kenyon he had way too much experience not letting his real feelings seep through the walls he'd put up so long ago. "No," he said steadily. "Of fucking course not."

Kenyon flopped down on the edge of the bed next to him. "Of course you wouldn't . . . I'm . . . I'm sorry. I shouldn't have asked you that. It's just that . . . I wasn't the only one sneaking out," he said softly.

"What?" Julian thought he understood what Kenyon was saying, but he couldn't quite comprehend that it might be true. "You mean, your coach . . . *Coach Dawson* . . . was sneaking out too? Sneaking out where?"

"I would love to know that," Kenyon said, "but he wouldn't say."

"Shocking," Julian said, meaning it both sarcastically and seriously, both at the same time.

"But he was real insistent that I not tell Beau, which makes me think . . . it's either someone Beau wouldn't approve of, or . . ."

"It's not a woman," Julian finished Kenyon's sentence.

"Yeah," Kenyon said. He sounded conflicted.

"You think Coach would really not tell his own son that he was queer?" Julian had seen the coach and his son together enough over the last six months that it seemed impossible that Asa would keep that kind of secret from Beau.

"It's not always that easy, you know?" Kenyon said heavily. "I didn't mind telling my mom, she was real easy, but my dad? Jesus, I hated to see the disappointment in his eyes."

"Was he?"

Kenyon looked over at him.

"Was he disappointed?" Julian clarified.

"No, no, actually he wasn't. But the fear he might be . . . I could barely get the words out."

This right here was the other reason Julian had told Kenyon they were only going to fuck.

He didn't do these kinds of confessions.

Even if he'd had the material, he wouldn't want to.

They were his secrets to keep, because nobody else was going to want to see the ugliness of them exposed to the light.

"What about you?" Kenyon asked, clearly not getting the memo that he didn't want to talk about it. That he didn't want to share. That they weren't supposed to be sharing.

"Did I come out to my parents?" Julian hesitated. "No." *Because they were dead.*

Kenyon nudged him with his elbow. "Real talkative tonight, aren't you?"

He wanted to say *because the point isn't the talking, it's the fucking*, but that was shitty even for him. The way it felt shitty to tell Kenyon even a half-lie.

How had they gotten to this place? Really, he should've cut this off months ago, but the sex was so good, he'd become more than a little addicted to it.

And to the risk.

Definitely not the man. Nope. No way.

"No, I didn't tell my parents because they weren't around much," Julian said.

Hoping that Kenyon would take the obvious explanation instead of digging further. Let Kenyon continue to believe he was some rich, spoiled trust fund kid, fucking around, instead of a graduate of too many foster homes, barely hanging on to the kind of life he desperately wanted.

Kenyon looked at him, eyes kind. He was a nice guy, underneath his bluster. More than nice, if the kind of money and resources he was rumored to funnel to his foundation were real.

How much more sympathy would he feel if he knew the truth? *Too much.*

Julian didn't need any free handouts or charity—and he definitely didn't need anyone to feel sorry for him.

"So, how did you leave it with Coach?"

Kenyon shrugged. "I didn't tell him what he wanted to know, if that's what you're worried about. He threatened me with sitting us down and making us listen to his whole speech, but I told him that wasn't necessary, 'cause it's not like that between us."

"Right," Julian said. It was just what he'd thought he wanted—what he'd been telling himself from the beginning he wanted—so the last thing he should've felt was disappointment, but he could taste the bitter edge of it in his mouth.

Kiss him. Kiss him and let him take it away. He'd do it. You've seen it in his eyes. He'll look down at your lips, and you know he's not thinking about them wrapped around his cock.

But things were already complicated enough, even though they'd set out to make them as simple as possible. Kissing Kenyon, as appealing as it sounded, would just fuck everything up more.

Instead, he put his hand on Kenyon's thigh, and then slid it higher. The kind look in his dark eyes—kind and fucking *sympathetic*—turned hotter the closer he got to his dick.

"You still up for it?" Julian asked, licking his lips.

There was a brutal honesty in his gaze, too much truth laid bare, when Kenyon said, "When am I not?"

Julian couldn't argue with that. He didn't know what Kenyon's sex life had been like before him—that was another subject they didn't touch—but it couldn't have been as plentiful as it was now. At first, they'd fucked maybe once a week.

But now, six months in, it felt like they were stealing time nearly every single day.

To the point where Kenyon was risking discovery by sneaking out after curfew the night before a game. Then there was the time they'd actually snuck into a janitor's closet in the Piranhas' stadium. They kept taking these risks, just for sex.

The sex isn't that good, even though it's fucking amazing. You know that.

Julian shut down his brain. He knew what it was trying to tell him, and he wasn't interested in listening.

Kenyon put a hand on his chest, pushing him back gently, fingers trailing down his chest. "You bring the lube?" They'd stopped using condoms ages ago, once they'd had the awkward conversation that they were actually having so much sex together that they could hardly be hooking up with anyone else on the side.

Julian fluttered his eyelashes at him. "Do I ever forget it?" He gestured towards the pillows at the top of the bed. "You wanna go grab it?"

"If you promise to behave and stay right here," Kenyon said, his voice growing darker, rougher, Julian's cock hardening at the sound of it. The kind of pleasure it promised every single time.

"I'll consider it." He'd learned when he put his smug, haughty persona on, it turned Kenyon on more than he wanted to admit.

"If you're gonna be moving, then turn over," Kenyon said.

There was a part of him that wanted to play a little harder to get, but this was what they were here for, wasn't it? But then the part who wanted more, who wanted Kenyon to work a little harder for his submission, was drowned out by the greedy part of him, the part who knew just how good it would be if he was just a good boy and did what he wanted him to.

He turned over and was rewarded with a deep groan from Kenyon as he trailed fingertips down his back and then gave his butt a light smack. "Fuck, I love your ass," he said, his tone hushed and reverent now.

Julian let himself get lost in the worship in Kenyon's voice, in the way his hands parted his legs like he was revealing the most precious thing in the world.

This is why the sex is so goddamn good.

He pushed the voice away. Focused on the feel of Kenyon's fingers, wet with lube, as they rubbed against his hole, and then began to push in.

The sex was fantastic enough on its own, but there was a part of Julian that liked this even more. Kenyon was detailed and thorough, and liked to have him sobbing against the mattress before he'd even consider putting his dick inside him.

Tonight was no exception. He fingered him nice and slow, his big thick fingers sliding against every sensitive nerve, coaxing every bit of pleasure he could out of him. One finger, then two, and then he was begging for the third, desperately trying not to hump the mattress and explode before he could even get fucked.

"I love you like this," Kenyon groaned as he slid a third finger in, his movements slowing even more until Julian was squeezing his eyes shut and nearly crying with the effort it took to not rub his hard, leaking cock against the comforter and get off just on that.

He said stuff like that a lot, liked to talk during sex, and all of it wound Julian up something fierce. Maybe it was because whenever they were fucking, it was like Kenyon thought he could get away with the kind of shit he couldn't any other time.

And he did. Julian never protested or told him he should stop, he just leaned into it, let the words wash over him and ratchet up his arousal even more.

Let them warm him in that cold, dark place deep inside.

"So gorgeous," Kenyon murmured as he leaned over him, deep and dark and perfect. "Think about this all the time."

Julian did too.

He thought about how it felt different every time they were together like this, a nearly miraculous reaction between two people with two unique lives. Sometimes it was like this, where Kenyon would overwhelm him until it felt like he couldn't quite breathe right or sometimes he'd push him down, to his knees, and demand he suck his cock, and he would. Or sometimes it would be mutual, getting each other off together.

It was never the same.

And yet it was always so good.

But right now, as Kenyon finally withdrew his fingers and slicked up his cock, his big body pressing Julian to the bed, it felt better than good. It felt vital, like if Kenyon didn't get inside him right now, he was going to *die*.

"Come on, come on, come on," he begged, shaking as Kenyon pushed inside.

A big strong arm wrapped around his waist and pulled him up, pulled him back. Braced against him as his cock slid in, deeper and deeper, until Julian's fingers scrabbled against Kenyon's arm, overwhelmed by the feel of it.

"You're gonna come," he murmured into Julian's ear, "when I say you can come."

Then he thrust hard, and Julian's knees turned into jelly. If Kenyon hadn't been holding him like this, he'd have turned to mush. Maybe with someone else, it would have felt like Kenyon was just using him, using his body to get off, exactly the way he wanted to, but instead, it felt like all of this wasn't for Kenyon at all—but instead, it was to make Julian feel as good as possible.

The angle was exquisite and he was so turned on, he found himself pushing back against Kenyon's body, meeting him thrust for thrust, until Kenyon's moaning was just as uncontrolled as his.

Then, he slid a hand down his chest, down his stomach and all it took was a single touch against his cock and Julian was coming, clenching hard around Kenyon's cock, sending him off until everything between them felt like an endless feedback loop of pleasure.

Julian collapsed against the bed, his knees completely fucking useless.

"That was . . ." Kenyon had hit the bed right next to him, careful to avoid the wet spot they'd inevitably made.

Julian knew he should get up and clean up, but he was fuzzy and warm and too fucked out to move.

Just when he thought it couldn't get any better between them, it got better.

"Amazing?" Julian rolled over and opened an eye, taking in the bliss written in every angle of Kenyon's incredible body.

"More along the lines of barely tolerable," Kenyon teased.

Julian grinned.

He'd never smiled as much as he had in the last six months, doing this with the man next to him.

He'd never imagined sex could be fun. That sex could be all-consuming like this.

No wonder they hadn't been able to quit each other.

At the beginning, during the first few months, he'd been sure that one day his phone would just go silent. That eventually, when he sent a text, Kenyon would just ghost him.

But it had never happened.

And what are you gonna do? Just keep going on like this? You know you can't.

Why couldn't they? Julian questioned his uncooperative brain stubbornly. They'd been doing this for six months now. No reason not to continue.

They lay there for another few minutes, in a comfortable silence.

At first, they'd always gotten up right away. Now, they didn't exactly cuddle, but they weren't in any hurry to leave either.

"At least it was definitely worth getting practically caught with my pants down," Kenyon mused.

"It kinda sounds like your coach should be giving himself the talk," Julian said drowsily. He didn't want to fall asleep, but he might, just like this, even though he needed to get up and finish his article so it could be posted before the game tomorrow.

"Seems like it," Kenyon said. "You know who I was thinking it could be?"

"Who?"

"That new guy. The new coach they just brought in."

"What, his old friend from Tennessee? Nah, they've known each other forever." Julian had done plenty of research on the new coach the Piranhas had brought in unexpectedly, hoping there might be a good story there. But there didn't seem to be. Scott Callaway was exactly what he seemed; another college coach with an excellent pedigree who'd been friends with Asa Dawson for twenty-plus years.

"Not everyone fucks each other on the first night," Kenyon teased.

"Everyone's who's got a brain in their head does," Julian retorted. He finally pulled himself together and went to the bathroom, turning on the shower. "Imagine waiting that long for sex."

This was usually when Kenyon got dressed and left, but to Julian's surprise, he walked into the bathroom, still gloriously naked, and leaned against the doorjamb. "Maybe it's not just sex," he said. "You know people do that, things that aren't sex."

This sounded like a risky line of conversation.

Julian could see danger signs and flashing red lights everywhere.

The only question was why Kenyon didn't just leave it alone.

He pulled the shower curtain back and got in, putting his head under the hot water, but annoyingly it didn't clear his head.

"You looking for satisfaction somewhere else?" Julian asked, raising his voice so Kenyon could hear him over the water.

He could still see the faint outline of Kenyon through the shower curtain.

He hadn't moved.

"You know I'm not," Kenyon said. "How could I possibly?" He sounded frustrated, like he knew Julian had purposefully misunderstood what he was asking.

"Yeah, I guess, maybe he's wildly in love with someone. That happens. I know it happens." *To other people.*

"I used to think that'd take up a lot of time, that wildly-in-love thing," Kenyon said. "But then I started hooking up with you, and it's not like *that* doesn't take up a chunk of time."

Julian finished washing up, but instead of getting out, he leaned against the cool shower wall. Hoping that it might resolve his conflicted heart. This wasn't fair; *Kenyon* wasn't being fair. Sure, he had these thoughts too, but he didn't *say* them. That was against the unspoken rules they'd laid out, at the very beginning. Just fucking. No kissing. No cuddling. No talking.

No feelings.

Julian just hadn't anticipated still doing it six months later or that after spending all this time together, even in bed, he'd like the guy so goddamned much.

Or that it might be mutual.

Nobody had ever really spent so much time with him before, even if it was between the sheets—or in hotels, or in janitor closets, or in empty classrooms—and still liked him at the end of it.

Julian didn't know what to do with that particular fact.

"You're being awfully quiet in there," Kenyon said. "You drowning? Taking on water? Need a rescue?"

It was the last word that shook Julian out of his stupor.

No, he didn't need a rescue.

After all, he'd promised Kenyon at the very beginning that he wouldn't end up needing to be saved, or crying in his arms like some pathetic damsel in distress.

He shut the water off and tugged the curtain over.

"I'm fine," Julian said. He pulled a towel from the rack and began drying off. "If you need more time for practice or for your foundation or something, you know you can take it."

"I know I can," Kenyon said. A little annoyed now. And yes, that was fair. Julian *had* deliberately misunderstood him.

"Good," Julian said. "I've got to finish my story. Get it filed before tomorrow."

"Don't worry, I'll get out of your hair. I know how much you hate it when someone sits there and watches you type."

There had been a night, not unlike this one, a few months back, when Julian had sent Kenyon the go-ahead text to come over, and then Nikki had assigned him a last-minute story.

"For good reason," Julian said, toweling his hair off. "It's incredibly annoying."

"Apparently," Kenyon grumbled. "I was *silent*."

"Except your thoughts are really noisy," Julian explained with a lopsided grin. "I told you this."

Kenyon chuckled. "How can thoughts be noisy?" But he didn't linger. Instead, he got dressed, and after one last inscrutable look at Julian, who was pulling his shorts back on, left, the door shutting behind him with a finality that shouldn't have annoyed Julian, but did anyway.

Julian tried to settle back down at his desk, but he was all agitated from the conversation, *and* on top of that, now he was thinking of all the times he'd relaxed the self-imposed rules. And how lately, Kenyon had been coming over earlier and talking longer before, and staying later after.

It wasn't just Kenyon either. When they weren't in the hotel for a game, Julian only went to his place, and thinking back, Julian could see himself doing the exact same things. Getting there earlier. Staying later. Even though he knew better.

Kenyon had made noise once or twice about going to his place, but Julian had put his foot down. He knew what kind of place Kenyon thought he had—and what kind of place it actually was. He wasn't ashamed . . . not really . . . but having to explain the difference would mean answering a lot of questions he didn't want to deal with.

They'd been slipping, *both of them*, for months now.

If Julian had been thinking about it, instead of just enjoying it, he'd have noticed.

At least that was what he kept telling himself.

But that was a cold comfort as he forced himself to sit and actually focus on the story.

He was going to have to change the status quo, and it was going to suck.

It might even be the end of them.

Julian told himself he didn't care, but the truth was so obvious even he couldn't deny it any longer.

"This is good stuff," Nikki said, popping a strawberry into her mouth and chewing as her fingernail flicked through Julian's story on her tablet. "In case I haven't told you, you're doing good work here. Real different from Walter, but good."

"There's a reason you gave *me* this job and didn't just hand it off to the next Walter clone in line," Julian pointed out dryly. "Has he stopped emailing you complaints yet?"

Only Walter, someone who had *quit,* would send his old boss endless complaints about how his replacement was doing his job. *Doing his job better*, Julian thought rebelliously.

"I had IT block him," Nikki said with a resigned sigh. "But not before I sent him a message explaining it was ridiculous he'd quit because he thought Dawson was headed towards a garbage fire but didn't think you should be asking him any tough questions."

Julian rolled his eyes. "Good riddance."

"He was right about one thing though. You'd have made a killer political reporter. But I'm not going to encourage you, because I don't want to lose you," Nikki said, tucking a stick-straight strand of blond hair behind her ear. "Did you see my email about the podcasts wanting to book you?"

"Yeah, I can do those," Julian said.

Podcasts weren't what he ultimately wanted, but Julian wasn't naive. He wasn't going to do a couple of months of killer work here in Miami and automatically get just where he wanted to be. It was a process, he was still young, and the fact that he'd gotten this promotion, and then paid off Nikki's hunch, that was a damn good start.

But it was just a start.

"I know, I know, you want to be on TV," Nikki said. She grinned. "*I* want you to move into TV, all your insanely good looks are totally wasted on print and on podcasts, but you gotta earn your spot, first."

"I know," Julian said. "It's not time. But it will be. Someday."

She shot him a look. "You are annoyingly pragmatic, you know? Anyone ever tell you that?"

Julian thought about last night, and the frustration in Kenyon's voice.

"Not directly, no."

"See?" Nikki chuckled under her breath. "Pragmatic to a fault. It's a wonder Dawson doesn't like you better."

Julian smirked. "I think I annoy him by asking him the kind of questions he wishes everyone would just pretend don't exist."

"You mean, you annoy him by being too much like him," Nikki observed. She finished her latte, and set the porcelain cup on the saucer. "You know I come do these checkups as a matter of routine, but I don't have any suggestions for improvements. Just keep doing what you're doing. Keep pushing. Keep digging. I think you're right on the cusp of really breaking through." She hesitated. "I noticed your social media follows were way up."

"I went from being an assistant to being the main reporter for the Piranhas," Julian said. "Of course they're up."

"They're up because you took my advice and put your stupidly attractive face on your accounts sometimes."

Julian shrugged. He wouldn't deny that being attractive helped, especially in the industry he was working to break into—but he found the focus on them annoying, because he was so much more than just a pretty face.

He had a brain, too, as well as killer instincts, and an unnatural willingness to work his ass off.

That was all *him*. He'd created all of that from nothing. His face was just what he'd been born with.

"That too," Julian acknowledged. He wasn't stupid, and it would have been to ignore the advantages he had.

"You know, sometimes I wonder if I'd be here, getting ready to watch you play, if you hadn't convinced me to hire you," Nikki mused.

"That was never going to happen," Julian said firmly. "I'd reached my ceiling. I wasn't going to physically get any bigger."

He'd approached Nikki his junior year of college because she'd made a reputation in the sports journalism industry for being both incredibly tough and scrupulously fair. And for being the best. Nobody else could sniff out a story like her, and damn if mothball misogyny or locker room politics or backroom deals were going to get in her way.

At the time, she'd told him what he needed to do. Where he should best focus his time and energy. She'd applauded his determination, and told him to come see her after graduation.

For three years after he'd finished school, he'd been her assistant, then he'd been promoted to field work, right before Walter had quit.

Julian knew he hadn't been the obvious choice to replace Walter—he hadn't had the experience yet—but Nikki had undeniable instincts, and he'd fit in well in Miami.

"Like I said," she murmured. "*Pragmatic*. It's the thing I love about you, Anderson. And the thing I kinda hate about you, too."

Even though Julian was trying not to think about Kenyon, he did anyway.

He had a feeling Kenyon felt the same as Nikki did.

But this was who he was. Who he'd forged himself to be.

Everyone can either take it or leave it.

In Nikki's case, he had a feeling she loved it way more than she hated it. It meant he worked hard. It meant he never took no for an answer. It meant he never stopped pushing. But for Kenyon, it meant he probably wouldn't get the answer he believed he was looking for.

"Don't worry though," Nikki said with a smile. "That attitude's gonna shoot you straight to the top. Right where you want to be."

It will, Julian promised himself, as he and Nikki gathered their bags and headed towards the lobby. *It better*.

Chapter Five

Two weeks later

"Can you believe we've made it to the second to last game of the season?" Tristan said with a grin as he collapsed onto the bench next to Kenyon. "It feels like it just started."

"Just wait til the *real* work starts," Logan teased from his other side. "The playoffs are a whole different beast."

"You ever been in the playoffs, Banks?" Kenyon asked, leaning back against the bench.

It was midway through the second quarter and the Piranhas were up 17 to 3 against the Commanders.

"Two years ago, the Vikings team I was on made it to the divisional round," Logan said with that irrepressible grin of his. Kenyon hadn't really expected to like his teammates—or to grow as close to them as he had.

"AFC Championship four years ago," Kenyon said.

"Oh, so you weren't on the Piranhas team that beat the Riptide in the Super Bowl two years ago?" Tristan asked.

"Nope, year after was when I came to Miami," Kenyon said.

"We gonna chitchat all day or look through the plays?" Pax asked, without much heat.

"We scored on our first three drives," Wade chimed in.

"Doesn't mean we can't be better," Pax said with a faux stern look, even as he wore that dopey grin that must mean that Davis was somewhere nearby. "We could've gotten a touchdown on that last drive, not a field goal."

"Yeah, Tristan, you should've caught that pass," Wade teased.

Tristan elbowed him in the side. "You mean the one Pax floated above me, when he was throwing the ball away? That *uncatchable* pass?"

"Was it really though?" Wade wondered.

Everyone looked over at Wade in surprise.

"Whoa? Trouble in paradise?" Kenyon questioned.

Kenyon wasn't usually the first to speak, but the thing that had remained the same this year, through thick and thin, through wins and losses, had been Tristan and Wade. Their connection, and their determination to find every available empty closet, had been consistent.

Looking at them throughout the season, Kenyon had been reminded of just how ridiculously in love they were, and how he and Julian weren't.

Maybe they did a few of the same things—that closet thing, it could come in handy, occasionally—but they weren't the same, not at all.

Especially now, now that Kenyon was pretty sure Julian was trying to push him away.

"No, no, that's not it at all." Logan was laughing now. "Do I have this right, Wade? You bet Tristan that he *could* set the rookie touchdown record? Is that correct? And he bet against you? For some goddamned reason? And the prize is . . . well, I'll let y'all come to your own conclusions about what it might be."

There was a collective groan up and down the bench. Everyone knew what Tristan and Wade would be betting on. It was inevitably something to do with sex. Something they'd no doubt hear about in extensive detail later.

Wade nodded enthusiastically. "You got it right."

Tristan rolled his eyes. "I'm three short. Unless we go off in the second half, it's not happening, 'cause Coach has already told me I'm probably not playing next week. And Kenyon here guaranteed it, 'cause he got the only touchdowns today."

"Sorry, Flounder," Kenyon said with a grin. "I'm runnin' hard today. Pax knows it, too."

"A bunch of us aren't probably playing next week," Pax said archly. "That's why we need to make it count *this week*."

Wade groaned. "Now you sound just like your boyfriend."

"Where do you think I get all my pep talks from?" Pax questioned archly. "These are all Abernathy originals."

"He chargin' you rent for those?" Tristan questioned lightly.

"If he is, we all know what he's payin'," Logan joked.

"What is goin' on here?"

They all looked up into the face of Davis Abernathy. Pax's aforementioned boyfriend, and the quarterbacks coach of the Piranhas. He was squinting, trying to look tough.

"Come on," Davis barked. "Defense is about to turn the ball over. Let's get ready."

Tough as a marshmallow, inside, Kenyon thought as he picked up his helmet, even though he knew Davis had a spine of pure fucking steel.

Nobody else could have survived those rumors about him, otherwise. But inside, especially when it came to Paxton, that spine didn't so much as disappear, as it didn't matter.

He was a good guy, solid as hell, and twice as loyal, and Kenyon had liked him from the first moment they'd met at training camp this summer.

He'd liked him even more when he'd found out that Davis had finally done something about that painfully obvious and completely mutual crush he'd had on their quarterback.

It took balls to break the rules. Especially the no-fraternization rule.

Except Pax and Davis weren't just fraternizing; they were balls-to-the-wall, crazy-in-love, ride-or-die for each other.

Kenyon wasn't sure he understood those kinds of feelings. He sure as heck hadn't ever felt that way about anyone before. But there was a part of him that not only admired Pax and Davis, but *envied* them.

What would it feel like to always have someone like that in your corner?

He had his parents, of course, and his sister, but friends always wanted shit from you, and romantic partners were even worse. Not only demanding something, but usually the most valuable commodity of all: time.

Julian hadn't done that.

Of course, he hadn't had to.

Kenyon had freely given him as much time as he was able.

Which was probably why he was a little pissed that twice this week when he'd texted that he should come over, Julian had texted back that he was unexpectedly busy.

Maybe he was, the season was winding down, and the playoffs would be starting soon, and maybe that meant he was locked up in his apartment—or wherever he lived, Kenyon was just now realizing that he'd never so much as *seen* wherever Julian lived—conceiving of more questions destined to give their coach heartburn.

Or maybe he was pissed Kenyon had tried to make a point that night, a few weeks ago.

That whatever they were doing, six months in, was definitely *something*. And it wasn't just sex.

The offense huddled up, and Kenyon pushed that thought out of his head. Maybe they were up fourteen points, but this was the last game he'd probably be playing in til the playoffs, and he needed to be focused, totally locked in.

"Let's go down the field, nice long drive, okay?" Pax said as they all leaned in. "Little over five minutes left. Plenty of time to get Tristan one of those touchdowns, yeah?"

Tristan rolled his eyes, but Wade high-fived Pax, clearly enthused about whatever it was he'd win if Tristan did in fact break the rookie TD record.

They jogged onto the field, and Kenyon felt the world outside the field fall away as he got positioned, leaning over, tensing his muscles, getting ready to unleash his speed on the field.

Since they were trying to burn clock, he wasn't surprised to see their coordinator call a run play, and then another run play.

The Commanders' defense was also not great against the run, especially not against the tough tenacity of the Piranhas' offensive line.

Kenyon had agreed to sign with Miami two years ago not only because they were willing to pay the most money for his talents, but also because they had some of the best offensive linemen.

Which meant, consistently, he'd get the best chance of decent yardage. Good yards every game meant he'd meet the bonuses built into his contract, which meant more money, and good yards also meant more visibility, which was even better than just dollars. Visibility brought attention to him, and as an extension, to his foundation.

Pax called out the snap count, and balancing on the balls of his feet, Kenyon leaned all the way to the left, then whipped his body to the right, the ball hitting him right in the hands as he took it, tucked it in an automatic movement that he'd been practicing since middle school, and pushed forward.

The play called for an opening in the line to the right, but with the way it had developed, Kenyon saw a *better* opening to the right, helped by Wade blocking the defensive end pretty competently, and he cut in, twisting past one of the Commanders' linebackers and then sprinting into the flat, legs moving, lungs moving, everything moving in perfect tandem.

He saw the safety cutting across to tackle him, and he had only a single moment to brace for the hit.

Then the guy was bowling him over, hitting him right at the waist, the breath knocked out of him, as he was pushed down to the turf.

Getting hit never felt good, but there was a good kind of satisfaction in the pain of being tackled in the flat, past the line.

It meant he'd gotten at least five yards.

That was the last thought he had, before the safety jabbed an elbow hard, right at the ball, and Kenyon hesitated, securing it only a second too late.

The ball popped out of his grip and he scrambled, trying to get his hands back on it, but it was too late.

The safety was already running with it, only twenty yards to their end zone.

Fuck.

The dance he did in the end zone was annoying and obnoxious.

Goddamn it.

Kenyon shot a glare in his direction before he jogged back to the bench.

He wasn't known for fumbling.

He should have been better. So he'd gotten two touchdowns today. He'd given one up, too. And instead of widening their lead, and giving Tristan one of the TDs he needed for the record, the Piranhas had conceded one, and the blame was all on Kenyon.

Coach Dawson grabbed his shoulder as he tried to slink by, wordlessly. "Hey, Ellis, that was a tough one."

There was no judgement in his tone or in his face.

Concern, yes, but judgement, no.

Kenyon almost craved the judgement, but Coach was too smart to give it to him now.

He'd be carrying a ball around all week, during practice, and all the defense players would be told to go for it, whenever they saw him. To make sure he knew how to protect the ball, to *not* give it up again.

That was a minor annoyance.

The crappy, nauseating way he felt, after glancing up at the scoreboard, was a major one.

"Yeah," he said shortly.

"Take a breather," Coach said, kindly. Still kind. Even as he benched him for this next drive.

Maybe he didn't know that the sympathy burned twice as bad as a nasty remark would have.

Whether he did or not, Kenyon had a feeling it wouldn't have mattered. Coach wouldn't be any different.

He slunk to the bench, and replayed in his mind, a dozen times, and then more, the ball getting punched out. Promised himself, each and every time, that it wouldn't happen again.

"Helen, you bringing Ellis out here?" Julian pasted on his most convincing, charming smile as Helen, the head of the Piranhas' PR, checked the microphone at the podium.

The Piranhas had won 36 to 10.

No doubt she'd be bringing out Coach and Pax, as the two leaders of the team, but often she'd have other players come to the podium to address media questions, too. Having scored two touchdowns today, it would make sense if Kenyon was one of those players.

But he'd fumbled too.

Julian had noticed that anytime someone underperformed or made a mistake, they almost never showed up at the podium.

Except Pax, of course, who, as the quarterback and de facto leader, didn't have the ability to pass the buck.

He got to face the media, no matter what, and Julian didn't envy him that particular task each and every week.

Helen looked up, and shot him a look that told him everything he needed to know. The staff protected the players at all costs. It wasn't a bad move; in fact, Julian respected it more than those franchises that *didn't* protect their players, and let them take the heat all by themselves. But it was his job to ask. To push.

His personal feelings didn't belong here, where he did his job.

"Nope, you're getting Coach and you're getting Pax," Helen said. "And you know that's the case, Julian. So stop trying to push."

He grinned at her. "But you like it when I push, Helen my darling."

She rolled her eyes, but she was smiling too. He knew she liked him, because he worked hard, much harder than, for example, Walter, who'd barely made an effort.

"You sucking up gettin' you anywhere?" Ed asked as he settled down next to Julian. Over the last few months, they'd become friendly.

Friends, Julian mentally corrected. *It's okay for you to have a friend.*

Sometimes Julian wondered what Ed would say if he knew he was sleeping with the Piranhas' starting running back, but the truth was, he already knew what Ed's reaction would be. Ed would lean back in his chair, steeple his fingers together, shoot Julian a look and ask, "What's the angle?"

And Julian would have to tell him there wasn't one.

That right there was the reason he hadn't told Ed the truth. Not just because it was a secret, even though it was, but because he hadn't wanted to endure Ed's knowing look after he confessed he wasn't sleeping with Kenyon for the insider info, or for an advantage, or for any reason other than he *wanted* to.

Than because he couldn't stop.

"Better than you," Julian teased. He knew Ed had a real soft spot for Helen. Would've liked to do something about it, even if it was a bad idea.

"Helps that you don't give a shit," Ed muttered. "You flirt with her 'cause it doesn't mean anything."

"Yep," Julian said cheerfully. "You should try it sometime."

Ed rolled his eyes, and didn't say anything, because they both knew he wouldn't be doing anything about it anytime soon.

Pax came out first, damp hair pushed back from his forehead. He gave the group of reporters an easy grin as he sat down and began to field questions.

It hadn't always been so relaxed, but a 12–4 season had given Paxton Kelly a lot of much-needed confidence.

Julian asked a handful of questions, not because he really had much to address, but because it was good practice to never be silent.

Then Coach took the podium.

Sometimes he had a lot to say, but today there wasn't much. "Just takin' care of business," Asa said. "Good, solid win. I like to see a good balance between run and pass, and that happened today. I'm sure y'all have the numbers, but I think it was a pretty equal split. Defense played great. Gave up a touchdown on that short field, but I was glad to see them push the Commanders to third and goal. Didn't make it easy on them to punch it in."

Julian got the first question. He was sure that everyone in the room, including Coach, and even *himself*, had been sure he'd ask about Kenyon's fumble, but instead, at the very last second, he changed directions.

Told himself it wasn't because he was still thinking of what Kenyon had brought up two weeks ago. He'd never let their thing intrude into his job, and he told himself it wasn't happening now, but it was kinda hard to deny.

"I know Nicholson is within a touchdown of setting the rookie touchdown record. He's tied for it right now, with Randy Moss, who set it in 1998," Julian said. "Any thought to playing him next week even though your playoff position is set already?"

Asa looked contemplative. "Is he that close? I didn't realize." Nobody believed that bullshit; Coach knew *everything*. "I'll say first that it says a lot about Tristan's talents, and his incredible work ethic that he's being mentioned in the same breath as Randy Moss. I know he really looks up to him. But we still haven't had any conversations about who's playing next week and who isn't. I know our number one priority is to get set and healthy for a deep playoff run. That's going to mean something different for every player. And I know Tristan understands that."

Julian knew then that Coach's complete non-answer meant that he was going to do what he could to get Tristan the record. And really, so did everyone else.

Maybe he'd wasted his question, but at least he hadn't gone straight for the jugular, pointing out Kenyon's mistake.

Didn't that count for something?

"Speaking of that short field, any thought on changing the balance after Kenyon's fumble this week? Maybe giving the backup some work?" Ed asked after shooting Julian a baffled glance. No doubt wondering why he hadn't pounced on that singular occurrence first thing.

Okay, he was definitely known for challenging Coach—and anyone else Helen brought to the post-game press conference—with the toughest kind of questions. Maybe he hadn't today, but that didn't mean anything.

Didn't mean he was losing his touch.

Didn't mean that he'd gotten soft, or stopped pushing.

Or that he'd lost his mind and developed *feelings*.

"Kenyon's been rock solid for us this year. He's delivering exactly what we've needed, in important situations. We trust him, and nothing that happened today changed that trust," Coach said.

Ed nodded, and the conference pressed on.

Normally, Julian might've challenged that answer. There were things he could say. Things he'd observed, over the last six months. Times he'd noticed that Kenyon hadn't delivered exactly what they'd needed, in those same important situations. So far they hadn't really cost the Piranhas any wins, but . . . well, as much as Coach hated luck, they'd been lucky that way.

As he packed up, and got ready to head out, Julian told himself that nothing had changed, but he knew it was a lie, even as he'd told it to himself.

He just hadn't wanted to . . . well, rag on Kenyon like that. He didn't need it, because from what Julian knew of him—and it was a lot, okay, even though at the same time, there was so much he *didn't* know about him—he'd be beating himself up plenty. He didn't need a pile on, on top of that.

Even though Julian told himself he was being stupid, that Kenyon didn't give a shit if he participated in that pile on or not, he just couldn't bring himself to do it. Not after that conversation he still felt guilty about shutting down.

Because that was it, wasn't it? He felt *guilty*.

And feeling guiltier with each passing day. With each passing invite of Kenyon's that he either turned down or ignored.

"You doing alright?" Ed asked as they walked out of the bowels of the arena.

Julian shrugged. "Didn't sleep well last night." It was the truth.

He hadn't slept well in two weeks.

How many nights had he lain awake wishing that he was different? A different kind of man? With a different sort of past? And a much different kind of future?

Too many.

Julian had finished filing his story as the conference had ended, and knew it lacked his usual bite. Nikki might mention it, or she might not, because even she could acknowledge that nobody could be *on* all the time, even Julian, even though he had been almost continuously.

But because of all that hard work, all that pushing, he thought this might sneak under her radar. He thought she might let it go.

Sure enough, as he reached the staff parking lot, his phone beeped, and there was a response from her. "Good work, as always," her message said.

But that didn't make him feel any better. Made him feel worse, in fact.

How had things come to this?

What he should do, he thought, as his phone dinged again, was meet up with Kenyon one last time and tell him that it was over. That they'd run their course.

But he didn't *want* to.

He didn't want to so fucking much that it should've scared him into doing it immediately.

But instead, he was hesitating.

He glanced down at his phone. **Meet me around the corner from the player parking lot.**

It was from Kenyon, and Julian didn't miss that instead of asking, he'd stated. As someone who worked with words for a living, he understood the intrinsic difference. He also knew he could just blow Kenyon off again.

Blow him off again or do what he didn't want to and end it.

Be there in a minute, he texted back.

He still didn't know what he was going to do.

Because there was definitely a third option: pretend like nothing was wrong.

And a fourth: lean in and kiss him and tell him that everything was changing, and he didn't care, he was here for it, here for Kenyon.

But is that really an option? Julian wondered as he shouldered his bag, said goodbye to Ed, and headed off to the corner of the parking garage that they both knew would be abandoned at this time after a game.

How did they know?

Well, it wouldn't be the first time they'd fucked in Kenyon's car after a game.

You're not gonna fuck now. You're gonna tell him that it's over. Clear and concise. No emotions. No regrets. Just . . . time to go our separate ways.

But when he opened the passenger door of Kenyon's car—it wasn't the ridiculous vehicle so many other NFL players drove, it was a plain black Tesla SUV, which, Julian could attest, had a very roomy back seat—Kenyon's look disarmed him almost immediately.

He didn't smile like usual. He didn't look happy to see him.

He looked . . . very definitely annoyed.

About the fumble? Julian wasn't sure.

"Get in," Kenyon said in a clipped voice.

Julian nearly turned and walked off, but the intensity in Kenyon's gaze drew him in—the way it had from the very first—and he slid into the car, shutting the door behind him.

"What?" Julian asked. "I gotta file my story still." Which was a lie. He'd already filed it. But the longer he sat here, in the cool interior that smelled just like Kenyon's cologne, with his big body taking up so much space, physically and metaphorically, the more he was going to want something else than to break it off.

He was going to want so much more than that.

How had they gotten here? He still didn't know. In fact, he was beginning to think that the only way they could've avoided any of this was never to start it in the first place.

"About?"

"What?" Julian didn't follow.

"What's the story about?"

Kenyon never asked what his stories were about. After all, he could read them, couldn't he? And then there was the fact Julian had told Kenyon at the very beginning he was never going to want to use him for a scoop. He only ever wanted to use Kenyon for his body, and his very fine dick. That was all.

"The game? What else would it be about?" Julian was annoyed. Even more annoyed than before. Why did Kenyon keep pushing like this? Couldn't he just leave it alone? Couldn't they keep going on like they had before?

You know you couldn't. You knew it yourself, you were just too scared to say anything.

"You didn't use your question to ask Coach about my fumble," Kenyon stated. Staring straight ahead. Right into the dark corner of the parking garage they were idling in.

"Oh, uh, well, I guess not," Julian never sounded this unsure. He knew it. But he sounded like it anyway.

He's breaking you down, down into pieces you don't know how to live with.

"Why the hell not?" Kenyon shot him a hot look. "You always go for the jugular. *Always.*"

"Thanks, I guess," Julian retorted.

"It's not a compliment. Well, it is, but it's also *you*. You do that. You don't sit meekly there and ask a question about Tristan getting his goddamned record. You don't let Coach pawn that other guy off with a bunch of bullshit. But you *did*."

"Maybe I wasn't on top of my game today," Julian said.

It was true. And the reason why was sitting right next to him. He was all fucked up. Turned up and twisted inside out.

Everything he'd thought he'd wanted was all flipped around. All fucked up.

Kenyon frowned. "Don't lie to me. You were. You were *fine*. You asked Helen if I'd be coming in for the press conference, and then when you had your shot with Coach, you *blanked*. If I'd been there, you'd have blanked even fucking worse. Why?"

Julian stared at the dash.

It would be so easy. He could cut this whole conversation off with one straightforward, simple sentence.

We're done. Have a nice life.

Okay, two sentences. And that was being generous. He didn't need to wish Kenyon a good life—or any kind of life at all. That was entirely optional.

But instead of saying any of that or just *leaving*, he stayed rooted in place, without any words at all.

He didn't want to lie, and the truth was completely, fucking impossible.

I didn't ask because I knew you'd be hurting and I didn't want to make you hurt any worse.

"What? You usually have *plenty* to say," Kenyon said.

That was fair. Julian deserved that. He *pushed*. It was what made him a good reporter.

"I didn't have anything to say about that. About . . . about you," Julian finally said. "So you fumbled, that doesn't make you a bad player. It was a bad moment. Even great players have bad moments, sometimes. You'll move past it. I knew it. Coach knew it. The whole goddamn team knew it. That's why I didn't say anything." He said the last part especially defiantly. "There wasn't anything to say."

Kenyon didn't respond. He'd been pushing for just this, for exactly this confession, Julian thought resentfully, and then he'd gotten it and he didn't even say fucking *thank you*.

His fingers tightened around the steering wheel, the leather creaking loudly in the silence of the car.

Then, finally, he looked over at Julian. He leaned close, and for a single heart-stopping second, Julian thought he was going to damn all the rules to hell, and kiss him.

But he didn't.

You are not disappointed.

But he was, kind of.

Conflicted, that was what he *really* was.

He was used to wanting things he couldn't have, and easily moving past them.

But Kenyon?

He was different. Different than anything else.

"See, that wasn't so hard. You think I'm a good player, huh?" Kenyon said softly, and then he was even closer. Julian could smell him, and he felt lightheaded with how much he wanted. His eyes were so dark, so compelling, his gaze capable of drawing everything out of Julian—even things he didn't want to give.

Julian rolled his eyes. Trying to deflect. "You know you're a good player. A great one, even."

"I like it when you're nice," Kenyon said. "I like prickly Julian, but nice Julian, he's pretty great too." And wasn't that the whole problem? Nobody else in the whole goddamn world even knew nice Julian existed.

"I wasn't trying to be *nice*," Julian said. "I was trying to be pragmatic. Everyone likes that about me. Including you."

Kenyon raised an eyebrow.

"I'm *likeable*," Julian insisted, even though the truth was more complicated. "You like me fine when I'm touching your dick. Like me even more when I'm sucking it."

"Yeah?" Kenyon's voice was dangerously rough. "That why you're here?"

Julian shot him a look. "I'm here because you *told* me to be here."

"That's right, I did. 'Cause otherwise, you might keep ducking me," Kenyon said.

So much for him not realizing the truth of what he was doing.

"I've been busy," Julian insisted.

"You," Kenyon said, and *God*, he was so close now, Julian could practically taste him, "are a *terrible* liar."

"Actually, I'm not," Julian said in a prim voice he barely recognized as his own.

What was he doing? What were *they* doing?

They never flirted like this, not without sex immediately following.

Julian couldn't quite make himself go for Kenyon's dick, though there was a part of him that definitely wanted to.

Was this what normal people did? Sit too close in a car and dare each other, not in so many words, to cross the line?

If that was the case, then Julian was beginning to understand why the idea appealed.

This was shockingly sexy, especially considering nobody was touching anyone's dick right now.

"It's 'cause you never bother to lie," Kenyon said, tapping his fingers on the steering wheel. "You're bad at it because you don't do it. So don't start now. Not now. Not with me."

You're wrong; I've been lying to you—been lying to myself—for months now.

"Fine," Julian said. "You want me to be honest about you? I can do that."

"That's all I want, fair treatment," Kenyon said. "I know this is . . . complicated for you. For me too."

It was an irony how much of an understatement that was, considering how insistent Julian had been at the beginning that if they only fucked, everything would be straightforward and easy.

"It's not complicated for me," Julian lied. "You really fuck up, don't worry, I'll call you and Coach out and everyone else I can. You'll be begging me to shut up."

"Thanks," Kenyon said dryly, with a sudden grin that made Julian's pulse accelerate. "That's real heartwarming. I appreciate it."

"Hey, it's what you asked for."

Julian wondered if he was going to ask for anything else.

It was insane that they kept fucking in these spots. Sneaking into each other's rooms the night before games. Hooking up in dark corners of the parking garage. None of this was normal, or safe or *sane*, and he knew it, and Kenyon surely knew it. But they kept doing it anyway.

But Kenyon didn't say a word, just kept looking at him, steady and loyal, and *goddamn it*, what were they doing here?

Not specifically in the dark corner of the garage.

Specifically, the point where if Kenyon asked, Julian willingly came to the dark corner of the garage.

If someone asked Julian how they'd gotten here, he couldn't have even drawn a fucking diagram.

But just when Julian felt drawn too tight, like he might implode if he didn't lean in another inch and finally figure out what Kenyon's lips would taste like against his, his phone buzzed.

Again.

And then again.

He yanked it out of his pocket, ignoring what he knew was disappointment in Kenyon's eyes, and glanced at the screen. "Shit, it's my boss," he said. "I have to take this."

Kenyon's look was wistful as he pushed the door open. Regretful.

Julian pretended he wasn't feeling it too, but like Kenyon had just said, he kinda *was* a terrible liar.

He shut the door behind him and walked away, towards where his own car was parked, and didn't look back.

Wouldn't let himself.

Wouldn't let himself wonder if Kenyon lingered there. If he'd hoped maybe Julian would come back.

They never just *talked*. Okay, maybe it had been a pissed-off kind of talking, but it was still *just* talking.

"Hey," he said, answering Nikki's call. "What's up? You said you got my story."

"Yeah, and look at you being all sweet and heroic, not dragging Ellis for fumbling. Your story today almost made me remember you were a human being."

"Thanks," Julian said. He should've known better. Nikki would never ignore him dropping the ball this way. She had killer instincts; it was how she'd gotten to where she was, despite the raging misogyny in sports journalism.

"I wanted to talk to you real quick about that podcast tomorrow."

"I'm set, all good to go," Julian said. He was always prepared. Nikki should know this, even if he'd had a human-ish moment.

"I never had any doubts," Nikki said.

"Then?"

Julian unlocked his car. His old, basic car. The car he was really hoping wouldn't break down on him because he was finally making some inroads in his savings with this better job and better salary, and he didn't want to waste money on a car. There was a reason he made sure that if they were going to hook up after a game, it was going to be in Kenyon's house. Or Kenyon's car. Or anywhere else associated with Kenyon.

It was bad enough they were toying with this line, seriously considering crossing it, even without discussing it. Kenyon finding out the truth about him would be even worse. Very few people knew what he'd come from, on purpose.

"I just wanted to make sure you were okay." Nikki never did that.

"What's going on?" Julian flipped the call to speakerphone and tucked his phone into the mounting bracket on his dash. He didn't have that fancy hands-free calling feature. Whenever he dreamed about a time when money wasn't tight, he imagined buying a car where that came standard.

But for now, this worked.

"Your moment of semi-humanity? You really worried about whether Tristan is gonna get the record?"

"He's gonna get the record. I guarantee it."

"Yeah, of course he is. Asa will make sure of it."

"Because nobody believed in him," Julian said, finishing her sentence. "And Asa knows what that's like. Nobody believed in either of them. It'll happen."

Julian pulled out of the parking garage.

It would've been convenient to live downtown, but he couldn't afford it, and so he'd rented a place about twenty minutes out, in a suburban apartment complex tucked between strip malls.

"Does it feel weird being surrounded by so many bleeding hearts?" Nikki asked. "Walter wouldn't have known what to do with it. It's better you're there. At least you can deal with it clear-eyed, without resenting it."

"Walter saw the writing on the wall," Julian pointed out. "Remember? He quit because he saw it."

"But seriously, you're okay? No issues? You seemed . . . distracted in your piece. It was good, of course, because it's you, and you're always good. But . . ." Nikki trailed off. Still so unlike her.

It was also very unlike her to call and make sure he was prepped for a work commitment.

Definitely unlike her to check up on him.

She knew Julian took care of Julian.

"I'm fine," Julian said firmly. Wanted to believe it, but didn't quite.

"Alright, good." She sounded relieved. "Just making sure. There're people who've got their eye on you, you know. Don't fuck this up tomorrow, not when you've got it in the bag."

He knew, and he absolutely wouldn't.

"I know," he said. "Screw something this big up? Not likely."

"The thought never occurred to me," Nikki said. Though it clearly had.

That alone should've scared Julian straight. Or not . . . *straight*, exactly, because that ship had *long* sailed, but scared him away from Kenyon.

But that pull was inexorable and automatic now. He didn't know how to disentangle himself from it.

The only way to do it would be a hard, fast, clean cut, and so far committing to that had been beyond even Julian's powers of self-control.

But tomorrow was another day.

"I'm almost home," Julian said. "I'll check in tomorrow, after the podcast's recorded, alright?"

"I'd say slay 'em dead, but you always do, so it seems redundant."

"Thanks, boss," Julian said dryly, and hung up just as he pulled into the apartment complex parking lot.

For a long moment after he turned the car off, he sat there and stared up at his building. Cataloging, even though he shouldn't, the differences between his life and Kenyon's.

The differences between the life he actually led and the life everyone assumed he led.

He'd learned, a long time ago, that the best way to not answer questions he didn't want to address was to pretend to be someone else. A person who nobody would ever interrogate because they wouldn't dare. Or because they thought they understood everything about him, so it would be pointless.

But neither of those things was technically the truth.

So on one hand, Julian thought as he trudged up to his apartment, Kenyon was right, and also, he was wrong.

He was a brilliant liar, because he'd deceived the world about who he was so well that everyone believed the lie.

But he was a terrible fucking liar when it came to Kenyon. He knew it, and yet he kept giving Kenyon chances to guess the truth.

Chapter Six

"Let's get this meeting going," Keisha, his beloved sister, the head of his foundation, and also an unbelievable pain in his ass, said. "I'm sure Kenyon has a hundred different places he needs to be."

She said it with affection, but also with a roll of her eyes.

Okay, sue him, he was busy.

So busy, between the foundation, and all the obligations it created, plus football, *plus* his hookups with Julian, it felt like he was barely keeping his head above water, but it wasn't like he slacked.

Keisha couldn't accuse him of that.

She wouldn't, either, because she knew what was good for her.

Kenyon flopped down on his chair and pulled over his laptop. "Alright," he said to the screen, "let's get going."

Once he'd realized that the foundation needed more attention than just he could give it, he'd hired Keisha, fresh out of Northwestern, and determined to make her mark on the world. She'd told him that she'd be willing to move wherever he did, but since he usually didn't spend more than a few years in any one city, it had made sense for them to establish a base of operations separate from where Kenyon played football.

They'd chosen Cleveland, and now every week, on his day off from practice, they met. The rest of the team sat in the small conference room in the offices they rented in a Cleveland suburb and Kenyon beamed in from his house in Miami.

"First order of business. The auction we did last week was a huge success. Send thanks to Paxton and to Coach, for their donations," Keisha said, consulting her notes. "But make sure to tell Davis that the jersey he sent along, with Pax's, was the biggest seller."

"Really?" Kenyon was surprised. Not that Davis was a solid guy, and a solid quarterback, but that people were able to get their heads out of their asses long enough to bid on something he'd signed.

Keisha shrugged. "There's been a lot of interest since he turned that job down with the Riptide. Lots of people think he should be playing somewhere, not just coaching."

"I think he's pretty happy where he's at," Kenyon said. He wasn't going to announce to his incredibly nosy sister and a handful of others that he knew, but didn't trust one hundred percent, that the reason Davis was so happy where he was had everything to do with the Piranhas' quarterback.

Pax and Davis' relationship wasn't public knowledge yet, though it was pretty much an open secret in the Piranhas' facility.

"Well, I'm glad for him," Keisha said. "And real glad he sent along that jersey, because it pushed the auction over the top, making it one of our best ever."

"That's awesome," Kenyon said. He'd never had any problem utilizing his NFL contacts to raise money for We Read. It was worth it, because he could see, every single week, how important the work they were doing was.

Keisha went through the rest of the agenda for the week. They were hiring another special education teacher for the downtown Cleveland tutoring center they ran. There was a short list of three applicants, and she asked him to take a look at their résumés, and the recorded interviews she'd sent him and give his thoughts.

He agreed, expecting another late night. But just like every time he found himself pulled in two incredibly different directions—one being football and the other the work he did with the foundation—he knew it was worth it. If he hadn't had that teacher in sixth grade who'd figured out that he was dyslexic, if he hadn't had a family who could afford tutoring to help him learn to overcome his disability . . . well, he didn't want to think about it.

The foundation focused mainly on general literacy, donating books to schools, especially in budget-cut inner-city schools, but they also provided important resources to teachers that helped them identify and assist kids who discovered that they didn't learn or read the way everyone else in their classes did.

It was good, important work, something that Kenyon had known he wanted to do from before he'd gone to Stanford.

And while he'd been in school, he'd taken a number of classes on not just business management, but specifically *nonprofit* management. He'd known he'd need them, because the point of going into the NFL wasn't the fame or the sport itself, it was the money and vital connections that he'd known he'd make.

It was why he kept chasing the highest bidder, switching from team to team.

He didn't care about winning a Super Bowl, though it wasn't like he *enjoyed* losing games. But he wasn't playing because he loved it. He was playing because he loved something else.

"Now," Keisha said with a reluctant tone to her voice, "there's one last thing we should probably talk about."

Their whole lives, she'd never been reluctant to kick his ass or tell him the blatant, blunt truth, and nothing between them had changed, so the way she couldn't quite meet his eyes across the screen made him nervous.

"What is it?"

Keisha shot him a look of pure annoyance. "You really going to pretend you don't know what it is?"

"What's going on?"

"We've gotten three calls about it already this afternoon," Keisha said. "Wondering what our comment is."

"Comment on *what*," Kenyon said with exasperation. "I had meetings and then a workout this afternoon. I don't even know where my phone is . . ."

"Find it," Keisha said with an earnestness that worried him.

He finally dug it out of his bag, that he'd brought home from the gym much earlier this morning. And, just like she'd foretold, it was full of missed calls. From some media contacts. And about a dozen of them from his agent.

Shit.

"What the fuck," Kenyon said, rapidly scrolling through his unanswered texts, and then his emails, trying to figure out what so many people were so worried and outraged about.

"Some reporter got on a podcast and made some comment about how you're not dedicated to the team, that you're half out of your job, because of *us*," Keisha said archly. "That we're distracting you from doing what you need to do, and the Piranhas should have found another running back who was completely committed."

"What the hell." Kenyon's jaw dropped open.

He knew, without being told, who this reporter was.

What had he just told Julian last night?

All I want is fair treatment.

Julian had agreed.

But what had he also said?

You really fuck up, don't worry, I'll call you out.

"I just need to know what to say, Kenyon," Keisha said crisply. "Nothing isn't going to cut it. We're going to have angry Piranhas fans overwhelming our social media—which you know is an important part of our outreach—if we don't address this."

"So this guy," Kenyon said. *This guy. This guy I've been fucking on the regular for the last six months. This guy I thought I really liked. Who I thought might actually like me back.* "This guy, he says shit, that doesn't mean anything. Journalists say shit all the time. Why this? Why does this even matter?"

"Oh, the guy he was talking to laughed him off, too, just like you're doing, because you know, the Piranhas are winning games, and you're kicking ass, and the reporter said, and he was serious and scary convincing, Kenyon, I saw the video, that he had *proof*."

Kenyon couldn't believe it.

Because he didn't have proof.

He couldn't possibly.

Because it wasn't true.

"I'm going to fix this," Kenyon said.

Keisha looked dubious. "Don't fix it," she said. "Just tell me what to do."

"Talk about you," Kenyon said. Feeling a little desperate. "Tell them everything *you* do, 'cause that's why I hired you, right? So I could focus on football. Worst-case scenario, maybe we'll get some extra attention. Negative attention is still attention, right?"

"Right." She didn't look any more convinced than he felt.

He was definitely going to kick Julian's ass. Betrayal and anger warred inside him; along with an insidious thread of uncertainty, inevitable concern that maybe Julian was right after all.

Maybe he wasn't committed.

He'd fumbled yesterday, hadn't he?

But they'd won so many games this year; games he'd been instrumental in. If he wasn't playing well, Julian wouldn't have been the very first person to say so, not when they were heading into the last regular season game.

He'd have been exposed long before this.

Coach would have been on his ass. And Coach wouldn't have been the only one.

"Well," Keisha said, "I sure hope you get this sorted out."

"It's gonna get sorted," Kenyon said, teeth clenched. "I'm gonna make sure of it, and anyone who's got an issue, who won't listen to what you're saying, you send them to me, alright?"

Keisha looked uncertain. "Really, but . . ."

"No," Kenyon said firmly. "You send them to me."

But first, before he dealt with any of these assholes who thought he was too busy trying to make sure that kids who couldn't read or didn't get the opportunities to read, didn't get their future sunk over it, he was going to deal with one asshole in particular.

The asshole he'd learned wasn't an asshole at all.

The asshole he'd come to trust.

The asshole he'd come to *care* for.

The asshole he was pretty sure cared about him too.

Julian Anderson.

It actually took longer than Julian expected for the angry text to come through.

It wasn't until hours after the podcast had been recorded and released for his phone to ding.

Well, that wasn't entirely accurate.

It had been making noise all day.

Nikki had told him in an awed voice that she hoped he knew what he was doing.

The truth was, he had no fucking idea.

He hadn't intended to say what he had. It hadn't been any-where in his notes.

But the problem with being obsessed with Kenyon Ellis was, he was *obsessed* with Kenyon Ellis. He thought about him all the time. He watched his film. He studied him. He obsessively charted his stats.

It was the worst possible combination of his job and his grow-ing feelings.

He knew what he'd said was true, but he'd never, ever planned to say it. Not out loud. Not even to Kenyon. And then it had just slipped out. The podcaster had been surprised, and then he'd pushed him, and Julian, so used to doing and saying the right thing, things he *meant* to say, dug himself into an even deeper hole.

It didn't matter that he was right. It didn't matter that he'd promised to call Kenyon out if he needed it.

Why, then, had he done it today?

You're so goddamn scared.

You're scared and obsessed and in so fucking deep.

He was.

Julian didn't like the way that felt. He was used to dictating the circumstances, to making the decisions, to charting the course of his own life, not *reacting* to other people charting it for him. He'd reacted today, a gut punch instinct to push away the one person who kept insistently worming their way in.

But understanding why he'd done it didn't make it right.

He hoped it might be a minor sensation and then go away, but he'd underestimated—something else he didn't normally do—the interest in the Piranhas right now. They'd gone from winning two games a year ago to clinching their division and heading to the playoffs. They were a hot commodity and he'd offered one of the most divisive takes on them.

One of the most divisive takes on one of the most famous players on the team.

Julian stared at his phone and tried to think of a way out of this.

You shouldn't even be thinking of a way out of this, he reminded himself. *You got more bookings for next week. Nikki's thrilled. Confused, but thrilled. And your phone won't stop ringing. You got what you wanted.*

Kenyon's never gonna talk to you again.

But had he?

We need to talk, the text said.

Julian was pretty sure what Kenyon actually meant was *I need to yell at you for stabbing me in the fucking back.*

He slid his phone back in his pocket and stared out the coffee shop window.

Julian was supposed to be working on a bigger article about playoff predictions that Nikki was compiling from a few different sources—it had been a big deal when she'd picked him as one of the reporters to chime in—but he'd been mostly staring at the screen for hours.

He stared at it for another hour, then finally the closing coffee shop chased him out.

When he got in his car, he had two more messages from Kenyon.

You really gonna ignore me now?

And then, twenty minutes after that text, came another one: **I thought you were a lot of things but I didn't think you were a coward.**

Julian hadn't thought he was a coward either, but it was undeniable that ducking Kenyon like this was akin to him pissing in his pants.

Afraid of what he'd say. Afraid of what he wouldn't say. Just plain fucking afraid.

He stopped by a fast-food restaurant on his way home, because drowning his guilt in fat and salt seemed like a better plan than popping open the bottle of vodka in his otherwise empty freezer.

Slinging his bag over his shoulder, he headed towards his building, ignoring his phone buzzing away in his pocket again.

He didn't want to talk to another person.

He just wanted to eat his burger and fries, ignore the vodka in his freezer, maybe put on some bad reality TV, and try to finish this story so he could get it off to Nikki.

Everything he could to avoid dreading tomorrow, where he'd be expected at the Piranhas' practice facility.

Where it was inevitable that he'd run into Kenyon.

He took the stairs, two at a time, but his feet froze on the top step.

Kenyon was leaning against the wall next to his apartment door.

Julian had two thoughts, nearly simultaneously:

1. Kenyon wasn't supposed to know where he lived.

2. He did not look particularly happy.

"This the place your boss rents for you?" he asked as Julian unstuck himself and approached, warily.

"What, not what you expected?" Julian knew his question was snarky, which wasn't exactly what he'd meant to start with, but at least he wasn't standing back anymore, letting Kenyon dictate their interactions.

What you need to do is take a step back and apologize.

"Just surprising." Kenyon regarded him steadily.

He stopped a few feet away from him. He had a dark blue hooded sweatshirt on, the hood pulled up. The zipper was partially open though, and he could see bare skin underneath.

How many times had he pushed his hands inside Kenyon's clothes to find bare skin? Craved the feel of the muscles underneath his palms?

Too fucking many.

He could remember all of them right now, blurring together in one pornographic video that flashed through his mind.

Sometimes, in his fantasies, he'd imagine Kenyon showing up like this. That he might press him to this exact door, and undo him.

"I'd ask why you're here, but I'm not going to pretend to be stupid now."

"Good," Kenyon said. "That would be pointless and exhausting. You gonna let me in?"

"No," Julian said, crossing his arms over his chest, his fast-food dinner in a bag dangling from his fingertips.

"Really?" Kenyon scoffed. "After . . . well, *after*."

Not expecting to be confronted by him tonight, Julian hadn't decided yet what he was going to say.

But in the end there was only one choice.

"I shouldn't have said it. I'm sorry. But no, you can't come in," Julian said. Because if Kenyon came in, Julian would fold the rest of the way, like a bad hand of cards.

"Really?" Kenyon looked frustrated, and even a little angry.

"Yes."

Kenyon threw up his arms. "You're the most fucking frustrating person I've ever met, hands down. Can't you just be . . . a human for a minute?"

"I'm trying to be," Julian said. And he was, goddamn it, he *was*.

Frankly, he was more human right now than he'd been in forever. He didn't like it, and he almost resented Kenyon for making him feel this way. For *making* him feel things again.

"You trying to be human is calling me out on a podcast?"

"You *asked* me to be honest." Kenyon had. Neither of them could argue with that.

"Oh, for fuck's sake," Kenyon argued. "That wasn't the same thing. I wanted you to give me a fair shake, not to deliberately throw me and the good work we're doing at the foundation to the wolves. I didn't want you to make up crap about me."

"I shouldn't have said it but that doesn't mean it's not true." Julian said this very matter-of-factly, because inside, something uncomfortable was churning in his stomach. Guilt, certainly. And regret. And a fatalistic inevitability that made him want to scream and/or cry.

"*What's* true?" Kenyon prowled closer. So close, Julian could smell him. So close his body believed that they'd be doing something else in a minute. That was the only way he could explain his growing erection.

His dick still thought he was going to get something he wanted, even if he'd almost certainly waved goodbye to the last orgasm that Kenyon was ever going to give him.

In the future, the only Kenyon-related orgasms were going to be ones he gave himself, while he fantasized about the man in front of him.

Julian shrugged. "You know it, deep down, it's why you're so pissed at me."

"That's bullshit," Kenyon argued. "You're just a reporter, you're not a football player. You're just talking out of your ass, trying to make a big story. Trying to get people to pay attention to what you're saying."

The funny thing—the most *ironic* thing in the world, actually—was that yes, for many reasons that Kenyon couldn't possibly know or comprehend, he was desperate to get people to pay attention to what he had to say, but that wasn't why today had happened.

Maybe, months later or even years later, Kenyon would realize the truth.

But he was too angry now to dig down, and see that Julian had only said it to piss him off. To end things because he hadn't been able to do it any other way.

Even now, the fact ached.

Not because he was in love with Kenyon or anything—he still didn't know him well enough for that, and Kenyon definitely did not know *him* well enough—but because the tantalizing possibility something more could develop had been hazy but damnably real.

He could've fallen in love with him, and Julian had known it.

Had been fucking terrified of it.

But now it was over, so none of that mattered.

"I'm so glad you've identified all my barely camouflaged asshole agendas," Julian said. "Now can you please move so I can get into my shitty apartment and eat my shitty dinner?"

But Kenyon didn't budge. Not an inch.

Julian wasn't exactly a slouch; he was small but strong. However, there was no way he was moving a brick wall like Kenyon.

Kenyon just stared at him. Like he was trying to read him. Like he was trying to understand him.

Too late for that.

"Here's the thing," Kenyon said. "You said you were right. Said you had evidence. They doubted you, and you dismissed their doubt. But you don't *know*."

"Guess that's up for debate," Julian said. He wasn't about to disclose all his qualifications—or his secrets—just because Kenyon thought he was totally clueless.

"You know something," Kenyon said, and suddenly he was right there, even closer, right in Julian's bubble. His fast-food bag dropped to the floor from nerveless fingers. Kenyon pressed right against him. Trying to intimidate him. Which was crazy, even crazier than this whole thing had been, because he should've known Julian didn't intimidate.

He *did* the intimidating.

Gathering his strength, he pushed Kenyon away. To his surprise, he went easily, stumbling a step away. Julian pulled his keys out of his pocket and unlocked the door.

"I know you're lying to yourself," Julian said, and then ducked inside, slamming the door and locking it behind him.

For a breathless moment, he rested against the chipped and stained wood. He could still *feel* Kenyon out there.

He hadn't left. Like he hadn't gotten what he'd wanted at all.

Dissatisfaction crawled through Julian's blood.

He'd wanted more, too.

He'd wanted to press his mouth to Kenyon's, their first kiss messy and maybe even a little bit angry before it morphed into something else entirely.

Their first kiss, and their last kiss.

But even then, he didn't move.

Moving felt like giving up, like finally severing this cord between them.

He felt the door shimmy. Someone leaning against the other side of it. *God, they were so messed up.*

A soft knock echoed through his head. Or his apartment? Was it real or just wish-fulfillment?

Julian wasn't sure until he heard the voice. It was Kenyon's, low and filled with . . . *God,* filled with hurt.

"Don't worry, I'm gone," he said. "Don't forget your dinner. You're too skinny. Skip too many meals 'cause you work too hard."

Then Julian felt him go.

He told himself it was better this way, but he didn't believe it. Not even for a second.

Kenyon wanted to believe that after settling things between them, he'd be able to fall asleep.

It was why he'd tracked down Julian's home address, and showed up at his apartment complex, surprised at how shitty and run down it was. Didn't his company pay for better housing?

But Julian hadn't answered that question. He also hadn't answered anything else.

So as a result, it didn't feel like they'd settled a thing.

Not a single goddamn thing.

Julian had been his normal slippery self, teasing him and ducking him, even as he enticed him to slide a little closer.

It was why he didn't want to give up on the guy.

You're pissed off, you've got every right to ditch the asshole.

But somehow, Kenyon couldn't convince himself that Julian *was* an asshole. Because even when he'd first thought it, nothing else had seemed to confirm it.

Yes, Julian could be prickly. He could be difficult. He'd drawn that line between them and then he'd stuck to it. Or at least *sorta* stuck to it.

But he'd never been an asshole. Not once.

There was something else going on, and damnit if it wasn't keeping Kenyon awake, staring at the dark ceiling as the hours passed.

When he headed into practice, he grabbed a second cup of coffee and even that didn't help.

When he hit the offensive team meeting, he was still yawning.

"You not sleep well?" Davis asked as he slid into one of the chairs.

"Not great," Kenyon admitted.

Davis' expression turned sympathetic. "I saw that shit the reporter said. Must have pissed you off."

"Yeah." Davis had no idea how badly it had. Because he just thought Julian was doing his job as a reporter, creating a story, even if it was at Kenyon's expense. Davis didn't have any clue that he *knew* Julian. That he'd wanted to know him even more, despite all the ways it could've bitten him in the ass.

"It'll pass," Davis said, sounding confident it would.

The email he'd gotten first thing from Keisha said that they'd temporarily turned off comments on their social media, and the tags on Twitter had gone down, even since the day before.

It was going to blow over, she was sure of it.

It wasn't like he doubted she was speaking the truth. Julian was a nobody—a nobody on the rise, sure, but still essentially a nobody—and with the Piranhas' win–loss record, the story wasn't going to have legs.

Maybe Kenyon couldn't figure out *why* he said it, but at least it wasn't even as bad of a hack job as had been done to Davis on a regular fucking basis.

The fact that he was still feeling sorry for himself was pathetic. Davis should've said that, but he was too nice of a guy.

Maybe he should just get over it, Kenyon thought, trying to pull his attention back to the meeting, because it certainly wasn't the right move, the morning after he'd been accused of not giving a shit, to look like he *didn't* give a shit.

Except all that thinking that he shouldn't be angry, that he should let it go—should just let *Julian* go—only stoked his fury even hotter.

He was gonna tell Julian he was wrong.

Even more, he was gonna *show* him.

By the time he finally made it onto the field, his temper was hotter than ever, and sharpened to a fine point.

Kenyon could tell because everyone was giving him a pretty wide berth.

Normally that was how he operated, but over time, he'd begun to let this particular team in, further than he had before. He'd gone to social events, he'd hung out with these guys, and he'd even count some of them as friends.

But most of them had taken one look at the hard look in his eye and avoided him. Kenyon couldn't even blame them.

He attacked practice like it had personally wronged him, pushing harder than he had in awhile. Hitting his marks, accelerating through the gaps created by the offensive line, tucking the ball away so tight it would take a bomb to dislodge it.

It was mostly a non-contact practice, because at this late in the season, nobody wanted to be the one to hurt a teammate. But when he'd caught a pass out of the backfield, he'd attacked the field, running hard, and when Sebastian came up to stop him, he put out his fist and pushing with all his strength, stiff-armed him to the ground.

He barely blinked, and then kept running.

Even though he heard Coach blowing his whistle, he didn't stop, plowing ahead until he crossed the goal line.

When he dropped the ball, it fell out of his nerveless fingers, aching because he'd been gripping it so firmly.

Turning, he was surprised to see Coach's . . . well, it was Coach's guy, wasn't it? Scott Callaway, who usually worked with the defense, standing there.

"Hey, hard running there," the guy said.

He was unexpectedly short of breath. Leaned over, tried to catch it. "Yeah." He had no fucking idea what Scott Callaway was doing down here.

Scott tucked his hands into the pockets of his shorts. He was still in exceptional shape for a guy his age, built like a tank, with these incredibly broad shoulders. But he had a nice smile, especially whenever Coach crossed over into his field of view.

"I guess you got somethin' to prove," Scott observed.

"You heard." What *he* heard was his own voice grow harder. Unforgiving.

Yeah, he was still a little pissed.

Or a *lot* pissed.

"Yeah, sure I did. Coach was sorta moanin' about it."

Kenyon shot him an unamused glance. Considered saying that he didn't think Julian was the only reason he was moaning lately, but he didn't, because nobody knew quite what to do with the fact that Coach—*Coach*—was not only in love, but *married*.

He'd heard Logan say in a confused voice more than once, "Does that mean we can give him shit? Like we give Tristan and Wade shit?"

The answer was almost definitely no.

Though Kenyon was real interested to see if Logan ever decided to take the risk.

"Anyone here tellin' you that you're not pulling your weight?" Scott asked.

Kenyon shook his head.

They wouldn't, you've been doing this long enough to know the difference between required and optional.

That was the whole fucking problem, wasn't it? He was threading the needle, doing exactly what was required of him, and nothing more.

Before his teammates had reached out, he'd even kept himself apart from them.

He saw the way Pax studied.

The hours Logan put in in the weight room.

Even Tristan had worked his ass off, learning how to run an NFL route.

Coach had gone to the hospital for a heart attack, because he'd been working so goddamned hard.

He felt the inevitable swell of guilt, and pushed it away, letting it melt into all his white-hot anger. Julian hadn't had any right to say what he had. Not about him. Not when he was technically pulling his weight.

Nobody here had pulled him aside and told him he needed to do more.

He'd made sure of it.

But, in the end, it was the making sure of it that bothered him.

"No," Kenyon said wryly. "But I made sure they couldn't."

"Not today," Scott pointed out.

"You here to give me the pep talk?"

"Actually, I came over to remind you that we need you fresh for the playoffs. Why? You need one?"

Kenyon wasn't sure. 'Cause a pep talk sure wasn't going to fix the guilt—or the certainty—that Julian was exactly right.

He even said he had proof.

Of course, that could have been total bullshit. But that wasn't like Julian. It wasn't like him to lie.

He wasn't even any good at it.

And he wasn't an asshole, he reminded himself again. No matter how much he put on that front, it wasn't true. Kenyon had been seeing through it for months now. Had seen through it from almost the beginning.

"No," Kenyon said. "I'm good."

But he wasn't.

He still felt like beating something—or someone—to a pulp.

But Scott was annoyingly right; pushing himself too far when he needed fresh legs for the playoffs wasn't going to help anyone.

Not even him.

Chapter Seven

Julian hated feeling guilty.

It was a waste of emotion.

A *distracting* waste of emotion.

He'd finally finished his playoff article and sent it to Nikki twelve minutes late, which was unlike him. She'd waved his tardiness aside, with a reassurance that she knew how in-demand he was.

He'd definitely been fielding calls and texts and emails for days, booking more podcasts to air this week, no doubt all of them hoping that he'd say something equally as incendiary and bring all kinds of attention to their media.

But Julian had already told himself—and Nikki—that he wouldn't be. He didn't even want to write an article about what he'd said about Kenyon, though she'd come perilously close to begging, which was totally unlike Nikki.

She could have ordered him to do it, and considering how well he knew her, she must have considered it, but in the end, she'd let it go.

"You'll find something else," she'd said, sounding confident that he would.

He knew one thing and one thing only: he wouldn't be giving any more quotes about Kenyon Ellis.

Not a single damn one.

Of course, Julian thought as he stared at his laptop screen, annoyed with himself, and even more annoyed with the guilt he couldn't stop feeling, the one had been enough.

Kenyon wasn't going to want to spend another second in his company if he could help it. While Julian kept thinking he should be relieved about that, relieved at the near miss, since he'd been so damn close to actually developing something called feelings, the actual truth was that he plain fucking missed the guy.

He'd known how much time they spent with each other, but he hadn't realized how much of his so-called "free" time their hookups had occupied.

How it felt so weird to not be able to text him.

How bizarre it felt to look at his phone and realize none of the messages in his inbox were from the person he wanted them to be from.

You are so fucked.

He didn't think this project occupying so much of the time he didn't have would really improve the situation, but he was staying up way too late every night, and getting up at insane o'clock anyway.

You're just looking for his attention. Even if it's negative.

The truth was, he could have left it alone.

He *should* have left it alone.

He'd not *wanted* to end it, but he'd known he should. And now it was ended.

But of course, he hadn't left it alone.

Because if Kenyon had disliked his quote on the podcast, he was really going to hate this, but Julian kept working on it anyway, until it was finally done. He sat back and scrubbed a hand across his face.

Was he crazy enough to actually show this to Kenyon?

How could he *not*?

He was going to hate him either way.

But maybe, just maybe, Kenyon might see something in here that would give him something. One last gift from someone who hadn't wanted to care about him, but did anyway: a truth he didn't know about himself.

So he packed up his laptop, locked the door of his shitty apartment, and got into his car before he could figure out that this was a really fucking bad idea.

It was late on a Thursday night. Julian knew Kenyon usually went to the offensive lineman dinner, because he benefited from their hard work just as much as Paxton did, but that afterwards, he almost always came back home to his house. Watched some TV. Usually had sex with Julian.

So the chances were, Julian thought as he parked in front of Kenyon's house he rented in Miami—not as big as some of the other guys' houses, but still big enough that it could fit his shitty little apartment ten times over—that he'd be home.

Home, and almost definitely still angry.

Julian got out of his car. Gripped his bag with trembling fingers as he walked up the steps to Kenyon's front door.

Knocked.

For a minute, for an everlasting minute, Julian thought maybe he wasn't home after all. Maybe he'd already found a new hookup partner, and he was off fucking someone else.

That shouldn't have stung, because *he'd* done this. He'd pushed Kenyon away, and then pissed him off. Maybe not entirely on purpose, but deep down, he'd known what would happen if he opened his mouth.

There was a reason he'd known this about Kenyon's play for months, but never said a word.

Then, he heard footsteps in the foyer, the echo of them matching the pounding of his heart, and abruptly, the door swung open.

Kenyon wasn't wearing a shirt, only a pair of low-slung athletic shorts and a pissed-off expression.

"What are you doing here?" he demanded.

Responding to anger with snottiness was a life failing. He knew it. But it was comfortable, even if it didn't always feel particularly intelligent. "Nice," Julian said. "At least when you appeared on my doorstep, I didn't yell at you."

Kenyon stared at him. "Really? You came *here*. What was the plan, Julian? To apologize again? To beg for my forgiveness?"

Yes.

His words burned Julian because they were true. He'd apologize a million times if it meant this could be fixed. If it meant the angry look in Kenyon's expression melted away.

"Yes," Julian said. He could be pragmatic yes, but that didn't mean he ever shied away from things he needed to do, and one of those things was apologize, again. "I shouldn't have said what I did, not like I did. I'm sorry it happened that way. I didn't mean to . . . but . . ." Julian hesitated. He didn't want to say *why* he'd done it, so instead, he moved on. "I thought it might help you if I showed you what I saw, that made me say it in the first place."

He tried to say it all matter-of-factly with none of the emotion swirling through him, but he wasn't quite sure he pulled it off.

Affection. Longing. Regret. *Guilt.*

There was that goddamned guilt again.

Kenyon was still staring at him incredulously.

"You said you wanted to see the evidence. Said you didn't believe me." Julian pointed to the laptop bag slung over his shoulder. It was dark brown suede, stylish and simple, a knockoff he'd scoured Amazon for, because there'd been no chance of him affording the designer original. Image was always important. "I've got the evidence right here, if you're interested."

Kenyon's gaze morphed into suspicion.

"Why should I trust you?"

That shouldn't have hurt so much but it did. Because before Julian had fucked this up, Kenyon had trusted him, implicitly. Julian knew it.

They *both* knew it.

"Because," Julian said, "it's not me you're trusting. It's the tape. It's black and white, right there on the screen."

"You seem pretty sure about this."

It made sense Kenyon might doubt him; he was just a reporter, after all. A pretty face. Kenyon didn't know about Julian's past, because he'd scrupulously made sure to never tell him.

Never thought he'd regret that—but he did now.

"I am," Julian said.

Kenyon finally shrugged, and pushed the door further open. "Might as well, I guess."

Julian had been arguing with himself for days over whether compiling this was even the right call. Tonight, he almost turned and walked away because as much as Kenyon's anger had hurt, it had been justified.

Kenyon's casual dismissal was worse.

He wanted to justify his words, sure. But that justification wouldn't be worth this.

But something about Kenyon drew Julian into the house, like he always had.

Usually they went straight to the living room. Or the bedroom. But tonight, Kenyon led him into a part of the house he'd never been in: the kitchen.

It was painfully bright; white tiles and white cabinets and white marble countertops. He barely stopped himself from shading his eyes.

"Yeah," Kenyon said with a short bark of laughter. "I always wanna wear sunglasses in here. If I wasn't renting, I'd have torn it all out."

"What would you have put in instead?" It was a stupid question for so many reasons—because everything between them had already fallen apart, because he wasn't here to discuss interior decorating, because he'd *never* come over to talk about Kenyon's kitchen and why would he start now?—but he found himself asking it anyway.

"Dark wood, I think. Green tiles. I like green. Relaxing color, green," Kenyon said thoughtfully.

Then, like he caught himself, his expression morphed from considerate to exasperated. "Why are you really here?" he demanded.

"I told you. You said you didn't believe me. And, I thought, now that it's in the open, whether either of us like it or not . . . I thought you should see." Julian pulled his laptop out of his bag and set it on the countertop. He opened it up, and clicked play on the video on the screen.

He'd picked out ten plays, starting from the preseason and continuing through to now, just so Kenyon couldn't accuse him of focusing too much on early games, when the Piranhas' offense had still been trying to find its footing.

For each play, he'd gone through the footage, analyzing it like he'd done in college, slowing down the video, and marking it up on the screen.

Then he'd added some voiceover—succinct, and clear, explaining what Kenyon could have done instead of what he'd actually done. He'd tried to keep his judgment out of his tone, but it had been hard.

From the way Kenyon's expression hardened as each segment played, he had a feeling he hadn't quite succeeded.

He would give Kenyon credit, though.

He watched every single play, not saying a word.

But the tenseness in the room kept escalating, until all Julian wanted to do was grab the laptop and run back to his car.

Why had he thought this was a good idea?

It was the supposedly adult equivalent of pulling Kenyon's metaphorical pigtails.

Not smart.

He could hear Nikki's voice in his ear, one of the first conversations they'd had after she'd hired him out of college.

You're painfully good looking, she'd said, *which you don't need me to tell you, but I will remind you that getting involved with players isn't only a bad idea, it's generally not tolerated. Don't do it,* she'd added. *Just don't do it, no matter how tempted you are.*

And you'll be tempted.

The one slim excuse he had was he and Kenyon had hooked up before he'd realized he was a player.

Did it excuse the hundreds of times after that?

No, no, it did not.

He'd been willfully stupid for six months now, but at least he had consistency on his side.

Tempted was an understatement.

The video finally ended, and the kitchen went quiet.

Kenyon didn't say a word.

Just stared at the last image on the screen. Reached out, clenched the back of one of his barstools—white, of course—with his hands.

Still said nothing.

Finally Julian, awkward and suddenly, inexplicably nervous that he'd pushed Kenyon too far, reached for the laptop but Kenyon grabbed his arm. Held him in place.

Not in any of the sexy ways he'd done it so many times before. This time his grip hurt.

Julian flinched, and Kenyon immediately let him go. He couldn't miss the shame in his eyes that he'd hurt him.

They'd not hurt each other, not like this, before now. Maybe you couldn't come back from that.

"Is this . . ." Kenyon took a deep breath, turning towards him just enough that Julian could see the anger and the humiliation in his eyes. He'd done this, *he'd* put that look on Kenyon's face. "Is this really what you think of me?"

"No, no, not really, no," Julian said hurriedly. "No, of course not. You're . . . you know you're a valuable member of the team . . . I just thought . . . God, I'm so sorry. So sorry."

What had he been thinking?

Right now, he couldn't formulate even a single reason why this had been a good idea.

Except that it meant he could talk to Kenyon one last time.

Good job, he just kinda hated you before. Now he really *hates you.*

"So you apparently think I'm a shit running back," Kenyon continued, like he hadn't even spoken. "Was I shitty in bed, too? You gonna make me some diagrams on how to fuck better? How to fuck 'less distracted'?"

Julian stared at him. Not sure what to say.

Didn't the fact that he kept coming back say it all? That they hadn't been able to keep their hands off each other?

He felt astonished, in the worst way possible. He'd hoped to *help*, and instead, all Kenyon felt when he saw the truth was shame. Like he'd been fucking up and hadn't even realized it.

"What? Nothing? You don't have anything to say *now*?" Kenyon retorted. "Though I guess that makes sense. 'Cause when it really mattered, you never had anything to fucking say."

"That's . . ." Julian wanted to say that wasn't fair. It was an entirely false and unfair accusation, but it wasn't.

"And," Kenyon continued, relentless, his voice so hard that Julian barely recognized it, "when should I expect you'll be publishing this? Tomorrow? Next week? Right before our first playoff game?"

"That's not fair," he finally got out. "I never . . . I *wouldn't*."

"No, you didn't, not til now, not til you came here and proved that you've been digging dirt on me since day one. Practically since the day we met." Regret and anger warred on Kenyon's face. "Maybe that was even a bullshit lie, too, how we met. I believed you, 'cause you never used me, not once, but now . . . now I'm not sure anymore."

"It was an accident." Julian interrupted him. "It was a fucking accident, you know that. You *know* that."

"Do I? *Do I?*" Kenyon's voice rose with each word and they were suddenly so close to each other.

Too close, you're too close, Julian's brain screamed, even as his dick did a little celebration dance that maybe, *just maybe,* he might get a little more of the pleasure he'd become so addicted to.

"I would've said you trust me, but maybe you don't. Not anymore," Julian said. "And that's my fault. I shouldn't have said what I did. I *know* I shouldn't have. I said other stuff, too, after, but you know nobody ever bothers to add context. About how good you are, how solid, how reliable. How you protect the ball. I . . . I never wanted things to be this way between us. I wanted . . ." Julian swallowed hard. "I wanted you to trust me. Like I trust you."

"Goddamn it, Julian, *I tried to.*"

That was the worst of all: he knew that Kenyon had tried. And he'd made it impossible.

Par for the course, pushing everyone who might give a shit about you away.

"I know," Julian said, turning his head away. He couldn't look at Kenyon's face anymore, at what he'd screwed up. At what he'd regret forever.

He would not cry. He never cried. Not for years and years and years. And now here was Kenyon Ellis, pushing him to that point.

Kenyon didn't move. Didn't speak for a long time.

Then suddenly, his hands were on Julian's arms and he was shaking him a little, his eyes wide with shock.

"You did this on purpose. You did this *on purpose.*" Kenyon was staring at him like he was seeing him for the first time.

"I don't know what you're talking about," he blustered, but the knowledge was clear and bright in Kenyon's eyes. He *knew.*

"Yes, you do. You were afraid. I was getting too close and you freaked out. You were freaking out, just like I was freaking out, and you lashed out. Not because you hated me, or didn't trust me, or wanted to humiliate me, but because of this . . ."

Julian froze, but Kenyon was already moving, then he pressed him up against the fridge. For a heart-stopping moment, they stared at each other, and he knew what was coming, but he'd already tried everything he could to stop it, and it turned out that he was fresh out of arguments against this.

"Goddamn it, Julian," Kenyon muttered, and then he kissed him.

It wasn't like he'd never been kissed before—before Kenyon he'd never been particular about not kissing his hookups, but *with* Kenyon it had seemed like an important line worth preserving—but he'd never been kissed by Kenyon Ellis before, and it turned out that was a monumental difference that he'd never considered, but now wouldn't be able to forget.

He was fucking amazing at kissing, lips soft but purposeful as his mouth moved against Julian's. The intimate knowledge of how insanely good Kenyon's tongue was still didn't prepare him for it when his lips opened and then it was right there, stroking against his own, leaving him lightheaded.

His solid thigh wedged against his own, and that was definitely his cock, pressing against him as Kenyon pushed him into the fridge, devouring him alive. Like he didn't even want to stop.

Don't ever stop. Don't let me think. Don't let me overthink.

Then, horribly, Julian felt him lift his mouth.

To take a breath?

To say something?

To suggest they stop?

To suggest they go upstairs before they ended up fucking on the kitchen floor?

Julian didn't know what he was going to say, but he wasn't ready for the spell to end.

He reached up, dug his fingertips into Kenyon's broad, muscular shoulders—*God*, he'd done this so many times, but how had he never taken this inevitable, obvious step and pressed his mouth to his?

He didn't know how he'd ever resisted it. If he'd known how good it was, he never could've. His self-control was ironclad and frankly legendary, but it evaporated entirely around Kenyon.

It was his smile, lighting up his eyes with kindness. He was sweet, but not too sweet. There was the way he loved how pragmatic Julian was. How he never wanted him to be different. How he didn't mind his snotty attitude, or his secrets, or the way he went totally boneless after sex.

It was the size of his heart, because the thing he did that wasn't football, the thing that he'd claimed distracted Kenyon from football, was one of the best fucking things in the whole world. This was a guy who cared not just what he could do on the field, but off it, too.

Lots of people had offered charity to Julian over the years.

But almost none of them had made it about him; their supposed generosity had always been about *them*.

But not Kenyon with his foundation.

How had he repaid that generosity? By calling him out publicly, in the worst possible way. It was a fucking miracle that he'd even let Julian into his house tonight, never mind that they were currently kissing against his also-white refrigerator.

Guilt swamped him again.

Guilt and something else.

Something that shouldn't have terrified him, if he was *normal*, but Julian wasn't normal. Never had been.

He pulled away.

For a long second, looked not at Kenyon, but over his shoulder, at all that blinding white.

His breathing wasn't normal, but neither was Kenyon's.

His cock was still a hot, hard line against his own thigh.

You should say something.

Something.

Anything.

"I guess . . ." Kenyon was chuckling under his breath, rueful and surprised. "I guess we should've done that awhile ago."

It wasn't like Julian disagreed.

Clearly it had been a *long* time coming, because it had been not just in the top five kisses of his whole life, it had been the best goddamn kiss he'd ever had.

So of course, it made perfect sense that he freaked out. *Again.*

Ducked right under Kenyon's affectionate stare, under his arm, grabbed his laptop and took off through the foyer, walking fast, hearing the footsteps behind him.

"What are you doing?" Kenyon asked, as he chased him.

See? He's not that pissed off at you. He's chasing after you, like some sappy romantic comedy.

But this wasn't a movie, it was Julian's life, and he'd already fucked it up badly enough.

He turned. "You don't want to do this with me," he said.

Kenyon frowned. "But I *just* did."

"Yes, but . . ."

"Why am I not surprised there's a *but* in there?" Kenyon interrupted, sounding darkly amused. "You are . . . well, a piece of work, you know?"

"I know."

Didn't he fucking know it?

Kenyon sighed. "Here's the other crazy thing. I'm not angry at you for it. I mean . . . that *sucked*. Watching that video sucked. I should hate you, for how humiliated you just made me feel, but I don't. I almost . . . and this is the kicker, the craziest fucking kicker, right here . . . I almost want to *thank* you for it. Isn't that messed up?"

Stop talking, Julian thought. He was terrified Kenyon was working his way up to a confession that he didn't want to hear. The reason why he didn't hate him.

"It's 'cause I give great blowjobs, isn't it?" Julian said flippantly.

Kenyon shot him a strange look. "No, actually, that's not why, though I'll admit it doesn't hurt your case."

"I thought so," Julian said smugly.

"It's 'cause I almost think you did it *for* me, which is wild, 'cause why would you think that insulting me means something? But you're *you*, so you might actually think that."

Julian didn't say anything.

He felt so fucking exposed.

How had this happened? He'd been so goddamned careful. He'd kept his distance—or *tried* to keep his distance. He'd not kissed the guy. He'd only fucked him, and let him fuck him back. He'd restricted their conversation before and after sex, though admittedly, he'd gotten rather lackadaisical about that particular rule.

He'd gotten rather lackadaisical about everything, honestly. The line had been blurred almost from the first moment. The first night they'd met.

"You must be more masochistic than I realized," Julian said in a frosty voice, "if me being an asshole turns you on."

But even that didn't scare him off. Even then, he didn't tell Julian to get out.

Instead, Kenyon shook his head, and he was still goddamn *laughing*. Like he couldn't quite believe it himself, and well, that made two of them, didn't it?

What was wrong with him?

Actually, Julian thought, *what is wrong with* you, *if you keep running away from a guy that actually gives a shit about you because you're a dick to him?*

"It's not that you're an asshole. 'Cause you're not. It's that you're ... I don't know ... yourself. No matter what. No matter if you want me to suck your cock or meet you in some dark corner of a place where we could absolutely definitely get caught doing something we shouldn't, you're still *you*. You're never anybody else."

"If you're meeting a lot of people who pretend to be someone else, you might want to work on that," Julian said.

"See?" Kenyon took a step closer, carefully, like he might spook him. And frankly, he wasn't all that wrong.

Julian's hand was still on the knob on the front door, and he was *this close* to escaping.

With his sanity intact.

Without Kenyon compromising any more of his heart.

"See what?" Julian said, swallowing hard.

Kenyon pressed against him again, chest to chest, thigh to thigh, and Julian felt the touch resonate through him. Trembled, against his will.

"See," Kenyon said softly, "even now, when you're still being your prickly self, I absolutely love it. I shouldn't. I should tell you to fuck off. I'm humiliated, and turned on, somehow, impossibly, at the exact same goddamn time. I wish someone would explain that to me."

Julian swallowed hard. "I can't."

Kenyon stepped away, reluctantly, and Julian had to grip the door harder, so he wouldn't reach for him. Convince him, any way he knew how—and he was plenty willing to play dirty—to come back.

"I had a feeling," he said.

"Oh." This was his cue to go, but he was still lingering.

Stupid, stupid, stupid.

"Maybe you could send me that video," Kenyon said.

"What?" Julian's jaw dropped. "*Why?*"

He just shrugged, though. "Maybe I'm feeling a little masochistic. And maybe you had a point, a few times. Not all of them, mind you, but a few. What . . ." He hesitated. "How did you learn how to analyze film that way?"

"Normal reporter school, you know," Julian said. "They teach it all to us these days."

Kenyon just shook his head, but he was smiling. "You're still such a bad liar."

Just when it comes to you.

"You'll figure it out," Julian said, which was even stupider. He didn't want to challenge Kenyon to dig into *him*.

But *stupid* was the one word that seemed to define every single one of his interactions with Kenyon Ellis. He kept taking all these risks, running right up to the line and praying that Kenyon wouldn't catch him and drag him right over. He would, someday. It was inevitable.

Self-preservation reared its ugly, annoying head, and Julian couldn't avoid the *other* inevitability. He ran away then, turning the doorknob and stumbling down the brick entrance to his car.

When he tried to put his key in the ignition, his hands were shaking so badly they dropped the whole bundle of them twice.

As he drove home through the dark streets of Miami, he had only one thought, repeating over and over through his stupid brain: that kiss hadn't felt anything like a goodbye.

"Hey, you got a minute?"

Beau looked up from where he was hunched over his desk—looking from Kenyon's view nearly the same as his father did, just with no gray strands in his dark hair—and smiled.

"Oh yeah, sure, what's up?" he asked as he straightened, stretching his arms above his head. "Gah, that's better. Sebastian keeps telling me I should set an alarm, to remind me to move every hour, but I forget."

Kenyon took the seat across from Beau's. Scrubbed his damp palms on his sweatpants.

He'd debated whether he should talk to Beau about this ever since Julian had sent the video over this morning, no subject line, no email content other than the attachment.

He hadn't known what he'd expected. Maybe something like, *wow, that was a long time coming, wasn't it? We should get together and kiss like that again, soon.* But of course, there was no way that Julian would ever say that, even if it was true.

The chances of Julian ever acknowledging what was brewing between them had probably gone right out the window the moment they'd kissed.

Probably if Kenyon tried to get him over again, he'd never come.

He was running scared.

Wouldn't admit that, either, probably, but Kenyon knew the truth.

Even if he didn't like it one bit.

"So?" Beau asked, raising an eyebrow.

"What did you think of what that reporter said the other day? About me and my commitment?" Kenyon asked.

Beau chuckled. "Did my dad tell you not to worry about it?"

"Basically," Kenyon said, though he hadn't cornered Coach to ask about it specifically.

Why hadn't he?

He hadn't wanted his *coach*—the man he undeniably respected more than almost any other—to sit him down and tell him the painful truth.

But then, if it *was* true, why hadn't he done that exact thing?

Kenyon wasn't sure.

Beau sighed, leaned back in his chair. "There's nothing wrong with how you're playing, Kenyon."

"I have a video that says otherwise." He hadn't meant to be so blunt about it, maybe hadn't really intended to tell Beau about Julian's work at all. But if he hadn't, why had he come here in the first place?

You wanted to hear what he thought. You trusted Beau to tell you the truth, just the way he told Sebastian a truth he didn't want to hear.

"A video? Someone gave you tape trying to say that you were playing distracted?"

"I think the idea was that my prep was distracted. I wasn't . . . as game-ready as I could've been."

"Would we send you out there not game-ready?" Beau asked, his tone mild.

"No . . . no, you wouldn't."

That was the problem.

But film didn't lie.

Kenyon couldn't stop thinking about it.

About the truths that Julian had laid bare, starkly obvious in the footage, and ultimately undeniable.

"But you don't trust that," Beau said thoughtfully.

"Not after what I saw," Kenyon said.

"What's this video?" Beau asked. "Can I see it?"

Kenyon had been anticipating this request. But he wasn't going to forward Julian's email to Beau—because that would create more questions than find him answers—so he'd emailed it to himself, and now he pulled out his phone and sent that email to Beau.

Of course there was the voiceovers . . . but fingers crossed, Beau wouldn't recognize Julian's voice. After all, what reason did he have? Julian mostly did print, and Beau never participated in press conferences like his father did.

"Just sent it to you," he said.

"Alright," Beau said, clicking on his laptop, pulling up the video.

It was hell, sitting there, taking in Beau's expression as he watched it.

It wasn't exactly damning, because if it had been, he wouldn't still be a starting running back on a team that was twelve and four and seeded third in the playoffs.

He just wouldn't be.

But there were some really good, really painful points that Julian brought up.

Spots that he should've known to go the other direction.

Instinctual plays he hadn't made.

When it finally ended, Beau's gaze fixed on him.

"Where did you get this?" he asked.

"Does it matter?" Kenyon retorted.

"Yeah, yeah, of course it does, because I'd fucking hire this guy in a moment."

"Uh, I think he has a pretty good job."

Beau sighed. "Of course he does. Because this is damn good work."

"I know," Kenyon said. It was why he was angry; and also, impossibly, why he wasn't *angrier*.

Julian hadn't just been talking out of his ass, trying to get attention.

He'd seen something, and he'd held back. Because he could've said it ages ago. And louder. Way louder.

"His voice sounds familiar, but I can't quite place it . . ." Beau trailed off. "Anyway, what he says isn't entirely wrong, Kenyon. You watched it. You know that."

Kenyon nodded. It hurt less than he'd expected, hearing the truth from Beau's mouth.

"But here's the thing, we wouldn't trade you for another running back. *You're* our running back. But maybe we could incorporate some of this prep into your routine. That's absolutely something we could do."

"We could," Kenyon agreed. But he thought, before he could stop it, that what he really wanted wasn't to do that at all.

He didn't want to work on football sixteen hours a day, like Pax did. Like Sebastian and Logan and even Beau.

He didn't love it with every fiber of his being like Dylan, determined to make it in the NFL no matter what it took, how many dead ends he hit.

That wasn't him. It hadn't ever been him.

He'd always known the truth, but this was the first time it had stung.

Maybe he was doing the Piranhas a disservice.

But we're twelve and four.

He'd given what was needed to get them there. Was he supposed to feel bad he hadn't opened a vein and bled out for them, too?

That wasn't part of the employment contract.

But even that undeniable fact didn't erase his guilt.

"Just a thought," Beau said. "I can do this for the last game, send you the footage, or we can do a meeting . . ."

"Send me the footage." He didn't have time for more meetings. Not with the end of the season coming up, because Keisha always ramped up his responsibilities with We Read then. Normally he didn't worry the team he was on going deep into the playoffs, but that was the unspoken excitement around every corner in the Piranhas' facility.

Nobody said the words, but it was obvious *Super Bowl* was on everyone's mind.

They wouldn't say it and jinx them, because football players were a fucking superstitious bunch, but Kenyon knew they were all thinking it.

It would make his schedule even tighter over the next few weeks.

"Alright," Beau said. He hesitated. "I want you to promise me you aren't going to obsess over this, okay?"

Kenyon shot him a baleful look.

"Okay, okay, I *know* what asking that is like," Beau said. "I live with a football player who overthinks the way he ties his shoes, but I mean it. It's not going to make you play better. Just lean into the feeling. Into your best instincts. They've gotten you this far, they're not wrong."

"But they're not right every time."

"No," Beau acknowledged. "But every time Pax throws a pass, it doesn't get caught either. Not every pitch is a strike. Some of them are balls, on purpose. It's okay. There's enough you're doing for us, I don't worry about every single one of your runs being five yards or more."

"Okay," Kenyon said. He didn't think Beau was wrong. But knowing it wasn't wrong, and believing it were two different things. "Thanks for taking the time." They shook hands.

Beau smiled. "It's what I'm here for, Kenyon. It's fine."

As Kenyon walked away, he realized that Beau had been telling the truth. It *was* what he was here for, to maximize the potential of every single goddamn player on the team, and had he ever even considered taking Beau up on that?

No. No, he had not.

Chapter Eight

WHAT AN ABSOLUTE FUCKING disaster.

Nothing—and everything—had gone right in the two days since he'd been stupid beyond imagining and had let Kenyon kiss him.

Let me? He could hear Kenyon's voice observe in his head. *You wanted me to do it, and you fucking loved every second of it.*

Which was really the whole problem, because yes, Julian had. He'd not only loved every moment, now he wanted more.

Julian leaned back in his chair, in front of the desk he'd set up his laptop on in the hotel room, and groaned as he stretched.

It was the night before the last game of the year.

And for the preceding sixteen games, he and Kenyon had established a routine.

After curfew, Kenyon would leave his room, take the stairs, and knock on his door. They'd spend a few hours losing themselves, ignoring both of their jobs and every internal voice warning them they were currently making a whole series of mistakes.

But that wouldn't be happening tonight.

It was a good run.

But had it been?

Whenever Julian thought of the last seventeen weeks, he was swamped with regret.

You should've kissed Kenyon a long time ago.

Seventeen goddamn weeks ago, to be specific.

He hadn't heard from Kenyon after he'd sent the video, as promised, and he didn't expect to.

He'd pushed him away, time and time again, and then to top it off, he'd betrayed him.

Anyone with a single molecule of self-preservation would leave Julian alone.

That was why he was so surprised to hear his phone beep.

It's not Kenyon, he told himself as he glanced over. *No matter how much you want it to be.*

But it was.

Let's find a bar nearby and grab a beer, he'd texted.

It wasn't like they hadn't ever fucked in a bar bathroom. They had, the very first night. But Julian was sure that wasn't why Kenyon was asking to meet him.

He stared at the message on his phone's screen for a long moment.

Did he know what he wanted to say?

Oh, he knew.

Yes, please, let's get a beer and then make out in the bathroom. I want to kiss you again.

But his fingers hesitated on the screen.

Instead, he typed: **Anyone ever tell you that you're too goddamn persistent?**

Masochistic, too, Kenyon replied right away. **Why else can't I get you out of my head?**

Head, that's why, Julian typed back. **You're thinking about head with your head.**

No, Kenyon typed back. Nothing else, just *No.*

Like he knew it was so much easier for Julian to reduce what Kenyon felt—what *he* felt—to sex.

Of course, he wasn't delusional enough to think that was all it was.

But admitting it to himself wasn't the same thing as admitting it to Kenyon. That wouldn't be happening, not ever.

First off, they were an impossible couple, even if either of them had the vaguest idea they might want to be.

Second off, at some point, Kenyon was going to remember just how pissed he should be at Julian. It was inevitable.

Or Julian would do something, either inadvertently, or more likely, totally, completely on purpose, to piss him off. Then he'd be mad, either way.

Inevitable, Julian reminded himself, as the regret throbbed inside him, persistent and painful.

But a beer, that sounded good. At least if he went down to the hotel bar, he'd know that ninety-nine percent of whoever he saw there would be totally off-limits. He'd learned better than to ever troll for a hookup in any kind of proximity to the Piranhas.

The hard way.

He stood, checked his hair in the mirror, and grabbed his wallet and room key, heading downstairs.

It was nearly curfew, and there were a few knots of people, sitting around the various darkened corners of the hotel bar.

He saw Asa Dawson, Scott Callaway, Beau Dawson and his boyfriend, Sebastian Howard, sitting around one of the high-top tables with Micah, the rookie corner. They were all laughing.

Julian ignored them, took a seat at the bar, and ordered a beer.

The bartender brought over his drink and he took a sip, his eyes scanning the TV, turned to ESPN, for any late-breaking stories.

There weren't any.

The ticker at the bottom of the screen was full of headlines about all the big NFL stars who wouldn't be playing in the last game of the season.

For so many teams heading to the playoffs, their seeding was already determined by their record, and tomorrow's game didn't matter. It had become routine for teams in those positions to sit their star players, resting them for the playoffs.

The Piranhas would be doing the same thing.

Paxton, the normal starting quarterback, wasn't playing. Neither were Kenyon or Sebastian or a few others.

Tristan was dressing, and everyone knew he'd be trying for the rookie receiving touchdown record, and he'd probably get it because there was no way both Dawsons hadn't worked out a way to make sure he would.

It would be a major coup for Nicholson, whom nobody had believed before the draft could be a quality wide receiver in the NFL. But he'd proven them wrong, one game at a time, and now he was going to be one of the most important pieces in the Piranhas' game plan moving forward. If they went deep into the playoffs, Julian had already predicted—and written it in his playoff predictions article—it would be because Nicholson kept getting better, not just with his own skill set, but his chemistry with Pax.

They could be, he'd written, one of the best new quarterback–receiver combos in the NFL, and might even make their own mark on history if they kept playing together.

But Tristan was smartly nowhere to be found downstairs tonight. If he was going to be playing, he was probably already tucked into bed, or at least in the vicinity of the bed, if rumors about how loud and insatiable he and Wade Lewis, the Piranhas' tight end, were, could be believed.

"Hey, this seat taken?"

It was a deep, sexy voice. Objectively, Julian knew that before he even turned around.

And then he did, and kinda wished he hadn't.

The guy was undeniably hot, and also undeniably, reminded him of Kenyon.

Even worse, Julian recognized him.

This was Micah Rose, a rookie corner on the Piranhas, and Julian was the last person he should be hitting on.

Five minutes ago, he'd been sitting with both Dawsons and their partners, but now that table was empty. Still, Micah should most definitely not be hitting on him.

Julian shot him a look. "Yes."

Micah looked confused. "But it's . . ."

"Julian Anderson, reporter for CBS," he said, enunciating each word clearly. "And you're Micah Rose, and you should definitely not be sitting next to me."

He'd learned that one the hard way.

Micah looked resigned. "That's too bad."

"It is," Julian agreed. Though he didn't exactly feel terrible about it. The guy was hot, yes, but everything about him reminded him of Kenyon. While, *yes*, he needed to fucking get his head—and the rest of him—past Kenyon, this was not going to be the right way to do it.

"Well, how 'bout I sit a few seats down, and just look at you? 'Cause . . . *damn*."

Julian smiled, surprised. He hadn't heard that the new Piranhas' corner was queer.

"Thanks," Julian said wryly. "I think?"

"I might be shitty at this, anyway," Micah said, settling down the promised few seats away from Julian. "Never done it before, so, yeah, that might've sucked." He shrugged self-consciously.

"Never hit on a guy?" Julian *was* surprised now.

"Yeah," Micah said. "Never thought I . . . well, that I could. Or that I *should*, but a friend keeps telling me to get out there. To . . . I don't know, *be myself*, I guess. You were hot and I wanted to, so I did. Of course you're a reporter."

"It figures, doesn't it?" Julian sipped his beer.

"It fucking does," Micah said with resignation.

"Let me give you a little advice, which it sounds like your friend already knows. Nobody's really going to care who you hit on. You marry your old assistant coach out of nowhere? You hook up with the coach's son? You get outed by a nasty ex? That's when people give a shit, but the truth is, people *still* don't care," Julian said.

He should stop talking to this guy. But he had a sweet face, and nice eyes—though neither were as sweet or as nice as Kenyon's—and Julian felt a little sorry for him.

Was it easier to be queer and in the NFL these days?

Absolutely.

But that didn't make it *easy*.

"Scott keeps tellin' me that," Micah said. "And I guess he should know."

"Scott Callaway?" Was that the "friend" Micah had kept referring to? It must be. That was some kind of friend, that was for fucking sure.

Micah looked sheepish. "Yeah."

"He should know," Julian pointed out.

"I'm just so antsy about tomorrow. Couldn't stay in my room, worrying about it."

Julian raised an eyebrow. "It's a game that doesn't matter."

"Yeah, maybe not for you. Or for our record. Or the playoffs, but . . . Sebastian's not playing tomorrow. I'm a little bit . . . well, on my own, I guess."

There was a terrified vulnerability hiding underneath Micah's bravado. Julian shouldn't find it attractive; he didn't, not really. Because Kenyon had the same thing in spades, and it was Kenyon who he really wanted.

It was Kenyon who he really wanted.

Wasn't that just the worst thing in the world?

"You're going to get there. Rookie year's always hard," Julian said. "It's sorta my rookie year, too."

Micah's gaze assessed him very frankly, head to toe. "You're the youngest, and honestly, the hottest reporter I've ever seen. So not too much of a surprise there."

"Thanks?"

"I'm just telling the God's honest truth here."

Julian chuckled. "Thank you, with no question marks attached. I'll accept the compliment."

"Good," Micah said.

Frankly, if the vulnerability hiding in his gaze was the truth, then maybe just being able to hit on him had been a major step for Micah. Which, *God*, Julian didn't want to give a shit, but he was still human, wasn't he? He wasn't a cold, heartless asshole. Kenyon had proved that, hadn't he?

Maybe he was just a lukewarm asshole with a shriveled sliver of a heart.

As Julian sipped his beer and Micah stared up at the television screen above the bar, he considered a question.

If he'd met Micah first, in a bar just like this, and he hadn't known Micah was a player, and he hadn't already been fucking nonstop with Kenyon, would he have let him sit next to him? Would he have let him hit on him?

Would he have taken him back to his hotel room? Let him work out all those nerves in bed?

No.

Because yes, Kenyon had been convenient. He'd been right there, and irresistible and supposedly string-less. Even after discovering he *very* much had strings, his irresistible attractiveness hadn't dimmed one bit.

Ten out of ten times, Julian would've wanted him. No matter what. He'd kept wanting him, hadn't he?

Because Kenyon was beautiful. Inside and out. He might not know him as well as he wanted to, but he *knew* that.

That truth fucked him up.

He pulled his phone out of his pocket.

The last text Kenyon had sent was just one word. **No.**

No, it wasn't just about Julian giving great head.

No, it wasn't just about sex.

Julian tapped his fingers against the wood of the bar. **But you have to admit,** he typed before he could change his mind, **that it's weird not to be hooking up tonight.**

It wasn't what he really wanted to say, which was that he should've taken him up on the offer of a beer and a make-out session. But it was something. A tiny sliver of an olive branch.

He drank more beer. Pretended to watch the TV. Pretended that Micah wasn't eyeing him every five or so minutes, like he wished in the interim Julian might've changed jobs.

"Hey."

The voice was similar. But it hit Julian different.

So fucking different.

He'd heard this voice whispering dirty pleas in his ears. He'd heard this voice angry and sad and happy and frustrated and contemplative.

So many times, in so many unique contexts.

He glanced over. Kenyon was leaning against the bar. Not moving to sit. Just standing there, not even looking particularly surprised.

That should be it. Kenyon wasn't even surprised when he was an asshole. Accidentally *or* on purpose.

But he was still standing there, wasn't he? He hadn't left. He didn't even look particularly pissed.

Resigned, yes. Angry, no.

Resigned—Julian understood that all too well.

"You said you wanted a beer," Julian said.

"And you said you didn't."

"No," Julian said crisply, "I said you were too damn persistent."

Kenyon lowered his voice. Slid a little closer. Maybe he didn't know what that did to Julian's heart rate, but then maybe he did, and he didn't give a shit. Maybe he even wanted his pulse to start racing, even though nothing was going to happen.

Nothing is going to happen, Julian reminded himself.

"And then *you* said, and I quote, *isn't it weird we aren't hooking up tonight?*"

"I'm a creature of habit," Julian lied, "it's been seventeen weeks, and it feels weird to do something else."

"We didn't on the bye week," Kenyon said.

Except . . . they sorta had.

Kenyon had called him, and growled in his ear, all the nasty, filthy things he wanted to do to him when he got back from LA, until Julian had exploded, messing himself all the way up his chest.

"Except . . ." Julian didn't even need to finish the sentence.

"Alright, okay, we kinda did still." Kenyon's smile was lopsided. Charming. It was absolutely not doing anything to his stomach.

"You want a beer?" Julian asked.

Kenyon glanced down the bar, just noticing Micah now. The Dawsons and their partners had cleared out, a bit ago, and it was just Micah now, who knew exactly who Julian was, and of course, he knew Kenyon.

"Rose," Kenyon acknowledged him with a dip of his head.

"Ellis," Micah responded. "What brings you here?"

"Need a distraction." It was unlike Kenyon to be so honest. "Not playing tomorrow. Makes me antsy."

Julian would've said that didn't matter. Kenyon always needed a distraction, it didn't matter when or why.

But then, maybe that had just been the little white lie they kept telling themselves so they could keep meeting like this.

To keep not giving a shit about all the very valid reasons they should stop.

"Right," Micah said. He didn't sound very convinced. He eyed Julian again. "Bet you've got just the thing." He tossed a twenty-dollar bill on the bar, covering the ginger ale he hadn't really drunk. "Good luck with that."

When Micah was all the way out of sight, Kenyon turned to him. "He hit on you?"

Julian raised an eyebrow. "What if he did?"

"Didn't think he swung that way."

"Then maybe he was just sitting here."

"No, I saw the way he looked at you, when he was about to leave. I know what that look feels like."

"Thanks, I think?"

Kenyon rolled his eyes. "For the millionth time, there's no point in pretending otherwise, because you know how hot you are."

You know how much I want you, even though I know better. I wouldn't be here otherwise.

Kenyon didn't say the rest of it, but Julian heard it, loud and fucking clear.

"You must really be as masochistic as you claimed," Julian said dryly.

"I must be." Kenyon sighed. "Come up with me."

"Why?" Julian finished his beer. Found some cash. Left it on the bar, underneath his empty glass.

"Because you want to? Because I want you to? Because we both want to? Take your pick."

"It's a bad idea." Julian stood and started walking towards the elevator bank. Knowing that Kenyon would follow.

Hoping he would.

Hoping he wouldn't.

"It was a bad idea for the last six months, and we kept doing it," Kenyon pointed out under his breath as Julian hit the up button.

"Why do you even want me? Because I'm hot? Because I suck your dick really good?"

Kenyon looked annoyed now.

Julian couldn't even claim that he hadn't said it with that end goal in mind.

"Yes, and yes, and for some fucking insane reason, I want to talk to you, too."

The elevator doors opened. "Why?" Julian asked, stepping in. It was too much to hope that Kenyon wouldn't follow him.

That he wouldn't make saying no almost too much for Julian to handle.

"Are you trying to get me to say you're an asshole? Because I really don't think you are. Not the way you want everyone to believe."

"I'm not?"

"You try really hard to prove you're just a jerk, but I'm sorry, Julian, I'm just not buying it."

Julian didn't reply to that particular assassination of his character. Just leaned against the back of the elevator and crossed his arms over his chest.

"I just want to know what's underneath," Kenyon murmured. "Under all this . . ." He waved towards Julian. "All your attitude and your gorgeous hair and the killer brain. I know there's something there and it's fascinating."

"It's really not," Julian said. Annoyed now that Kenyon had given him such an incredible compliment and he wasn't even *right,* so he didn't feel okay accepting it.

He wasn't fascinating.

He was fucked up.

There was a fundamental difference between the two. Clearly Kenyon didn't recognize it, because he wasn't seeing it clearly. *Yet.*

But someday he would, and that's when everything was bound to get ugly.

Julian's floor was only four away.

Would he get out of this elevator without losing his mind?

Without losing the last of his self-control?

"This is me," Julian said, when the elevator came to a stop with a ding and the doors began to open. He took a step, but Kenyon caught his arm.

"See, that's where you're wrong."

Julian couldn't quite look away from the dark look in Kenyon's eyes, couldn't be one hundred percent sure, but he was fairly certain that he was holding down the "door open" button even as he leaned in and gave Julian a kiss he wouldn't soon forget.

It was fiery and needy and . . . weirdly sweet.

Kenyon lifted his mouth off and Julian found himself speechless. "I don't blame Micah for kinda losing his mind over you," he said. "I did. I *do.*"

Julian loosened his arm and straight up jogged out of the elevator.

You have got to stop running away, he thought as he walked at a furious pace down the hallway to his room. *You keep doing it. And one of these days, he's going to take the invite and actually follow you.*

Julian was exhausted.

He hadn't slept last night.

Instead, he'd lain awake, staring at the ceiling, wondering what the fuck he was going to do.

It didn't matter what he said. Or even worse, what he *did*. Kenyon wasn't going to accept being pushed away.

You should be happier about that, Julian told himself.

But somehow, he didn't feel happier about it at all.

No. All he felt was tired.

But he still had to do his goddamn job. The game had been fairly uneventful. The Piranhas hadn't scored as many points as normal, because a lot of the normal starters hadn't been in.

But Tristan Nicholson had gotten his touchdown, early on in the first quarter, because like Julian had figured, neither of the Dawsons—or frankly the rest of the team—was going to accept the fact that he might *not*.

They'd wanted that touchdown for him, probably more than the rest of the team.

Julian had known that was true, but watching it unfold on the field drove the point home.

Everyone on the bench, even the players who hadn't dressed for the game, had poured onto the field, surrounding Tristan and lifting him up in the end zone.

The NFL allowed celebrations. These days they were even pretty damn tolerant of extended celebrations.

But the crowd surrounding Tristan had been so happy and so caught up in their pride for one of their own setting such a monumental record—which had stood for almost twenty-five years—the refs had actually thrown a flag for excessive celebration.

But Coach, who, like every other coach, hated penalties with a fierce and unyielding passion, had just kept grinning even as the flag fell on the field.

He still looked happy, Julian thought, as he took the podium for the press conference, but he looked tired, too.

It had been a long season already, and it wasn't over yet. Though the fact that the Piranhas had still managed to eke out a win, without half of their starters, said a goddamn lot about how good they were.

How deep they could potentially go in the playoffs.

Julian thrust his hand up first, and Coach just chuckled under his breath. "Yeah, Anderson, what's your deal? You gonna question that call to go for it on fourth and one in the third quarter?"

He shook his head. "That was a good call, actually?"

Coach laughed. "You *would* say that. Your momma know she raised such a contrarian?"

She couldn't possibly, of course, but Julian still hoped, in that tiny hopeful, idealistic part of his brain that remained, that she did, anyway.

"I actually wanted to know how you approached Nicholson's record this week. Was it a consideration for who you asked to dress or who you sat down? He was targeted a whopping twelve times in the first half, and didn't play in the second half at all."

Asa put his elbows on the podium. "You sure keep track, don't you?"

Julian nodded. He did. It was his goddamn job, and he took it seriously, because what else did he have? No relationships. No friendships. No family. No real fucking life.

Just his job.

But even he knew that wasn't quite true anymore. Because he had Kenyon now, whether he wanted him or not.

And he did, *desperately*, even if he didn't know what to do with him.

"You want the truth? 'Course we talked about it. That's a record that's stood for twenty-four years, set by one of the best receivers to ever play the game. We all wanted it for Tristan, to own that little slice of history. And you know what? He came to me early this week, and told me that I could do whatever I felt was fair. If I wanted him to sit out this game, keep him fresh for the playoffs, then he'd respect my decision." Asa smiled, like he was thinking about it now. "And let me tell y'all, that kid is a major talent. You can't contain him. So I didn't really try. But, I'll add, if I *had* tried to sit him, the parade of players through my office this week, begging me to play him, would've changed my mind in a second. This whole team loves him, and wanted him to have that record."

Julian could see it.

He'd seen the celebration. The penalty flag that had finished it. The way nobody had given a shit when the ref had thrown it.

It was something special, even in a team sport, to see players who gave more of a shit about their teammates than they did themselves.

"What about the penalty flag?"

Coach chuckled.

Ed, sitting next to him, did too, and elbowed Julian in the side.

"You want me to say it was worth it? You journalists are gonna have a field day if I do."

"Probably." Julian couldn't contain his own smile anymore.

"Then we'll leave it at this: we're all real happy for Tristan. Happy and, honestly, couldn't be prouder."

"Did you see that Randy Moss tweeted about it, warning Jerry Rice about *his* record, for the most career receiving touchdowns?"

"No, but I'll just say if I was Jerry Rice, I'd be worried."

After Coach moved on to the next question, Ed leaned over, and murmured in Julian's ear, "I can't believe you didn't go for the fourth and one question."

Julian shrugged. "That wasn't the story. The story is Tristan Nicholson becoming the next Randy Moss or Jerry Rice."

"You forget Ja'Marr Chase, he got close last year." Ed referenced the new star receiver for the Cincinnati Bengals.

"But he didn't get it, Tristan did," Julian said. "Now, I *could* say that was because Chase had other solid players around him, which meant that Burrow spread the ball around more. Pax doesn't have as many solid targets. He had to throw to Nicholson. Which . . . maybe I'll add that, too. A little extra wrinkle." He made a note on his phone, even though he had no intention of diminishing Tristan's achievement that way.

Would he really add it?

He thought a few months back, he'd have done it without blinking, but now?

He wasn't sure he *could*.

Ed shook his head, surprise blooming across his face. "You are stone cold, Julian. Just stone fucking cold."

Maybe he used to be, but the more he looked at himself recently, the warmer he seemed.

Was it because he'd actually changed?

Or was it the way he saw himself was different now, all because Kenyon was looking at him and seeing something else?

"It's the job, isn't it?" Julian said.

He knew it was.

This is what you signed up for. This is what you're good at.

But that voice, that had always felt so goddamned sure, from the very beginning of when one of the visiting professors had told him he had the brains—and the looks—to be a journalist—didn't feel as certain as it once had.

Chapter Nine

Kenyon's phone was burning a hole in his pocket and he couldn't pretend otherwise.

The Monday evening victory party at Hibiscus was a team tradition at this point, and he'd come, because he'd known he should.

There'd even been part of him that *wanted* to, but then there'd been that other part that wanted to get up in front of the majority of the team, gathered here tonight, and apologize.

I'm sorry I've been distracted. I'm sorry I haven't been playing up to my standard—or yours. But mostly I'm goddamned sorry, because the truth is, I'm still distracted.

I still wish I was somewhere else.

With someone else.

Kenyon sipped his beer, and tried to ignore the weight of his phone in his pocket. And the text that Julian hadn't returned. *Again.*

With anyone else, he'd believe Julian's lack of response meant that he wasn't really into him. Or into the idea of more.

But with Julian, it was clear that wasn't the case at all.

He wanted it so much, he denied it.

One hundred percent it was fucked up, and one hundred percent Kenyon was into it.

"You shouldn't be standing over here, glowering."

Logan stopped next to where he was leaning against the bar and nudged him with a shoulder.

"I'm not glowering," Kenyon argued. Even though he definitely was.

He was pissed. He was distracted. He was distracted *because* he was pissed.

That, somehow, impossibly, made him even madder.

It was a nasty little cycle.

And the only way he wanted to work out all that excess frustration was to lure Julian back to his bed. Even though by this point, neither of them could possibly ignore the truth: it wasn't just sex.

Kenyon wanted it even more—wanted *him* even more—because of it.

He'd never wanted a relationship before. He wasn't even sure Julian would *do* a relationship, but surely there was some middle ground that they could work with.

"Yeah, you kinda are," Logan said. "What's wrong?"

"It's not that I'm not . . . happy or whatever. I am. I just never . . ." How to possibly explain that winning and losing hadn't ever changed his life? That he wouldn't work himself into a frenzy if he did the latter more than the former?

That football wasn't the defining pinnacle of his existence?

How could he possibly explain that to Logan, who lived and breathed and *existed* for football? Who was one of the very few sets of brothers who all played in the NFL? But then, Kenyon reminded himself, Logan hadn't *just* signed with the Piranhas because he'd seen a chance to play at the high level he expected from himself, but because he'd seen an opportunity to live as his authentic self.

Maybe he couldn't explain to Logan about the football stuff, but he *could* talk about what else was bothering him.

Julian.

"I just never expected to be here, that's all," Kenyon finished. "But that's not the issue so much as . . . how did you know?"

Logan raised an eyebrow. "How did I know what? That we were gonna go to the playoffs? That Pax and Davis were meant to be together? That Coach was gonna go get married?"

Kenyon laughed. "All of the above? But really, not to sound horribly cliche because goddamn, it *is* a cliche, but there's this guy . . . and I swear to God, I just can't figure him out. So I guess the question is, how did you know Dylan was the right one for you?"

Logan's smile took on that sweet, private edge that it always did when Dylan came up. It was romantic and adorable and kind of nauseating.

At least, Kenyon had always felt that way about it.

Now, he felt . . . well, *envious.*

Wasn't that the fucking worst?

"It's not going to help to say I always knew, is it?" Logan had the nerve to look sheepish.

"No, especially because you *didn't* know. You kept telling everyone that it wasn't real, but all of us knew better," Kenyon said. He took a long drink of his beer. Wished it was something stronger, but the fact of the matter was, one of the most important games of his career was coming up in less than a week, and sadly, whiskey was not going to help him play any better.

"Here's the thing," he added, "I thought it was just . . . you know, hooking up. Just sex. It was just sex for a long time, and somehow, suddenly, now it's not, and I don't know what to do about it. But I know enough to know I can't just walk away."

Logan tilted his head. Looked thoughtful. "What is it, then, if it's not just sex? You like this person?"

"I think I could, yeah, but he won't let me get to that place, you know? He keeps pushing me away. All the fucking time." It was worse, Kenyon decided, because he knew he wasn't alone. He was pretty damn sure Julian felt the same way he did.

"I did that."

That surprised Kenyon. "What?"

"I knew I liked Dylan like that, from almost the beginning, and I spent months pretending that I didn't. It was . . ." Logan pursed his lips, like he was remembering it. "It was easier if I didn't think about it. But it seems like you're past that, now. The pretending."

"Yeah, *I* am, at least." It felt good to say it out loud.

"Don't get me wrong, I thought about it a thousand times, *what if I just kissed him?* Before the whole 'pretending to my boyfriend' thing. Would've cut through a lot of the confusion. But I know now *he* wasn't ready. He was coming to terms with the fact that he liked me too, and I wasn't what he was used to. I guess what I'm saying," Logan said with a sigh, "is that sometimes you've got to be patient. Makes things easier, in the long run."

"Harder, too," Kenyon said, speaking from experience. Because nothing about this situation with Julian had been easy.

He didn't want to be patient with Julian. He wanted to drag him, kicking screaming, across the line he'd set all those months ago.

He wanted to pin him against the nearest vertical surface and kiss him and touch him and wear him down, until he couldn't help but admit what was going on between them.

But that, unfortunately, was not the advice Logan was giving.

"Yeah, yeah, it *is* harder," Logan agreed. "But if you like this guy, if you could care a lot about him, then it's worth it, right?"

"I don't know if I could be that patient. But I know . . ." Kenyon sighed. "I know I'm not okay just letting him go."

"Then you shouldn't. He feel the same way you do?" Logan picked up the beer the bartender set in front of him.

"I think so. He's prickly. Hard to read. Keeps pushing me away and then deliberately provoking me." Kenyon could see it now, the things Julian had done that had pissed him off, they'd all been to get his attention. Positive *or* negative.

"Don't let him get away with it," Logan said. He paused. "Hey, I've got an idea. Something that might help you two take things to the next level."

"What is it?" He didn't mean to sound suspicious, but this was the same guy who'd dumped a metric ton of glitter in Coach's office *and* hired a cleanup crew to remove every single speck.

Logan might possess one of the most open, friendliest faces that Kenyon had ever seen. But he'd be dumb to not know that smile hid a devious brain.

"Just trust me on this one," Logan said, patting him on the shoulder. "You're going to be fucking grateful because there's no better way to get to know your guy than with this."

"I swear to God, Logan, if it's some weird sex toy, I will . . ."

Logan raised an eyebrow. "Do y'all need help with that?"

"No, *no*," Kenyon said emphatically. Not just because they'd definitely never had trouble in the sex department, but also because they weren't even having sex right now.

Which . . . that was a whole other problem.

If he thought about *that*, then patience wasn't going to be in the cards.

"Well, that's something, right?" Logan grinned.

"I guess," Kenyon grumbled.

"I'll bring it in tomorrow. You just gotta convince him to do it, but . . ." Logan teased, "I think you can figure out how to do that on your own. I'm sure you got something he wants."

I sure fucking hope so.

"But," Logan continued, "you can't give up, okay? Patience, that's what you're going for. Give him some time to come around. *Woo him.*"

But what if he doesn't?

Logan shot him a sympathetic look, and Kenyon realized he'd said that deep-down fear out loud. *Shit.*

"I don't know," Logan said with a shrug, "*but* I do know if you push too hard, too fast, he definitely won't. If I'd done that with Dylan, we wouldn't be together now, and that would be a goddamn shame."

"Yeah." Kenyon looked out into the club, across the rooftop. Davis and Pax were dancing, and Tristan and Wade were trying to follow their steps, laughing so hard they could barely stand up straight.

Tristan especially had been lit up like a lightbulb all evening, full of pride and happiness that he'd broken the record—but not just that, Kenyon figured, it was more than that. It was how happy everyone else was *for* him. It was the shining look in Wade's eyes whenever he looked at his boyfriend. The way Pax had led him out on the dance floor, and promised he'd teach him a few steps. The half a dozen toasts they'd already had, all dedicated to the best rookie wide receiver in the league.

Sebastian appeared next to Logan, probably because he needed a fresh beer. "Hey, Kenyon, how's it going?"

"He's got romance problems," Logan answered for him.

Sebastian looked interested.

"It's . . . it's nothing," Kenyon stammered.

"Oh? Doesn't seem like nothing. Even Beau noticed you were over here, sulking. I think that's what he called it."

"I wasn't *sulking*." Except he had been.

Micah fucking Rose had been hitting on Julian. Had he been interested? *Would* he be interested? He hadn't seemed to be, but Kenyon wasn't going to pretend he knew every thought that flashed through Julian's head.

"Right," Sebastian said dryly. "I guess it's your turn."

"I am not going to just . . . couple off," Kenyon insisted. Even though that was kind of what he wanted, wasn't it? He didn't know how he felt about the term *boyfriend* or *relationship*, but that was ultimately what he wanted, right? To belong to Julian, and for Julian to belong to him.

Definitely the latter, the more he thought about how Micah had looked at Julian. What made it even worse was he *got it*. He looked at Julian like that every single fucking time. The thing was, yeah, he was hot. Smoking hot. *Want to pull all his clothing off with his teeth* hot. But it was more than that, too. He was funny and charming and so incredibly smart. Kenyon would rather die than admit it to him, but he'd read every single one of Julian's articles, and damn, he was good at what he did. He *always* had some nugget of analysis Kenyon had never considered before.

Even though that video had been humiliating, it had been spot on. What had Beau said? *Can I hire him?*

"What's wrong with coupling off?" Sebastian asked.

He would say that.

He was cozied up nice and pretty with the coach's son. Everyone could see it.

Kenyon rolled his eyes. "'Cause I'm not into that, normally."

"Even though you *want* to," Logan said. "It's not a ding, Kenyon."

"It is, when everyone's talking about it," Kenyon pointed out.

"We don't even know who it is, though . . ." Logan's smile went wide. "We'd *love* to."

"Nope," Kenyon said. He'd have turned down Logan's offer to learn more, even if Julian wasn't one hundred and ten percent off-limits because of his job.

"It's your secret, for now, anyway," Sebastian said, patting his arm. He grabbed his beer and turned towards the dance floor. They all watched Tristan dancing with Davis for a moment in silence.

"I remember how he looked when he showed up to preseason camp," Sebastian said slowly. "Looks totally different now."

"He's got his confidence back." They all nodded.

"We gotta do something about the NFL sucking it out of our rookies," Logan said.

"Well, that's on you 'cause I've got enough on my plate," Kenyon said. Though he agreed. All these guys had been told their entire lives that they were the best player in the world. And then they got to the NFL and they weren't, and so many of them couldn't handle it.

So many of them broke down.

The Piranhas didn't let that happen, but then, Kenyon had been around enough teams to know they were special, and *why* they were special.

Kenyon had never been around a team that felt so much like a family.

It was why he felt so guilty at the thought of letting them down.

"You do enough," Logan said. "You do *plenty*."

But did he? Kenyon always wondered.

Wondered if he could do more.

"Something to think about," Sebastian said thoughtfully, and Kenyon recognized his tone. Wouldn't be surprised if next year, Sebastian Howard came back to the Piranhas with a whole plan on how to better integrate rookies into the system.

"Come on," Logan said, gesturing towards Kenyon. "We're supposed to be celebrating. Let's celebrate."

His tone was nice and friendly, as always, but Kenyon heard the steel underneath it.

The *stop sulking* was loud and clear, even though Logan hadn't said it.

"Alright," Kenyon said. Set his beer down. "Who's gonna teach me to salsa?"

Julian would be lying if he said he wasn't nervous.

First thing this morning, Nikki had called him, saying that the Piranhas had reached out, and wanted a private meeting.

Had someone found out about him and Kenyon?

Well, if they had, he could tell them—and it would be mostly the truth, anyway—that it was over between them.

What had that kiss been last night?

Julian still didn't know. Or what any of their other kisses meant.

But he could stand in front of Coach Dawson and tell him that he wasn't fucking one of his players anymore, at least.

When he'd asked Nikki what the meeting was about, she'd just hummed, under her breath. "Not sure," she'd said. "But Helen asked for you specifically, so probably some kind of story she'd like you to write. Or some quote she wants to leak. Congrats, Julian, you've really made it if Helen's wanting you."

"Thanks," Julian said dryly.

He reminded himself of this particular fact—that he'd *made it*, whatever the fuck that meant—as an assistant showed him into Helen's office.

She ran all the public relations for the Piranhas, and had an ageless face, a short blond bob, and an absolutely killer instinct.

A fact that Julian wasn't going to forget anytime soon. The first time he'd met her, at preseason camp, his heart had nearly seized, just from a bit of friendly conversation.

"Makes your balls shrink up, and you want to thank her for it, every goddamn time," Ed liked to say.

But truthfully, he did. He *liked* Helen.

Not really when he was getting called to her office like a naughty schoolboy, but still, it had to be something good. Nikki hadn't seemed worried at all.

Surely, if this was about him and Kenyon, it wouldn't be *her* office he'd be summoned to.

"Thanks for stopping by," Helen said briskly as she walked in. "Coach will be by in a moment, but I wanted to check in with you before that."

"Coach?" Julian told himself that his voice didn't squawk at the implication, but it kinda did.

"Don't worry, you haven't asked him one too many difficult questions," Helen said as she settled behind her big glass and wood desk. "We've actually got a story for you."

"What kind of story?"

She waved a hand. "Oh, a football story. With a bit of a personal angle. I was going to use someone else, but the tougher you are on Coach, the more scrupulously fair you've been, the more I realized I needed to use you. That you'd be perfect for this story."

"Thanks, I think?" Julian said.

She nodded. "Fair is important. I don't want you to make this look pretty, because it's not necessarily pretty. A great story, yes, but not clean and nice. And if we cleaned it up . . ."

"You'd look complicit," Julian finished for her.

Helen nodded. "Yes, exactly."

A moment later, Coach walked in. He was frowning, and that frown deepened when he saw Julian sitting there.

"Ugh, really?" he said, flopping down on the chair next to Julian. "You said you'd take care of it." He directed that comment at Helen.

"Yes, I did," she retorted crisply, "and I *am*. Julian's the right guy for this. He's fair. He's honest. He digs. All of which we want, here."

"Do we?"

Helen shot him a look. "I offered you one of two options. This story, or you and Scott. And it seemed fairly obvious that you didn't want to go there yourself."

"I don't," Coach said bluntly. He turned to Julian. "You know I got married, right?"

Everyone on the whole fucking planet knew he'd gotten married. It had also come as an enormous shock to just about everyone on the planet. Especially when he'd married his old assistant coach from Tennessee. But Coach hadn't asked if he'd been shocked by it, only if he'd known.

"Yes . . . sir?"

"I thought so," Coach said. "Everyone knows. There's nothing to talk about."

"No," Helen said, amused, "*you* just don't want to talk about it."

"That is also true," Coach admitted.

"That's why we're going with the other story," Helen said. She turned to Julian. "You know Paxton Kelly?"

"Yes," Julian said, his curiosity undeniably piqued. What was going on with the Piranhas' starting quarterback?

"Of course he does," Coach inserted.

Helen shot him *another* look. "Asa," she said, "you promised me you'd let me take care of this."

"I know." Coach sighed. "I'm just . . . are we making the right decision? This is going to change their lives forever. And well . . ."

"It's their decision, and they're on board. They *wanted* to do it."

"They're?" Julian questioned.

"They're," Helen confirmed. "I'm sure you also know Davis Abernathy, who is our quarterbacks coach."

Julian couldn't figure out where they were going with any of this. "Is he leaving? Heading to a different team?"

"No, he's one of us now," Coach said firmly.

"I said it had a bit more of a personal angle ..." Helen hesitated, which was totally unlike her. "Actually, it turns out that Pax and Davis are . . . involved."

She said it so obliquely that at first, Julian wasn't sure he'd heard right or that he'd understood exactly what she was saying. But . . . if he'd guessed right, the implications of this were through the roof.

This would be the story that blew the lid off his career.

And he was ready for it.

"They're together," Julian said bluntly. "Like together-together, holding hands, the *I love you's*, white-picket-fence kind of together?"

"Yes," Helen said.

"And you want me to write about it."

Helen nodded. "Not just about their sexuality, though that's obviously a component. I want you to get to know them, talk to them, talk about how their process works. How their personal relationship impacts their professional relationship and vice versa. This is a big story. We all know its implications. I want you to show there's nothing we need to hide."

Julian digested this. "You knew," he said, turning to Coach, "and you didn't fire Davis."

"Davis has been fucked around with enough in his career," Coach said with finality.

"Yeah, but that wouldn't matter to anyone else."

"I'm not 'anyone else,'" Coach pointed out bluntly. "I'm never gonna be. I'm me, and this is how I coach my team. You got issues with that? You think I should have fired Davis, when he was coaching the hell out of my second year QB, who had so much potential but who'd been lost and aimless after his rookie year?"

"No, sir," Julian said firmly. Holding his ground. It was hard, because Asa Dawson was Asa Dawson, and had that stern look in his eyes that promised retribution if he fucked this up, but Julian wasn't worried. He already knew he wasn't going to.

This was too big of a story to fuck up.

Coach's face relaxed. "Good, neither do I." He turned to Helen. "He'll do."

Julian rolled his eyes, even as he acknowledged that if Coach had decided he *wouldn't* do, he'd currently be being seen out of the building by Helen.

But *holy shit*, this was a huge story.

A quarterback dating his coach?

A coach not getting fired for dating his quarterback?

Julian could barely wrap his head around it. Yeah, the Piranhas were a different kind of team, but this was a development he never could have seen coming.

He wondered, because he couldn't help it, if Kenyon had known about them.

If he texted Kenyon now and said, *holy shit, your quarterback is in love with his coach, with Davis freaking Abernathy, how did you not tell me?* if he'd even answer.

Julian guessed not, because he'd pointedly ignored the last three texts Kenyon had sent.

"I'll be forwarding over a schedule we've set up where you can do some interviews. And there will also be some opportunities to watch practice this week. The hope is, with Nikki's blessing, we'll air this story next week. Do you have any specific questions for me?" Helen was such a professional, but Julian totally believed she was hiding a huge shit-eating grin under that calm, emotionless facade. No doubt greatly enjoying the way Julian's jaw was still partially dropped in shock.

Air?

Did that mean he was actually going to get some airtime?

"The hope, of course," Helen continued, "is that there will be both an in-depth article, as well as a long interview feature before the playoff game next week. Capitalize on everyone's interest in the Piranhas."

Julian was having trouble getting up to speed, his mind racing a million miles an hour.

For a second, he almost asked Helen if she was sure, if she really believed he was the right person for this job. He didn't have a lot of broadcast experience. Sure, he could write the shit out of an article, maximizing the human potential of the story, and adding in a decent dose of football analysis for good measure, but an interview? On TV? He hadn't done that before. Sure, he knew he *could*, but it was such a big story to leave to chance—or, Julian supposed, in the hands of a newbie.

"Makes sense," he said instead.

Surely he had something else to add?

But apparently his brain had been shocked to smithereens, because he didn't have any other thoughts worth mentioning.

"No questions?" Helen asked, raising an eyebrow.

"Uh, I guess . . . when can I meet with them?"

Not that he hadn't met either of them before—though he'd only had a reason to exchange a few passing pleasantries with Davis, who was understandably suspicious of most reporters—but the sooner he could see them, *really* see them, the quicker he could get a better handle on how he'd present this.

Julian was already thinking of how he'd start the story. How he'd frame it.

Coming out stories in professional sports had become rather . . . well, *regular* . . . these days, which was something Julian was not only profoundly grateful, but thankful for as well, especially towards the few guys at the beginning who'd made all of this possible.

But Pax and Davis would be fundamentally different.

Not only because Davis had a difficult history in the NFL. Not only because he'd been a player. Not only because Pax was one of the most exciting young quarterbacks in the NFL. But because they'd broken that one ironclad rule: players and coaches weren't allowed to date, *ever*.

"Oh, look," Helen said, and she was smiling now. "I think that's them right now."

And sure enough, with Julian still with a deer-in-the-headlights expression plastered on his face, reeling from the secret he'd just been read in on, Pax and Davis walked into Helen's office.

Julian pinned her with a look. "If you ever wanted to organize the world . . ."

"I know," she said smugly. "I'd just need to say the word."

"Seriously," Julian agreed.

He stood and shook Davis' hand and then Pax's.

Ignored the way Davis was eyeing him like he smelled bad.

"This guy?" Davis said, not sitting down in one of the chairs, but instead prowling over by the window. "He just threw Kenyon under the bus."

Oh, if Davis Abernathy only knew what he'd done to Kenyon over the last few months.

"That was . . ." Helen started to say, but Julian held up a hand. It was time to prove why she'd called him for this assignment.

"Yeah, I know I did," Julian said calmly.

Davis' gaze narrowed. "You know you did? Just easy as that."

Davis had been betrayed in the worst ways by people he should've trusted to always have his back. Julian wasn't particularly surprised he was suspicious of him. If he hadn't been, Julian would've questioned why that was.

"Davis—" Pax cautioned under his breath.

"No, I really want to hear this," Davis said, crossing his arms over his broad, muscular chest. It was an admirable chest. Julian had definitely spent more than his share of time thinking about it.

Of course he hadn't expected to admire it while it was currently paired with such a hard-ass look.

"I stirred the pot a little. Ellis needed that." Julian reminded himself to use Kenyon's last name, because using his first felt way too personal, way too close to what they might actually be to each other. Whatever the fuck that was. "He even called me up and thanked me for setting him straight."

Okay, he hadn't in as many words, but if questioned, Julian had a feeling Kenyon would agree with his interpretation.

"He *thanked* you?" Davis asked incredulously.

"We worked it out," Julian said. Refusing to squirm in his chair at the thought of just how they had.

Kenyon pressing him against the fridge. The way the handle had dug into his back, his firm, muscular thigh wedged against his cock, his mouth moving so hot and sure against his own.

It was a visceral memory.

"Besides," Julian added, clearing his throat, "you want me to be honest. You want me to tell the whole story. You want me to dig in, and dig down. You don't want some fluff piece. You want something with substance. Something that convinces the world that you're not just a coach who took advantage of his vulnerable player."

Fury flashed across Davis' face.

Sometimes being an asshole did not pay off.

If Davis punched him in the face—and Julian would put it at about fifty-fifty odds he might—it wasn't going to today.

Oh well.

"Davis," Pax said again, the warning clear in his tone.

It shouldn't have hurt that Davis said, *"This* guy?" To Helen, *again.* Yes, it had kind of stung when Coach had said it, but it made some kind of sense because he spent every Sunday giving Coach hell.

Good job, now you're pissing everyone else off. Excellent work. A+. All the gold stars for you.

But it wasn't Helen who answered.

It was Pax.

"Yes, this guy," Pax said bluntly. "Because he's not wrong."

"He just implied . . ."

"No, he implied that people are gonna think that, and you already knew that people might think that. We talked about it."

Julian had spent the last seventeen weeks watching Pax get his sea legs. When the season had started, he could barely look out past the podium. Now, he had a quiet, commanding sort of confidence.

And he was using it now.

On Davis.

Wasn't *that* interesting?

It was even more interesting that Davis totally freaking buckled. "Yeah, we did, but . . ."

"No buts," Pax said firmly. He turned to Julian. "I for one am game for you to dig. There's not much I hide, at least now that we're talking about *this*."

Julian chuckled. "We'll see how much of an open book you really are."

"Not *that* open," Davis grumbled. But it seemed that he'd been at least partially mollified by his boyfriend's words.

"All I want," Julian said clearly, so there would be absolutely no mistake, "is to tell your story in a fair and true way. That's all. Present it so that everyone who reads it and watches it can hear the truth. No unnecessary drama mongering. No twisting words. Nothing that isn't real."

For a long moment, both Pax and Davis were silent. Then Davis gave Julian a begrudging nod. "If that's all you want, that's what we want too. Just . . . to tell our story. Let everyone know, and then get back to football—and our lives."

"Then we're agreed," Julian said. Even though he already knew it was going to be hard as hell to fight to tell the unadorned, unembellished truth. Nikki would push for drama—he loved her, but he knew she would, because drama would get clicks and viewers—but it was his story, damnit. Even though enough guys had done this that it shouldn't be a big deal anymore, every single player who came out in the NFL deserved a fair and equal chance to tell their story.

This one? Even more so.

Julian knew what he was committing to when he shook Davis' hand and then Pax's, and then finally Helen's. But he did it anyway.

He was an asshole. He'd always known it, and in some corner of his mind, he'd always hoped it might be for a reason.

Maybe it was for this reason.

Chapter Ten

Kenyon's first indication that something was wrong—okay not *wrong*, but different; very, *very* different—was Julian appearing at practice.

The second indication was he was ignoring Kenyon completely. Didn't once glance his direction. Not once. Which Kenyon knew because from the moment he appeared on the field, his distinctive blond hair waving in the winter Miami sunshine, he hadn't once looked away.

Maybe he was being way too obvious. Warning bells were clanging away in his head, but he couldn't make himself focus on anything else.

That had been the problem with Julian from the very first.

He glowed so brightly—even when he was driving Kenyon nuts, he was a glowing, irresistible person who drove Kenyon nuts—a part of Kenyon always wanted a piece of it for himself.

Okay, who was he kidding? He wanted *all* of it for himself.

Kenyon ground his teeth together.

"You alright?"

It was Wade, coming over to him after he'd finished his individual stretches.

Kenyon hadn't even started his yet.

No, he'd been too busy glowering at Julian, who was currently laughing with Pax and Davis on the sideline.

Pax and Davis.

Seriously, what the fuck was up with that? When did they get so buddy-buddy with Julian?

He was definitely not jealous.

Not one bit.

Just like he hadn't been jealous of Micah, hitting on Julian without any idea of how even one night with the guy could ruin you for anyone else, ever.

"No," Kenyon said.

He was categorically not alright, and he was really tired of pretending otherwise.

It wasn't just because Julian had caught him; it was because Kenyon was pretty fucking sure that Julian hadn't even *wanted* to catch him. That he didn't even like that he'd caught him.

It was galling Julian was all ready to throw him back into the sea, like a too-small fish.

"You keep glaring over at the sideline," Wade said.

Oh, he knew.

He also knew Julian hadn't once noticed.

"It's that blond reporter, isn't it? The one who said that thing about you on the podcast." Wade hesitated, like he wasn't sure what he was about to say would actually improve Kenyon's mood. Bless Wade, he was so tactful, unlike everyone else on this goddamned team, bulldozing with the subtlety of a jackhammer into everyone's business. "Tristan heard he was doing some big interview with Pax and Davis. You know, doing their big reveal."

Wade did jazz hands on the last bit, and Kenyon laughed out loud, unable to help himself.

"Tristan hears everything, doesn't he?" Kenyon said. Still watching the trio, but in a new light now. Not that it had ever been likely that Pax and Davis had decided to add a third to their relationship, or that they would pick Julian, *or* that they would bring him to practice as a test run.

None of that had been even remotely likely.

Hadn't stopped his stupid, too-desperate mind from thinking it anyway.

Now, he looked again—or *kept* looking—and saw Julian working all his reporter skills to try to set both Pax and Davis at ease. He was clearly at his most charming, laughing and gesturing, tossing that criminal head of hair, working every inch of what God had given him.

He's never worked that hard for you.

But then, he'd never had to. Kenyon had been easy; from practically the first moment, he'd been putty in Julian's hands.

"Listen," Wade continued, setting his hands on his hips, "I know you've got shit going on. But you can talk to us, you know?"

"Give you more fodder for the gossip machine?" Kenyon retorted wryly.

Wade shrugged. "I wouldn't tell anyone, if you didn't want me to."

"Even Tristan?"

Everyone knew how they were practically sharing a brain these days.

"Yeah, if you didn't want me to, I wouldn't."

Kenyon considered this for a moment.

"You ever want someone who didn't really want you back?" Wade chuckled.

"No, scratch that," Kenyon said, before Wade could answer. "You're young and hot and rich. Every person in existence ever probably took one look at you, and fell at your feet."

"And it's any different for you?" Wade asked archly.

Truthfully, it had never been any different for him, but Julian had been a humbling experience. "Well . . ."

"Does this person know you feel . . ." Wade hesitated, scratching his chin. "However you feel? You like them? Or love them . . .?"

"Like," Kenyon said very firmly. "Just *like*. I don't know them well enough for *love*. Not even close."

"Then maybe you should just tell them. Maybe they don't know. Maybe they don't *want* to know. It's not easy dating one of us. You know that."

It would be tougher for Julian, too. There was an inherent risk with him that didn't exist with anyone else. Kenyon could at least acknowledge that.

"Thanks," Kenyon said, patting him on the shoulder. "That's good advice, Wade."

"I don't know shit about love, except that I'd fight with both hands to hold on to it, and"—Wade shot Kenyon a lopsided grin—"it sure seems like you're glaring over at him long enough that maybe he's worth really fighting for."

Damnit, Wade had guessed.

Of course, Kenyon could admit he hadn't been exactly circumspect.

"Yeah, yeah, that's true," he said dryly.

It *was* true, and Wade wasn't wrong.

It was weird being the one to chase after someone, but wasn't Julian special enough for him to put his ego away and make that effort for once?

There was all that buried under his charming, too-smooth exterior, so much that Kenyon could sense but couldn't understand because Julian wouldn't ever let him in. Just for that alone he was worth fighting for. Because someone hiding so much clearly hadn't had a lot of loyalty or trust in their lives.

Not for the first time, Kenyon wondered if that easygoing, privileged wall Julian put up was that—a *wall*.

Designed to keep everyone else out.

Coach Randy, the offensive coordinator, jogged onto the field, clapping his hands, and they all circled up, including Pax and Davis.

Julian stayed back, on the sideline. From Kenyon's vantage point, he saw him exchange a few words with Beau, Beau smiling as he walked away.

Coach Randy put them through their paces, working on a few new wrinkles in their plays. It was the first day of practice, but it was more intense than Kenyon had been expecting, which, once he thought about it, moving towards the locker room, made sense. The Piranhas' first playoff game was Sunday. They were favored, barely, but Kenyon knew the team they were playing wasn't going to go down easy.

They'd have to fight for every first down. Every turnover. Every point.

"Hey," Beau said, stopping Kenyon as he exited the locker room, "you get the email I sent you?"

Kenyon had. He'd briefly looked at it, before moving on to several others from Keisha currently lingering in his inbox.

One of the tutors they'd wanted to hire had started a negotiation and he'd needed to research and determine a ceiling for how high Keisha could go on his salary and benefits.

That had taken him a few hours, and by the time he'd finished, he could barely keep his eyes open.

Leaving him no time and, frankly, no inclination, to deal with Beau's email.

"Not yet," Kenyon admitted.

"It's got a link to some footage I analyzed for you," Beau said, and Kenyon wished he didn't feel that inevitable pulse of guilt.

Maybe he should've been doing that instead of working on We Read problems. But those problems were life-changing. If they could hire this guy as a tutor, Kenyon knew the kind of difference he could make.

"I'll take a look at it today." He would, he promised himself. In fact, he'd do it before he even left the building. The running back room would be empty, because they always had their meeting before practice. He'd duck in there, and watch the film.

"Awesome, you let me know if you have any questions, alright?" Beau said. "Good practice today. You guys are lookin' good."

"Good enough for the playoffs?"

Beau shot him a lopsided grin. "Well, it's a start, we'll say that much."

"Ouch," Kenyon said. He shouldn't be surprised.

You just aren't sure you got any more work in you.

And that was the problem, wasn't it?

The Piranhas were asking for a hundred and fifty percent commitment to the cause. And Kenyon felt comfortable giving only a fraction of that.

Maybe it'll feel different, if you watch this stuff from Beau.

But it didn't.

Instead, Kenyon settled down in the empty running back room with his laptop, and when he watched the first two plays with their analysis that Beau had put together, he felt his eyes glazing over.

He was tired. He was bored. He didn't *want* to be doing this.

Was this what falling out of love with football felt like?

You never loved it. Not like you should've. That was in Julian's voice. His self-important, smug, and utterly charming voice.

Kenyon smashed the pause button on the laptop and pulled out his phone.

You still around? he typed out.

Julian hadn't answered the last few texts Kenyon had sent. But those were explicitly about hooking up. Maybe he'd scared Julian off. Maybe he needed to hit a combination of Logan's and Wade's advice. Let him know how he was feeling *and* wait for him to come around, with a patience he still wasn't exactly feeling.

But he remembered what Wade said, and wasn't Julian worth that kind of effort?

Kenyon couldn't deny it any longer. He *was*.

He watched the third play, and was halfway through the second viewing of it, scribbling down some notes when his phone dinged.

Yes, Julian had responded. **I'm still here, and still in disbelief at how good of a liar you are.**

For a split second, Kenyon froze, fingers hovering over the screen, not sure why Julian was calling him a liar. Then he realized what he was saying.

He was surprised and impressed he'd known about Pax and Davis and not said a word.

They deserved to do whatever they wanted, Kenyon typed back. **Without you media vultures ruining their happiness.**

I should be annoyed you said that, but it's unfortunately all too true, Julian texted. **Don't worry,** he added, **I won't fuck them up.**

Kenyon typed out, **You'd better not,** but before he could send it, he realized Julian *wouldn't*. It wasn't in his makeup. He didn't ever want to sensationalize a story. He just wanted to tell the truth. To report the real nitty-gritty. Sometimes it wasn't a particularly comfortable truth, but it was still the truth.

It was why Kenyon respected him, and he hated most other reporters.

It was also why a lot of people thought Julian was an asshole.

But why Kenyon had always trusted him. Even from the beginning.

Kenyon deleted his original response and instead typed, **You done with them yet? Ready to decompress from all that loved-up-ness?**

Yes, was all Julian said. **Save me. Please.**

Kenyon grinned. **Room 213. Right down the hall from the QB room.**

Was it kosher for Julian to be hanging out in the Piranhas' private meeting rooms? Well, it was probably kosher that he'd been to the QB room. After practice, Davis and Pax always went over the footage from the practice scrimmage, without fail, so he knew he was probably stuck in there, between them, and Kenyon knew from experience how all that intensity was exhausting.

Was Julian technically allowed to come down the hall to another room? Probably not, but Kenyon wasn't going to be the one to report him.

A minute later, there was a soft knock on the door, and a second later, there was Julian, popping his head in.

Kenyon didn't move, just watched, silent, as Julian glanced around the empty room, with its mini fridge, snacks stacked on the far counter, the big whiteboard with several plays worked out on it, from their meeting earlier today. Finally he settled against the wall, choosing to lean against it, instead of taking the other chair, right next to Kenyon's.

"I can't believe you didn't tell me," Julian said. Then made a face. "No, actually, I can. I actually can. But it sort of pisses me off that you didn't. You didn't think you could trust me."

"Wasn't about you. Nobody knew. Not even most of the team," Kenyon said. "I only knew because I was part of their first attempt at hosting Thanksgiving together. Davis asked me to come and I felt bad that I was always ducking team events to hang out with you and so . . . I went. And yeah, it was immediately obvious they were fucking."

Julian raised an eyebrow. "Just fucking? Have you *spent* any time around them?"

"I *play* with them, Julian. On the same goddamn team."

"Yeah, that's what I mean," Julian said. He pushed off from the wall and started to pace now. "It's clear they aren't just fucking. They . . . I don't even know how to describe it. They practically vibrate on the same goddamn frequency. It's . . . well, it's really crazy."

Kenyon knew it. He'd seen it from nearly the beginning, because Pax and Davis had always been a little bit this way. Then they'd gotten a *lot* that way.

"Yeah," Kenyon agreed.

"But Jesus, I intercepted more than one look, when Davis wanted him to do something and Pax pushed back . . ." Julian fanned himself with a palm. "It was *hot* and . . ."

"And you've been ducking my texts," Kenyon finished for him. He was pretty sure Julian wasn't having sex with someone else. So chances were, he was horny. Spending hours with Pax and Davis and their sexual tension couldn't have helped any.

Despite knowing better, Kenyon sure hadn't been sleeping with anyone else either. Because the person he wanted was Julian, and if he couldn't have him, he didn't want anyone else.

It was annoying as hell.

Julian shot him a look. "Yes," he said crisply.

"You gonna tell me why?"

"Because things got . . . complicated," Julian said. "And I thought we weren't doing complicated."

Kenyon couldn't help it, he threw his head back and just laughed.

"Oh honey, we were *made* to be complicated."

Julian made a face. Didn't answer him, but he didn't have to. He must see it too. Every single one of the lies they'd told themselves from the beginning.

"So, why did you text me?" Julian asked instead.

"Can't I just enjoy your company?"

"Sure," Julian said sarcastically, rolling his eyes.

It was more of that wall deflecting. Kenyon knew it. But he still almost believed it, for a second.

But he knew better now. Knew what to look for.

"I was watching some tape Beau sent over," Kenyon said. "Stop sulking and come over here, and help me figure out what he's saying."

"You know what he's saying." But Julian came over anyway, which Kenyon had counted on, and leaned over the desk, eyes on the screen.

"Maybe, but you still explain it better," Kenyon said, which was one hundred percent the truth.

Also, it was a lot nicer to look at Julian.

Not that there was anything wrong with the way Beau looked.

He looked fine. He just didn't have blond hair he was dying to tangle his fingers in, and those blue eyes that plain and simple, *glowed*.

They watched the first play Beau had pulled, and then Julian leaned in, and clicked replay.

"You see what you did here?" Julian pointed to the screen.

Kenyon tore his eyes away from Julian's face. Tried to focus on where he was pointing. "Yeah, the line was pulling one way, to one side, and I took the other, because that seemed like the easier route in the moment."

"Yeah, and it was the way the play called for," Julian said. "*But* you didn't identify where JJ Watt was going to be. You gotta account for him, every single damn time. And he tackled you for a loss, instead of you getting through the hole."

"He didn't buy into the play," Kenyon said, realization dawning. "Not the way he needed to."

"No," Julian said.

They watched the second, third, fourth, and finally the fifth play, and every time Julian was able to explain exactly what he'd missed.

It was clear as day—at least to him.

Not so much to Kenyon.

"Well?" Julian asked, as he rested against the back wall. "Did that help?"

But instead of answering that question, Kenyon asked another one. "How do you know how to do this?"

"Do what?"

"You're as good at this as Beau. Maybe better."

Julian opened his mouth but Kenyon pressed his palm to his lips before he could speak. "No, don't give me that reporting bullshit again, I know most—if *any*—reporters don't analyze game film this way."

"Maybe I want to be better than most," Julian said, his chin sticking out stubbornly.

"Maybe you do, but that's still not why. You gonna tell me, or do I need to google you? Hire a private investigator?"

He might actually be forced to, but what he *truly* wanted was for Julian to just tell him.

"Fine, fine," Julian relented. "I played football in high school and college, okay? You happy now?"

He'd known it. He'd *known* it. But it was something else to have Julian confirm it.

"You played running back, didn't you?"

Julian glared. Like this was too much sharing, too fast. But as far as Kenyon was concerned, it was high time. "Yeah, I did. So?"

Kenyon looked him up and down. He'd seen him without a single stitch of clothing more times than he could count. Had touched every inch of him. "You weren't very big."

"Nope." Julian didn't look particularly pleased he'd pointed it out. "But I was fast."

"And you spent a lot of time studying film. Optimizing your carries."

"It's annoying how smart you are," Julian complained. Except the look in his eyes didn't match his voice. They were soft. Grateful. Like it felt good that someone finally understood.

"Yeah, you like it," Kenyon murmured. He put a hand out. "Come 'ere."

He expected Julian to resist for a moment, which he did. He also expected Julian to give in, which he *also* did, pushing off from the wall and fitting his body into the space Kenyon had made for him.

Kenyon tucked his arm around him, tugging him closer. "Why'd you quit playing?" he asked.

"You know why," Julian said. Still fighting this every inch of the way. But he was still giving enough, bending enough, that it was clear now to Kenyon he *wanted* to be here.

Maybe he hadn't intended to catch Kenyon. Maybe he didn't know what to do with him now that he had.

But he didn't really want to throw him back. That much was obvious.

Kenyon just had to win him over, one little bit at a time. He could take Logan's advice, and be patient. He could also take Wade's, and tell Julian the truth.

"Yeah, maybe, but *maybe*, I also want you to tell me."

Julian sighed. "I knew . . . I knew I wasn't going to get the chances I needed. I was just too small, the NFL scouts all said it, all told me I'd need to be so much bigger, and I was tired. So tired of trying to be someone else," he admitted. "I was on my own, and needed to do *something*, and I finally acknowledged that wasn't going to happen for me with football. Fall semester my senior year, I took this intro to journalism class for my communication major, and the professor pulled me aside and said I had a real knack for digging out the truth in people. I did, I guess, because I never wanted them to talk about *me*, so it was always easier to get them to talk about themselves."

Julian looked surprised. Echoing the surprise that Kenyon felt. That he'd shared so much? That he'd started talking and hadn't stopped?

"We're gonna talk about that last thing, even though I know you don't want to, but tell me something else. It was just that easy for you to quit football and trade it for journalism?" Kenyon asked firmly, even as he could feel Julian tense, and begin to squirm. He wanted to move away. Kenyon could feel it. But he held him one moment longer, just because he could.

Then, to his shock, Julian actually relaxed into his embrace again.

"Not *easy*, because I'd devoted a lot of time and energy to being the best. But in the end, it was the right choice."

"Where'd you go to college?"

Julian shot him another one of those snooty, undecipherable looks. "Northwestern."

"Am I gonna find you if I google you?"

Julian's stare promised pain and suffering. Or as much edging as Kenyon could stand, the next time he got him naked. "Probably," he said begrudgingly.

But Kenyon already knew he wasn't going to be googling him anytime soon. He wanted Julian to be the one to tell him everything he could find out so easily on the internet.

"So you don't miss football?"

"I'm around it all the time," Julian pointed out dryly. "And as a former player, I certainly understand it a hell of a lot better than your run-of-the-mill reporter."

Kenyon stroked his hand up Julian's back. The muscles tensed under his touch and then relaxed again.

"Why," Julian asked, "do I get the impression that some of these questions weren't just a replacement for you googling me?"

Kenyon shrugged, even though he already knew he'd probably given himself away. "Just thinking about the future, that's all. Can't play forever." Running backs in particular always had a shorter shelf life. He'd made plenty of money, and saved most of it. The foundation was on solid footing. He'd made his mark.

Was this the end for him?

Kenyon hadn't really considered it, but the deeper he got into his time with the Piranhas, the more exposed he felt. The more revealed his lack of commitment became.

Julian's gaze narrowed. "You're not old, not even close."

"Can still fuck you into the mattress, for sure," Kenyon said.

Watched as Julian's eyes dilated. Just thinking about it made every molecule in his goddamn body tingle. It had been so long—*too* long. Why had they waited again? Oh, right, because their situation was complicated.

"I'm not sure I still want that," Julian said primly, backing up. This time Kenyon let him go, but he followed him, getting up from the chair. He watched as Julian's gaze lowered for just a second, saw his hard cock, clearly outlined in his workout shorts.

Then he pressed him up against the wall.

Felt Julian's breathing hiccup.

Met his stare, but didn't move an inch.

Didn't kiss him yet.

Even though he was dying to.

"I know just what you want," Kenyon murmured.

The heat in Julian's gaze wasn't frustrated anymore, it was something else entirely.

"I thought we weren't doing this anymore," Julian tried to protest again.

Not very successfully.

"You just have to say the word," Kenyon said, "and we'll do this all night, every night. 'Cause I want to. But you have to want to, too."

Julian licked his lips.

Kenyon couldn't stop himself from looking, watching the way his tongue darted out, the way his lips glistened afterwards.

Couldn't stop himself from remembering the way they felt against his own.

He broke down and leaned in. Brushed a brief kiss against Julian's mouth. Quick and sweet.

Only that, and Julian trembled, like he'd just been electrocuted. Had anyone ever been sweet with him? Had anyone ever just wanted him for him? Or had they wanted him because he was hot? Because he was a football player? Because of what he could give them?

It was a tough question. Kenyon didn't know if anyone had ever wanted *him* for him.

Maybe Julian did. Maybe he didn't. But Kenyon knew one thing: he was committed to finding out.

"I thought . . ." Julian's voice dropped to a mere whisper. "I thought you said it was up to me."

"Kissing, that's different," Kenyon said, even though it wasn't. But also, it *was*.

They'd spent all this time *not* kissing, and it felt like he was making up for lost time now. That, and wooing Julian properly, the way he deserved to be wooed.

The way, Kenyon suspected, nobody ever had before.

"Is it?" Julian questioned.

Kenyon was done talking though, and ready for *something*. He was practically vibrating with the need to touch him. To kiss him.

So he did. Framed Julian's gorgeous face with his hands and leaned in. This kiss wasn't brief or sweet. It was hot and needy, Julian moaning almost immediately, mouth opening up underneath Kenyon's.

Every single goddamn time he kissed Julian, he couldn't imagine it could be any better than he'd imagined, but somehow, it was.

Julian's hands slid down his back, and then lower, lingering right above his ass. Just when Kenyon was about to go out of his mind with desperate want, he finally touched him. Squeezing gently, even as his tongue stroked Kenyon's in a way that lit a fire in his belly.

Kenyon had never understood how some of the guys on the team couldn't fucking control themselves. How they ended up finding handy janitor's closets, empty rooms, etcetera. But he felt it now. Could imagine taking Julian right here, right now, bent over this desk.

It would feel amazing.

Julian begging for it would be even better.

From how Julian kept thrusting into Kenyon's thigh, hard and needy, he knew he'd plead for it. He'd want it fast and hard and *now.*

But this isn't supposed to be just a quick fuck anymore.

The thought was ice-cold water, dumped all over his head.

Kenyon wrenched his mouth off Julian's, and took a step back, and then another.

Because Julian looked so gorgeously wrecked. His hair a mess from Kenyon's hands, his mouth red and wet, those beautiful eyes dilated til almost no blue remained, his cock a hard line in his jeans. He was panting, breathing unevenly, and eyeing Kenyon with something like wonderment.

Kenyon squeezed his fists together, trying to find a control that didn't really want to be found.

"I don't think the kissing was all that different," Julian said. Then, licked his lips again. Like he could still taste Kenyon, and he wanted more.

Wanted it all.

"It was . . . something, that's for sure," Kenyon stuttered. It was a miracle he was putting together coherent sentences at all. His cock ached.

Julian didn't say anything.

"I meant it, though . . ." Kenyon continued. "If you want me, you just have to say the word."

"Do I? Or are there strings now?"

"Honey," Kenyon said, grabbing his bag from the chair, "there have *always* been strings. Even if you didn't want to see them. You know where to find me, if you want me."

He turned and left then, shutting the door behind him firmly because if he stayed, he was going to absolutely, one hundred percent bend Julian over that table, and even *he* knew that was no way to prove to Julian how valuable he was. That Kenyon wanted him for more than just fleeting physical pleasure.

Chapter Eleven

Julian was absolutely *NOT* going to call Kenyon.

Nope, he was not.

He was not going to call him. He was not going to text him.

He was definitely, absolutely not going to get in his car, go over to his house, and collect on all the promises Kenyon kept making.

Kenyon had already learned some of his past. If Julian went over to his house tonight, if he gave in to the fire that they'd started earlier, Julian knew he'd inadvertently reveal even more.

Would he finally ask, *Why do you keep looking at me like I'm special, when I've never been special, the only person who ever truly believed in me was me?*

He might.

He might ask that, and a lot more, if only Kenyon would touch him again.

Julian flopped back against his couch.

Right now, if he had friends—or any actual family—this would be a great time to talk to them. But he had always been alone.

There was Nikki, who sometimes felt more like a friend than a boss, but he also knew how hard she'd clawed to get to the top, and he'd be stupid and naive to think that she'd place their friendship above her job.

The moment he asked her about a guy, she'd want to know who it was.

And the moment she found out who it was, it was all going to be over.

Normally, Julian wouldn't mind keeping his private life *private*, but he needed someone to unload to.

This is why you need friends. Or at least a friend, singular.

Julian pulled out his phone. He and Ed chatted regularly, though usually only about work. But he knew how the other reporter felt about Helen.

He'd seen him watching her.

Teased Ed about how he looked at her.

About how he flirted, even though it was pointless, and they both knew it.

He wrote, **If you had a chance with Helen, a real chance, would you take it?**

But instead of Ed texting him back, his phone rang almost immediately.

"What are you talkin' about?" Ed demanded the moment Julian answered.

"I'm just asking a philosophical question, and honestly, what does your generation have against texting?" Julian complained.

"What does *your* generation have against talking on the goddamn phone?" Ed retorted.

"Fair," Julian said.

Ed sighed. "This about you and Ellis?"

Julian nearly dropped his phone. "What? You . . ."

"Son, you'd have to be blind to not see the looks you and Kenyon been shooting each other all season. Just saying."

"That's nothing."

"Lie," Ed announced cheerfully.

"I don't even know if I *like* him," Julian said, trying again.

"And there's your second lie."

"You're annoying," Julian grumbled.

"I thought you were all about the truth," Ed said.

"That's *work*. I enjoy lying to myself and everyone else about my personal life—or complete lack of personal life—a hell of a lot more."

"Nikki would string you up if she found out," Ed said.

"I'm less worried about that," Julian said, which was saying something because Nikki would one hundred and ten percent make it hurt, and *bad*.

What did that say about him that he was actually way more worried about Kenyon breaching all his walls?

Nothing good.

Ed chuckled. "Then what *are* you worried about, if it's not Nikki killing you slowly?"

What was he afraid of?

Being exposed. Revealing himself, a little bit at a time, until Kenyon could see all of him, as he actually was, and then not liking what he saw.

Making Julian fall in love with him and then leaving him.

Kenyon falling in love with *him*, and then him panicking and breaking Kenyon's heart.

Julian was silent for a moment. "That I might really like him," he finally said quietly. "That this might not be about sex at all."

"Sounds serious," Ed said.

"I think that's what he wants. Something serious. What if . . ." Julian's voice caught, and normally he'd have been humiliated by the emotion in it, but Ed wasn't anyone else. He was the closest to a friend Julian could remember having.

"What if you end up actually happy and settled?" Ed retorted kindly. "God forbid."

"I know," Julian said with a reluctant sigh. "It's not what I ever thought I wanted."

"Don't keep lying to yourself. We all say we don't want it. That we're happier alone. More freedom. Can walk around the house buck-ass naked if we want, drink milk from the carton, don't worry about shoveling out any of the clutter from the dining room. But what it really means is that you're *alone*."

Julian looked over at the kitchen table—that he'd bought and assembled from IKEA—and its pristine surface. No clutter in sight. But that wasn't because he didn't have anyone to see the mess, it was because he didn't live enough of a life to *have* a mess.

"I know what being alone is like," Julian said. He'd gotten used to it. Did it feel *good*? Not really. But it was comfortable, at least. *Safe*. "Better than most."

"Then maybe it's time to try it the other way," Ed said gently.

That was what he'd reached out to Ed for. Not necessarily permission, because he was Julian Anderson, and he'd been taking care of himself, without anyone's input, for a very long time now. So not permission exactly, but the other side of the argument.

There were so many ways this could go wrong, so many ways he could end up somehow *more* alone than he'd ever been before, he'd needed the reminder it might not be all bad.

He could be happy. *Really* happy.

Look at Pax and Davis. They'd taken a chance, a real serious risk, and all he had to do was stand near them to feel their bliss.

"I think . . ." Julian took a deep breath. "I think you might be right."

"What's that? I might be right?" Ed chuckled. "I should've recorded that."

"You should've, 'cause I'm not sure it'll happen ever again," Julian retorted mildly.

"Probably not," Ed said, "but that's alright. I just want to be right in this one situation. You'll tell me if I am?"

Julian hesitated. This was why he didn't have friends. They wanted updates. They wanted to chat. Make friendship bracelets. Swear undying fealty to each other. That was not his style. Though, frankly, that wasn't Ed's either.

"Yeah, I'm sure I'll see you Friday."

"For the press conference, yeah," Ed said. "But don't hesitate to text, okay? He's just a football player. Feet of clay, just like the rest of us."

After saying goodbye and hanging up, Julian considered this as he pushed himself off the couch. Kenyon was just a man. A football player, sure, but hadn't he been one of those, too?

He wasn't that scary. He was *just a man.*

A man just as affected by Julian as Julian was by him.

He froze, on the way to the bathroom, the realization hitting him hard. Didn't that make Kenyon vulnerable in the exact same ways?

He reminded himself of that particular fact half a dozen times as he fixed his hair and threw on a sweatshirt, ducking out of his front door and heading to his car.

On the way to Kenyon's house, he made every single argument, and then discarded each one in turn.

Okay, there'd be strings now.

He could deal with that. He hadn't been sleeping with anyone else, he wasn't interested in sleeping with anyone else, and he knew Kenyon was the same.

Okay, Kenyon might want to do a relationship now.

But what did that really mean anyway? They couldn't see each other publicly. There wouldn't be any big romantic dates. Julian poked at his own emotions and decided he wouldn't mind Kenyon saying some of the things *he* was feeling out loud.

Okay, Kenyon was definitely going to discover some of the things about himself that he didn't normally share.

But Julian couldn't deny he trusted the guy. They trusted each other. They couldn't have done this, in their precarious position, for six months, without some form of trust.

What was it Kenyon had said earlier?

Honey, there were always strings. Even if you didn't want to see them.

Julian was beginning to see them now—clear enough he couldn't continue to ignore them the way he always had.

All his arguments demolished, and his realization that they'd ended in the exact same vulnerable position, Julian parked in front of Kenyon's house. Glanced up at the house. It was lit, like Kenyon was still here.

You know where to find me, if you want me.

Julian couldn't deny it any longer. He wanted Kenyon.

By the time he made it to the front step, he was trembling, nearly shaking with the effort it took to not turn tail and run back to the safety of his car.

Once he knocked on the door, everything would change.

He raised his hand to knock, but it never connected with the wood of Kenyon's front door. Instead, it swung open, and there was Kenyon standing there.

He raised an eyebrow, his gaze questioning, but he said nothing.

You just have to say the word.

At the last second, Julian's courage failed. Which was stupid, because hadn't he worked through all of this with Ed, and on the ride over?

But like an idiot, he opened his mouth to speak and nothing came out.

But, a sly voice added in his head, *Kenyon never said you had to say the words out loud.*

He didn't think, because thinking meant that he'd *overthink*. Instead, he took a chance, and launched himself at Kenyon, who caught him, settling a pair of hard, powerful hands under his ass, his legs wrapping around Kenyon's waist.

Julian felt the *whoosh* of the door closing next to his head and then Kenyon was pressing him against it.

The look in Kenyon's eyes was serious. Earnest.

He'd been right.

There'd always been strings.

Julian kissed him.

It had always been incredible between them—full of heat, their sexual preferences lining up nearly exactly, in that they didn't care who did what to whom as long as it felt good—and Julian hadn't known to expect any differently now.

But it was so much fucking better.

It was the kissing, and it was so much more now, too. That he *liked* Kenyon. Liked talking to him. Liked texting with him. Liked the way he felt when Kenyon's gaze fell on him. That he wasn't just a lover, but kind of a friend, too.

Kind of more, too, if he was being really fucking honest.

It was the emotional mixed with the physical, and it blew Julian's mind.

He dug his fingers into Kenyon's shoulders, and groaned into his mouth as Kenyon's grip tightened.

Then the door was gone and Kenyon didn't stop kissing him as they moved through the house.

He knew it was coming, but Julian still felt the loss of Kenyon's mouth acutely when he landed on his back, the softness of Kenyon's bed breaking his fall.

Kenyon stripped off his shirt, Julian's mouth watering as he took in all his delectable brown skin, those broad, muscular shoulders, the firm pecs, the chiseled six-pack abs. He looked so fucking incredible and he was all Julian's.

"You caught me," Julian murmured.

Kenyon smiled.

It was sweet. It was dirty. It was full of promise.

"I sure did," he said.

"Don't you dare say anything about not wanting to drop precious cargo." Julian was prepared to go so far, but there was a definite line and cheesy romance was *far* across it.

"I wouldn't dare." But his smile had grown even brighter, and his dark eyes were soft and amused, like he hadn't expected any less from Julian. Like he *liked* him this way—a little prickly and rough around the edges.

"Good," Julian said. He toed off his shoes, then his socks, eyes never leaving Kenyon's. "What do you want?"

"What do *you* want?"

"Oh God, are you gonna be that kind of lay now?" Julian complained.

Kenyon's eyebrow ticked up. "What kind is that?"

"The kind that's all conscientious and thoughtful, always wanting me to get my own way because of some misplaced sense of romance?"

"Does that sound like me?" Kenyon asked, chuckling.

"Kind of," Julian said, suspicious.

"Well, how 'bout this . . . you good with what I said earlier?"

Julian swallowed hard. He knew exactly what Kenyon was referring to. "You want to fuck me into the mattress?"

He nodded, wordlessly.

"Yes," Julian said primly, which was so stupid, because Kenyon was already moving towards the drawer in the bedside table, pulling out lube. They hadn't used condoms in ages, and Julian felt a pulse of something that must be affection that even though they hadn't had sex in weeks, Kenyon hadn't found someone else to satisfy his urges.

Considering Kenyon, with his kind eyes and sexy smile and fucking incredible body, could have anyone he wanted, it was . . . well, it was something.

Something Julian wasn't sure he wanted to give a label to, just yet.

Kenyon tossed the lube on the bed, and then he was there, too, straddling Julian, his pulse increasing the nearer he got.

"Fuck, you're so . . ." Kenyon's voice was worshipful as he reached out and popped open every button on Julian's shirt, slowly, deliberately.

"Hot, gorgeous, beautiful?" Julian tried to employ a non-snide voice, because he knew Kenyon believed he was all of those things. He could see the truth of it reflected in Kenyon's eyes now.

"Sexy as hell, and not just 'cause you look like this," he said, spreading his shirt open, running his fingertips down his chest, down his stomach, down to where he strained, hard and ready, against his jeans.

"Why, then?" Julian asked.

He'd spent the last six months trying to keep the bedroom talk to a minimum because that had seemed . . . safer. More like they were just fucking.

But now it seemed to just blossom out of him, without effort.

Like he'd been waiting all this time for the chance to be a brat, and for Kenyon to punish him in a hundred sexy, creative ways for every single rude comment he made.

Kenyon chuckled.

"You're so goddamned smart, for one. Snarky too, I like that."

"You like that?" Julian couldn't temper his disbelief.

"God, I *love* it," Kenyon said, his expression fierce and fervent. And undeniable.

He fucking *meant* it.

Then he was working Julian's jeans open, yanking them down, and Julian froze, aching with the need to be touched. To be touched by Kenyon, specifically.

"You want this?" Kenyon traced a teasing finger down Julian's cock, covered by just his briefs.

"*Yes*," Julian hissed.

"Then turn over." Kenyon backed off him, letting him move, and Julian wasted zero time.

He knew how good this was.

He knew how much he'd be crying and begging for it, the moment Kenyon touched him.

But Julian had been lying facedown on the mattress, with *nothing*, for long enough that he nearly turned around to ask Kenyon what was wrong.

But he didn't because one of those hard, capable, calloused hands traced down his back, right down his spine, making him shiver then, and then his fingers were pulling his briefs down, tracing over his curves.

Julian wasn't proud of it, but his knees buckled a little. It felt so good already, as good as it had always felt, and frankly, exactly the goddamn same.

Honey, there were always strings. Even if you didn't want to see them.

It was annoying how right Kenyon was, even as Julian loved every second of his touch, pushing into his hands.

Kenyon gave him a little smack on his ass cheek. "Stay still, or I'm not gonna be responsible for what happens next."

"What is that? Can you describe it to me, in detail?" Julian asked hopefully.

He laughed then.

It does feel different, Julian realized, *because there aren't any more rules. No more expectations. Or guidelines. Just me and him.*

He wiggled then, and Kenyon smacked him again, lighter this time, and that was when Julian felt it, one of those fingers brushing up against his hole, wet with lube.

Groaning, Julian relaxed and let Kenyon work the first finger in him.

He was so worked up, because he'd been having fucking amazing sex for six straight months, and hadn't had any for three weeks now.

This promised to be *very* good sex. Every touch of Kenyon's lit him up inside, every brush of his cock against the bedspread making him shake with desire.

"God, I love you just like this, needy and desperate for me," Kenyon murmured as he worked a second finger deep, brushing right against Julian's prostate, making him tremble.

"I'm needy and desperate because you won't get on with it," Julian said.

Kenyon was big, and it would burn a little if he wasn't properly prepped, but he'd been waiting too long as it was.

"Don't want to hurt you," Kenyon reminded him. Paused. "And not for some stupid romantic reason, either, but because I want to do this again and again and *again*. Til you can't even fucking walk straight tomorrow."

Julian moaned. He wanted that too. He wanted to feel branded by Kenyon's cock. Owned by it.

He slid another finger in, stretching him further. Julian pushed back against his hand, wanting it deeper, wanting so much more.

"Come on," he chanted, "I'm ready, if you think you can still fuck me good enough . . ."

It was all he got out before there it was—Kenyon's cock, hard as Julian had ever felt it—right against his hole, beginning to push in.

"Yeah, I've got you," Kenyon said, and the smug satisfaction in his voice would've been annoying, if Julian hadn't been wailing with the pleasure of it as he began to do just what he'd promised: fuck him into the mattress so good he'd be begging for it.

He *already* was.

Because that was definitely his voice now, babbling incoherently, a mix of pleas and swear words, as the pleasure began to overtake him.

Kenyon knew the rhythm he liked, the exact right angle. His strokes were long and steady, and then right when Julian thought he'd taken everything he could and couldn't take another moment of Kenyon's safe fucking, he lost his reins—or purposefully let go of them—and started fucking Julian hard and wild, just the way he'd always craved it.

It was Kenyon losing that control, or maybe it was that jacking off by himself had been lackluster at best, when compared to the smorgasbord of sexual delights he'd been enjoying during the last six months with Kenyon. But almost too late, Julian realized he was right there, hovering on the edge, so close to orgasm that he could nearly taste it.

"Fuck, I'm close," Julian wailed, and even before he could reach for his cock, to give himself the stroke or two he needed to send him over the edge, Kenyon's hand was there, his grip perfect, the pleasure overwhelming, and he spasmed hard, trembling as his orgasm went on and on.

Kenyon didn't give him a break, didn't slow down or even hesitate. He just fucked him through it, until his grip tightened, and he groaned, shaking as his cock emptied out.

Julian slumped to the bed, not giving a shit if he made a mess.

He'd never felt so goddamned fucked out in his whole life, and it was glorious.

If this was what sex with strings was like, he'd gladly let himself be tied up like a freaking marionette.

Kenyon collapsed next to him, but nothing was more surprising than hearing him laugh.

Laugh, and *keep* laughing.

Julian found the energy to turn his head. "What is it?" he demanded.

Kenyon slid an arm around Julian and dragged his body against his own. "Nothing, just . . . why didn't we do that from the beginning? Are we stupid?"

"Speak for yourself," Julian said. Rolled his eyes. "I . . ." Suddenly he didn't know what to say. Because it had been amazing. Transcendental, even.

Maybe they had been a *little* stupid.

"I thought so," Kenyon said, and he was doing that smug thing again, and Julian couldn't even hold it against him.

Annoying.

Adorable, but definitely still annoying.

"So," Kenyon said after a moment of what Julian had been *so* sure would be awkward, painful silence, but actually wasn't, at all.

"So," Julian repeated, tilting his eyes up, meeting Kenyon's. Kenyon's gaze was warm. Affectionate. His cheeks were hurting, and he realized, almost belatedly, it was because he was smiling so goddamn hard.

"What do we do now?" Kenyon asked.

Julian laughed. *Also* unlike him, though Kenyon had been making him laugh like this almost from the beginning. Which . . . maybe he should've guessed sooner what was really going on between them. But how could he have? He didn't have experience with any of this.

"This was all *your* idea," Julian reminded him. "Remember? All that *you just have to say the word* garbage."

"Hey, it wasn't garbage. It worked, didn't it? Can't be garbage if it worked."

Julian rolled his eyes. "Maybe it wasn't your crappy line, but the promise of your frankly amazing dick."

"Thanks, I guess?"

Julian laughed again. How did this keep happening?

He was supposed to already *be* charmed. Not continually be shocked at how freaking adorable Kenyon was.

"I mean it though," Kenyon continued stubbornly, because that was one of Julian's most favorite things about him, and also his *least* favorite thing, too, "what are we going to do about this?"

"Keep having sex?" Julian asked hopefully.

Kenyon elbowed him in the side. "Definitely that, yes, but what else?"

"If you wanted to whisk me off on some romantic Caribbean vacation, complete with new wardrobe that you took me shopping for, *Pretty Woman*-style, I wouldn't complain."

"No?"

Julian shrugged. He'd said it because he knew it wouldn't happen. Those types of big romantic gestures weren't for guys like them. He'd given up on those kinds of blind fantasies a long fucking time ago.

"As long as we draw the line at rose petals on the bed," Julian said.

"I don't know," Kenyon said thoughtfully, "I kinda like the idea of rose petals. Something soft, to go with all your . . ."

Julian made a face and interrupted before he could continue. "If you're gonna say all my *softness*, please don't. I don't need romance, you know that."

Kenyon was quiet for a moment. "You know," he said finally, "I don't think anyone needs it. But it's nice to get, you know?"

"Is that what you're asking?"

Oh my God, Kenyon's gonna try to romance me.

The worst part wasn't that it might happen, the worst part was the undeniable thrill working its way through him.

"Would you kick me in the balls if I did? If I wanted to?"

Julian nearly rolled away. This conversation had gotten so serious so quick, and he was suddenly, inexplicably out of his depth. Which . . . he didn't even have to remind himself that didn't happen, *ever.*

"You seem to be laboring under the assumption I'm a rather violent person," Julian said slowly.

"You wouldn't?"

"I might want to use your balls later," Julian said.

"Right."

Was that disappointment lingering in Kenyon's eyes?

"I wouldn't . . . I wouldn't hate it," Julian said hurriedly. Without thinking. Added, "If you did it. If you wanted to. That is."

Kenyon smirked. "Alright. Does this mean you'd go on a date with me?"

"A date?" It wasn't like he'd never been asked before. He was prickly, sure, and could be a bit of an asshole, but he was hot. He got asked. A lot.

He'd just never said yes before.

"Yeah. A date."

"We couldn't . . ."

"Go out somewhere, yeah, I know."

"And I have the big story about Pax and Davis . . ."

"Yeah, that too. But you can spare me a few hours, can't you?"

He could.

The only question was if he wanted to.

But that wasn't it either. It wasn't a matter of wanting, it was a question of that fear pressing against his breastbone, all those ugly thoughts about his real worth he had never quite been strong enough to banish.

Would Kenyon eventually believe them? Or could he see past them?

"I . . ." Julian cleared his throat. He'd never let fear control him with anything else, and he was already halfway in this . . . whether he wanted to be or not—and he *did*, that was the real kicker. "I could. Make the time, that is."

How many ways and times had Julian seen Kenyon smile? So fucking many.

But his smile had never looked like this before. Slow and sweet and *real*.

And it's all for you.

"Good," Kenyon said.

Maybe he was still a little smug, but frankly, Julian thought he deserved it. After all, he'd convinced *him*—who'd never willingly dated in his life—to not only go on a date, but that it was actually a good idea.

"I'm looking forward to it," Kenyon said.

Julian shot him a look. "Don't push your luck."

Kenyon chuckled, and his fingers dug into his skin, which was all the warning Julian had before he was rolling him underneath his big, muscular body. Then his mouth lowered onto his and Julian relaxed into his embrace.

This he understood.

This made sense.

Chapter Twelve

It would be silly and tacky to run around for the next day doing a fist pump whenever Kenyon thought about how Julian had actually come to him. Had come to him, his heart in his hands, and had actually agreed to a date.

They were *dating*.

Just the thought it was happening kept blowing Kenyon's mind into tiny little pieces.

Only with an extraordinary kind of focus had he been able to fix his attention where it belonged, on today's practice and on the playoff game this weekend.

As practice came to a close, Beau approached where he was stretching on the sideline, working out the kinks in his muscles.

"Hey, you watched the video I sent," he said.

Kenyon glanced up. Didn't question how Beau knew, because Beau was the sort of guy who could always tell if you'd done what you were supposed to. He'd inherited his father's scary accurate skill in that particular area.

"Yeah," he said.

"That second cut you made in the last play, that was brilliant," Beau said.

Kenyon didn't want to admit that he'd never have seen the opportunity if it wasn't for Julian.

"Couldn't have done it without that film," Kenyon said, which was true, because if Beau hadn't put it together, he never would have gotten Julian's unique perspective either.

Between the two of them, he was learning more than he could've dreamt about this position that he'd been playing for over fifteen years.

"Well, it's about implementation, too," Beau said, patting him on the shoulder pad.

"God, I swear that's your new favorite word," Sebastian said, jogging over and collapsing onto the bench next to Kenyon. "I think I'm hearing it in my dreams, these days."

"Then I must not be doing it right," Beau said with a grin at his boyfriend. "Though, that's not what you were saying last night."

Sebastian swiped a towel over his damp face. He was grinning. "Guess not."

Before, all this . . . painfully obvious togetherness would've made Kenyon nervous and awkward. He never knew what to do with it. But now he looked at Beau and Sebastian, at the obvious affection they had for each other, the love in their eyes, and thought he might recognize a little of himself there, these days.

Wasn't that crazy?

Kenyon resisted the urge to randomly fist-pump.

"Oh, I forgot to tell Scott something."

"Better go tell him now, and not later, when he and your dad . . ."

Beau shot his boyfriend a freezing look and took off.

Sebastian was still laughing as Kenyon took a seat next to him. He'd hoped to talk to him one-on-one, without making a big deal out of it, and this was his perfect opportunity.

"What's that about?" he asked Sebastian casually.

"Oh, I think Beau's still traumatized from discovering his dad and Scott together in well . . . we'll say a private moment."

"In an apron?" Kenyon had heard this story. He was pretty sure *everyone* had heard this story.

It wasn't unusual for Scott to show up at his office and discover an apron hung on the doorknob. He thought it was hilarious. Coach was a trickier nut to crack. He usually just pursed his lips and rolled his eyes.

"Yep, that's the one," Sebastian said.

"And Beau's still . . ."

"Oh, he loves them together, he'll be the first to admit it now," Sebastian said, lowering his voice, "but can you blame him for not wanting to think about his dad having sex?"

"If it's with Scott . . ."

Sebastian cackled, and they fist-bumped in agreement.

"Coach has good taste, I'll give him that."

"Don't let him hear you say that," Kenyon warned. Logan had said it once, and had ended up running drills for nearly an hour.

"Oh, I know," Sebastian said, sounding like he too had learned about Coach's propensity for privacy the hard way.

"You looked good out there today," Kenyon said. "I might've gotten the edge, couple of times, if it wasn't for you."

"You make it hard," Sebastian said, which was a high compliment, coming from him.

"But you're still doing it." It wasn't the most slick segue of all time, but it would do. "Why?"

"Why didn't I pack it in?" Sebastian shot him a sideways glance, dark eyes knowing.

"Yeah," Kenyon said.

Sebastian shrugged. "I wasn't ready. I love playing, just had to figure out a way to keep doing it."

That was not helpful.

Kenyon was going to have to dig deeper, and that wouldn't be casual. Sebastian was way too smart to believe it was.

"You could've said, I don't want to play safety, I'm gonna call it quits, but you didn't."

"Safety's a new, different challenge, you know? I'm not great at it yet. Could be, though. Keeps me pushing, keeps me moving, keeps me on my toes. That's all I want. Someday that won't be enough, someday I'll have to find something else to do that." Sebastian's gaze narrowed. "Like you. You already got that thing. The foundation."

He did.

And that was the problem, wasn't it? Both of them—football and We Read—deserved one hundred percent of his attention, and because math was never his friend, he could only manage fifty percent for each, on a good day.

"Yeah," Kenyon agreed.

"You're really good at it. Giving without making it about you, making it about the people who need the help. Assisting kids who nobody gives a shit about. Taking care of our community, being there for those young kids. Better, maybe, than you are at football," Sebastian said thoughtfully.

Like he knew just what Kenyon needed to hear.

Not what he *wanted* to hear. But then, he hadn't come to Sebastian for sugarcoating.

He was absolute shit at it.

Maybe that's why he liked him.

Maybe that's why he also liked Julian.

Julian wouldn't know sugar if it came up and bit him in the ass.

But then, because of that, he never had to question him.

"Now you're just showing off," Kenyon complained.

Sebastian grinned. "Now's the point where I say you could do anything you goddamn wanted to do. So the question is . . . what *is* that?"

"Could be both. Used to be both," Kenyon admitted.

"You been chasing big contracts, not great teams," Sebastian pointed out. Kindly. But bluntly. "You never cared about a ring or a trophy."

"Some people don't," Kenyon argued.

"But you gotta ask yourself why that is," Sebastian said, and stood with a groan, stretching out his back. "I better go, before Beau kicks my ass."

"He do that?" Kenyon had always kinda believed relationships meant there was no more ass-kicking, that it was more ass-*licking*, but then he'd met Julian and he couldn't imagine Julian not routinely kicking his ass, just because he could or because Kenyon needed to be set straight about something or other.

"Absolutely," Sebastian said, smiling like he actually enjoyed it.

And that, Kenyon thought as he stretched his legs out, watching as Sebastian headed towards the locker room, was something else to think on.

Maybe romance wasn't just rose petals and *Pretty Woman* shopping sprees and extravagant Caribbean vacations. Maybe it wasn't just the date box that Logan had slipped him before practice. "No fail," Logan had told him seriously. "These are *personally* responsible for at least three relationships on this team."

Kenyon should've been way less pleased about Logan's guarantee but instead he took the box like it was the golden bullet he'd been promised, and carefully tucked it into his locker.

He'd promised Julian a date. This would make that easier, right?

"Let's go over this one more time," Julian said, not only to the camera crew behind the monitor, but to Pax and Davis, sitting in front of him on two uncomfortable chairs—at least if theirs were anything like his own.

He gave both of them credit. Pax barely blinked, and a passing annoyance crossed over Davis' face, but he reined it in.

Julian couldn't say he had any familiarity with wanting something so badly, with having something so goddamned precious in your life that you'd go to any lengths to protect it, to cherish it, to make it last.

But he was beginning to see what that might look like, just from watching Paxton Kelly and Davis Abernathy.

The director gave the cue, and Julian turned to the pair in front of him.

"What do you want to say to the critics who claim you can't be together and play your best football?"

Davis' smile reminded Julian of a shark. With lots of teeth. "That they're homophobic," he said bluntly.

This was the last piece they were filming for the big feature this weekend, airing before the Piranhas' first playoff game. He'd written a piece, too, and it was currently sitting on Nikki's desk, no doubt waiting for her to tear it apart, and build it back with a hell of a lot more drama.

Julian wasn't looking forward to that conversation.

But before that, they needed to get this footage in the can so they could edit it and have it ready for Sunday.

"Not just that," Pax added, shooting the camera a charming, quiet smile. "But that they've equated two things that just aren't the same. That I'm gay and I play—or *can't*—play football. Because you don't ask Patrick Mahomes if he can't be with his wife and be an MVP and a Super Bowl champion."

"Surely Sam Crawford and Heath Harris have gone a long way to proving that's untrue. Not to mention all the other out players in the NFL," Julian pointed out.

He'd promised that he would take it easy-ish on them for this part. But that he wouldn't pull his punches either.

They'd agreed, because they both knew it mattered that Julian pushed.

Or rather Pax had agreed and Davis had continued to glower.

"Yeah, they have. Every single person who's come before us has made it a little easier on everyone who came after," Pax said. "But that doesn't mean it's *easy*."

Davis nudged him. He was smiling. "Pax here never likes it when it's easy, anyway."

They wrapped up the interview with a few more cute exchanges, and then it was done. In the can. Julian let out the breath he hadn't realized he was holding, watching as Davis helped Pax divest himself of his microphone. Even as Pax tried to bat his hands away, protesting that he was totally capable of doing it himself.

That was the other thing Julian was beginning to learn about this whole relationship thing: even when you knew your partner could handle their shit—because Davis *knew* Pax could handle his shit, Julian had personally watched him know it, over and over again, during the last week of practice and game prep—but that didn't preclude you from wanting to protect them anyway.

Julian had finally identified the gnawing guilt he'd felt over giving that quote to the podcast about Kenyon.

He hadn't protected him.

He'd been frustrated and confused and annoyed.

He'd felt like everything was changing, and he'd fought the change, tooth and nail.

But now, the idea of what he'd done stung, in a deep, dark place he normally avoided.

Especially after what he'd seen this week between Pax and Davis.

It wasn't that he wanted what they had—he'd go nuts, spending twenty-four seven with someone else, even if that someone was Kenyon. He'd been independent too long; he needed that space now. But the care they took with each other? The way Pax didn't even look before he'd leap into something, because he knew Davis was there, knew that Davis would always have his back?

That was something special; something *enviable*.

"In the spirit of emotional honesty, I have to tell you I've never been on a date before," Julian announced the moment Kenyon opened his front door.

Kenyon grinned as he opened the door wider, letting Julian in. "Let me guess, you just spent the afternoon with Pax and Davis."

Julian shot him a look. "That obvious, huh?"

"The answer is yes," Kenyon said as he led him into the kitchen, "they make everyone feel completely, totally jealous of their super-duper extra-special love, while at the same time making every single person want to do everything possible to earn their own."

Julian chuckled.

"And they're so damn cute together that you're not even mad," Kenyon said. "That's the truth. No—you're not alone. Yes—everyone feels it, even Coach. I've heard him muttering about it, even though he's practically on his goddamn honeymoon." He turned, leaning against the big white island. "So . . . your first date, huh?"

Julian had told himself he was not nervous.

Nerves would mean he cared how this turned out.

Because it was just an experiment, right? They were just trying this on for size. If it was a complete disaster, they could always retreat to the bedroom. Absolutely zero pressure.

"Yes," he said.

Regretting telling Kenyon at all, because now he looked smug and way too pleased with himself. Like he should win an award for being the one to finally bag a date with Julian Anderson. When in reality, was it really that wonderful? Julian wasn't sure.

"I'm just surprised, 'cause I bet you were in high demand."

Julian shrugged, shoving his hands awkwardly in his pockets, because he didn't know where else to put them. He'd assumed they'd be staying at Kenyon's house, because it wasn't like anyone could actually see them out and about, and while Kenyon believed he wasn't recognizable . . . he definitely was.

At least Julian would never make that mistake again.

"Oh come on," Kenyon said with an irrepressible smile, "don't be shy, it's so unlike you. I bet I was like the hundredth guy to ask."

"Why should I tell you? You're just going to be even smugger about it," Julian countered.

"Because that's what people who date do . . . they *share*," Kenyon said.

"Fair," Julian said. He knew Kenyon was right, and it wasn't like he'd really believed he'd be satisfied with the truth about why he'd become a reporter.

It might be big to him, but Kenyon wouldn't understand that.

"So," Julian continued, "have *you* ever been on a date?"

Kenyon froze.

"I didn't think so," Julian said. It was definitely his turn to feel superior. "And no, sorry to disappoint, but not even close the hundredth, most of the time because I never let it get far enough for them to ask."

He tried to say it casually, like it didn't matter. Like it wasn't a big deal. Like it wasn't already freaking Julian out, this thing had been going on between them for six months already—when any previous hookup had only lasted a few weeks, *at most*.

"Ah," Kenyon said knowingly, but Julian was grateful he didn't say anything else about it. What was there to say? They were both putting themselves out there. No need to draw even more attention to it.

"What's that?" Julian asked, pointing at the nondescript cardboard box sitting on the island. It was the only thing breaking up the unrelenting white surface, so it had caught his attention almost immediately.

"Our date," Kenyon said.

Julian raised an eyebrow. "A date in a . . . box?"

"Logan gave it to me, I guess he got a subscription when he started dating Dylan, and when he heard we were doing this . . ."

Julian fought the panic spearing through him. Logan was the center for the Piranhas, and the last thing they needed was to become a source of team gossip. Because there was *definitely* team gossip. He hadn't needed to spend the last few days with Pax and Davis to know that. "You told a player on your team?"

"That I was going on a date, yeah. Not who it was with. Don't worry." Kenyon reached for him, and Julian allowed himself to be reeled in. "It's gonna be fine."

It *felt* fine, just being wrapped up in Kenyon's warm embrace, and when had that ever happened before?

Never. It had never happened before.

"You good now?" Kenyon asked quietly. Julian let his head fall to Kenyon's shoulder.

"Yeah."

"So, yes, I did tell Logan I was going on a date, with a guy I really liked," Kenyon said, like the phrase *guy I really liked* didn't make Julian's heartbeat accelerate all over again, "and he said, I got something that's gonna make it easy. Well, not *easy*, but easier, so here we are. You wanna open it and see what we're going to do?"

Julian couldn't deny it, he *was* curious.

"It's a whole date, in a box?"

"That's what Logan promised."

"Well, I guess we might as well open it, then," Julian said. Like he wasn't dying to look inside.

"Not eager at all, huh?" Kenyon teased. He reached over and pulled the box closer to them.

Julian popped the lid off, and to his surprise the box was almost entirely full, and lying right on top was a card, with a few doodled illustrations of wine, cheese, and a . . . a *boot?*

"Welcome to your Italian date night," Kenyon read over his shoulder. "You're going to be exploring some of the best experiences Italy has to offer. Included is a mix to help you make your own pizza, just add tomatoes and cheese—*shit*." Kenyon paused. "Do I have tomatoes and cheese?"

"I don't know," Julian said with a sniff. "The box *says* you needed to check the list of ingredients before the date, and let me guess, you didn't do that."

"Hush," Kenyon said, pressing a kiss to his cheek. "I can take care of it." He pulled out his phone, and in a few clicks, he was smiling just as smugly as he had before. "There," he said. "*Done.*"

"Did you just order tomatoes and cheese from Postmates?"

"Hell yes I did. And basil. And some Italian wine that you'll drink and I'll get to watch you drink."

"What, you don't want to even taste it?"

Kenyon's gaze turned dark and intent. "Oh, I'll get to. Don't worry about that."

Julian nearly leaned in and kissed him then, the anticipation for it already rising in his blood, but Kenyon just chuckled and nudged him. "Don't you start that," he said. "If you do, we'll never make a pizza."

"Have you ever *made* a pizza before?" Julian asked skeptically.

"Nope, but there's always your first time. You're smart, and I'm at least reasonably capable of following directions. Surely between the two of us, we can figure out how to do this."

"I guess we'll find out," Julian said. He pulled out the rest of the items from the box. There was a bag of flour, a recipe card for the pizza, as well as a deck of cards, labeled in Italian, and then several other printed pages, which after careful examination, proved to be flowery compliments and terms of endearment all accompanied by their Italian translation.

"Ooooh," Kenyon said, reading the card as Julian finished scanning it. "*Tesoro*. I like that one. Yep. *Tesoro*. It fits you."

Julian glared. "Don't call me that."

"Why not?" Kenyon still seemed pleased with himself. Even more so now that he'd found Julian a nickname.

"I told you, no cutesy nicknames." He probably hadn't but then he hadn't thought he needed to.

"It's Italian, so it can't possibly be cutesy," Kenyon argued. "It's literally not possible."

"I think the Italians would probably have something to say about that." Julian grabbed the paper and shoved it, not caring a bit if it crumpled, into the pocket of his jeans.

Not that it wasn't entirely possible for Kenyon to physically take it back, but it probably didn't matter because Julian was afraid the damage was already done.

Kenyon already knew a term of endearment he both loved and hated.

Treasure.

He definitely wasn't a treasure. Someday Kenyon was going to discover that, too.

"So, *tesoro,* how are we going to make this pizza dough?" Kenyon slid the recipe card across the counter. "I think we can get started on this, before our delivery gets here with the rest of the ingredients."

"It says we need a big bowl. Pour the flour in it, add the salt and sugar. Then the yeast. Then the warm water."

"That sounds easy enough."

"You have a big bowl?"

"I'm sure . . ." Kenyon froze. "I'm sure I do?"

They spent the next ten minutes going through every one of Kenyon's cupboards, looking for a big bowl, and settling for something that . . . well, Julian wouldn't have personally described it as large.

"It's going to be just fine," Kenyon argued.

Julian eyed the metal shape critically. "It's more medium size, if I'm being perfectly honest."

"Eye of the beholder and all that," Kenyon pressed. "My medium size might be someone else's large."

"You just keep telling yourself that."

"Hey, you've never complained," Kenyon teased. "In fact, the last time, there was quite a bit of groaning about size, and it wasn't exactly negative . . ."

"Yes, yes, fine, okay, the size is just fine." Kenyon shot him a look. "*Your* size is just fine, alright? It's perfectly . . . adequate."

Kenyon laughed.

It was so weird doing all this togetherness without sex, never mind that Kenyon kept mentioning it. Like all this was normal—and it wasn't. Not even close.

They hadn't even gotten the flour into the goddamned bowl yet, and already Julian wanted to tell him to forget it, that this was pointless, just as pointless as using *tesoro* as his nickname, and they should just head to Kenyon's bedroom.

But if he did, that would mean he blinked.

It would mean he was the one who gave up and said that he couldn't do this—and Julian was too stubborn to give in.

Instead, he ripped the top off the bag of flour and dumped it unceremoniously into the medium bowl, where it exploded into his face in a cloud of flour dust.

"Whoops," he said, coughing. Kenyon was laughing as he passed him a wet paper towel to wipe the flour residue from his face.

Next, he much more carefully added the salt and the sugar, and then the yeast.

Now, they needed warm water. But not *too* warm.

"The water needs to be one hundred and five degrees *exactly*," Julian insisted as Kenyon stood by the sink, testing the water flowing out of the tap.

"Exactly?" He sounded dubious.

"Don't you have a thermometer?"

"I'm a football player, not a chef," Kenyon griped. "I get all my meals delivered. I didn't have a large bowl. Of course I don't have a thermometer."

"Well, your best estimate, then," Julian said.

After Kenyon finally came over with the pitcher—which had taken them another ten minutes of searching to find—he slowly poured the water in, as Julian tried to stir the flour mixture with a wooden spoon.

"This is a lot harder than it seems," Julian complained as the dough didn't come together into one smooth ball, the way he imagined dough just *did*, but instead congealed into a huge sticky lump around his spoon.

"Maybe you should've taken one of those hundred guys up on a date before now, and then you'd know how to do it," Kenyon teased.

"Make pizza dough? I doubt *any* of those guys would've expected me to cook my own goddamn dinner," Julian said as the spoon got completely stuck.

"It's fun, though, isn't it, *tesoro*?" Kenyon asked, and there was that hopeful look in his eye again. Like he was actually enjoying this, and he wanted Julian to, as well.

Despite no large-sized bowl. Despite no thermometer. Despite the fact that they weren't currently naked, intertwined in Kenyon's bed.

Julian huffed. "Yes, sure," he said. And realized, belatedly, that he really meant it.

He hadn't laughed as much in the last month as he had in the last hour.

Even without the right-size bowl, or the right equipment, and even with that stupid nickname which made Julian's heart flutter rebelliously every time he heard it from Kenyon's lips.

There was just something about the way he crooned it, his accent no doubt terrible, but heartfelt, like he really meant it.

"I know you like the naked parts, but this is good too, isn't it?" Kenyon said, taking over spoon duty. Just when he'd almost managed to get the mass moving again, a massive *crack* echoed through the kitchen.

"You just broke the spoon," Julian said, peering into the bowl. "Right in half."

Kenyon grinned, and flexed. "It's these muscles, *tesoro*. They can't be contained."

Julian sighed.

"Alright, let me figure this out," Julian said, nudging him to the side.

The doorbell rang, and Kenyon waved towards it. "I'll grab it," he said. "It's probably our delivery."

Julian extracted the broken halves of the spoon, carefully scraping the sticky dough off, managing to get more of it onto his own fingers than into the bowl.

By the time Kenyon returned, he'd gotten the spoon out, and had not only started to slowly knead the dough, but it was actually starting to look like what Julian imagined pizza dough was supposed to look like.

"Look at that!" Kenyon exclaimed as he walked back into the kitchen. "I knew you could do it."

Hands full of dough, Julian could only shoot him a hot look as Kenyon set down the bag on the counter, pulling out cheese and basil and several containers of tomatoes. He even opened the wine and poured it into a glass.

"A glass, even," Julian pointed out as Kenyon set it at his elbow.

"I have *dishes*," Kenyon said. "What do you have in your kitchen?"

Julian didn't have to think about this very long. "Not very much," he admitted.

"Alright, then," Kenyon said with satisfaction. "I'm glad we did this here, then."

Julian wasn't about to say that there was no way he'd have allowed them to have their date at his shitty apartment.

To his surprise, after several minutes of kneading, the dough really began to come together.

"Wow, look at that," Kenyon said, sounding really impressed.

"It's just pizza dough. It had like five ingredients," Julian said casually, like it wasn't as big of a deal as it felt.

"You still did it," Kenyon said softly but firmly. Not letting him deflect the compliment.

"It says here, it needs to sit and rise for an hour." Julian changed the subject. "And while it rises, we're supposed to play the card game." He looked down at his hands, covered in little clumps of dough and flour and laughed. "It's going to take me an hour just to get my hands clean."

He had just shoved them into the sink, into the warm stream of water, when Kenyon came up behind him. Pressed his lips to his neck, Julian trembling, even though he'd have never admitted it.

"You *are* a *tesoro*, even if you won't admit it," Kenyon murmured into his ear.

Julian's hands flexed under the water. He felt so vulnerable like this, a mess, unable to get clean yet and unable to get away. He didn't have a choice but to stand here and just *take* whatever Kenyon wanted to do or say to him.

"This is why you wanted a date, huh?" Julian tried to brazen it out, but his voice wasn't entirely steady—and not just because Kenyon's big, strong body was warm and steady behind his own.

Solid, that's what Kenyon felt like.

Like if Julian ever couldn't handle his own shit, Kenyon could take over right where he left off.

But you're never going to not *handle your own shit,* Julian reminded himself. *You've been doing it forever, and you're going to keep doing it.*

"Honestly?" Kenyon's voice dropped even further. "Yeah. I *like* you, Julian."

It was right there on the tip of his tongue to say it back. Because it was true, he liked Kenyon. He liked how steadfast he was. How funny. How supportive. He liked the way he laughed. The way he smiled. The way he gave a shit about people. Definitely the way he fucked. Julian even liked the way he stood on the sideline, tall and upright, a force in a uniform. The way he tucked the football away when Pax handed it off.

Now that he thought about it, he could think of a hundred things, some big, some minor, he downright *loved* about Kenyon.

"I . . ."

"It's alright," Kenyon said, and strangely, it sounded like he really believed it was. "I know. You like me too."

"Trust me, I wouldn't be here otherwise." That much was definitely a truth he could say. Should he be able to say more? Probably. But sue him, it was only their first date. He was still dealing with that—*liking Kenyon* and *saying it out freaking loud* was a whole new complexity he hadn't quite figured out how to address yet.

But, at least, he could even admit, perhaps under duress, he even liked how Kenyon was having them make this stupid pizza.

Or how Kenyon didn't move away, not until long after Julian's fingers were clean and beginning to turn prune-y.

"I like this," Julian said, turning in the circle of his arms as Kenyon began to release him.

"Me too." Kenyon's eyes were dark and serious.

It felt natural to close the distance between them now and press his lips to Kenyon's.

This is just kissing, Julian reminded himself, but it didn't feel just like kissing.

He felt the pulse of arousal he always did, when he touched Kenyon—he'd have to be dead not to feel it—but there was more too, a melting of his mind, his body, his soul, like he could slip right into Kenyon and never notice or care that it had happened.

"God, *tesoro*," Kenyon murmured as his lips slipped down, kissing his neck again.

Julian felt the echo of that feeling, those words, somewhere deep down, somewhere he'd ignored for a whole lot of years.

Too many years, he could almost hear Kenyon tell him.

It would be so easy, to just slip his hands down, find Kenyon's cock in his jeans. He knew exactly what made him tick. Exactly what would make him moan. He could blow him right here, in the goddamned kitchen, and it would be spectacular, for both of them.

Julian nearly did it.

Every past Julian beyond the age of sixteen would've done it without hesitation.

But he hesitated, now.

Sex was part of this. It couldn't not be part of this, not when it was so utterly amazing between them. But it was just a part of this other, brand-new thing they were building, and suddenly, Julian was unsure where sex belonged.

Maybe it didn't belong in this moment at all.

"I like you too," Julian said, instead, his voice so low that maybe Kenyon wouldn't hear him at all.

Maybe they could pretend he hadn't said it.

But then, Kenyon eased back an inch, and the happy contentment in his eyes told Julian that he'd not only heard it, but that it had been exactly the right thing to say.

"Hey, let's play that game," Kenyon said.

The game was simple, but fun, and Julian was so competitive, Kenyon discovered he couldn't rest for even a second.

Even though he had his own share of winning drive, there was nothing quite like seeing Julian flush with victory, crowing about it as he danced around the kitchen, no doubt trying to rub it in, but only endearing himself to Kenyon even further.

The truth was, he'd never expected to have anything like this.

The other truth was, he'd never, in a million years, expected that it would be with Julian.

A prickly reporter, and to boot, a guy he'd tried to tell himself many, many times he was just fucking.

"Oh shit."

Kenyon, absorbed entirely by Julian's beautiful face, hair flopping over into his eyes, didn't realize what he was pointing out for a long second.

Then he glanced over towards the medium-sized bowl, sitting over by the stove, where Julian had determined was the "warmest" part of the kitchen through five minutes of experimentation, and the dough was totally overflowing one side.

"See," Julian said triumphantly, which somehow even *still* managed to be charming, "I told you it was the wrong-size bowl."

"Yeah, yeah, you did," Kenyon said, and grabbed him briefly, smacking a kiss against his cheek. "I thought we established, though, that it was the perfect size . . . for *you*."

Julian shot him an unamused look and wiggled free.

"We established," he said, "that we were making this pizza. And we're going to make it."

"I'll buy you a hundred pizzas," Kenyon said, and realized he meant it.

Julian looked even less impressed then.

And Kenyon realized, like a shot, whether Julian had—or the most likely possibility, *did not have*—money, he was still completely, totally uninterested in Kenyon's.

It wasn't like Kenyon had worried about it, specifically, but the thought was always there, in the back of his mind, with every person he met, every connection he made. Did this person like him for him? Or were they just trying to get into his sphere so he could provide influence? Or were they just trying to get into his pockets?

But Julian was different.

He might be prickly, and a little bit of an asshole sometimes in his dogged pursuit of the truth, but he'd never, not once, seemed interested in what Kenyon could do for him.

Not with his position with the Piranhas, and not with his money.

Who, or *what*, had made the guy so fiercely independent? Kenyon had a feeling he'd end up dragging that particular truth out of Julian one tiny bit at a time. But he no longer wondered if Julian would ever tell him.

He knew Julian would.

Because the reason he was here, the only reason he was here, in Kenyon's kitchen, critically examining the dough currently overflowing the medium-sized bowl, was for Kenyon.

Kenyon the man.

Not Kenyon the football player.

Not Kenyon the millionaire.

"Hey, it's seriously all good," Kenyon said, approaching where Julian was standing. "I'm sure it's fine. I'm sure it'll taste great, still."

"I guess," Julian said dubiously. "I suppose we need to shape it and then bake it and we'll find out."

Except that wasn't nearly as easy as it sounded— and definitely not as easy as the directions made it seem.

"Well, that looks sort of like a pizza," Kenyon said ten minutes later.

Julian had given up, and was sitting at the kitchen island, drinking his wine and supervising, offering comments every minute or so as Kenyon tried to wrestle the dough into something resembling a pizza.

"I think," Julian said, watching as Kenyon opened the mozzarella, "that wasn't supposed to be so . . . watery."

"The directions say mozzarella, don't they? I got mozzarella."

"I guess." Julian didn't sound convinced, and Kenyon was right there with him. But he laid the wet slices of mozzarella all over the lopsided circle of dough covered in the tomato sauce. What else was he going to do?

"Now what?"

"You preheated the oven, right?" Julian asked.

"Yes," Kenyon retorted. "You told me to do that ten minutes ago."

"Oh, right," Julian said, and then let out a very un-Julian-like giggle.

Glancing over at the bottle of Chianti he'd had delivered, he was surprised to see it was more than half gone.

He hadn't noticed Julian refilling his glass.

But now that he was looking, he definitely looked a bit flushed. Adorably so.

"So, into the oven, then?" Kenyon prompted.

"For thirteen minutes," Julian read off the recipe card.

Kenyon shoved the pan into the oven, said a little prayer, and then returned to where Julian was sitting.

He took his glass of wine and took a long sip. It was good. Fruity. Very drinkable. Which was probably why Julian had been drinking so much of it.

"I think," Julian said with quiet dignity, "you're trying to get me drunk. On wine. And on . . ."

Kenyon raised an eyebrow. Set the glass down. "On?"

"You," Julian murmured. It was absolutely a no-brainer to lean in and kiss him again.

Julian's mouth tasted like red wine and all the confessions he hadn't really wanted to make, but hadn't been able to help.

They kissed and kissed until Kenyon felt his self-control hanging on by a thread. Julian was so pliant like this, not really different from his normal self, but a slightly altered version, softer and a tiny bit easier, and Kenyon was beginning to realize the kind of Julian didn't matter.

He just liked Julian.

When they broke apart, Julian's lips were red and wet and his eyes were blown wide.

"I said that, didn't I? *Out loud.*"

Kenyon grinned. "You absolutely did, and you can't take it back now, *tesoro.*"

"I . . ." Julian looked like he might want to. But then he straightened. "No, I suppose I can't. But at least I'm not using a cheesy Italian nickname for you right now."

"True," Kenyon said wryly. "But it *is* accurate."

"According to you."

"Yep, according to me," Kenyon said. "And it turns out that my opinion on this subject is the only one that matters."

Julian didn't even look annoyed at that. Instead, he looked pleased—and like he was trying, poorly, to hide it, and failing.

It was just their first date but Kenyon had a feeling it would be far from their last.

A few minutes later, the timer dinged and Kenyon pulled the pizza out of the oven, and eyed it with concern.

It didn't look anything like any pizza he'd ever consumed, and he'd been a college student, so he considered himself a semi-expert on all-things pizza.

"Well," Julian huffed as he peeked over Kenyon's shoulder. "What happened?"

"Us," Kenyon said, chuckling because if he couldn't laugh at this, then he might actually be annoyed they'd failed so spectacularly. "Us happened to it."

"Hey, I read the directions *very* well," Julian reminded him.

"You definitely did an exceptional job supervising," Kenyon said, patting him on the shoulder. "Should we cut it? Try to eat it?"

"It can't possibly taste as bad as it looks."

With that optimism in mind, Kenyon pulled out a knife, cut the pizza and picked up a piece, chewing his first bite slowly.

"Well, it's the worst pizza I've ever had," Julian announced. Clearly he'd lost his brain-to-mouth filter, or maybe he'd never had one.

"It's . . . weirdly chewy, but also weirdly doughy and wet," Kenyon agreed. He took another bite because maybe the second would be better than the first.

It wasn't.

"And no flavor," Julian chimed in. "None whatsoever."

Which was how they ended up in Kenyon's living room, eating a Domino's pizza, and sharing the rest of the wine in one glass, a movie playing on the TV.

"Well, that was the worst pizza in the world," Julian said drowsily, his head leaning onto Kenyon's shoulder.

It kinda had been.

But also the best, too.

"But the best, too."

Kenyon started, surprised at the words coming out of Julian's mouth and how they'd echoed his own thoughts almost exactly.

"Yeah?" he asked hopefully.

"And," Julian said, blinking sleepily at Kenyon, "I think you're kind of a treasure too."

Chapter Thirteen

When Kenyon woke up the next morning, Julian was already gone—which did not surprise him at all.

He'd protested plenty when, after nearly falling asleep on the sofa downstairs, Kenyon had carried him upstairs to his bed.

Why was he already thinking of it as *their* bed when this was the first night they were truly sharing it? Kenyon didn't know, but that was a problem for a different day.

Still, he'd absolutely expected Julian to bolt.

One hundred percent because he'd freaked out that they'd had a date, and not actually had sex.

But, to Kenyon's surprise, when he came downstairs, there was a cup of coffee, still warm, from his favorite shop down the street, and a note scribbled in Julian's handwriting. *I'm willing to do it again*, the note said, *as long as you're willing to risk potential food poisoning again.*

He'd signed the note, *Tesoro.*

Kenyon laughed.

It had been one of the best evenings of his whole life.

The thought they could do it again and again and that maybe, when his career came to a close, it wouldn't be just him and the foundation, that he could have a life too, filled him with a kind of hope that was entirely new to him.

"You're grinning at your locker," Logan said. "That's kinda weird, you know."

"Hey, we're about to play in the playoffs. *Us*. The Piranhas. That's worthy of smiling, isn't it?" Kenyon retorted.

Frankly, if someone had told him last year they'd be here, he wouldn't have believed them.

But the Piranhas were not only here, ready to play in their first playoff game since winning the Super Bowl three years ago, they were ready to win.

"Yeah, not ever gonna argue about that," Logan said, leaning against his locker. "But you got an especial glow about you. That date box treat you real good?"

Normally, Kenyon would've said an evening that ended with Domino's pizza, Julian snoring away in bed next to him, and no sex whatsoever was a total fucking failure. But it had been *so* dang good anyway. And fun, in a completely unexpected yet fantastic way.

He'd actually gotten Julian to relax. And once he had, once he stopped being so damn afraid of what could happen, he'd *enjoyed* what could happen.

Kenyon knew he had.

"It was great, actually. Thanks, man." He pulled Logan into a quick half-hug. "Appreciate it a lot."

Logan grinned. "I had a feeling. Those date boxes, they never fail. The irony, my brother sent them to me as a joke. But he's sure not laughing now."

"Guess not," Kenyon said, chuckling.

"What Levi needs to do is send one to himself," Logan huffed. "*And* send one to Landry. Scratch that. He needs to send about a million to Landry."

Kenyon knew Landry, Logan's eldest brother and a tight end for the Buffalo Bills, a little. They'd played together in the Senior Bowl, and hung out during the week-long festivities. Sure, that had been years ago, but Kenyon still remembered what a solid guy he was. Just like his brother. "Why does Landry need one?"

"Oh, he just hates dating. Thinks it's a waste of time." Logan grinned, nudged Kenyon. "Don't know who else that reminds me of. Maybe you should call him up, set him straight."

Kenyon thought if Landry didn't have a Julian of his own, that was probably why he was uninterested in dealing with the dating scene.

"Maybe he just hasn't found the right person yet," Kenyon said.

"And he's not going to, by refusing to even look," Logan argued.

"Hey, maybe he'll meet the love of his life when they desperately need a place to stay," Kenyon teased. "'Cause that worked out so well for you."

"Maybe." Logan sounded skeptical.

But before Kenyon could ask why, Coach walked into the locker room.

"Y'all ready to get some work done today?" he asked. Didn't even have to raise his voice, but already the players were hollering, and clearly Kenyon wasn't the only one excited to play in this game.

"I thought so," Coach said. "Just remember . . . we're playing for today, not next week. Not the week after. Not five weeks from now. *Today.*"

A cheer went up through the room. "Let's make it count, okay?" Coach said.

Kenyon intended to.

He jogged out onto the field, helmet hanging from his fingertips, and for a second, just took in the raucous atmosphere surrounding them in the Piranhas' home stadium.

The roar as he and the rest of the players made their entrance seemed even louder today, and maybe that was because Miami was really freaking glad to be back in the playoffs or just maybe . . . Kenyon knew Julian's interview with Pax and Davis had aired before the game—and he knew, because Julian had told him, all tucked up next to him on the couch two nights ago, they'd also be showing the interview in the stadium, on the big screens.

Pax always brought up the rear.

"Last," he liked to say wryly, "but not least."

The avalanche of sound as Pax entered the stadium made it clear that while *yes*, Miami was damn glad about the playoffs, they were even happier with their quarterback.

There were scattered chants of, "*four, four, four,*" throughout the stadium as Kenyon began to warm up.

That, he knew, was for Pax's coach and partner, Davis Abernathy.

He'd worn number four when he'd played for the Charleston Condors, before they'd thrown him away like yesterday's trash.

But the thing was, Kenyon thought with smug satisfaction as Davis finally emerged from the tunnel, and the shouts grew louder, apparently nobody was unhappy at this new development, the Condors might not have appreciated him, but the Piranhas had from the very beginning.

Kenyon finished his stretches and headed over to where Davis was standing by the bench.

"Hey," he said, giving Davis a quick hug. "You holding up okay?"

Davis' smile was wry. "You mean because now everyone knows? Yeah, actually. It's better than everyone *not* knowing."

They listened to the next round of, "*number four, number four, four, four, four.*"

"Pax is gonna get jealous, think they want Coach to start you and not him," Kenyon teased. Only because there was no possible way that would ever happen.

Davis had made it abundantly clear that his playing days were over, and he was happy about it.

Kenyon envied the man's certainty—and that quiet smile on his face whenever he glanced over at where Pax was throwing warmup routes to the wide receivers.

"He won't, because he freaking started it," Davis grumbled affectionately.

"You know," Kenyon said, and then hesitated because *of course* Davis knew. If they won today, and the Condors won *their* playoff game tomorrow, then they'd be facing off, again.

The first time had been an absolute fucking bloodbath, and, Kenyon believed, a little bit of sweet vindication.

But the Condors weren't slouches.

There was very little chance the Piranhas would catch them sleeping again. They'd learned, the hardest way possible, that it was a massive, and potentially season-ending, mistake to under-estimate this team.

"I know," Davis said. His voice had grown harder. But not angrier. More resolute. More determined.

Kenyon couldn't blame him. If a team treated him the way the Condors had treated Davis, he'd want to exact every single bit of revenge he could.

"We'll be ready, if it comes to that," Kenyon said. Believed it.

"You heard Coach," Davis said gruffly, but he patted him on the shoulder as he said it. "Focus on getting today's job done."

"Right," Kenyon agreed. He turned away, to finish his warmup. He always liked to catch a few passes, too, keep his hands fresh, even though with the dynamite receiving crew the Piranhas were fielding, he wasn't nearly as involved in the passing game as some running backs were. But before he could go, Davis caught his arm.

"Hey, you know that reporter we talked to? About us?"

Kenyon wanted to say his insides didn't congeal—but he'd be fucking lying if he did.

"Yeah?" he asked as casually as he could. "What's his name?"

"Julian," Davis said firmly. "His name is Julian, and you know his name. Don't front with me." Davis lowered his voice. "Not with me, okay?"

Kenyon swallowed hard, and nodded.

"You know, Pax and I stood in the shadows in the tunnel, watching as they played the interview on the big screens."

Kenyon nodded again. He hadn't known, actually, but now that Davis said it, it made sense.

It was a big moment. One of the biggest of their lives. They'd want to see it. Gauge the reaction.

"Julian said something in the intro package, something about how he knows how tough it can be to be involved with a player." Davis stared at Kenyon. "What's that about?"

"What's what about? Why are you asking me? Ask him."

Davis shot him a look. "Oh come on, Kenyon. I saw him go down the hall, the other night, and end up nowhere near the bathroom but at the running backs' room."

"Maybe he was lost."

"Or maybe he was found," Davis said.

Kenyon rolled his eyes, but the feeling wasn't there, and he knew it. "Just because you're so happy with Pax doesn't mean . . ."

Davis held up a hand. "Don't lie to me. You don't have to tell me the truth, okay, I get that. If you're involved with him, it's maybe worse than me and Pax dating, and nobody's sure how far Coach's grace extends."

"Not that far," Kenyon murmured under his breath.

"But," Davis continued, stressing the word, "if you were . . . I really like him, okay? He's a good guy. And I wanted to tell you he said that 'cause everyone's gonna be lookin' out for who it is he's with now."

"Yep, they sure are." The next time Kenyon saw Julian, they were going to have words about that, for sure.

Words, first, and then a lot of kissing, and hopefully even more than that, because just the thought of Julian going out on a limb and committing *publicly* to him, or the idea of him, made him happier than Kenyon could remember being.

He knew Julian, knew how he was, and as a result *knew* they had to be serious for him to even consider going as far as they had, but here was rock-solid proof.

Undeniable proof.

He wasn't falling alone. Julian was too. Maybe he was already there, and didn't even know it. After all, he'd spent six months insisting they were just fucking, when it was *clearly* more than that.

Davis patted him again. "Watch your back out there, okay?"

"Will do," Kenyon said.

Julian spent the first half of the game fielding a dozen calls.

Starting and ending with his boss.

"Why am I just now finding out about this?" she asked testily the moment the segment had aired.

Why *had* he said that?

He hadn't intended to.

It had just . . . well, not *slipped out,* because it had been more intentional than that, he'd known what he was saying when he was saying it. But he'd not been thinking—now for the *second* time in his life, the podcast being the first—of the consequences. He'd only been thinking of how great their date had been. How much he hadn't wanted to leave Kenyon's bed—and Kenyon. And how much he just plain *liked* him.

It's more than that, the voice inside him had whispered.

Julian had remembered just how upfront Kenyon had been about his feelings. *I like you a lot*, he'd said. Bluntly and baldly, without an ounce of game-playing.

He hadn't been the same. He'd hesitated. Tried to make up for it later, sure, but had it had the same impact as Kenyon's honesty?

Not really.

So he'd sat on the studio stage and swung for the fences. Stupidly, maybe.

It had been offhand, yes, casual, even.

"Dating a player can be really tough," he'd said. "Or else that's what I keep hearing. I wouldn't know anything about that, right?"

It hadn't been a direct admission, but it was close enough that it hadn't been exactly tough for Nikki to read between the lines.

"You're just now finding out about this because there's not much to say," Julian told her.

"That doesn't seem possibly true," Nikki said. "I'm already pissed because you kept wanting to do this crazy thing called stick to the bare bones of truth for the Pax and Davis story, and think of the clicks we'd have gotten if we leaned into the drama of it . . . even a *little*."

He'd known. He hadn't cared about the clicks.

It hadn't seemed fair to serve Pax and Davis up for that kind of additional media scrutiny, when he knew the reality of them.

"You knew it was wrong, which is why you gave in," Julian said. He'd debate all game with her, if she wanted, about the Pax and Davis story. It was already a sensation. His rapidly filling email inbox told him it was. His social media gaining thousands of followers a minute told him it was. Didn't matter if he hadn't sensationalized a goddamn thing.

"Don't change the subject," Nikki snapped at him. "Who is this player you're dating?"

"I never said I was dating a player," Julian said.

"You said you *understood*."

"No," Julian insisted steadily, "I said dating a player can be tough, and that I wouldn't know anything about that. I don't know how you can go from that sentence to believing I'm dating a player."

Nikki made a sound of frustration. "Julian."

"Seriously, if I was, would I tell you? Would I tell millions of people on-air?"

"Apparently," Nikki said sarcastically.

"There you go," Julian said, and the temple of truth was preserved, because he hadn't actually directly lied to her face.

She'd hung up on him then, but he knew her grace—or whatever it was—was short-lived.

He'd fielded six more calls, from various other sources. Some wanting quotes. One of them wanting to interview *him* about his interview. Another wanting to offer him a new job, which he rejected as graciously as he could. He wasn't interested in leaving Miami right now. Not when the Piranhas were heading into what might be a deep playoff run and then there was Kenyon . . .

Who was probably going to blow a gasket when he found out what Julian had said, but he'd threaded the needle carefully, and genuinely, he didn't think there was anyone who knew the truth.

They'd been careful.

Ish.

Julian sat in the media booth, and watched as Pax threw for two touchdowns, and Kenyon ran for a third, dodging and weaving between defenders.

The Piranhas went into the locker room with twenty-one points, but it was still close.

The Rams had scored twice, and then kicked a field goal. The Piranhas were only up by four.

They'd need to figure out a way to stop the Rams' relentless offensive assault *or* keep scoring.

Both tough challenges.

Julian was contemplating this, typing some notes into his laptop, when his phone rang again.

It was Nikki again.

"You think you're pretty clever, don't you?" she asked, but it didn't sound like a demand, instead she sounded resigned about it.

"I like to think so," Julian said. "And I like to think that's something valuable for you, too."

"Usually, it is," Nikki said.

"Then what's the problem?"

He knew exactly what the problem was. They both did.

The trick, Julian thought, was going to be continuing to talk around it like it didn't exist.

"If I ask you directly if you're dating a player, what are you going to say?" she challenged.

Not so resigned now.

"No," Julian said.

It was splitting hairs, but she'd said *if* I ask. She hadn't asked directly.

He hadn't really believed he'd get away with not lying about it.

At some point Nikki's boss' boss would call him up and he'd have to lie.

Especially if he wanted to keep dating Kenyon.

Maybe eventually, if Kenyon retired and they actually, miraculously *kept* dating, then they might be able to be truthful about their relationship.

But Julian wasn't stupid or naive enough to believe that would be happening anytime soon.

Kenyon was still in his prime. Heading down the backside of his prime, maybe, but there were still plenty of teams that would pay for him. There were no indications that the Piranhas wouldn't be on that list, too.

"Alright, then," Nikki said. "I thought so."

She thought he'd lie.

Which . . . well, she wasn't stupid.

"Anything else?" Julian asked innocently.

He could practically *hear* her purse her lips.

The shitty thing, Julian thought, as she said no, and hung up, was that he *liked* her. He still liked her. She was a good boss. Aggressive, yes, but then that's how she'd gotten where she had in this business, by being the toughest, pushiest person in the room, male or female.

"You good?" Ed leaned over and nudged him. "Created a firestorm for yourself, huh?"

"Couldn't just take a good thing, apparently, and accept it," Julian said wryly.

He should've bought himself an eternity's worth of goodwill with how well he'd pulled off the Pax and Davis story. Instead, he hadn't been able to help himself. He'd added that wrinkle in.

Added something potentially personal about him.

Which, not only had he been taught *not* to do in journalism school, but was a rule he'd never once been tempted to break. Not talk about himself? That, he'd thought so many times, would be a piece of freaking cake.

Apparently not with Kenyon showing up on the scene. He was unwinding Julian a little bit at a time, so slowly and so *carefully*, that Julian couldn't even dislike it. Couldn't even be angry at it.

It wasn't that Kenyon hadn't anticipated that this would be a tough game.

He'd known it would be.

Coach was Coach and so he'd prepared them more than adequately. Set their expectations. Been brutally honest not only about their chances, but what they'd have to overcome to beat the Rams.

But it was one thing to know it, and it was another to be standing in the huddle, deep in the fourth quarter, down six, needing a touchdown to take the lead, and know that if they didn't, this would be the last game of the season for the Piranhas.

"You ready for this?" Pax asked, his direct gaze meeting every single one of their faces in the huddle.

Tristan's, to his left. Wade's. Logan and Rob and the rest of the offensive line. Carter's. Then finally Kenyon's.

There was a chorus of approvals, of agreements, and a determined stare on every single face. Kenyon could feel the echo of that sentiment deep in his heart.

He wasn't quite ready yet for his last play.

His last game.

"Then let's get this shit done," Pax said and clapped, breaking up the huddle.

They were starting out on the five-yard line, because the Rams had boomed an absolutely fucking dynamite punt.

Let's see you run the whole length of this field, their defenders seemed to be saying with every smug look they shot the Piranhas' way. *You haven't scored more than two field goals in this half, we shut you down, and we can do it again.*

The first two plays of the drive were pass plays, Kenyon pushing off the line at the snap of the ball, blocking against a defensive end on the first and running on a route on the second as a distraction, setting up Pax to throw for a fifteen-yard gain to Wade.

Then, on the next play, it was his number being called.

The whistle blew, Logan snapped the ball and Pax turned, and he felt it hit his hands.

There was only a split second to view the field, to see where the blocks had held, and where they hadn't. Only a moment, a single blink of his eyes, to take it in, and make a decision.

He darted right, legs churning as he passed Logan, and then Wade, blocking for him, squeezing between them. One of the defenders they were holding swiped at the ball but he had it tucked away safe and sound, and it didn't budge.

Kenyon had been playing running back for nearly twenty years, and he thought his vision was as good as it could possibly be, but watching the film with Julian this week had helped give him a different perspective.

He jumped to the right, spun past another linebacker, and saw *nearly* empty grass in front of him.

There was one last holdout, the Rams' safety, hanging back as he tried to figure out which way Kenyon was going to go so he could take the best angle to stop him.

It was late in the game, but he dug down deep, found his energy reserves and burst with speed down the sideline, watching as the safety started to cross over to him, hoping to intercept him twenty yards before the end zone.

Kenyon knew he was coming.

Prepared.

And when he was just within an arm's length away, he reached out and, with every bit of strength he had, shoved him away and down.

The roar of the crowd echoed in his ears as they registered that he'd just given the guy a stiff-arm he wouldn't soon forget.

Clear and open field greeted him as he ran the last twenty yards in for the touchdown.

Wade was the first one to smash into him the moment he crossed over the line.

He realized then, that Wade must have been blocking behind him, every step of the way, as he'd made his way down the field.

"Fucking killer, man!" Wade yelled as he lifted him high, ball high above his head.

It was the touchdown—and the momentum swing—that the Piranhas needed to close out the win.

After the touchdown, setting them a point ahead, the defense came out strong and ready, energized by Kenyon's nearly eighty-yard touchdown run, and sacked their quarterback on the first play.

Kenyon didn't see it, he was still too busy trying to suck down oxygen on the sideline, but Tristan shouting next to him and leaping to his feet told the whole story.

The Rams never got their own drive started, because Micah knocked away a deep pass, and then it was fourth down.

Kenyon watched, breathless, and not only because he'd just run nearly eighty yards, but because if they didn't stop the Rams now, on fourth down, they'd get another chance to score. Another chance to get into field goal range and win.

The quarterback threw, a shorter pass this time, hoping to just get the first down and keep the drive alive, but Sebastian was right there and tackled the receiver two yards short and refused to let him budge.

Tristan screamed next to him, and to Kenyon's surprise, he was yelling too, smashing into the big group rushing onto the field, time expiring from the clock.

They'd done it.

The Piranhas had faced their first test and beat it.

"You think they're gonna give us Ellis?" Ed asked as he and Julian took their seats for the press conference.

Julian shot his friend a look. "Why are you asking me?"

"No reason. No reason whatsoever. Just was curious about your entirely professional opinion."

"He played lights out, okay? That fucking stiff-arm? That's all you're going to see on ESPN for the next week." Julian couldn't quite keep the pride from his voice. Personal pride, not professional. Because Kenyon had kicked some serious ass today.

One hundred and twenty-four yards on the ground and the touchdown that had sealed the win for the Piranhas.

And then there was that epic beatdown he'd given to the Rams' safety in the middle of that touchdown run.

"Yep. That ,and if the Condors win, how there's going to be another epic rematch."

"It'll be an ugly game if they play each other again," Julian predicted. "Dirty, is my best guess."

"The Piranhas don't want to do it," Ed said. "They want to avoid them, if they can. The Condors are spoiling for a fight since the last game, and yeah, dirty is the best-case scenario here."

"We'll find out later tonight, I guess," Julian said. He shouldn't feel apprehensive. The Piranhas weren't *his* team—he didn't even have a team. But he'd gotten to know Pax and Davis, and of course, Kenyon, and he didn't want them to have to fight down and dirty in the mud with the Condors.

And he knew, without Davis ever having said, because he wouldn't ever, that playing the Condors had been hard the first time around. It would be worse the second.

"We're gonna be packed with work all week," Ed said, and he sounded like he was actually looking forward to it, when just a few months back, he'd actually had the audacity to say he hoped the Piranhas wouldn't make the playoffs so he'd have less work to do.

"Yep," Julian agreed.

Though he already had one thing set in stone he refused to budge on.

Davis had invited him to the potential victory celebration the Piranhas players threw every week at Hibiscus. "Because," Davis had said, "you did such a freaking great job telling our story, you're one of us now. I know how hard you probably had to fight for it to stay the way it was."

No, it hadn't been easy, but it wasn't the breadth of the fight that bothered Julian.

It was that the fight had happened at all.

He couldn't say when he'd decided to go into journalism, he'd expected it to be pretty and sweet and clean. He'd been prepared to fight.

But what the last year had taught him was everything had an angle. Every story could be told two different ways, and sometimes those ways were fundamentally opposed.

It shouldn't work that way, but it did.

Julian had considered turning down Davis' invite, even if it had meant a *lot* to get it in the first place, because surely he shouldn't be showing up to players-only events when he was trying to hide—albeit not very well—that he was dating a player.

But Kenyon hadn't been the one to invite him. It had been Davis. They were friends now, Julian thought, he and Davis and Pax. It was only right he come to help them celebrate a great playoff win, and an absolutely fucking amazing season.

Ed had been right—Helen brought Kenyon out first.

Especially after what he'd said earlier today, Julian knew he couldn't take it easy on him, so his hand was one of the first up.

But Kenyon's gaze slid right over him, and he instead pointed to Ed, who asked him about his vision for that 80-yard touchdown run, which was a dang good question.

After Kenyon finished answering, Julian nudged his friend. "Learning from the best, huh?"

Ed rolled his eyes. "Wasn't that I couldn't, it was more like I didn't give a shit. But you're young and eager and maybe rubbing off on me a little."

Julian grinned. "Just a little?"

"Fine, fine, a lot, alright? You happy now?"

Julian stuck his hand up again, and this time Kenyon's eyes landed squarely on him. "Julian," he said.

"Was there any hesitation today because of your fumble a few weeks back? I know that safety could've gone for the ball not for the tackle . . ."

"No," Kenyon said before he could even finish the question. "Not in the slightest. And yeah, he probably *thought* he could take it from me, but that wasn't happening."

Julian hadn't thought so either.

But there was always a chance, and it was his job to ask the tough questions.

Even if he hated the way the shadow of memory of that one bad play swept over Kenyon's face, even for a moment.

"That's all for Kenyon today," Helen said, clearing her throat.

Julian pulled his phone out. Opened up his messages to Kenyon. Typed, **You're right, no way could he have gotten the ball from you then. Also, I thought maybe the sexiest thing in the world was you pinning me against your front door, but**

I was wrong. It was that goddamned stiff-arm. I'm gonna be jerking off to that for the next thousand years, thanks.

MONDAYS WERE ALWAYS BUSY for Kenyon. During the season, Julian knew he dealt with a lot of foundation business on Mondays, because that was his one truly "off" day every week.

Julian knew it, and before, when they'd been hooking up, he'd always tried to give the guy space. Now he was *still* trying to give him space, even though it was the last thing he wanted.

I don't know, Kenyon had texted him back last night, **I still think the sexiest thing in the world is a guy who proclaims he really likes you on national television.**

Even, Julian texted back, **when it was pretty stupid to do?**

Especially when it was pretty stupid, Kenyon had replied almost immediately. Then he'd sent a second text. **Did you get into big trouble?**

Julian thought about those two phone calls he'd had with Nikki. She'd sent him a handful of texts and an email since, but they'd been terse and to the point.

She was mad, there was no doubt about it, but she also had no proof, and wouldn't fire him without it because he was too valuable right now to dispose of.

Sort of, Julian responded finally. **I handled it.**

I guess this means we should really go on a second date, Kenyon texted back. **Wednesday night? You free?**

Wednesday was a packed day. But Julian knew it wasn't just him. Kenyon would be crazy busy this week, so the fact that he was making time for him this week was a big deal.

Just about as big of a deal as you declaring in front of millions of people you're dating a player.

I can make the time, he wrote. **We doing another one of those date boxes?**

Nope, not gonna make you cook your own dinner this time.

As long as you don't let me fall asleep before we have sex, Julian typed out.

It's a deal, Kenyon replied. **See you Wednesday.**

Julian stepped out of the Uber he'd called to take him to Hibiscus, where the Piranhas held their weekly victory parties. Of course, Kenyon didn't know that he'd been invited tonight.

He'd considered telling him, of course.

But in the end, Julian decided it would be so much more fun to surprise him.

Davis had told him he was on the list, but he still didn't quite feel like he belonged as he headed towards the nondescript front door, with its smoked glass and subtle gold lettering.

He was still surprised when he got waved in, and then headed upstairs to the rooftop of the club, where the Piranhas always held their get-togethers.

"Hey," Pax said, walking over the moment he spotted Julian. "I'm so glad you came."

"Hey, congrats, man," Julian said, and they hugged briefly. "What a win."

Pax's eyes lit. "I know, wasn't it? And honestly, I know you're not here in an official capacity, I promise, but you gotta know, we are *fired up* to play the Condors again."

News of the Condors' win had come in late, as Julian was driving back to his apartment. He'd felt an inevitable pulse of excitement at the news—and also a horrible foreboding.

Could the Piranhas take them on and win *again*? That first win had been so unexpected, so unprecedented, so completely and utterly non-competitive, that it had taken the NFL world by storm.

Julian was worried this next game was going to be anything but the easy cakewalk that the first had become.

The Condors, humiliated and shamed last time, were going to come to Miami with a chip on their shoulder.

But Pax looked unconcerned about the challenge, and even *excited* for it.

It really proved football players were, nearly without exception, insane.

"Really?"

Pax laughed. "You look skeptical."

"Skeptical? Or concerned?"

"It's gonna be fine. We handled them last time. We're just going to do it again."

Julian remembered a time, not very far back, only a few months ago, when Pax's lack of confidence had been obvious to everyone.

He'd come so far since then.

"Look who it is," Davis said, joining them and handing his boyfriend a beer. "The man of the hour."

"All I did was let you tell your story the way you wanted to tell it," Julian protested.

"And how many reporters would've let us do that?"

"Anyone with an ounce of soul," Julian said. And realized, almost after he'd said it, that this now included him.

There'd been a point, when he'd been not only metaphorically young and hungry, but nearly *actually* hungry as well, when that might not have described him. When Nikki had first picked him up, he'd been ready and willing to do whatever it took.

Whatever had happened to him this year in Miami, he was different now.

Julian wasn't sure you could use the word *ethical* to describe him, considering he'd been secretly banging a player for the entire season, but the truth was, he liked the sound of it anyway.

Besides, was it unethical if it was more than just sex? If they actually gave a whole bunch of shits about each other?

Julian was steadfastly refusing to use any *L* words to describe their relationship. *Like* was hard enough for him to wrap his head around. Anything else was impossible.

But it was hovering there, in the back of his mind.

How could it not be, after he'd essentially painted a target on his back just to . . . *Oh, God,* just to make some big romantic gesture?

Because that's what it had been.

"And none of this, none of this 'soul' you're calling it," Davis said, chuckling, "could possibly have anything to do with the fact that you're in love with one of us?"

Julian flushed. "Don't use that word," he insisted, mild hysteria building. "That's a bad, bad word."

Pax laughed. "Oh, I can see why you guys are friends now."

"Davis doesn't think the *L* word is bad. In fact, we just did a whole segment about how he thinks it's the greatest thing since sliced bread."

"Ahhhh, but he didn't start out that way. You guys who think you can avoid it, you're cute." Pax patted him on the cheek. "Real cute."

"Thanks, I think?"

"Don't thank him," Davis clucked. "He's wrong. We're big and manly and awesome. Not cute."

Pax shot his boyfriend an irrepressible grin. "Not even a little."

"Really, though, we wanted to say thank you, a lot," Davis continued, expression turning more serious. "It could've been very different. But it wasn't, and we can move on with the rest of our life, now, without worrying about who's seeing what."

"Right, yes, well, thank you, too. It was a big opportunity for me."

"Didn't think you were the right man for the job, initially," Davis said, putting out a hand and Julian shook it. "But I'm really, really glad to be wrong. Anyway, enjoy the party. Have some drinks. Maybe you'll even see that guy you're not dating."

"Weirder things have happened," Julian agreed.

The first time Kenyon spotted Julian at the Piranhas' victory party was the moment he walked up the stairs to the rooftop bar, and to his shock, he discovered his current hookup-boyfriend-what-ever-the-hell-they-were-to-each-other standing next to Pax and Davis, and they were all laughing together, like somehow during the last week they'd all become best friends.

Okay, yeah, he'd done their story, so that made a little sense. And it made even more sense because Julian had done a great fucking job, but then Kenyon had never doubted that he would because Julian was Julian, and nobody ever committed to a story like he did.

The *second* time Kenyon spotted him was twenty minutes later, after a lot more people had shown up. When he went to go grab himself a second gin and tonic from the bar, there was Julian surrounded by Tristan, Wade, and Micah, and now it was *they* who were laughing at something he'd said.

You are not annoyed. You are not even frustrated. You are defi-nitely not jealous.

Except he was definitely a little bit of the latter.

He also got it.

Because he'd gotten a little taste of Julian—of his self-depre-cating charm and humor, and all that wicked-sharp intelligence, and the way his smile seemed to include you, always—and he only wanted more.

"Imagine finding you here," he said, when Tristan and Wade finally faded away, probably to head to the dance floor, and Micah ventured off to ask Sebastian something—and then Julian's head turned and he realized it was him, standing there.

Waiting, Kenyon knew. He'd been waiting.

And while, yeah, he'd felt a little jealous, he didn't mind waiting for him.

Because in the end, he knew he was going to get all of Julian.

The snarky Julian. The slightly drunk Julian. The caustic Julian. The sleepy Julian. The Julian who wanted to micromanage him making a pizza. The truth warrior Julian, who'd fought, it was clear to everyone, for Pax and Davis to tell their story the way they wanted it told. The *right* way.

"Imagine seeing you here," Julian said, flushing a little. He slid his drink closer to Kenyon's.

Kenyon raised an eyebrow. "It's a Piranhas' victory party, and I'm the Piranhas' starting running back. However . . . last time I checked, you weren't on the roster."

"Wrong," Julian said. "Davis said I was an honorary member, and I'd think Davis gets to say, because he's a coach."

"Or because you totally defended Pax's honor," Kenyon teased. "Usually he's all about that, but he doesn't mind when other people do it, too."

"True." Julian smirked at him. "Feeling a little envious?"

"Not even a little." He wasn't, not from the moment Julian had turned all that incredible charm on him, and Kenyon had realized that as much as Julian glowed around others, there was no contest with how brightly he shone when he was with Kenyon.

Did it make him feel a tiny bit smug?

Absolutely.

"Oh." Julian looked disappointed, like he'd hoped that maybe Kenyon might be jealous.

Kenyon slid a little closer. "No, I'm not envious," he said, "because I see you around them, and then I know how you look at me, even when you try to hide it, even when you try to pretend you don't. I see it anyway."

Julian gazed up at him, his beautiful face mesmerizing in the low light on the rooftop. Were those stars reflected in his eyes or was Kenyon just imagining they were?

"You caught me," Julian said quietly.

It would be so easy to just kiss him right here. Close that last inch between them. It would be so good. So right.

So completely insanely fucked up.

Everyone would freak out, if he kissed a reporter in front of them.

He'd seen Beau, earlier. And Davis had told him that he'd invited Coach and his new husband, Scott, and fully expected them to show at some point during the evening.

Wouldn't that be the best possible timing, for Coach to walk in, just at the right moment to see Kenyon kiss the reporter who had been giving him headaches all freaking year?

"Come on," Kenyon said, his voice rough, and he wrapped a hand around Julian's forearm and tugged him in the direction of the bathrooms.

He just needed one kiss.

Sure, Julian would be going home with him—there was absolutely no question he'd be getting Julian naked in his bed later; in *their* bed—but he needed something to hold him over.

It was risky, sure, but how often had Beau snuck around with Sebastian. Everyone had known it was happening, but there hadn't been any solid proof.

Kenyon could work with that.

"What are you . . . we *can't*," Julian hissed under his breath. Kenyon didn't let go, but slid Julian's body in front of his own, theoretically hiding *most* of where they were connected.

Kenyon raised an eyebrow. "Oh, you mean, like we couldn't tell anyone on national television that you're dating a player?"

Julian looked flustered. Gorgeously, perfectly flustered. Nobody else worked him up like this, Kenyon was sure of it. And he fully intended to work him up some more. Now, and definitely later.

"I *didn't*," Julian hissed under his breath.

No, okay, he hadn't. Kenyon had watched the segment, listening for the exact wording, and true to form, Julian had covered his ass spectacularly. But the insinuation had been there.

In fact, it had been enough Kenyon had been surprised the whole team hadn't gotten an email blast from Helen reminding them what a terrible idea it was to date a reporter.

He didn't need an email to remind him. He already knew.

Yet, here he was anyway, dragging Julian away from the bustling party, in front of all these players and even a handful of coaches, towards the nearest dark corner that he could find.

They reached the hallway that led to the bathrooms. It was blessedly unoccupied.

Kenyon didn't think—he was a little beyond thinking, right at this moment—he just leaned down and tugged Julian towards him. Their mouths collided, Julian staggering backwards, back hitting the wall, but Kenyon was with him every inch of the way, his body pressed against Julian's.

He felt Julian's tongue slip into his mouth, and he shivered. He didn't know how it was this good, every time, but it was.

Julian had so much fight in him, but even when they kissed it wasn't like the fight left him. The fight just evolved, morphing from *Julian-versus-the-world* to *Julian-versus-mediocre-sex*.

That was the kind of fight Kenyon could get behind.

He reached out blindly, and yanked the bathroom door open, barely getting them inside before Julian wound his arms around Kenyon's neck and kissed him hard, groaning the whole way.

He'd only dragged Julian in here to work him up some for later, not to actually have sex, but now with Julian climbing him like a tree, and his cock aching in his jeans, it didn't exactly seem like a terrible idea.

Even with the whole Piranhas team milling around outside.

But it is, you know it is, and the problem is you don't give a fuck anymore.

It seemed like he wasn't the only one. Hadn't Julian thrown his own share of caution to the wind?

He heard Julian flip the lock, and then he slid down Kenyon's body, boneless and sweet.

Pressed a palm against Kenyon's hard, aching dick, and he groaned.

Trying, at least a little bit, to keep it down, but not making the kind of effort he probably should be.

Kenyon glanced down as Julian made quick work of his jeans, shoving them down, along with his boxer briefs, and *God*, he could be so soft like this. His hand drifted down, cupping Julian's head. Tangling his fingers in his hair.

Julian nipped at his thigh in response, a reminder that *one*, Julian was not exactly sweet, even like this, which Kenyon discovered he *liked*, and *two*, that he was not supposed to mess up Julian's hair, not when they were going to have to leave this bathroom after and pretend that nothing had just happened.

Then his mouth was on him, hot and wet and so fucking perfect.

Kenyon groaned, his head hitting the back of the door, as Julian began to suck, with long, earnest strokes of his tongue, punctuated with short, teasing bites, never letting Kenyon get comfortable and fall headfirst into the pleasure.

"Fuck, just like that," Kenyon groaned, trying—*sort of*—to keep his voice down. They didn't have all day, or even longer than a few minutes, and he needed to have enough time to put his hands all over Julian.

The thing was, Julian liked a long leisurely blowjob, working Kenyon up, making him crazy with lust, but that wasn't in the cards. Not today.

In fact . . . Kenyon realized just as he hit the point of no return, fingers tightening carefully in Julian's hair, that this was the first time they'd fucked in a bathroom since the first time.

They'd fucked plenty of other places.

But not a bathroom, not since the first time.

Julian did something unbearably good with his tongue, and he slid right into his orgasm, the pleasure overwhelming him.

But it wasn't so much it could drown out the thoughts he was having.

He was paralyzed by the thoughts of affection and care and how much he always wanted to see Julian.

It was big and vast, that desire, but not just to see him on his knees or bent over their bed—though Kenyon wouldn't ever argue with those, either—it was so much more.

His heart was beating in triple time, like he'd been trying to outrun the truth, not just have an orgasm, as he lifted Julian up and fitted their mouths together.

Julian was wiggling, squirming almost, as Kenyon pressed a hand against his hard cock.

Kenyon's lips slid to his neck, nibbling at the tendon there, the one that always drove Julian insane, the sensitive spot he hadn't wanted Kenyon to find at first.

That was the thing about Julian—he always hid those vulnerable places. And hid them well, because Kenyon didn't think anyone else ever saw them.

But he couldn't *unsee* them.

Julian moaned a little, and shifted further, Kenyon's fingers undoing his belt, his jeans, sliding them down his thighs.

It was usually pretty easy to work Julian up—he was so responsive, so turned on just by Kenyon touching him—but today felt like a new high, Julian frantically pushing against his hand as he slowly, tightly squeezed his dick and started to jerk him off.

"You know," Kenyon murmured, "we did this for the first time, in a bathroom, kinda like this one."

"No," Julian said, his voice high and breathy, panting on each stroke. "You clearly do not remember that bathroom well. It was disgusting. This one is . . ."

"A little better, huh?"

"Yeah." Julian gave a happy sigh, as Kenyon tried to draw it out, slowing down with his strokes, leaning in and nipping at Julian's bottom lip.

"Maybe," he said, "I'm just feeling all nostalgic. Nostalgic and affectionate."

Julian's eyes grew impossibly wider. "Are you? I thought you were trying to give me a handjob."

"Why can't a man have both?"

"Both?" Julian squeaked it, as Kenyon's hand sped up. Tugged him harder. He could see as the pleasure blurred his vision, and his eyes fluttered closed.

"Didn't realize it at the time," Kenyon said, "but that was the beginning of a very good thing. A life-changing thing."

That was the truth, he realized. His life had changed, completely and irrevocably, the moment Julian had stepped into it.

He hadn't realized it at first, because the change had been so gradual, so slight, but now, looking back, he could see both the beginning and the thousand tiny steps they'd taken to get here.

And the walled-off Julian he'd met that summer evening?

He wasn't the same either.

There were still walls. They hadn't all come down, but Kenyon had started helping Julian to demolish them, brick by brick.

Because the truth was, they both wanted Kenyon inside those walls.

Julian moaned and then he was shaking in Kenyon's arms as he worked him through his own orgasm.

They cleaned up in silence.

Kenyon was afraid maybe he'd said too much, especially when Julian was single-minded about finding paper towels and using them and then straightening his hair in the mirror.

He kept waiting for Julian to stop him, to say something, but instead, he reached over and unlocked the door instead.

"Alright, then," Kenyon mumbled to himself, tossing the last paper towel into the trash and heading out into the hallway, a few steps behind Julian.

Later, he would realize that if he hadn't been a dozen feet behind Julian, everything could've been so much worse.

He had a close eye on Julian, wondering where he was going, what he was going to do. He hadn't explicitly told Kenyon to follow him—but they both knew he would. So the only question was where Kenyon was going to be following him to.

But then, out of the blue, Julian froze, hesitated, right in the mouth of the hallway, before he reached the rooftop proper.

It took Kenyon a moment to catch up and realize who it was that had stopped Julian in his tracks.

Coach.

Asa Dawson, in the flesh, at the victory party, and heading to the bathroom just as the two of them were leaving it.

Oh shit.

This had happened once before, on a stairwell, in a hotel they were staying in the night before a game. Coach had caught him sneaking out, though later, when Kenyon had found out about Coach and Scott, the fact that he was *also* in that stairwell had made a hell of a lot more sense.

But now, Coach was not only catching *him*, but Julian, too.

Close enough, with the bathroom right there, that there was very little chance he'd call this a coincidence.

That was the thing about Coach—he was brilliant, which was awesome ninety-nine percent of the time, and during the rest, the absolute fucking worst.

"Julian," Coach said politely, and they extended hands, shook. "Didn't expect to see you here." He craned his neck around. Caught sight of Kenyon.

Kenyon couldn't miss the way his eyes practically fired at that. *Double shit.* "And, Kenyon, too, what a coincidence." Coach said it mildly, like it might actually *be* a coincidence, but there was no way he really believed that. He was, Kenyon knew, way too crafty to truly believe it.

He was just lulling them into a state of calm before whipping the curtain back, unexpectedly, and revealing all their dirty secrets.

And there were a lot of them. Dirty secrets, that is.

"A coincidence, yes," Julian said weakly. Then he straightened. Tried to sell it. Kenyon gave him full points, but if it had been just the two of them, he'd have told him it was pointless. "I just happened to be running to the bathroom at the same time as Kenyon here."

"Yep," Kenyon said. What else could he say?

"Yes, I can see that," Coach said, still steady, but with those eyes that saw *everything* narrowing in on Kenyon.

He was probably remembering now how he'd caught him in the stairwell.

Probably also remembering what Julian had said about dating a player, only a few days ago.

No doubt, he was currently adding two and two together and getting the correct answer—because Coach didn't get wrong answers.

"You excited for the fireworks?"

In any other situation, Kenyon would be amused at how high and semi-panicked Julian sounded. Julian, who didn't get intimidated by shit, freaking out that Coach had discovered them practically in the middle of fucking.

But this was not funny because things were still so unsure between them. The last thing Kenyon wanted was for Julian to freak out about the consequences of them dating and bail.

And he would.

Maybe he'd be right to. But this thing between them, it was so good, it was so . . . different from anything Kenyon had ever had. Different, he knew, from anything that Julian had ever experienced. That was why they kept leaning into it, wanting more of it, even when any sane person would've stopped it ages ago.

Love, Kenyon realized with a jolt, that was what love was.

Would Coach bench him if he figured out that he was with Julian? It was a possibility. Slim, yes, but a possibility. There were other running backs, hungry for an opportunity, sitting just behind him in the depth chart. They weren't as good as he was, and some of them were totally unproven, but Kenyon had broken one of the cardinal rules. He'd be punished for it, not given the nice, friendly chat that the other couples on the team would get. That even Pax and Davis had gotten.

He was doing all of this, in spite of every good reason not to, because he fucking loved Julian.

It wasn't that he couldn't give him up. It was because he *wouldn't*.

And, he was pretty sure, from the deer-in-the-headlights look Julian shot him when Coach walked past them to the bathroom, that Julian loved him too.

Julian *admitting* it was a whole different story, but there was something that settled, deep and inescapable, inside Kenyon now that he knew the truth. And that something didn't care if Julian admitted it now. It only cared that his feelings existed, and that he too, had basically given a big middle finger to everyone in his life who would absolutely give a thousand shits that he was dating a player.

"Well, that was not ideal," Julian hissed as they headed out into the club. The sun had set, now, and the lights had cast a warm glow across the rooftop. In the center, there was the dance floor, and it was packed, full of Piranhas players and their partners. He could see Pax and Davis leading a whole group in some kind of salsa.

The bar was packed, Logan in the center, holding court as he gestured with a beer bottle in one hand, and his other arm wrapped around his boyfriend, Dylan.

Scott was over by the low-slung couches, talking earnestly to Beau and Sebastian and Micah was there, too.

Kenyon took Julian's arm, not even caring who saw at this point, because the person who they'd *most* needed not to see, had already seen enough.

"No, but . . . it's going to be fine," Kenyon said, even though he wasn't sure that was true. Was it going to be fine? It was. No matter what the fallout was, they were still going to have each other.

Even if Julian tried to cut and run, Kenyon was going to stick tight to him, like glue.

He couldn't get rid of him now, not when he knew the truth.

God, he loved him.

Just looking at him now, under the glow of the lights strung across the rooftop, it all felt different than it had only a few minutes ago.

He'd wondered what that feeling was, pressing against his breastbone, the one that made him feel slightly breathless every time Julian turned those light blue, otherworldly eyes on him. But now he knew.

It was love.

Julian knew he should be freaking out right now.

Coach was going to come out of the bathroom, pull out his phone and call Nikki and say, *guess what I just saw,* and then Julian wasn't going to be able to pretend anymore.

Pretend that Kenyon hadn't somehow become the most important person in his life. Pretend that walking away from him wouldn't nearly kill him.

Or you could just . . . not do that.

Julian wasn't sure he was going to have a choice.

If Nikki found out the truth, she was going to want him to do one of two things: *one,* use the relationship to give him an edge, or *two,* break it off.

He wouldn't do the first one.

Even if it didn't feel wrong, even if it didn't feel *earned,* he wouldn't ever do that to Kenyon. His trust was a precious thing, and the idea of letting him down, of breaking his heart by betraying him was unthinkable.

And the second one?

It would hurt.

It would hurt so fucking much.

"Hey, you just zoned out there for a moment." Kenyon had tugged him over to an empty corner of the rooftop.

He'd tried to let go of his hand, but Julian had hung on.

Tenacious, even at the end.

But was it really the end?

There's a third choice. You could tell Nikki to suck it. Quit. Quit to be with Kenyon. He'd encourage you both off the cliff, you can see it in his eyes right now. He . . . he really fucking cares about you.

This particular option should've hurt just as much—should've hurt *more*—than walking away from Kenyon, but it didn't.

He'd had a feeling for awhile now that what he loved about his job wasn't the actual reporting, but, Julian considered, this must confirm it.

Before Kenyon, it hadn't mattered. He'd committed to this job, to this career path, and so many things were riding on that commitment.

"Aren't you freaking out?" Julian demanded.

Because Kenyon wasn't really. He looked . . . really happy.

Satisfied and calm.

"Yes. And no," Kenyon said cautiously. Like he was afraid Julian would.

But Julian wasn't either. Not really.

"There's still no proof," Julian said.

"If Coach benches me . . ." Kenyon shrugged. Like he wouldn't care.

Julian understood what that felt like, because he'd just discovered the same disinterest in the possibly forthcoming punishment.

"Same," Julian said.

"Huh," Kenyon offered. "I'm not sure what that means."

It was a lie.

A *nice* lie, a lie to preserve Julian's lack of freak-out, but it was still a lie.

Kenyon knew what it meant.

He wasn't stupid, and Julian wasn't either.

"You know," Julian said. "It means if the shit hits the fan . . . we're choosing each other."

Kenyon's gaze was inscrutable.

"You know what that means?"

Julian rolled his eyes. "I'm not an idiot. If I tell Nikki to fuck off, I know exactly what that means."

No job, no money, no way to support yourself.

Exactly the position he'd sworn he'd never find himself in.

Dependent on the man he was in a relationship with.

Of course, he'd never believed he'd even make it that far with any guy, never mind commit to him and accept his help.

But he'd do it. Swallow all his significant pride, and take the handout, if it meant they could be together.

"The shit might not hit the fan," Kenyon said.

Julian squeezed his hand. Stared out at the Miami skyline, all lit up.

"You said it," he finally said, his voice not exactly as steady as he'd hoped it might be. "This is life-changing."

It was undeniable, because Julian was making all kinds of decisions he'd never have made before.

He turned to Kenyon to say so, to see the look in his eyes when he was honest about how he felt, no matter how terrified he was, when a *boom* shook the air, and then light and color exploded across the sky.

The crowd on the dance floor dispersed, all heading towards the edge of the roof, watching with *oohs* and *aahs* as the fireworks burst above them.

Reluctantly, Julian let go of Kenyon's hand, and moved away from him. Not far, but far enough that if anyone saw them together, they wouldn't think they were *together*.

It sucked. If things went down the way he thought they might, then it wouldn't matter—but right now, at least they had plausible deniability.

Right now, it would have to be enough to gaze up at the sky, at the cacophony of color and sound, and be at least a little part of this team and its accomplishments this season.

Nobody knew about the most solid way he was connected, but that was okay.

Better, at least for now, if they didn't.

Kenyon glanced over at him, and it felt like all of Julian's thoughts were reflected in the darkness of his eyes, color blooming in them as the fireworks exploded above them.

"I..." Julian took a risk and a step closer, and kept his voice low.

But Kenyon gave a little shake of his head, an affectionate and knowing smile on his face. "I know," he said. "I *know*."

Maybe he did.

But did that mean Julian didn't get to say it?

Maybe it's better if you don't. You haven't committed yet. Maybe Coach won't call you. Maybe Coach won't call Nikki.

CHAPTER FIFTEEN

IT WAS A NICE thought while it lasted.

Instead, first thing in the morning he got an email from Coach, asking him to come into the Piranhas' practice facility for a meeting about, "an exciting opportunity."

The email in Kenyon's inbox didn't even bother with the subterfuge of the exciting opportunity. It just told him to be in Coach's office this morning at nine AM sharp.

Same time as Julian.

"He knows," Julian said bleakly, staring into his coffee cup.

"Well, no shit," Kenyon retorted. "Yeah, he knows. But there's no proof. He'll yell and bluster, but what's he going to do?"

Julian looked up from the eggs he was pushing around his plate, his appetite gone. It was one thing to make promises to yourself and to the man you . . . well, that you cared a whole heck of a lot about . . . in the romantic light of a fireworks show. It was entirely another to face the music under the cold, hard light of day.

"Bench you?" Julian suggested. "Tell Nikki who will absolutely fire me if I don't cooperate?"

"Cooperate?"

This was *another* conversation Julian hadn't wanted to have.

"She won't fire me, not right away, not until she figures out I won't . . ." Julian hesitated. He hated to say it out loud, because he couldn't take it back then. Not that Kenyon probably hadn't considered it at one point—they wouldn't be in this place, right now, if he hadn't. "If I won't use you for source material."

Kenyon frowned. "Would she really want you to do that?"

He really liked Nikki; he *did*. She was a really good boss and had been an excellent mentor, but the problem was the industry. It rejected women, in general, and when a woman *did* manage to weasel her way into the good ol' boys club, she was considered valuable only for her looks and sex appeal, not for anything she had going on upstairs.

That attitude, over time, had made Nikki hard and a little bitter, and frankly, Julian couldn't even blame her.

So, would she expect him to sell Kenyon out to gain an advantage? She would. She wouldn't even blink twice before ordering him to do it, and probably say something along the lines of, "But isn't that why you started dating him in the first place?"

"Yes," Julian said.

It was easier to be frank about this. Lay it all out in black and white, even as he wanted, desperately, to pretend it didn't exist.

Pretend that the whole world wasn't stacked against them, rooting for them to fail, or at the very least, to betray each other until their relationship exploded in a fiery cataclysm of drama and lies.

"You know, I never . . ."

"I know," Julian said.

Kenyon stared at him. "You just wouldn't. It's not who you are. You . . ." He chuckled under his breath. "You wouldn't want it to be that easy."

In case he was wondering if Kenyon really knew him, there was hard and undeniable proof right there. He *wouldn't*. It would be an advantage, sure, but it would be an advantage gained the wrong way and it would never sit right with him.

"You're not wrong," Julian said wryly.

Kenyon skirted around the gigantic kitchen island and nudged Julian, slipping an arm around his shoulders. "Not that I wouldn't give you something, if it would help you."

Of course he would.

"Keyword there is *give*," Julian pointed out.

"Yeah, well, you might be an asshole sometimes, but you're not a backstabbing asshole, and here's the other thing." Kenyon pressed a kiss to the side of his head. "You're kinda my asshole now."

"I like being your asshole." It was true. Bizarre, but *true*.

It shouldn't feel so easy to settle into Kenyon's embrace, like he was meant to, like they were designed for each other. He'd never thought he'd feel so comfortable with another person. But he did, with Kenyon. Only Kenyon.

He could handle his own shit, but if he ever couldn't . . . he could trust that Kenyon would be his knight, his hero, and would go out and slay every snarling demon threatening him.

How could he possibly repay such loyalty?

"Today," Julian said, his voice muffled by Kenyon's shoulder, "let me do the talking."

"He's *my* coach," Kenyon said dryly. "And he doesn't really like people knowing it but he's a soft touch. Got a heart, beating under all that overachiever exterior. Didn't he let Pax and Davis stay together?"

"Still . . . I might be able to convince him it's just . . . well, that we're a little bit less like them."

Kenyon pulled back.

"It wouldn't be true," Julian said hurriedly.

"You want to lie to my coach." Kenyon didn't sound happy about this.

"Not *lie* per se, just . . . bend the truth a little bit. Pretend this is like . . . three months ago, when we were still pretending."

Kenyon stared.

"I know you can't," Julian added. "So let me do this, okay?"

Maybe he couldn't prove his loyalty the same way Kenyon did, every single day, every single moment they were together, but he *could* do this. Save Kenyon's starting job at least.

"Alright," Kenyon said.

Kenyon knew he was going to regret agreeing to let Julian handle this meeting.

He'd only done it because Julian had been so anxious about it. It wasn't like he *wasn't* anxious about it, because he'd not only broken the rule about dating reporters, he'd entirely fucking demolished it. But he still didn't think Coach would bench him. Yell at him, sure, but bench him? Coach wasn't that stupid. He was playing the best he had all year, and if he was being honest, a big part of that was Julian. Of course, he didn't really want to tell Coach that, either. Because that would mean explaining that it was *Julian* and not Beau or any of the other coaches who had helped him get there.

But as he settled down in the chair opposite Coach's big desk, covered in a flurry of papers, Kenyon couldn't help feeling nervous not about Coach finding out the truth, but nervous about the way Julian was going to handle it.

Coach looked tired. Happy, but tired.

Resigned, too.

"Glad you two could come this morning," he said, clearly getting the social niceties out of the way. It was just like Coach not to ignore them completely.

"I'm very interested in this exciting opportunity you mentioned," Julian said.

Coach leaned forward, onto his elbows and shot Julian a very frank look that Kenyon had personally been on the receiving end of a time or two. He was impressed how Julian barely blinked at the fierceness of it, because he knew how that look felt.

"You two know why you're here," Coach said. "And as far as I'm concerned, it's a formality. Kenyon—you *know* better."

He did. He really, truly did, and that hadn't made a damn bit of difference.

"I thought maybe when I caught you, few weeks back, you'd have realized what you were doing was a mistake." Coach sighed heavily, and Kenyon felt his disappointment deep down, down to his toes. "But I guess not."

"Coach, sir, I have to say, it's not what you think it is." There went Julian again, trying to throw himself on the ticking grenade.

Kenyon had to give him credit, he was tenacious and more loyal than he'd even realized. His boss could try to get him to betray Kenyon, but Kenyon had never worried about it, even for a moment, because Julian just wasn't built that way.

He'd rather blow himself up with the bomb than let Kenyon take any amount of well-deserved flack.

"Oh?" Coach raised an eyebrow. "What do I think it is?"

"I know a lot of your players, and frankly, *you*, sir, have found love this year, but we're just . . ." Julian gestured between him and Kenyon and Kenyon desperately tried not to cringe at what was about to come next.

"You're just?" Coach questioned.

"Fucking, sir," Julian said earnestly. "We're just fucking."

Kenyon was a grown-ass adult. He could own his behavior and his decisions, but Coach was *Coach*, practically more of a father figure than his own father, and here was Julian talking about them *fucking* in front of him.

He'd known it was coming, but the reality still made him want to drop through the floor.

For a long, interminable moment, Coach didn't say anything. The silence drew out, and Kenyon fought the urge to squirm in his chair.

Julian, who was apparently made from much tougher stuff, didn't even bat an eye.

Not for the first time, Kenyon thought that Julian must've been forged in a fire. He didn't know exactly what kind yet, because he was still waiting for Julian to tell him—and he knew he would, someday, when he was ready—but the fact the fire existed was undeniable.

He'd been through his own share of tough times, but Kenyon knew the heat of his own fire hadn't been nearly as hot as Julian's. It was partially why he'd started We Read, because some people wouldn't ever have access to the resources he had. As soon as his parents had realized what his poor grades were really hiding, he'd gotten coaches and tutors. He'd learned how to overcome his learning disability. But so many kids never did. There was a whole community of young minorities who'd never gotten a chance because they'd never been given one.

He'd been handed one, and he'd never forgotten it.

But Julian was a whole different story. That much was clear.

Finally, Coach leaned back in his chair, and sighed.

"I wish I could believe that's true," he said, "but I'm sorta an expert on this now, through, I might add, *no* desire of my own."

"But it is true, sir," Julian repeated, wide-eyed and innocent, like talking about fucking was equivalent to crocheting a goddamn afghan.

Why had he decided to let Julian handle this?

Because he asked, nicely, and you knew he wanted to do this for you.

"Son, I just got married. And I promise I did plenty of fucking before we said our vows."

It was 100% official. Kenyon wanted to die.

"So, *no*," Coach continued, "I know what that looks like, and it doesn't look like you two. It sure doesn't look like you marching in here ready to deflect any anger from my player."

Julian, smartly, shut up.

Coach turned that killer gaze onto Kenyon.

He prayed he didn't look absolutely horrified at the thought of his coach fucking anyone, never mind his husband.

Sex was a subject they should *not* be covering. Not in this office. Not in this whole fucking building.

It was bad enough they had all started knocking on every door before they went in. First, it was because of Tristan and Wade, and now . . . well, it seemed half the team had paired off, and it was just smarter to be safe than sorry.

"You have anything to say about this, Kenyon?" Coach asked mildly. Not angry. More resigned than anything else.

"Yeah, I actually do. First, maybe it was at the beginning, I won't deny that. When I was . . . uh . . . in the stairwell, that one time, and we ran into each other, that wasn't a lie I told you." That was important to Kenyon. He wanted Coach to know that he hadn't lied to his face that night. Sure, things were becoming increasingly complicated, but it still hadn't been a lie. Julian was still steadfastly insisting at that point that they were just hooking up, and they hadn't even kissed yet.

"I understand," Coach said, and he sounded like he did. "Sometimes things are . . . complicated. But . . . as much as it pains me to say it, this relationship is not in either of your best interests. There it is, plain and simple."

Kenyon knew there were a lot worse ways he could've said it.

It should've helped that Coach had gone out of his way to be nice.

It didn't.

Because he already knew he wasn't going to be giving Julian up.

He'd fight for him, every single step of the way.

"It's not," Kenyon said. "But that doesn't change anything. I love him."

He was acutely aware of Julian next to him when he said it. Heard Julian's squeak of shock, and sharp intake of breath.

"I see," Coach said.

He would. Because Logan loved Dylan, and Beau loved Sebastian, and God knew, Pax and Davis loved each other, and then . . . then there was Coach and his own husband, and everyone and their aunt knew there was a real story there.

Love was the one bulletproof shield Kenyon possessed.

And it just so happened to be the complete truth.

"You *what*," Julian hissed under his breath.

Kenyon expected when he turned towards Julian, he'd see shock on his face. Maybe even a dire need to run away.

He'd prepared himself for it.

What he didn't prepare himself for was the sheer wonder on Julian's face. He was shocked, yes, but it wasn't the bad kind of shock, but instead, it was astonishment and utter awe that not only did Kenyon love him, but that he'd taken the grenade from his hand, and tossed it away.

That he'd said, *I got this, too; we've got each other, here.*

Julian didn't even need to say the words, he didn't even need to believe they were true. Because Kenyon could see them in his face.

Love was written on every beautiful angle.

"Yeah, you heard me," Kenyon said, and reached out, taking Julian's hand and squeezing it with his own.

"I . . . I guess we're gonna have to talk about this." Julian sounded like he actually wouldn't hate it. It was amazing that just a month ago, they hadn't even kissed and Julian wouldn't even have a conversation that didn't involve sex.

"Guess you will," Coach inserted, clearing his throat. "Well, that puts everything into a slightly different perspective."

"I thought it might," Kenyon said.

Of course, he hadn't thought of it at first, because he'd been too panicked, and then too agonizingly embarrassed by Julian's tactics.

But of course being in love would change Coach's perspective.

"This is going to be really difficult for you. I won't lie about that."

"I know." Julian sounded like he believed it. "I just don't want you to punish Kenyon for his feelings."

Coach's face softened. "I know. I wouldn't. Kenyon, you're our starting running back. Nothing changes that."

Kenyon thought there were definitely a handful of things that *might* change that, but this wasn't the time, and, anyway, he wasn't completely decided yet.

"Thanks, sir," Kenyon said. "That means a lot to me."

"You're going to be in for a lot more pressure," Coach said, directing this comment towards Julian. "But I suppose if anyone can handle it, it's probably you."

Julian nodded.

"He won't be handling it alone," Kenyon promised.

"As it should be," Coach said. He was smiling now. "If you need anything, you know where to find me." He paused. "Should I give you the 'talk' now? Is that something you need? Seems to me that it would be a little pointless, since this has been going on . . . well, how long *has* this been going on?"

Kenyon watched as the flush climbed up Julian's neck.

God, seeing him flustered was one of his all-time favorite things.

Even when they were sitting in Coach's office and he couldn't do a single thing about it.

"Long enough?" Julian said sheepishly.

"Since the summer," Kenyon said. He had no issue being honest with Coach now. He deserved to hear the truth, since he'd essentially offered to help support and shield them.

Clearly, he'd not been prepared for that honest of an answer, because he did a double take. "The *summer*? Like . . . training camp?" Coach asked.

"Yep," Kenyon said, enjoying Coach's shock probably more than he should be.

"Well, you can't say you two aren't serious about each other," Coach said.

"I guess . . . I guess you're right," Julian said, sounding surprised himself.

"There you go," Coach said. "Now, get out of here, before I do something intelligent, like change my mind and read both of y'all the riot act."

Julian couldn't quite believe that had just happened.

Okay, he could.

He could totally believe it.

Kenyon was just that kind of guy who didn't think he was romantic, who'd spent his whole lifetime denying he was romantic, but now he'd realized it wasn't so bad, had completely, utterly, totally embraced the sappy side to his personality.

Kenyon was still looking at him like he was afraid he might bolt.

Coach had been right about one thing: they were clearly serious. Serious people in serious relationships told each other they loved each other and didn't . . .

Julian swallowed down the emotion bubbling up inside of him.

They told each other they loved each other without making it a big deal. Without . . . *oh God,* sobbing all over each other.

If he cried—and he really, *really* did not want to cry, not now, not in front of Kenyon, not in the hallway of the Piranhas' practice facility where anyone could see—it would make everything weird again. Just when they'd managed to *un*-weird it.

"Why are you looking at me like that?" Julian had hoped to make it slightly less of a belligerent question, as they headed down the hall towards the front of the building. Kenyon would be sticking around, because he had meetings and practice, but Julian had his own job to deal with, now that they'd diffused the coach situation.

"I told you I loved you," Kenyon said softly.

"Yes, you did, I was right there." Maybe if he kept talking, he could keep all these tears in. He'd never expected Kenyon's confession to hit him this hard. It wasn't crazy that Kenyon *might* care about him. In fact, Julian reasoned, it made perfect sense that he would, because why else would you want to spend so much time together? Go on dates? Sleep next to someone without any sex involved?

But he'd been thinking only in abstracts, not specifics.

This was very specific.

Kenyon loves Julian.

Julian . . .

He couldn't quite finish the thought.

Not because he didn't want to, because if he did, that onslaught of emotion that he normally held back, that he always kept in check, was going to wash over him, and he would much rather be alone, in his car, when that happened.

Actually, he'd prefer it not happen at all, but it seemed that choice had been taken entirely out of his hands.

"I just wanted to make sure you knew I wasn't expecting anything out of you," Kenyon said gently. "This stuff is new to me."

Julian sniffed. Resolutely. "It's new to me, too."

"Yeah," Kenyon said, and *God*, how had Julian not seen it written in huge, flashing letters before this? Kenyon's eyes were full of love and his voice was even brimming with it.

There was no question. Julian knew he was losing it. The wall was crumbling, right in front of him, and he didn't know how to stop it. His eyes stung, his throat closed over and he felt it working hard, as he desperately tried to at least hold it off.

He was never going to get over crying not only in front of Kenyon—but in the middle of the freaking hallway at the Piranhas' offices.

In a second, Kenyon would look at him, and he'd know.

Everything.

Every single bit of himself he tried so hard to keep hidden.

They passed by a door, and the discreet tag on the side identified it as a supply closet.

Julian didn't hesitate. He *could* cry in front of Kenyon. It was not ideal, but he trusted him. And after all, wasn't he crying *because* of Kenyon?

But he was not going to do it in the middle of the Piranhas' facility, where anyone could see.

Yanking the door open, he grabbed Kenyon's arm with his other hand, and pulled them both into the dark, cramped space, shutting the last of the light out behind them.

"Wha . . ." Kenyon only got half the word out before Julian lost it.

He tried to keep his sobs quiet, but it was so much flooding him, the emotion overwhelming him, he couldn't. He could only latch on to Kenyon's big, strong frame and fucking *cry*.

To Kenyon's credit, he didn't hesitate. He put his arms around Julian and just held him tight, until finally, his tears slowed.

"You wanna tell me what's wrong?" he finally asked in a soft, careful voice.

Julian nearly shook his head, because he *didn't*, but *one*, Kenyon wouldn't even be able to see if he did, it was so dark, and *two*, he'd just cried all over the guy, hadn't he? Surely that deserved some kind of explanation.

The truth, his brain reminded him, *he deserves the truth.*

"It's not anything that's wrong," Julian said, sniffing. "It's just . . . nobody's ever told me that before."

He felt Kenyon tense. "What? Surely . . ."

"No," Julian said unequivocally. "Never. Nobody's ever loved me. Well . . . that's probably not true, I'm sure my parents, while they were alive, loved me. But I don't remember them, and I don't remember them telling me . . ."

"Wait," Kenyon interrupted. "Your parents . . ."

Julian sighed. "They died when I was four. I don't really remember them. A vague impression, maybe. But there wasn't anyone to take me, so . . . I ended up in the foster care system. And nobody loves you there. Some places weren't so bad, but I was always . . . it's not like a real family. Not like a real family who loves you, who *tells* you they love you."

The emotion threatened to wash over him again. He'd never truly belonged anywhere, except here. Tucked into Kenyon's arms.

Those arms squeezed him tighter, like they didn't want to let him go.

"Well, this I can promise you. *I* love you, and I will tell you every single damn day going forward."

Julian laughed wetly. "If I let you."

"You'll let me," Kenyon said confidently. "Because . . . I think when you're ready, you'll say it back to me."

How could he be so sure? Just listening to Kenyon say it had totally broken him apart. He wasn't sure he'd ever be ready to say them back.

But Kenyon believed he would. Kenyon believed in *him*.

He freaking loved him.

"I like how sure you are," Julian said, words muffled by the front of Kenyon's shirt.

"Of you? Always." He hesitated, and Julian found himself holding his breath for a long moment. "It was really sweet how you thought you could deflect Coach's anger. Sweet, but also stupid."

It's just what an idiot in love would do.

But Kenyon didn't have to say that part, because Julian still heard it, loud and clear, echoing in his own head.

"It was kind of stupid, wasn't it?" Julian sighed.

"You talked about us *fucking* in front of him." Julian could feel Kenyon shake his head. "I may never get over that."

He laughed then, because *oh my God, he had.* Several times. Without an ounce of shame. He'd been so focused on trying to save Kenyon—and to a lesser extent, himself. Or, as Kenyon would probably say, he'd been trying to save *them.* "Sometimes, I just start down a path and I'm too stubborn to abort."

Kenyon was chuckling now, as he stroked a warm line up and down Julian's spine. He felt better. Emptied out, but better.

Before this morning, he'd believed that they were in this for the long haul. That they'd make it work, mostly because anything less was unacceptable, since he'd already figured out he didn't want to live without Kenyon, that he *couldn't* live without Kenyon. But now, they felt unbelievably solid.

They'd taken a risk on each other, and unbelievably, it had paid off.

"I can't imagine you ever being that stubborn," Kenyon said, amused.

"Oh, you can, you're just being nice." Julian rolled his eyes.

"Nice? Me? I think that's you."

"Liar. I've never been nice."

Kenyon was still laughing when his phone rang.

But he was. He *was* nice. It was funny, once they stopped fighting each other, and started fighting *for* each other, everything had changed. Even Julian himself.

Kenyon fumbled in his pocket, pulled out his phone and answered it.

"Yeah," he said. "I'll be there in a minute."

"Oh shit," Julian said, as Kenyon hung up. "Did I make you late?"

"Yes, and no, it doesn't matter. Pax just wanted to make sure I was on my way."

"I'm sorry." Julian hated to move away from Kenyon even a fraction, but he did it.

"No, don't be. I'm not," Kenyon said, reaching out for him, tucking his fingertips under Julian's chin. "I'm glad you told me. I'm even glad you cried on me."

"Really?" He couldn't help but be skeptical.

"Yes. I love you, you know."

His smile was so big, so wide, it nearly hurt. "Yes, you mentioned that."

"Now, I gotta go be awesome, and so do you. But that should be easy for you."

Julian pressed a quick kiss to Kenyon's mouth. Anything longer and they were never going to leave this supply closet.

"You too," he said. "And . . ." He wanted to say it. The words were on the tip of his tongue. But he didn't.

Kenyon squeezed his arm. "I know," he said, and unbelievably, it seemed like he really did.

Chapter Sixteen

"Thanks for making time for me," Keisha said, voice slightly distorted through the laptop as Kenyon skirted around the kitchen island, trying to get the plates and silverware set up for the meal that would be delivered for him and Julian shortly.

"I only have a minute," he said.

"What are you even doing? Are you . . . *oh my God,* you're setting a table. With *two* places. You have a date, don't you?"

"Maybe," Kenyon hedged. He hadn't told Keisha about Julian yet, because he wasn't sure exactly where to start. In fact, he hadn't told *any* of his family about Julian, not because they wouldn't approve—though they certainly would be *very* surprised that the guy he'd ended up falling for was a prickly, white journalist—but because they'd be *too* excited.

"Oh, come on," Keisha said, both amused and annoyed. "Don't be so secretive. Who's the guy? Or is it a girl?"

Keisha knew that he didn't have a real preference for sex, and that he'd casually dated both, though he usually ended up with men.

"It's a guy," Kenyon said. He set out the silverware. Then went to get the glasses from the cupboard. He'd enjoyed the last date with Julian, but this one, he was going to spoil him a little. That had always been the plan, and now it was even more of the plan, once he'd heard a little more of Julian's past.

Unlike what he'd believed about the guy at the beginning—that he was spoiled and rich and smug—he was actually the opposite. Nobody had ever given a shit about him, which was unbelievable to Kenyon, because he gave *all* the shits about him.

"You gonna tell me anything else? Where'd you meet him?"

"At work," Kenyon said shortly, setting the glasses down. There was a champagne flute, for the sparkling wine he'd ordered that was supposed to be the *best*. And then a red wine glass for the insanely expensive red wine he'd bought, too.

There'd be candles scattered across the kitchen, and he'd turn the lights down. There were a dozen white roses, sitting in a crystal vase, right across from where he'd set up their plates.

"You're dating another *player*?" Keisha said, sounding shocked. And yes, okay, he had always been cautious about hooking up with people he played with, or worked with at all. Anonymous had always been more his kind of thing.

The irony was at the very beginning, this whole thing with Julian was *supposed* to be anonymous, just some random guy he'd met at a bar.

"Not a player," Kenyon said. Then finally broke down. "Even worse, actually. He's a reporter."

"Dad is going to freak out when you tell him." Keisha sounded like she was looking forward to this. Which made sense, because their parents were constantly despairing over her finding a suitable partner. They'd never been happy that she was more married to her work than even he was.

But at least Keisha *dated*, like she was actually trying to find someone.

Kenyon had never really intended to find anyone. Julian had fallen right into his lap before he'd even realized how amazing he was.

"I haven't told them yet, so don't be the one to break the news, alright?" Kenyon warned her. "Did you actually have something you needed or was this just an opportunity to grill me about my personal life?"

She grinned on the laptop screen. "Oh, that was just a happy coincidence. I wanted to ask you if you'd looked at that new proposal I sent over."

"Not yet. Sorry," Kenyon said, trying not to sound testy. Keisha had said she needed it soon, when she'd emailed it over. This was the time of year they always tried to implement new programs, because this was usually the time of year he was mostly free from his other football-related obligations. But not this year.

"It's alright," Keisha said. "You don't need to apologize. Especially not for going to the playoffs. That's pretty damn cool. You think . . ."

"I'm not going to talk about the Condors game and jinx us," Kenyon said.

"When did you become so superstitious?"

Kenyon sighed, and looked straight into his sister's gaze. "It's this team, okay? I don't want . . . they matter to me."

"You don't have to apologize for that either," she said. "Nobody ever said you shouldn't care about who you play for. *You* made that choice. *You* decided that it shouldn't matter."

"And it was the right choice, I know it was," Kenyon said. He still believed it. "But if . . . if this is my last chance . . . I want it to count for something."

It was the first time he'd said it out loud.

Keisha's gaze softened. "You're thinking it's your last year?"

"Can I keep going like this forever? No. I can't. You know that."

He didn't want it to be true, but there was another life beckoning to him now, a meaningful change he wanted to embrace. But it would still hurt like hell to leave these guys behind.

Sebastian said he'd find something that meant something to him, and he had. We Read, of course, and then there was Julian. He wasn't stupid enough to believe that he could balance all three, and Julian deserved more than just scraps of time. He deserved someone willing to build a life with him.

Even if that scared the shit out of both of them.

"Doesn't mean it doesn't suck," Keisha said. "You're going to miss it, I know you will."

"Yeah. But I want this last . . . if it *is* the last . . . to count for something."

"Of course you do. The proposal can wait."

"But—"

"No," Keisha reiterated in a firm voice. "It can wait. We Read is part of who you are, because frankly it wouldn't exist without you, but football is part of you, too."

Kenyon didn't know what to say. Emotion clogged his throat.

It was. As much as he thought it was time to move on, the tug of it was strong. And stronger now than it had ever been, because this team was special.

But before he *had* to answer her, the doorbell rang. "Just a sec," he said, clearing his throat. "That's the food."

It was still too early for Julian, after all, so it must be the caterers coming with the fancy surf and turf he'd ordered.

But when he got to the front door, he opened it, and to his shock, it wasn't the caterers at all, but Julian, here early.

"Hey," he chattered away, the moment he stepped inside, the door shutting behind him, "I hope it's okay I got here early."

"It's . . . it's fine." Kenyon wondered if he could run back to the kitchen before Julian wandered in there and he and Keisha met, accidentally.

But maybe it would be okay.

Maybe it was time for his sister, the second most important person to him, to meet the guy he'd fallen in love with.

"Come on," Kenyon said gesturing after they kissed briefly. "There's someone you should meet."

"Meet?" Julian's nose crinkled adorably. "Someone else is here?"

"Kinda," Kenyon said, leading him into the kitchen. He waved at his sister, still on the screen. "Keisha, this is Julian. My boyfriend."

Keisha's jaw didn't entirely drop, which he gave her full points for, but she did look pretty damn shocked.

"Nice to meet you." Julian grinned at the screen. "I wondered if I would get to, someday."

"You're . . . you're Julian Anderson."

"Oh, yes, you've heard of me, then."

"You said that shitty thing about my brother." Keisha frowned, then glanced over at Kenyon. "*This* is the guy you're dating? Please tell me you weren't dating him at the time?"

"Oh no, we were just fucking then," Julian said cheerfully.

They were really going to have to come up with a better story for when people asked how they met—just fucking in a shitty bar bathroom was not going to hold up.

"Ah well, I see." Keisha's tone was cautious. "That's . . . that's nice."

"We really need to work on your willingness to tell the world that we were only fucking," Kenyon said, chuckling under his breath.

"I don't know, I think it's kinda cute. And then you fell in love." Keisha sighed happily. "Kinda gives me hope for the future, you know? If you can fall for someone who told the world you're a shitty running back, then *anyone* can fall in love."

Julian flushed. "That wasn't *exactly* what I said."

Keisha's stare was frank. "Oh?"

"I knew he could do better. I wanted him to do better. I wanted *him* to want to do better."

"And you wanted his attention," Keisha added, smirking.

"Alright, a little of that, too," Julian admitted.

Kenyon had never thought of it that way before. Julian *had* wanted his attention, that's why he'd said it. Everything had begun to get weird between them then, but instead of pulling away, instead of running away, Julian had pulled out the stops to get all of Kenyon's attention.

What Julian hadn't known was that he didn't need to do any of that.

He'd *always* had all of Kenyon's attention.

"Well, I'll leave you two to your fancy date," Keisha said. "And whenever you do get a chance with that proposal, give it a look, okay?"

"Soon, I promise," Kenyon said.

She grinned. "Hopefully not too soon. I'm rooting for you guys to make it all the way. Kick some Condor butt for me, okay?"

"Uh," Kenyon said, but she'd already closed her video chat window, and there was nobody to chastise for possibly jeopardizing their win.

"So, that's your sister, huh?" Julian leaned against the island and regarded him sharply. "She seems . . . nice."

"Same way you're nice, huh?"

"Hey, those of us who fight for what we want, it makes us a little punchy. That's okay."

"That what you had to do?" Kenyon crossed over to the fridge and pulled out the champagne. "Fight for what you wanted?"

He'd been thinking about Julian's confession about his past, for the last twenty-four hours. Seeing everything that had happened between them in a totally different light as a result.

"Every single day," Julian said steadily. Didn't offer a single additional detail.

Kenyon wasn't surprised he'd try to downplay all that hard work. All that sacrifice.

Julian had been a queer foster kid who'd been not only the best football player at his high school, without any advantages the other students took for granted, but the best player in his whole county. Then he'd been recruited to Northwestern, with a full ride.

It was an unbelievable accomplishment, and he shouldn't be downplaying anything, but that was Julian for you. Doing the extraordinary and acting like it was normal.

"So when you said you quit playing football because you couldn't make it, that was why."

"I was always going to choose the path that got me where I wanted to go. That wasn't football."

"It could've been." Kenyon loosened the cork on the bottle with an expert motion, heard it pop, and then began to pour into the two flutes on the counter. "You could've gone into coaching."

"And tell players what to do? That isn't me."

Kenyon shot him a baleful glance. "It absolutely *is* you. Don't you tell me what to do, and enjoy every goddamn second of it?"

Julian flushed happily as he took the glass from Kenyon's hand. "Maybe," he allowed. "What's this? You trying to spoil me now?"

"Every moment I'm allowed," Kenyon admitted.

"What are we having for dinner? You did promise I wouldn't have to cook it."

"You won't. The caterers should be here in a few minutes."

"Caterers?" Julian's eyebrows shot up. "You really did go fancy. You know you don't have to do that; I'm a sure thing by this point."

"Doesn't matter. You're worth it, every bit of it," Kenyon said, and tugged him into his arms.

Julian scoffed, but he still melted into his embrace.

"I love you." Kenyon brushed a strand of that gorgeous hair away from his ear, and murmured into it.

"You gonna keep saying it?"

Kenyon chuckled. "Yeah, I am, and I'll enjoy it every time, and so will you, even if you pretend otherwise."

Julian didn't say anything for a long moment, just laid his head on Kenyon's chest.

"It's annoying," he finally said in a quiet voice, "but also kind of amazing, how well you know me."

Kenyon thought that it had been both the easiest thing in the world to discover the man underneath, and also the toughest.

So maybe they were even.

"Also," he added softly, "that you still want anything to do with me after I sobbed all over your shoulder."

Kenyon squeezed him harder. "I was surprised, yeah, but it was fine. Nice, even. To hear something about you."

"You mean, hear something about me I didn't want to tell you?" Julian asked wryly, tilting his head back and looking right into Kenyon's eyes.

He should be used to the flare of attraction whenever he looked at Julian now. He'd been feeling it for months now, and it was the very first thing he'd felt for him.

But now it felt tougher to resist than it ever had before.

It reminded him, *hard*, that they'd both been really busy with work during the last week, with almost no time to get naked.

He shifted his body, trying to keep his hardening cock away from Julian, because if he felt it, he would not only try to reduce their connection to just sex, he'd also take this emotional moment and make it about sex.

What's wrong with that? Kenyon's brain squawked.

And okay, maybe he was a little bit horny.

Or a lot horny.

Julian squirmed against him, and then he reached up and kissed him. And it wasn't a sweet, nice, loving kiss either. It was a hot, dirty kiss.

Kenyon stumbled back against the counter and groaned deep in his throat as Julian's hands were suddenly everywhere, touching him everywhere he wanted them to be—except one.

"Come on," Julian said, after he broke the kiss. "Let's go up-stairs. Or we can do it right here, I know how much you like bending me over things."

It was impossible not to groan, because Julian was one hundred percent right. He *did* love to bend Julian over things. Tangle his fingers deep in that hair and just listen to him scream as he filled him up.

And, extra bonus, it would be a lot more fun than sitting, without touching Julian, through an entire semi-fancy meal.

Of course, that was the moment the doorbell echoed through the kitchen again.

"Shit," Kenyon said and tried to extricate himself from Julian's touch, but naturally, that was *also* the moment where he finally went for his dick.

Which meant there was absolutely zero chance he'd be able to answer the door without embarrassing himself.

If he knew Julian at all, that was probably on purpose.

He took two steps away, putting some space between them, before he decided answering the door was overrated.

They didn't need dinner. Just the two of them, no clothes, and a bed.

Or, maybe Julian had it right, and all he needed was something to bend him over . . .

The doorbell rang again.

A sound couldn't be passive aggressive, but it sounded like it to Kenyon as he took a deep breath, shot Julian a heated look, tried to pretend the smug expression on his face didn't turn him on even more, and headed out of the kitchen to deal with the caterers.

Ten minutes later, the dinner was deposited on plates kept warm in the oven, and Julian was perched on one of the barstools, sipping his champagne, looking delighted with himself as he sampled some of the appetizers the caterers had prepared.

Kenyon told himself he was delighted too.

Dinner was good. Dinner had been the plan, after all, Kenyon reminded himself.

"Come try some of these little crab puff things," Julian said. "They're fucking delicious."

Kenyon was trying *not* to think about what else was delicious.

"You just look really keyed up," Julian continued, gesturing with his champagne flute. "Sit down and stop glowering."

"I wasn't…*glowering*." He definitely wasn't. Pouting because they were actually going to sit down and eat this dinner he'd meticulously planned was silly.

Conceding, he flopped down onto the barstool next to Julian and picked up one of those crab puffs he'd been rhapsodizing about.

"They're good," he agreed, after chewing and swallowing. "Thank God I'm not like Keisha and allergic to seafood."

"Ugh, that would be the worst," Julian agreed. "No allergies, then? Nothing I should worry about, or brush up on my CPR skills for?"

"Not . . . not exactly." Kenyon sighed. It was high time they had this conversation, and he'd even intended to share, so that Julian wouldn't feel like he was the only one putting himself out there—but saying it out loud, no matter how long it had been, was still hard. "You know why I started We Read, right?"

"You wanted to do lots of good things and not take credit for them?" Julian teased.

It was true; he rarely wanted to be the mouthpiece of the organization, even though he was a driving force behind the scenes.

Kenyon rolled his eyes. "No."

"You're going to tell me you were dyslexic and couldn't get the help you needed."

Kenyon supposed he shouldn't be surprised. Julian knew everything about everyone.

"What, of course I googled you," Julian continued. "It was literally my job to know why."

"Yes to the dyslexic part, no to the getting the help I needed. I got plenty of help, once they figured out what was wrong." Kenyon hesitated. "It was other kids that didn't. Everyone else I saw. Once I'd been diagnosed and coached to be able to deal with it better, I noticed other kids who struggled too. I recognized the same kind of problems I'd had. But nobody was lining up to help *them*. I asked teachers. They couldn't really help. My parents were comfortable, but not made of money. I couldn't ask them either. But there were all these people, good and smart and *young* kids, who I knew had learning disabilities, just slipping through the cracks. And it made me . . . *God*, so fucking angry. So I decided to do something about it. I think everyone thought I was kidding. Not serious about it. But I was dead serious."

Julian gazed at him steadily. "You saw an injustice, a gap, and you worked to correct it."

"I didn't want to play pro ball. I enjoyed it in college, sure, but it became clear pretty early on that I was going to be scouted, and when agents started sniffing around, talking big money, I thought . . ." Kenyon knew he shouldn't feel guilty about this. Everyone played for different reasons. He didn't have to love the game the way some of the other guys on the team did. That wasn't a requirement.

"You thought you could use the money to do some good," Julian finished for him.

"At first, yeah," Kenyon said. "And then I realized it was more than that. I could use my fame to funnel investors and donations to the foundation. Keisha graduated with her master's in business administration and I hired her. She's been invaluable, helping guide things, but in the future . . ." Kenyon hesitated. Not sure how much to share. It wasn't that he didn't trust Julian; he did, with his life, and with his heart, but this was big. Breaking this story would continue to change the trajectory of his career.

Julian's gaze softened. He reached out and put his hand on Kenyon's knee. Kenyon couldn't help it, he wished he'd put it a little higher. But that wasn't what they were doing right now. "I promise that anything you tell me, it's to me, *Julian*, not Julian Anderson, reporter." He made a self-conscious grimace. "I realize I should've said that ages ago, but I sort of thought . . ."

"You thought right." Kenyon squeezed Julian's hand. "I do trust you. I know you wouldn't. I just . . . I haven't said this to anyone, really. Just to myself, when nobody else could hear."

"You want to retire after this year?"

Kenyon laughed; he couldn't help himself. "I guess I spend all this time bragging about how well I know you, but you know *me*, too."

"I can't tell you how many times I've watched you and known you were thinking about it." Julian shrugged. "Nobody else could see it, but I could. So this is it for you?"

"I'm divided, between something I'm incredibly passionate about, that does a whole hell of a lot of good, and something that I do love, but I'm not fully committed to. It makes it hard to have any kind of life, when I'm balancing the two, and also . . . I get the feeling I'm not giving either the best part of me."

Julian nodded, serious and understanding. Then he grinned, suddenly, and slipped off his chair, positioning himself right between Kenyon's legs, and then his warm and firm hand was suddenly right where he wanted it, the pressure incredible against his cock.

"I don't know about all that," Julian said, "but I kinda think *I'm* the one who gets the best part of you."

Kenyon had been trying so damn hard to be good. To be loving and romantic and not even *think* about laying Julian out over the nearest flat surface, but maybe they'd actually moved right past thinking and into the doing part.

The way Julian was touching him now, gazing up and him and licking his lips made it clear what *he* wanted.

"Don't you want dinner?" Kenyon asked, making one last ditch effort to be good.

"Can't it keep?" Julian's fingertips were stroking his cock now through the fabric of his jeans, and while the pressure was welcome, it wasn't even close to enough. "I don't know about you, but I ate plenty of those crab puffs. You can feed me the rest later, while we're both still naked."

Kenyon didn't need any more excuses—or any more motivation. He didn't hesitate; he scooped Julian up, and while Julian squawked in protest, he sure wasted zero time in attaching his mouth to Kenyon's neck, biting and sucking, and making Kenyon weak in the knees as he carried him upstairs.

Depositing Julian at the edge of the bed, he squawked again as Kenyon took a step back, but his objection didn't last long as Kenyon shed his shirt and then reached for Julian's, tugging it out of his jeans.

"Someday," he said, panting a little as Julian's hands found all the bare skin he'd just revealed, skating lower and lower on his stomach, "you're gonna tell me why you dress like such an asshole frat boy."

Julian stuck out his tongue. "Someday," he said with delight, as he made quick work of Kenyon's jeans, dragging them down his thighs.

"It's alright, I like you better naked anyway."

Julian *was* a revelation like this, soft milky-white skin over the perfect set of lithe muscles. Then there was his face—absolutely stunning—and Kenyon was still a little obsessed with his hair, and then, finally, it was the way his blue eyes narrowed when he thought Kenyon was taking too long to divest him of the rest of his clothes.

His fingertips trailed down one of Kenyon's bare thighs, tickling. But Kenyon didn't move, didn't even flinch, because he was so close to being right where Kenyon wanted him.

Finally, Julian's knuckles finally brushed his cock, and pleasure flashed through him.

"Yeah, you *do* like that," Julian said smugly.

"What gave it away?" Kenyon found he was nearly breathless with anticipation.

Julian's fingers drifted lower, casually like he didn't have a particular destination in mind. Briefly they cupped his balls, and damn if he didn't love Julian just like this: bratty and provocative.

Then his touch ventured lower, brushing against his hole. Kenyon swore.

"What about this?"

"You damn well know I like it." Kenyon heard the rough desperation in his voice.

"Yeah, yeah, you do," Julian said. His eyes narrowed, and it was something else to be caught in the crosshairs of all that intense focus. It definitely ratcheted his arousal up to another level, which since this was Julian, was exactly what he'd intended. "You gonna get on the bed, let me take you apart, baby?"

Julian had been adamant since day one that there would be *no* pet names or cute nicknames, in bed or otherwise.

But the way he was so dialed in made it clear he didn't even realize he'd said it. It had just slipped out, Kenyon realized as he made himself comfortable on the bed, shucking the rest of his clothes as Julian stretched out, grabbing the lube from where it sat in the drawer next to Kenyon's bed.

Kenyon felt breathless with anticipation as Julian settled between his thighs, and popped open the cap, every movement slow and deliberate, until Kenyon was close to losing his mind and actually snapping at him to hurry the fuck up.

But he didn't, he kept his mouth squeezed into a tight line, because if he said anything, Julian would go even slower, and that was the last thing he wanted.

Finally, Julian bent low and Kenyon keened as he touched him exactly where he'd been dying for him to touch him.

But did he give him everything he wanted?

No way.

His touches were still light, barely brushes against where Kenyon wanted him to push his fingers deep, make him ache, make him scream.

"Don't tease," Kenyon finally panted, as the fingertips on Julian's other hand trailed up his hard, aching cock, straining for a firmer touch.

"But you like it so much," Julian pointed out slyly.

He wished he could deny it, but considering the way every single nerve on his body was alight with promise, he couldn't.

Julian was right; but then he was almost always right, wasn't he?

Finally, he slid one finger in, only to withdraw it almost immediately, but it was *almost* enough. Kenyon's head hit the pillow and he groaned.

He knew better than to try to fuck himself onto Julian's fingers, but it took every ounce of self-control to hold back from doing just that. He clenched his fists in the sheets and held on as Julian fucked him with one finger, achingly slow, and then when Kenyon was reduced to begging gibberish, finally added a second.

He knew this, and knew Julian would keep him forever, leisurely stretching him out, hitting all the spots inside him that sent flashes of bright pleasure shooting through him, until he was nearly mad with it.

But to Kenyon's surprise, that didn't happen—well, it *did*, but before Kenyon could really sink into the idea of staying here for awhile, being lit up from the inside out, Julian added another finger, sliding it alongside the rest.

He pulled himself together, trying to focus, and his eyes fluttered open, and to his shock, Julian was panting, face flushed, eyes wild.

Almost as turned on as Kenyon himself, just from doing this to him.

Kenyon's head fell back and that razor-sharp edge he was balancing on suddenly felt even more perilous.

"Please," he begged.

He almost never bothered, because Julian typically did not give a shit about his begging. Oh, he liked to *hear* Kenyon beg, but it never swayed him. He had a plan, and he stuck to it.

But now, Kenyon watched as his plea hit him, like a soft-edged bomb, and he visibly shuddered with the implications.

"Come on," Kenyon coaxed. "Come fuck me. I know you want to."

Julian withdrew his fingers, but instead of sliding his cock in, he leaned over Kenyon, straddling him, their chests pressing together and then they were kissing, hard and messy and perfect, Julian groaning into his mouth.

Sex with Julian had always been great.

That had never been up for debate, but it was unbelievable how much better it was now. How he couldn't pull Julian close enough, like any amount of kissing wasn't ever enough, like he'd tuck him inside his body, if he could.

"Fuck," Julian said breathlessly as he pulled back a fraction, leaving Kenyon chasing his lips with his own.

"That's the idea," Kenyon said. "Come on. I'm . . ."

"Me too," Julian panted as he leaned back, and gripping Kenyon's knee, positioned himself, sliding in one miniscule inch at a time.

There was nothing on earth like being fucked by Julian.

He was slow, he was deliberate, he had an insane amount of self-control when he was in charge and the tables were turned, and it seemed to be his goal to wring every bit of pleasure out of Kenyon that he could.

Tonight was the same, but different, too.

Julian's strokes were as smooth and well-controlled as ever, sending Kenyon into a gasping, groaning mess. But he was shaking too, his fingers trembling on his skin. His head thrown back, his bottom lip bitten red.

Neither of them was going to last, Kenyon realized, at almost the second he *did* lose it. It felt so goddamn good, he only needed a little to push him over the edge, and he reached down, barely grazing his hard, leaking cock with his thumb.

Normally, Julian would've batted his hand away.

But he leaned into it now, eyes fluttering closed as Kenyon fell into his orgasm, Julian moaning so loudly, hips stuttering so wildly, it was clear he'd followed right behind him.

Julian collapsed on the bed next to him, as usual not caring if they made a mess.

His eyes were soft as Kenyon's gaze met his own.

He shouldn't keep saying it, but the words came, unbidden. "I loved that. I love *you*," Kenyon murmured, reaching out and pulling Julian close, tucking him under his arm.

Julian sighed. "You keep saying that, and I'm gonna get mad at you."

"No, you won't," Kenyon said, and realized he believed it. Julian wouldn't. The words demolished his walls a little bit every time he said them.

That was what Julian hated.

He was exposed and vulnerable now.

But did he really hate it?

Feeling as Julian nuzzled closer, his lips brushing over Kenyon's skin, he realized he didn't. Not even a little. It was foreign to him. Strange, maybe. But Julian trusted him. Trusted that he'd keep his heart safe.

Trusted that Kenyon would worship him with the last breath in his body.

That he'd put him first.

That he'd love him with every single thing he had.

It was what had him so befuddled. Because nobody had ever done that for him before, and as far as Kenyon was concerned, that was a goddamn crime.

It was a crime that *he* hadn't realized at first what a treasure Julian was.

"No, I won't," Julian echoed, proving Kenyon's thoughts right. He traced a pattern on Kenyon's bicep with a fingertip. "I'm usually so in control, of everything."

"Of everyone," Kenyon corrected softly.

"Yeah, yeah, of everyone. But not you." Julian seemed mystified by this. "I'm . . . at your mercy and I don't hate it."

Because I love you.

This was why Kenyon didn't need Julian to return the words. He didn't have to, to make it abundantly clear he felt the exact same way.

"It was hot, you losing control like that," Kenyon said.

Julian smiled. "You make me lose control all the time."

"Yeah, but not when you fuck me."

"I can't . . ." Julian hesitated. "I can't compartmentalize you anymore."

He knew.

"There's part of me," Julian continued, "that wants it to go back to the way it was, but I wouldn't like that, would I?"

"Julian, I hate to tell you this, but it was *never* like you thought it was, between us."

Julian sighed.

And that was answer enough.

They lay there for a minute longer, and then Kenyon groaned as he finally straightened up, pulling a wad of tissues from the box next to the bed, and doing a rudimentary cleanup.

He'd take a shower, in a minute, Kenyon promised himself, but right now, it felt too good to lie here like this with Julian.

"You going to stay tonight?" he asked.

He knew the answer, but he asked anyway.

Julian shot him a look. "You want me to," he said.

It was hopeless to not be honest. "Yes."

Julian sighed again. More resigned this time.

"I guess it's too late to pretend that I don't want to."

"Not too late, but here's the thing," Kenyon said, pressing a quick kiss to Julian's forehead. "I want you to have what you want. That's most important to me. So if that's you leaving and going back to your apartment, that's fine. If it's you staying and making out with me in the shower and then sharing dinner naked, in this bed, then that's what it is."

Julian shot him a look. "You don't play fair, do you?"

"Did you want me to?" Kenyon grinned.

Julian didn't answer, but the gleam in his eyes as he got up and tugged at Kenyon's arm, was answer enough.

Chapter Seventeen

"They're gonna kill each other out there."

The thing was, Nikki didn't even sound displeased by the level of intensity happening on the field below them. She sounded like she *loved* it. More stories, more clicks, more ad revenue. Julian could follow, from one step to the next, her thought process.

If it wasn't his boyfriend down there, having the shit kicked out of him by the Condors, who'd shown up to the Piranhas stadium, ready to exact a pound of flesh for every indignity and embarrassment they'd suffered in their last game, maybe Julian would feel differently.

Maybe he'd be more like Nikki still, watching objectively, not giving a crap at how many cheap penalties and shots the Condors kept taking.

But deep down, Julian knew he wasn't like that.

It was painful to admit he just lacked that particular killer instinct, that he actually had a little more empathy than he'd ever imagined.

He could imagine Nikki laughing and telling him maybe he wasn't as cut out for sports journalism as she'd thought, if he'd found a soft spot in his armor.

It wasn't a soft spot, though, it was so much more than that.

It was his *heart*.

And, Julian wanted to believe discovering his most vital organ after ignoring it for the first twenty-six years of his life would actually make him a better journalist, but that was naive.

He couldn't hold back his grimace as one of the Condors' defensive ends slammed Kenyon down on the turf.

The Condors had already taken two "roughing the passer" penalties on Pax, and now apparently they'd moved on to Kenyon, playing as rough as Julian had ever seen.

He knew Kenyon would live through this, even as his heart pounded and protested the beating he was taking. But would the team live if all this intimidation and abuse worked and the Condors won?

Julian didn't know.

"If I didn't know any better, I'd say they have a hit out on Ellis," Nikki said.

How she could say it so cold-bloodedly, he didn't know.

He wanted to scream about how unfair it was, how shitty it was, how it went against every ounce of sportsmanship.

But then, it was clear the Condors hadn't ever cared about that, considering how they'd treated Davis Abernathy.

"Pax *and* Kenyon," Julian said reproachfully. "Pax is getting the shit kicked out of him."

After the last drive, which had been a hard-fought battle down the field, with three third-down conversions and even a fourth-down conversion that Pax had taken himself, running hard to get the last yard they'd needed for a new set of downs, had ended in a thirty-six-yard Dylan Leonard field goal, Pax had jogged back to the sideline and removed his helmet. Everyone had seen the blooming reddish-purple bruise on his cheek and the cut on his forehead.

Davis had looked absolutely furious as he'd sat down next to his quarterback and boyfriend.

Obviously, from up here in the media suite, he hadn't been able to hear what Davis was yelling about, but it was clear it wasn't *at* Pax. He hadn't done anything wrong. Well, he'd certainly confronted the Condors head-on, and not let them just run him over, but he was definitely the victim in this scenario.

Which, considering that Kenyon was apparently now the target, made Julian understand how Davis might feel about that.

Of course the Condors hadn't treated Julian like shit, and then signed a domestic abuser to take his job, bad-mouthing him to anyone who would listen, either.

Davis had plenty of reasons to be pissed off, and today's campaign against Pax was just the beginning.

"Think about what a great article this is gonna make, though," Nikki said, sounding excited about it, even as Julian's stomach roiled uncertainly. "And the interviews! We're going to be able to mine this, whether they win or lose."

"It's an epic battle," Julian agreed, weakly. And it was.

Good versus evil.

Right versus wrong.

Of course it wasn't ever as simple or as cut and dried as that, but watching it, watching the guys and the guy he loved—oh God, the guy he *loved*—out there, taking the beating, made it feel just that clear cut.

Because yeah, if he hadn't thought he'd loved Kenyon before, watching him like this, as he ran for another hard-won two yards, only to have the defensive end practically sit on him at the end . . . the sick, agonized feeling in the base of his stomach would convince him he couldn't be anything else but wildly, completely, totally in love.

"You don't sound that excited." Nikki's gaze narrowed. "Why?" It was technically a question, but it sounded more like a statement.

A declaration, even.

"It's crappy," Julian said. "There's no finesse. It's just brute strength trying to match with brute strength." He didn't add that when it came down to it, while the Piranhas were a strong team, they weren't defined by that strength.

They were crafty and sly, smart and prepared. They won with not only their strength, but with skill and intense prep work.

And no amount of practice could have prepared them for this.

Was this going to be the end of the Piranhas' completely unexpected and totally glorious season?

Julian knew it was bound to come to an end at some point, but he didn't want it to end this way. Not at the hands of *this* team.

"Come on, come on, stay sharp, stay with the game plan." Coach clapped as they walked—no, more like *slunk*—into the locker room at halftime.

Kenyon, who considered himself to be in the best shape of his life, sharp and fluid and conditioned, felt like he'd just been run over by a truck.

His ribs ached, his ankle, which he was pretty sure had at least a mild sprain, was killing him, and his head was pounding, his lungs burning.

He flopped down onto the locker room bench, next to Logan. His head was in his hands, and he looked exhausted. Sweat matted his hair to his skull, and his eyes were sunken, his skin gray.

He'd been battling as hard as any lineman Kenyon had ever witnessed, to keep the onslaught of the Condors' defensive line at bay, but it nearly hadn't been enough.

How many times had Pax been sacked?

Kenyon had lost count.

He'd lost count of how many times he'd been slammed into the grass, extra hard, for good measure.

Most teams didn't want to injure you. They just wanted to stop you.

But the Condors?

They wanted revenge.

To them, the best way of winning this game would be to knock Pax out. To knock Tristan out. To knock Wade out.

To knock him out.

Well, he was made of stronger stuff than that. He wasn't going to give in, and let them push him around.

So they were tackling dirty. He was just as strong, just as tough. He could give it right back.

Maybe.

"I know you're tired, this game is . . ." Coach trailed off, and Kenyon saw him glance over at Beau, who looked equally as frazzled.

They'd expected a similar version of the Condors team they'd faced a month or two back.

They had not expected the Condors to come out fighting so viciously, though maybe they should've.

It was the biggest miscalculation Coach had made all year.

Sure, he always expected opponents to play them tough, but he also had an inherent streak of absolute fairness in him.

It never would have occurred to him to play dirty.

Or that a team would show up to play them, and intend for it to be as dirty as possible.

It went against everything that Coach was.

Everything Coach had ever told them about playing the game of football.

"This is war," Beau spoke up. "This is war, but it's a war we can win. We're only down three. We just have to hang with them."

Davis' face, every time Kenyon had glanced over at him during the game, had been a mask of anger and frustration.

And ultimately, resignation.

He alone, Kenyon realized, had worried about this possibility.

Not that he wouldn't fight it. Not that every single one of them wouldn't fight it with the last bit of energy they possessed, but sometimes it just wasn't enough.

If you start to think that way, you've already lost.

Kenyon could hear Julian's admonishing voice in his head, telling him a truth he didn't want to hear.

A truth he wasn't ready to face.

He dragged himself up, his ankle aching.

"Beau's right," he said, pitching his voice so it carried to every bit of the locker room. "We have to fight. We can win this. We *need* to win this."

I don't want this to be my last game. Logan, dejected and gray. Pax floundering. Me, hurting.

It had ended that way for so many players out there, he knew it. Quarterbacks who'd thrown one last pass, and it was picked off. Running backs tackled for a loss. Receivers who'd let the ball just barely graze their fingertips before it fell away, un-caught.

Kenyon felt the energy in the room perk up a little. He kept talking. Maybe this was what they needed. One of their own to believe.

"We won two games last year. *Two.* If we win this game," Kenyon said, raising his voice, "we're going to win as many *playoff games* as we won regular season games. This team is my family, and I'll give the last bit that I have, to you guys, because when we came together, everything changed." He turned to Pax. "You became our leader. Found the confidence to stand tall, that you didn't have before. We got rookies. We got veterans. And we all came together for one purpose. To win, yeah, and we're going to do everything we can today to grind out the win we want, so we don't go home, but it's more than that. You know what our purpose is? It's each other. It's Logan and Rob and the rest of the linemen blocking so I can get another yard. It's Wade, throwing his body out there, so he can get the first down. It's Pax, pushing himself to find every single damn opening he can find. It's Coach, always believing in us, and never letting us down."

Kenyon took a breath. It was a long speech, and an even longer speech for him.

But the whole team was upright now, they were all staring at him, and there was a palpable energy and excitement that there hadn't been only a few minutes earlier.

"Two more quarters, guys, and if you hold on for those two quarters, play your fucking hearts out and refuse to bend to the Condors' will, we'll defy every expectation, every odd, every pronouncement. Don't you want to prove them wrong? Because I sure as hell do. But even more than that, I want it for us. Because we've earned it."

A cheer went up through the locker room.

Coach came over and patted him on the shoulder. "I couldn't have said it better myself," he said. "Let's go Piranhas!"

It was clear when they took the field again, the Miami fans cheering for them as they came out of the locker room tunnel, that the Condors hadn't expected it.

They'd expected them to slink out defeated, tired, washed up, kind of like they'd been at the end of the half.

We're made of stronger stuff than that, assholes, Kenyon thought as he did his warmup stretches, ignoring the painful throb of his ankle. He'd iced it, after his big speech, and one of the medical guys had asked him if he wanted a shot, to dull the pain, help him get through the rest of the game, but he'd said no.

He didn't like the way those shots made him numb. Unresponsive. And his ankles were his greatest asset—they allowed him to pivot on a dime. To change course to a better path. To will this team to victory. If he was numb, he wouldn't be as sharp.

He wouldn't be able to get it done the same way.

So, he warmed up and ignored the pain. In his ankle. In his ribs. Focused only on the field and the feel of the ball in his hands.

Even the thought of Julian, up in the media booth watching him, faded away.

Everything but the next play, the next carry, the next first down.

The first drive after halftime, the Piranhas' offense moved the ball pretty well. It was still a struggle, there was no question about that, but Kenyon could see the whole team coming together, working their hardest, the moment they faltered, someone else stepping up.

Pax was sharp, throwing first for a twenty-yard gain to Tristan, and then Kenyon got the next two carries, eking out a four-yard carry, and then digging in, he pushed, spinning through the line, darting to the left, and then again to the right, weaving through the defensive tackles, just eluding their grasp, and then finally, they brought him down with a sharp tug of his jersey, after what Kenyon thought had to be at least a ten-yard carry.

Thirteen, actually, he realized as he glanced up at the scoreboard.

The rest of the drive they moved the ball the same way. Sometimes getting stopped, but never giving up, pushing and pressing for every single goddamn yard.

Finally, the unit made it to the red zone. It had been a long drive. Kenyon's breath was short, every hard intake making his lungs ache, but the pain focused him.

Made him want it even more.

They thought they could intimidate him. Knock him out. They were so fucking wrong.

Pax dropped back, and Kenyon blocked, as well as he could block a two-hundred-and-fifty-pound linebacker, trying with every ounce of will to get through Kenyon and to his quarterback.

But Kenyon refused to budge, setting his feet in the ground and using all his strength to push back.

The ball flew out of Pax's hands and into Wade's, who evaded two defensive players who would've tackled him, jumped over a third and went crashing through the fourth right into the end zone.

It was way too fucking easy to forget about the pain in his ankle and his ribs as he and the rest of the offense ran towards the end zone, Logan lifting Wade up as he fist-pumped into the air.

After the celebration ended, they all jogged back to their sideline, which was electrified. Davis was the most emotional Kenyon had seen him in ages—maybe *ever*—putting both of his hands on Pax's shoulders, as they shared a moment.

"Goddamn, that was a great drive," Coach exclaimed, distributing shoulder pats and butt slaps around the guys, making sure they all knew how important the seven points they'd just scored had been.

But he didn't need to, because they all knew.

Somehow this drive hadn't just become win or lose and go home.

Or one team against another.

But good versus evil.

Legitimate sportsmanship versus none at all.

Kenyon knew they all felt it.

He flopped down on the bench, his lungs burning with each fragmented breath, his ankle aching like a bitch.

Two more quarters, he told himself. *It's just pain. You can play through it. You've done it before.*

But the two more quarters proved to be a grind that challenged even Kenyon's toughness.

The defense stiffened again, the linebackers overwhelming the line, until Pax was running for his life nearly every play, and every time Kenyon touched the ball, he was lucky to grind a yard or two out.

The only silver lining was that the Piranhas' defense, struggling to find an identity and to fully utilize all its pieces for the whole season, had seemingly come together as one cohesive unit, and they were playing fucking lights out.

Still, even though they bent, but never broke, pushing Tom Taylor and the Condors to the brink every single time they took to the field, Kenyon could read the exhaustion in every defensive player's face as they returned to the sidelines.

At some point, something was going to break, and it might be the Piranhas.

And if they did, the Condors would score, taking the lead, and with the clock ticking away, the number of chances the Piranhas would get dwindling down, a heavy panicked weight settled in Kenyon's stomach.

They needed to make something happen this drive, he thought, as they took to the field, the scoreboard proclaiming there were only six minutes to go.

If they scored a touchdown, they'd be up two scores.

It wasn't enough, not when faced with Taylor and the normally explosive Condors offense, but it would *have* to be, today, if they had any hope of making it through this game and making it to the AFC Championship.

"Nice long drive, that's what we need," Pax told the huddle. "But you take what you can get, okay? I know you guys are gettin' beat up out there."

"Not like you aren't," Tristan said.

Pax just shrugged, brushing it off.

It was really unbelievable, seeing the change between him today, and this time last year. He'd been dejected and anxious, a complete wreck, because nobody, even Pax, had believed he could be a franchise quarterback in the NFL.

"We're gonna get it done," he said, with confidence. With certainty.

Like he truly believed it.

And as he met every single player's eyes around him, going from one to the next in the huddle, Kenyon saw him transfer a little of that belief to them too.

Pax held his eyes last. "One last drive," he said.

Kenyon knew he wasn't the only one hurting. Pax had to be one big bruise, but he couldn't see any of that in his eyes. Only rock-solid belief, not only in himself, but in this team.

"One last drive," Kenyon agreed.

They were not only trying to score, but to use more time, which meant that he'd get the ball as much as Coach Randy felt comfortable with.

Kenyon bent over, waiting for the snap, and the handoff, and steadied his breathing. Focusing. Dug his cleats into the turf, and the moment Logan snapped the ball, he took off, feeling the ball hit him right in the stomach. He gripped it hard, and ran hard, whipping around Rob, and through the line, dodging a defensive lineman there, and spinning past another, cutting back and finding his lane, legs churning, breath fracturing in his chest.

He saw the safety crossing over to him only a moment before he was on him, tackling Kenyon to the ground.

He hit with a breathless gasp but hung on to the ball even though the pain shot through him in a dizzying rush.

Definitely bruised ribs, if he was lucky.

If he wasn't lucky . . . well, he wasn't going to think about that right now, because they had a game to win.

Then he did it again and again, slowly but surely moving them downfield in a chunk here, five yards there. Every once in awhile, Pax would mix in a pass, or even a designed run of his own, hoping to keep the Condors on their toes.

It was an impossible grind, a painful drive, taking the rest of everything they had left. Kenyon knew it. He saw the players' eyes in the huddle, the draining energy in their gazes.

The way they were pinning every single hope on this one drive.

On the thirty-yard line, the drive stalled.

Third down and twelve.

Kenyon had been tackled for a loss, as a defensive end had shot the gap on first down. Then Pax had tried a pass that the safety had batted down.

They lined up, Kenyon knowing he'd be called on to block this down, so Pax would have as much time as possible to throw.

The end zone, Kenyon realized as Pax called the play. *We're going for the end zone.*

Maybe they'd gotten a little cocky. Sure of themselves. Believing so completely in their own skill and capability that they thought they could finish the Condors off now.

Pax dropped back, scrambling to his left, Kenyon with his hands full with a defensive back almost twice his size, doing his best to hold him even for a few precious seconds.

He didn't see Pax throw the ball.

Or Tristan try to catch it, only to have it knocked away at the last second.

But he saw Tristan's dejected face as they headed back to the bench together.

Saw his anxiety as Dylan jogged out onto the field to make a field goal.

It wouldn't give the Piranhas a two-score lead.

But when he hit the ball right through the uprights, as solid as a fucking rock, it did give the Piranhas a seven-point lead.

The defense would have to hold the Condors one last time. There was just over three minutes on the clock.

"I should've caught it," Tristan muttered as he dropped to the bench next to Kenyon.

"Nobody could've caught that ball, I'm telling you," Wade said, from his other side. "Stop beatin' yourself up, okay?"

"Yeah, you had that one great catch earlier. I didn't know how you even stayed in bounds, it was a real toe-touch catch," Kenyon reminded him. But Tristan's dejected expression didn't waver.

"I think you're only allowed one magnificent career-making catch a drive," Wade said wryly, reaching out and wrapping his big arm around Tristan's shoulders. "It was a hard game."

"It *is* a hard game," Kenyon reminded them. It wasn't over yet.

The defense was going out there, and maybe they'd pull out a miracle.

They'd *need* one.

"I just hate sitting and watching and knowing there's nothing else I can do," Tristan said.

Kenyon felt it as the minutes ticked by.

It wasn't like the defense was giving Taylor and the Condors much to work with, but they were making plays happen anyway. One miracle catch. Then their running back broke through containment for a fifteen-yard gain.

Slowly but surely, they moved down the field, too. Just like the Piranhas did.

And then they were at the twenty-five-yard line, and Kenyon didn't think he could watch anymore. It hurt too much.

They'd given everything, and it hadn't been enough.

Don't give up yet, that voice in his head that sounded exactly like Julian reminded him. *They've got something left. They haven't gotten into the end zone yet.*

But they were right there, knocking on the door.

First and goal.

Then second and goal, Sebastian coming up to tackle the running back before he could barely get a chance to grab the ball.

Third and goal. Taylor scrambled around, the Piranhas' linebackers in pursuit, and eventually tossed the ball away.

Fourth and goal.

Taylor launched a pass right down the line, a laser shot, right to the corner of the end zone, right to where Micah was defending their best wide receiver.

They sprinted down the sideline, and Kenyon didn't think he breathed as at the exact perfect moment, Micah turned, and jumped, a half a second ahead of the receiver, and he came down with the ball.

The sideline erupted, everyone jumping and cheering at the last-second save.

Kenyon saw, though, before the view was totally obscured by a laughing and crying Tristan, that Micah was kneeling in the end zone, time expiring, with four fingers held up on his right hand.

One last tribute to Davis.

He'd come so far from that angry, punk kid who hadn't wanted to be part of a team, who'd believed he was an island.

But he wasn't anymore.

That, Kenyon thought, as he wiped away a few tears of his own and watched the whole defense gather in the end zone, all holding up their fingers for Davis, felt righter than anything else.

Chapter Eighteen

"Are you really sure this is a good idea?" Julian asked as they got out of the Uber.

"Introducing you to my teammates?" Kenyon shrugged, apparently over having this discussion. When he'd found out, after the game, that Davis had issued Julian another invite to the Piranhas' victory party on Monday night, he'd insisted that this time, Julian should come with him. "Nobody's gonna tell your boss," he'd said.

It wasn't like Julian didn't believe him. He did. It wasn't like any of the Piranhas were going to go running to Nikki to tell her the truth about Julian's relationship with Kenyon. But this was a big step. A *serious* step, and even though Julian knew he was ready, there was still that little warning bell at the back of his mind going off. *What if it goes wrong? What if Kenyon gets tired of you? What if you can't find a new job? What if you become aimless and your general dissatisfaction with everything ruins you and Kenyon?*

They were fears he couldn't quite dismiss.

But he was afraid Kenyon was really fucking tired of reassuring him—God knew he was tired of reassuring himself—so instead of admitting that had been exactly what he'd meant, he said, "No, your ankle . . . your ribs . . . should you really be out celebrating?"

"You're worse than Logan, and that's saying something," Kenyon said, but his voice was affectionate, and his gaze as it latched on to Julian loving as they walked up to the Hibiscus entrance. "I'm gonna be fine. I promise I will sit most of the night, and you can fetch me drinks like a good little boyfriend."

Julian made a face.

"Seriously, I can't spend the next seven days in an ice bath. It'll be fine. Either I'm ready to play or . . ."

Kenyon didn't finish that sentence, because Julian knew he wasn't ready to face the alternative.

He was a reporter, and as a result, was intimately familiar with the Piranhas' injury report. He wrote articles about it nearly every day. Especially this week, as the whole NFL was interested to see who exactly would be facing the Riptide in next week's AFC showdown.

Right now Kenyon wasn't practicing. He was listed as doubtful.

They hadn't really talked about it, because Julian didn't know how to even begin.

The one time he'd really thought about the possibility that the man he loved might not play in his last game, not be standing in solidarity with the brothers he loved, he'd gotten real choked up about it. And if he nearly cried just *thinking* about it, there was no way he could look at Kenyon and talk about it.

Even if Kenyon really *should* talk about how there was no question if he'd rather sit on the sidelines and just cheer his teammates on versus take the field—but in the end, he might not have a choice. He had a bad ankle, and bruised ribs. Those weren't minor injuries.

Julian wasn't a doctor, but he could see the nasty bruising on Kenyon's ankle. The swath of colorful patches across his midsection.

The way Kenyon moved slowly and deliberately.

The pain flashing in his eyes when he didn't.

Another reporter might not have the personal view he did, now. But now that he did, Julian couldn't write about the Piranhas in the same detached way. He just couldn't.

Nikki had slashed four sentences from today's practice recap, in the paragraph where he'd talked about the injury report, and who wasn't practicing.

"What's wrong with you?" she'd texted. "You aren't usually this *nice*."

That had stung.

He could be nice. It wasn't wrong to look over at Kenyon, and the hesitant way he was climbing the stairs, and feel something in the general chest region about it.

But he wasn't ready to tell Nikki the truth—or to tell her to go to hell.

"Come on," Julian said, faking enthusiasm. "Let's go get you settled, okay? And I'll grab us some drinks."

"Not so fast on the grabbing drinks," Kenyon said, whipping out a hand and latching resolutely onto Julian's arm, a reminder that while he might be injured, he wasn't weak in the least. "I wanna show you off, first." His gaze skimmed Julian's tight jeans, his blue short-sleeved button-up, and the way it hugged his chest, and Julian had to swallow hard.

He knew what that look meant.

Kenyon was totally picturing him naked.

Imagining stripping his clothes off one piece at a time, as slowly as Julian could handle.

He knew from looking in the mirror that he looked good, but there was no proof like that look in Kenyon's eyes to know for sure.

"You mean, you wanna tell everyone," Julian hissed under his breath.

"Yeah, I'm happy to be yours, and I think you're pretty happy to be mine," Kenyon retorted with a grin.

"Yeah, yeah," Julian teased, but the truth was, he *was*. Proud and happy and terrified, sure, but the fear only existed because the future was so unknown.

Would they hold on to each other like Pax and Davis had? Or would they fall apart because Julian was too fucking neurotic to have something good and real and true in his life?

"You keep thinkin' I'm gonna leave, if you get too *Julian*," Kenyon murmured under his breath, his arm turning from a leash keeping Julian tied to him to a caress as he led him towards where a lot of players were gathered on the set of low-slung couches near the dance floor. "But you miss that the *Julian* part is the part I love."

"The only part?" Julian asked archly, changing the subject, because the earnestness in Kenyon's voice made his throat close over with emotion.

He wanted so badly to trust nothing could fuck this up.

The problem was that was entirely out of his realm of experience.

"Hey, Logan. Dylan." Kenyon nodded towards their center and his boyfriend, the Piranhas' kicker. "Wade. Tristan."

Tristan's eyes narrowed in on the way Kenyon was holding Julian's hand.

"What's this?" he asked archly.

"Something a long time coming," Kenyon admitted. "I know that y'all know Julian."

"This is *reporter* Julian, isn't it?" Logan questioned.

"Yeah, I'm a reporter," Julian said. "Don't worry, your coach already knows, and he hasn't tried to kill me yet, so I think I might be safe."

"That's 'cause he's sneaky," Tristan said, leaning forward, eyes gleaming. "He's waiting until you're nice and relaxed."

"Real complacent," Wade added with a nod. "And then *boom*, he's gonna get you."

"Coach knows everything," Logan said sagely. "But hey, we're happy for you. Kenyon's been real happy these last few months, and we *knew* something was going on."

"You did?" Kenyon looked surprised as he took a seat next to Logan.

"Oh yeah," Logan said knowingly. "We knew."

Dylan elbowed him, hard. "You did not know. You aren't Coach, you don't know *everything*."

"Okay, not *everything*," Logan conceded.

"So you gonna tell us how you ended up falling for a re-porter?" Tristan asked. "'Cause I don't know about the rest of you who apparently know *everything*, but I sure don't, and I'm hella curious."

"I'm . . ." Julian didn't really want to witness the recitation of how messed up they'd started out. How he'd kept Kenyon at arm's length even though he'd known, deep down, that he felt something. "I should go grab us some drinks . . ."

But Kenyon looked up at him, dark eyes pleading, and Julian realized, as certain as he'd sounded about taking this step, he was still nervous.

It was easy to forget, with all his easy natural confidence, that Kenyon hadn't done this before, either. They were both rookies at this relationship thing.

"Or," Wade said, flashing him a smile, "you could stay, and wait for the waitress to come around."

"Yeah, come sit down," Logan said. He scooted over, and patted the couch next to him. "Unless you're afraid of us?"

Julian shot him a look. He should've guessed how this would go.

"Hardly," he scoffed.

"Julian's not afraid of anything," Kenyon pointed out dryly. "He's more the *bust your balls* type."

"Who is?" Beau arrived then, Sebastian trailing after them, holding a huge bucket filled with ice and beer bottles.

"Dig in," Sebastian said, setting the bucket onto the table in front of them. "You want one, Kenyon?"

"Sure," Kenyon said, settling back into the couch. Julian realized he'd asked him specifically so his idiot boyfriend wouldn't get up and put more pressure on his ankle.

"Oh, hey, Julian, I didn't see you there," Beau said, sitting down across from him.

"Kenyon's telling us how Julian likes to do . . . well, *something*, with his balls," Tristan teased.

Beau's eyebrows rose nearly to his hairline. "Oh? That's . . . that's new, isn't it?"

"Not that new, I don't think."

Julian glanced up, to see Davis and Pax arriving. Everyone shifted on the couches, making room for their quarterback and his coach.

"Seriously? You told *them*!" Tristan exclaimed.

"More like I guessed," Davis said dryly.

"And he told *me*," Pax said with a chuckle.

"Of course he did," Tristan grumbled.

"You want to hear about it or not?" Kenyon interrupted. "'Cause we can definitely *not* share details . . ."

"No, no, I'm curious now," Beau said. "Does my dad . . ."

"He knows," Julian said. He'd almost lied, because wasn't it weird that Coach hadn't told Beau? But then . . . he'd said it was their secret, and Julian supposed that when Coach made a promise, he kept it. Even when it involved his own son. "He figured it out."

"Of course he did," Sebastian said. "Nothing's a secret from that man. Did you think he was gonna kill you?"

"He *still* might kill him," Tristan warned. "Like I said, Coach is sneaky. Lull you into complacency and then . . . *strike*."

Beau laughed. "I'm gonna have to tell him that one."

"Just make sure he doesn't bury you under the field," Sebastian chimed in.

Dylan blanched. "Tell me this isn't a thing. Coach wouldn't do that."

"He wouldn't have dared threaten you," Beau said, still chuckling. "Logan would have his ass, and he knew it. Besides, we all knew y'all were dating before you did. He couldn't really be mad about that."

"I think," Kenyon said, "he wasn't really mad when he found out about anyone dating, actually."

"I don't know," Davis said. "I told him about me and Pax at eight in the morning and at first he said nothing, just went and grabbed a beer."

There was a round of *ahhhhhs* around the circle, punctuated with more laughter.

"So what *did* Coach say to you two?" Sebastian asked, cracking open a beer of his own, after distributing half the bucket around the group.

"Uh, well . . ." Julian had told himself he could tell the truth without issues. After all, hadn't he faced Coach and had zero issue telling him he and Kenyon were just fucking?

"Oh, you don't want to know." Kenyon's voice was wry. "He insisted we were just fucking."

"*No*," Tristan said in a dramatic voice. "He said . . . to *Coach*?"

Kenyon nodded. "It was . . . well, it was true at some point, and it was kinda sweet, babe, how you wanted to protect me, but . . ."

"Oh my God," Dylan said. "I would . . . just die. Drop through the floor and die."

"Hey, you didn't get *interrupted* a few months back, with Coach knocking on your door, and telling you to turn it down," Wade said.

"Yeah, whose fault is that," Davis stated, rather than asked. Because they all knew the answer.

"He actually did catch me, sneaking out to Julian's room, once, and it was really, really awkward," Kenyon said. "Made even more awkward by the fact that he was totally sneaking off to Coach Scott's room."

Beau groaned. "I did not need to know that."

"Yeah," Sebastian said with an understanding grin. "We know. You already know too much."

"Seriously," Beau said earnestly. "You didn't see Scott wearing *only* an apron, making out with my dad."

"I told you, you should've taken a picture," Tristan wailed. "Have you *seen* that man's ass?"

"Unfortunately yes," Beau said, nodding gravely. "And if he was *your* surrogate father, you wouldn't be so excited about it."

"So I guess you figured out how it wasn't just sex, then?" Davis asked Kenyon, the corner of his mouth quirking up.

Julian frowned. "You told Davis it was just sex?"

"You *insisted* about a hundred times it was just sex, babe," Kenyon teased him. "You're mad I told *one* person that?"

Julian rolled his eyes. "No. Of course not. I wouldn't be mad about that. No way."

He kinda was, though.

Even though he *knew* better.

"Yeah, Julian's not afraid of anything," Logan teased. "Except maybe feelings?"

Julian considered this. Didn't like it. But could see the argument. "Fair," he admitted. "That's fair."

"More than fair," Kenyon argued. "You wouldn't even kiss me!"

Julian set his beer bottle down. "You didn't *say* you wanted to kiss me!"

Kenyon rolled his eyes, shooting him a loving, playful look. "I didn't think I *needed* to. It was fucking obvious."

"No shit," Pax said.

"What? Not you too," Tristan said with resignation. "How did I get so disconnected from the best team gossip?"

"Too busy fucking your boyfriend," Beau said.

Tristan made a scandalized noise.

But from what Julian had heard, that was *also* true.

"In their defense, once Davis told me his suspicions, it *was* kinda obvious," Pax said, almost apologetically. "In the press conference, you wouldn't even look Kenyon's way. But with the rest of us? You were so hyper-focused. It was just . . . well, it was obvious."

"I'm gonna guess the no-kissing thing didn't last that long," Logan said.

"Yeah, I think *you* lasted less than a week, after we 'practice kissed,'" Dylan teased his boyfriend, making air quotes with his hands.

Logan rolled his eyes. "You start practice kissing, that's a slippery slope, just saying. And I was *not* the one to suggest we try it."

"Uh, actually about six months," Kenyon answered Dylan's question, and in response to everyone's shocked gasp, he continued. "I know, I can barely believe it either."

"Me either," Julian admitted, exchanging glances with Kenyon.

How many times had he wanted to kiss him and hadn't?

Way too many.

If he'd been smarter, he wouldn't have been nearly as stubborn.

"I don't know, I think I need to see some real-life proof," Logan said, the doubt in his voice in direct conflict with the twinkle in his eyes.

Julian raised an eyebrow, and Kenyon smiled. It was all the encouragement he needed. Setting down his beer, he crossed over to the other couch, and leaned over, Kenyon's arm snaking around his waist and tugging him closer as their lips met.

Julian had intended to keep it fairly G-rated, as this was their first public kiss, and their first kiss around Kenyon's teammates, but it was clear from the first moment Kenyon's mouth met his, that he had no intention of playing it safe.

Julian groaned in the back of his throat as Kenyon tugged him closer, tilting his head a little so his tongue could move deeper.

When he finally pulled back, everyone was grinning widely.

"Fuck," Tristan said. He stood. "Come on, Wade, I think there is . . . uh . . . something I need you to look at. Right now."

"You know what that means?" Logan asked as Julian settled back down onto the couch. Picked up his beer. His throat suddenly felt dry, and his pants too tight.

"What?" Julian really didn't know.

"It means that you're one of us now," Logan said kindly. "Not just because of Kenyon, though we'd accept any guy he brought around. Any guy that made him happy. But you're one of us because you're officially awesome. And extra bonus, you've turned Tristan on. In case you didn't know, that's like the test that you didn't realize you had to pass."

Julian could barely process that sentiment. For a time, when he'd been in college, he'd been part of a team. And he hadn't realized how much he'd missed that, when he'd moved from playing football to just reporting about it.

Nikki probably would say they were a team, but Julian knew better.

The moment he didn't do something she wanted—or even worse, did something she didn't like—she'd cut him out. And that wasn't the way you treated a teammate.

"Someone should warn Coach that the bathroom will be occupied for the next . . ." Pax checked his watch. "Ten minutes."

"Fifteen, at least," Davis argued. "I saw that gleam in Tristan's eyes."

"Good news," Julian pointed out. "The door definitely locks."

Beau started to laugh. "Of course you know it does."

Kenyon shrugged innocently. "I won't take a poll of everyone who knows that the door locks, but I bet there isn't a clueless person here."

Even Pax and Davis looked sheepish.

"Hey, at least we aren't fucking in the quarterback room," Pax offered weakly.

"Small blessings," Beau said. He turned to Julian. "Something about you is so familiar. Did you play college ball?"

He was half tempted to lie about it, but the truth was out there, easily google-able for anyone with two hands and a Wi-Fi connection.

"Yeah, I did. For Northwestern," Julian admitted.

"Huh. That must not be it, then. We never played Northwestern." Beau hummed out loud. "I really can't place it. But there's something . . . something about your voice."

Julian didn't know he'd gotten so attuned to Kenyon, but he was now, it was undeniable. Especially when he felt Kenyon tense, all the way on the other couch.

"I'm sure you'll figure it out," Sebastian said, wrapping an arm around his shoulders. "You're like a goddamn bloodhound. Nothing stays a secret for long."

"Chip off the old block that way, huh?" Beau said sarcastically.

"Absolutely." Sebastian said it with feeling. Like it was a beautiful thing. Like it was something he loved about Beau.

And that, Julian realized, was what Kenyon meant when he said he loved Julian *for* his Julian-ness, not in spite of it.

Other people would have been put off, or been suspicious of Beau's constant digging for the truth but Sebastian liked it. He *loved* it.

Julian might not be brilliant yet at feelings, but he was getting better at them.

He glanced across the table at Kenyon, whose gaze was on him, warm and accepting.

Little bit at a time, I don't care how long it takes, he could imagine Kenyon saying, if they were alone, *as long as you're mine, and I'm yours.*

That was why this mattered, Julian thought. Why it mattered to be able to tell the people who mattered to them. Well, he amended wryly, the people who mattered to Kenyon. He was still trying to find his people. Or maybe he'd just begun to get to know them.

He certainly hadn't expected to have any of these guys accept him as readily and quickly as they had.

"Wait." Beau's voice was tight. Anticipatory. "I think I've got it." He looked over at Julian, and in that moment, Julian thought he might have realized the truth, too.

Kenyon must have showed Beau the video he'd made. With his voiceover, talking through the analysis.

Beau had just realized that was *his* voice.

Well, the good news was that if he got fired, it wouldn't be completely out of the blue. He'd totally fucking expect it.

To Julian's shock, Beau didn't say a word. Just swallowed the realization and shot Sebastian a brilliant smile. "Come on," he said. "You haven't danced with me yet tonight."

Slowly, the rest of the group dispersed, leaving just Julian and Kenyon. He'd joined Kenyon on the other couch, surprisingly enjoying the way his arm curled around his shoulders. Before, he'd have argued it would've felt like Kenyon was publicly staking his claim, but in reality, it just felt . . . nice. Like Kenyon was proud of him and happy with him, and happy to *be* with him.

"You showed Beau that video, didn't you?" Julian asked in a low voice.

Felt Kenyon tense again.

"If I did?"

Julian hadn't told him not to. But then he never would've expected that he would. It seemed the opposite of circumspect.

"We really sucked at keeping this a secret," Julian said flatly.

"Hey, in my defense, it was just your voice, and Beau wasn't as familiar with you then as he is now. And we *did* keep it under wraps for six months. That's pretty good."

"I guess it doesn't matter now." Julian accepted he was almost definitely going to get fired. "His dad knows. He knows. He just didn't know . . . well, about that."

"He thought it was a really solid piece of work, and honestly? It was. You know it was. There's nothing to be ashamed about."

Julian raised an eyebrow. "Even if it was really to get your attention?"

"Worked, didn't it?" Kenyon grinned.

It sure had. Way better than he'd ever imagined when he'd been putting it together.

"Hey," Kenyon continued, his expression growing concerned, "if you're worried, it's going to be okay. I promise you, Beau won't make a big deal out of this. In the bigger scheme of things, it hardly matters what you did or didn't do to point out all my flaws."

"I guess." Julian could hear the dubiousness in his own voice.

"Come on," Kenyon said, tugging him closer. "This is our celebration. Not just the Piranhas' victory party, but our coming out. I've got you, you know that."

Julian did.

And he was really beginning to understand what that truly meant.

CHAPTER
NINETEEN

JULIAN WAS JUST PACKING up his stuff after the press conference, right before the team flew to Los Angeles for the
AFC Championship, when Beau stuck his head into the media
room and blew all his well-designed, thought-out platitudes
about how it wasn't going to be a big deal if Beau knew the
truth, to absolute bits.

"Hey, you got a minute?" he asked Julian.

Julian tried not to look suspicious.

He did consider saying that no, he did not.

But he did, and Beau probably already knew it, and pretending he wasn't free was only going to prolong the agony.

"Sure," Julian said. He swung his bag over his shoulder, said
a quick goodbye to Ed, and followed Beau out into the hallway.

"Thought I'd grab a coffee and that we could chat," Beau
said. His voice was free of any inflection, no judgment, no
anger whatsoever.

But it was still incredibly hard for Julian not to tense.

When would he stop seeing the worst around every corner?

When good shit starts really happening for you, his brain
supplied.

Good shit *was* happening for him now. He and Kenyon had found each other, and had dispensed with the stupid charade of just sex. He was good at his job. About to get fired, probably, but good enough, with a high enough profile he could probably get another one. And he had *friends* now. A team, watching his back.

Why then did he feel like it was all one bad moment from being jerked away? Why couldn't he trust it?

Julian knew how the other players had begun to feel about him. How he was becoming folded into their family. But would they feel the same way about him—would *Beau* feel the same way—if they realized just how far he'd gone after the podcast interview? If they all found out about the video?

"Hey, feel free to help yourself to coffee," Beau said as he headed to the coffee station in the cafeteria, pouring himself a cup.

Julian already felt jittery enough with nerves, but he still filled a paper cup, preferring to keep it black.

He sat down opposite Beau and tapped his fingers nervously on the tabletop while Beau doctored his coffee with cream and sugar.

Finally, he leaned back in his chair and regarded Julian with a speculative glance.

"I looked up your college stats," he said.

That was not exactly how Julian had expected this to begin, but Beau was smart. Slippery, like his dad, but really fucking smart, too. He'd planned this, whatever *this* was, that much was clear.

Beau continued, not giving Julian a chance to answer or ask why the hell he cared what he'd done in college. "You started two years at Northwestern and were a backup for a third. You shortlisted for the Doak Walker award. And you didn't come out in the draft. Didn't even go to the combine. They wouldn't confirm you'd been invited, when I asked, but I can't imagine you weren't invited."

He'd been asked to the combine, just as Beau suspected, and turning the invitation down had been one of the toughest things he'd ever done. He'd wanted it, so fucking bad, but he'd known he wouldn't make it. He'd go in a later round, probably barely make an opening day roster, maybe get cut by half a dozen teams a half dozen times, and jump from practice squad to practice squad before finally, nobody really wanted him at all, and he faded into obscurity.

That was never how he'd wanted his career to go.

Now, he could've switched to journalism after a handful of years trying to make it in the NFL, but he'd decided against that because if he was going to commit to making this change, he needed to *commit*.

Plus, there'd been Nikki, encouraging him to intern for her, and painting a picture of a brilliant future.

She hadn't lied. Not exactly. He *did* have a potentially brilliant future ahead of him, and if he hadn't met Kenyon, hadn't fallen in love with him, he probably would have continued on that exact same path Nikki had planned for him to take.

But no longer.

"I was invited," Julian said. He considered lying. He considered declining to answer, but if he drew this out, he had a feeling it would only feel worse. "I decided not to go. That wasn't the right future for me."

"See, that's where we disagree. You were an *exceptionally* productive running back. Undersized maybe, and quick rather than fast, but you made yards where any other back would've been tackled for a loss." Beau leaned forward, eyes suddenly gleaming with interest. "You studied a hell of a lot of film, didn't you?"

Julian shifted in his seat. This conversation had only ever been headed one direction, but now they were heading there in earnest. "Yes."

"Because you were undersized. And quick."

"Partly, yeah. I had decent instincts, but they were even better when I primed them with information, so to speak," Julian admitted.

At least that was something Beau couldn't fault him for.

"You also did that video Kenyon had, a month or two back, didn't you?"

Here it was.

Julian really considered saying it hadn't been him, but Beau *knew*. And not just because he'd apparently recognized his voice, but because he'd done his research after, and he knew exactly why Julian could put something like that together.

He nodded.

"I thought so," Beau said with satisfaction. "It was brilliant, by the way. Absolutely fucking brilliant."

That was *not* what he'd expected Beau to say.

Julian took a sip of coffee to try to cover up his surprise.

"It was . . ." He cleared his throat. "It was a stupid thing to do."

Beau leaned in, elbows settling onto the table. "You were right, though."

"It wasn't my place."

"You did it because he didn't believe what you said about him on that podcast, yeah?"

It was annoying and a little bit painful how this guy kept digging and just refused to stop. Julian probably hated it more than anything because the person it reminded him of most was himself.

Fucking hell.

"Why does it matter?" Julian retorted.

"I bet too that when I sent over the film for Kenyon to study, he didn't analyze it alone, did he?" Beau didn't answer his question, but instead asked another one.

Julian refused to let himself squirm under the intensity of Beau's gaze.

The way he seemed to see right inside him; the way he effortlessly picked him apart.

But Beau could pin *him* all he wanted to. There was no harm in it, really. The chance of him being anywhere near the Piranhas next year was slim to none. He knew it, even though he hadn't been forced to face it yet. However—he certainly wasn't going to sell Kenyon out.

"I don't know what you're talking about," Julian said. He didn't like lying, but this was *Kenyon* and he was already uncomfortably aware of what he'd do to protect him.

"Yeah, yeah, you do. And I'm not even mad. I've been trying to get Kenyon into the film room for ages, trying to get him to study for ages, and he wouldn't, but then you came along, and I'm not exactly sure why it was different with you, but it was."

"Yes, you do," Julian retorted before he could stop himself. "It's exactly the same reason why Sebastian agreed to play safety."

Beau laughed then. "Okay, yes, I do. I do. I get it. But . . . it's more than that, too. There's something about you, Julian."

How many times in his life had he been told that?

Julian, you're so annoying. Julian, you're so frustrating. Julian, why don't you just listen? Julian, why don't you just do what I say?

The only explanation he'd ever been able to come up with was that he just *couldn't*. He was himself. It was all he knew how to be.

"I know," Julian said dryly.

"No, no," Beau said hurriedly. "I mean, there's something *amazing* about you. Something that's so fucking talented, a way you can look at a play and break it down, find the advantages and disadvantages, that it elevated your mediocre physical skills and made you one of the best college running backs. And it's not just that." Beau was waving his hands excitedly now. "You are *really* fucking good at convincing people to listen."

"Kinda why I became a reporter."

"I know, I *know*, but God, you could be so much more. I . . . honestly, I wanted to talk to you because I wanted to do this and I thought it was crazy, but the more I think about it, the more I talk to you, the less crazy it seems."

"What do you mean?" Julian asked flatly.

It was cruel to prolong this, and say what you wanted about Beau Dawson, he wasn't a cruel person.

"What I mean . . ." Beau shot him a lopsided smile. "What I mean is that I want to hire you."

Julian stared at him in shock. "What?"

"I told you, it's crazy, but it also makes a hell of a lot of sense. It's what you should've done from the beginning, I think. 'Cause you're brilliant at this."

Julian didn't know what to say.

"You want . . . to *hire* me?"

"Yes." Beau shrugged his shoulders. "And frankly, you're probably going to need a job. Sooner rather than later. I'm gonna guess when your boss finds out the truth and *then* discovers you're not particularly interested in selling Kenyon out to get the insider scoop, you're definitely going to be unemployed."

He was not wrong.

There were so many things Julian wanted to ask, but he thought he'd start with the most obvious.

"What's the job?"

"At least at the beginning, you'd be working for me. I'm trying to put together a few more people in my department—which this year consisted of basically *just* me—and you'd be the first hire."

"You don't think it's weird to hire a reporter to analyze film?"

Beau shook his head. "I think it's more weird that you ended up becoming a reporter when you are so damn good at this."

"Oh." Julian hesitated. "And your father . . . uh . . . *Coach*, he's on board with this?"

"You've been around this team long enough to know that we don't do things the traditional way."

"No shit," Julian said. "This is the weirdest job interview I've ever been on."

Beau grinned. "It really is, isn't it? It's not even an interview really, because I knew I wanted to hire whoever made that video the moment I saw it. You can ask Kenyon because I told him."

That surprised Julian, too. "What did he say?"

"That the person who made it already had a job. And you do, well, at least for as long as the rest of the season lasts . . . and you're a damn good reporter, too, for the record. You did great work on

Pax and Davis' story. They love you, especially Davis, who . . ." Beau hesitated.

"Has been treated like utter shit by the media?" Julian inserted.

"Yeah. He really has. But you did right by him, and by Pax, and Davis is the kind of guy who doesn't give his loyalty easily, not anymore. But he did, to you, and Kenyon is also a fantastic judge of character, and he'd never commit to someone who wasn't worthwhile . . . definitely wouldn't risk everything for someone who isn't worthy of him."

It wasn't like Nikki *didn't* appreciate him.

She did.

But there was always a catch. Always an angle. Always the question of how Julian could be used to her own advantage. He'd never faulted her for that because *one*, she was his boss, and *two*, he knew how hard she'd had to work to be taken seriously.

But Beau's words were given freely, with no expectations. No questions.

He just *genuinely* thought Julian was great, and coming from Beau Dawson, that meant something.

Even if he didn't take the job—and he would be frankly stupid not to, he could see that right away, from the first moment, when the shock had begun to fade—he'd not forget this conversation for a long time.

Beau pulled out a piece of paper and slid it across the table. "Here's the salary and benefits, the job description, which I'll freely admit is something I threw together really fast, this morning. We can work on the language, on the specific tasks. I'd probably want you to work closely with the scout team *and* the advance team. I'd want someone like you to touch as many facets of the

Piranhas as we can manage, because I've lost count of how many advantages you could bring us."

Julian glanced down and felt his heart begin to race. The number on the paper was three times the salary he was currently making, and he'd get to focus on exactly the parts of the game he loved.

And he'd be part of this team, a *real* part of this team, an invaluable part, if he believed everything Beau was saying.

Normally, he wouldn't, but he knew *Beau* believed every word he was saying, so it was hard not to follow suit.

Beau was someone who made you want to believe.

For so long, the only thing Julian could believe in was himself.

"You really want to hire me," Julian said.

"Absolutely. I'm probably over-selling this," Beau said with a self-conscious shrug. "I'm hoping that I don't regret this later, but yes. I really want to hire you. Coach does too, for the record."

"Really?"

Beau nodded. "Definitely. He's one hundred percent on board."

"He told you you were crazy, though."

Beau hesitated. "A little yeah, but then he remembered that we don't do things the normal way around here. Which is how we're in this position, headed to the AFC Championship after winning only two games last year. We don't care about appearances. We don't care about normal. We care about results, and we care about our players, and our team."

It was an invitation, plain and simple, to be part of the incredible system they were building.

Julian would be the crazy one *not* to want to be part of that. Because he could already sense that the Piranhas were making history. Not just this year but in years to come.

He could be not just part of it, but an integral cog in it.

"I'm assuming who I date has no impact on this offer," Julian said.

Beau raised an eyebrow. "I think the whole team saw you kissing Kenyon last night. You've made it plenty clear who you're dating, and I still wanted to make you this job offer this morning. So no, I don't care who you date."

Julian wondered if Beau knew how closely Kenyon was contemplating retirement and if that had something to do with his acceptance of their situation, but then . . . the Piranhas had accepted Beau and Sebastian. Pax and Davis. Logan and Dylan. Even Coach and his new husband.

He knew he should say he'd think about it.

It was a huge life shift. An enormous change.

He'd contemplated changing his focus from football to journalism for weeks.

That decision had been hard and painful.

And this one felt easy, like the easiest choice he'd ever made.

"I'll take it," Julian said, before he could overthink and do something even crazier. Like change his mind.

Beau's face broke into a huge smile. "Really? Seriously?"

"Seriously," Julian said, and he stuck out his hand and Beau shook it, firmly.

"Goddamn, that is great news," Beau said enthusiastically. "I can't wait for you to get started."

Kenyon wasn't proud of it, but there was no getting around the fact that he was grumpy tonight.

His ankle ached. His ribs fucking ached, too, like a bruise he'd been pressing on for too long.

Though the thing that hurt the worst was watching his teammates practice without a shit ton of restrictions.

He'd been upgraded from doubtful to questionable, which meant that at least he was now at practice. Except his participation came with a ridiculous list of rules, most of which involved things he was not allowed to do.

The medical staff kept telling him his outlook looked "optimistic" but whatever that meant—if it meant he could play in a few days—he didn't know.

All he knew was that suddenly, it *mattered*. He wanted to join with his teammates one last time.

The pain, his frustration with the unknown, and also Julian's uncharacteristic reticence had all collided to make him seriously grumpy.

And even worse, as Julian picked at his salad, his hair bright under the lights of Kenyon's kitchen, he couldn't deny that he was even more frustrated because his boyfriend hadn't even noticed his bad mood.

"You okay?" Kenyon finally asked.

Julian's head shot up and guilt crossed his face immediately, before he tucked it away, like it had never existed.

Kenyon knew people thought he was crazy for dating a reporter, who he might or might not be able to trust, but he'd never worried about Julian's loyalty for a second.

He wasn't exactly *worried* now, but . . .

"It was a weird day," Julian finally said, setting down his fork. "A really weird day."

Kenyon thought it couldn't be weirder than him practically sitting through an entire practice.

Or Wade finally taking his helmet away because he wouldn't stop trying to get on the field.

"What happened?" Kenyon shoveled in grilled chicken and rice, barely tasting it.

Julian shot him a look. A *hesitant* look. Which was so unlike Julian, the anxiety in Kenyon's stomach throbbed. "Promise me you won't freak out," Julian said. *Pleaded.*

It must have been one hell of a weird day if Julian was pleading with him and sex wasn't involved.

"Did that bitch boss of yours find out about us? Demand you give some kind of tell-all interview about how I snore when I sleep? How I like ketchup but not tomatoes?"

"It's so weird you don't like tomatoes," Julian said. "And no. But I did talk to her this afternoon . . ." He took a deep breath. "She knows now."

"And you're still alive," Kenyon marveled.

"She knows because I quit my job," Julian said, dropping that particular bomb before Kenyon could even adjust to the fact that Julian's boss now knew the truth about them.

It wasn't entirely a surprise that Julian was currently unemployed. They'd both expected it would happen. But . . . this had definitely not been part of the plan—even the vaguely sketched plan they'd discussed.

"Oh." Kenyon swallowed his bite of chicken and rice. "That's . . ."

"It's 'cause I got another job, and I sort of didn't want to wait another moment before taking it. And I couldn't do that, until I quit the old one."

Kenyon felt his jaw drop. "You got another job? *Today*?"

Julian looked smug now. Like he was really enjoying dropping one bomb after another. Frankly, he probably was. "Yep, I sure did."

Kenyon leaned back in his chair. Stunned. "Seriously?"

Julian grinned. "It shouldn't surprise you that much. After all, he told you he wanted to hire me."

Kenyon nearly fell off the fucking chair. "*Beau* offered you a job? And you *took* it?"

"I sure did. It was a really great offer, and frankly . . ." Julian sighed. "I took it because I wanted to take it. I . . . I've *missed* football. And don't say it, I see it in your face. Yes, I was a sports reporter. Yes, I reported on football. But there's nothing about it that's the same."

Kenyon considered this, and could see that might be true. "You didn't realize that, when you switched?"

Julian shook his head. "'Course it might not have mattered. I was young and stupid and a little bit desperate. Thought I'd miss it too much—and I did, I really fucking did—but being a reporter was as close as I could get, still."

"You're gonna work for Beau." Kenyon tested this thought out, and kind of like Julian had explained earlier, he could see, immediately, how right this felt.

He might be retiring after this season, but he wouldn't be leaving the circle of the Piranhas family behind. Not with Julian being folded in.

Not if he decided to stay involved, and even without Julian, he knew he would've, to a certain extent, but now that Julian would be here, in Miami? There was no question.

"Yep," Julian said, and he was grinning so brightly, almost as wide as Kenyon had ever seen him. There was a light in his eyes too, that Kenyon had definitely never seen before when it came to Julian's work.

"Guess I should've told him before that it was you," Kenyon said with a grin. He held out his arms. "Come 'ere, babe, I'm so fucking proud of you."

"You could've, but . . ." Julian came, easily, sliding in to his embrace like he'd been made to do it. "It wouldn't have been the same. I did this. *I* did this."

"Yes, you sure as hell did."

For a moment, they didn't move. Just felt.

Then Julian pulled back a fraction. "That wasn't the weird part, though it was a little bit weird, I suppose. Having someone offer me a job and not even really considering it, just saying yes because I really fucking wanted to say yes."

"It was quitting." Kenyon didn't need to hear any more details to know it had probably sucked.

The look in Julian's eyes told the whole story.

"Your boss was pissed."

Julian sighed and turned back to his salad. "An understatement. She was fucking furious. And I even get some of why she's angry. She took a chance on me. She developed me. She stuck her neck out for me. How do I pay that back? I start dating a player and quit to work for the same team. So yeah, she felt betrayed." He made a face. "I can't say I blame her for it."

"I can," Kenyon said. "You weren't happy. You're going to try something else, something else that might make you happy. If she really cared about you, if she gave any shits about you as a person, or *your* career, that would be the most important thing."

Julian shoved his fork around his salad bowl. "That," he said quietly, after a long pause, "was the conclusion I came to as well. She worked really hard to get ahead, and . . . I guess got stuck in that mindset, you know?"

"It's not even a *bad* mindset, putting yourself first, filtering everything in through you and your goals, but . . ."

Julian's gaze met his. "It wasn't what *I* wanted."

"No." Kenyon couldn't help but agree.

Julian, who'd spent his life trying to close himself off from love and connection, had, despite all his efforts, an enormous heart. A brilliant mind, yes, but he brought so much more to the table than that. And now he was going to get a chance to share it, with his new family.

"This is good," Kenyon continued. "Just . . . the best news, honestly." He hesitated. "Wait, does this mean you aren't coming to the game?"

Julian rolled his eyes. "I'll be there, but not in my normal capacity. Beau asked me if I wanted to get started right away, and I told him there's nowhere I want to be more than the Piranhas sideline, especially for this game."

Kenyon grinned. "You better not distract me."

"Like I would ever tolerate that," Julian said dryly. "But honestly, I really hoped you'd be glad. I hoped you'd feel that way, but also I worried it might be a lot to handle."

Now some of his earlier reticence made sense. He'd been nervous about how Kenyon would take the news of him signing on with the Piranhas.

"So, let me get this straight," Kenyon said, forcing his face to stay solemn, "I was supposed to be okay with you losing a job you loved over me, over our relationship, but you didn't expect me to be pleased as hell that you found something else you loved even more? A great job where you're going to be appreciated and admired?"

Julian burst out laughing. "Well, when you put it that way . . ."

"Though, speaking of job changes . . ." Kenyon knew this was *truly* the reason he'd been grumpy earlier. He'd come to a decision and it was wonderful and it was also terrible.

Julian's expression turned almost unbearably empathetic.

"Yeah, I made up my mind," he continued, "so I guess you're gonna have to give me some real good advice about how to retire with dignity."

Suddenly his arms were full of Julian again and he was hugging him with all the strength in his body. "There's no way to do it with dignity, because it's shit from start to finish. But you're doing the best you can," Julian murmured. "I know it feels like shit, but I think we both know this is the right call for you."

"Doesn't make it feel any better," Kenyon muttered.

"It won't. But you know what will?"

Kenyon was sure Julian was going to say winning Sunday's game.

But he didn't.

"Knowing every single day that you made the right choice, even if it was hard."

"That how you feel?" Kenyon asked.

Julian pulled back. "I didn't always . . . but ever since I met you . . . yeah. *Yeah*."

"God, I love you," Kenyon said. And he knew that he'd miss his teammates and the adrenaline spike from the field, but he had this now. A *life;* a life with someone he loved very much. And not just that, but an ironclad purpose.

"I . . ." Julian looked him straight in the eye. "I love you too, you know."

Kenyon felt the joy of it surge through him. He'd *known* it, of course, because Julian wasn't nearly as mysterious as he wanted to be, but it sure felt good to hear it.

"I do know, but it's nice to hear the actual words," Kenyon teased.

Julian grinned. "I was saving them for a moment you needed a pick-me-up, and this seemed like as good of a moment as any."

"Yeah. *Yeah*." Kenyon pulled him close again.

After a long moment, Julian asked, "You tell Coach yet?"

"No." Kenyon hesitated. "But I don't think he's going to be all that surprised, honestly."

Julian hummed to himself, like he was considering this. "You know, probably not. I think sometimes he knows his guys better than they know themselves."

"He is way too perceptive," Kenyon agreed.

"But in this case, probably a good thing," Julian pointed out, as he pulled away. "Come on, eat your dinner, and then we'll ice your ankle. And your ribs."

Julian's conscientiousness might have bothered someone else, but Kenyon could see how much he cared, in every glance, in every solicitous suggestion.

He grinned, shockingly happy despite the heavy weight of the decision he'd come to. "Oh, baby, talk dirty to me," he teased.

Chapter Twenty

The night before the game, Kenyon got cleared to play.

"Be careful on that ankle. We'll wrap it tightly. Give you the shot . . ." The PT glanced up when Kenyon made a face. "I know, you hate those, but you're gonna need it. And the extra padding for the ribs, while we're at it."

"Makes me slower," Kenyon grumbled, but he wasn't going to argue with what the doctors wanted him to do, because if he did, then maybe he *wouldn't* get cleared to play, and now that he knew this could be his last game, he wasn't going to take the risk he might not be on that field.

"You just finish with the doctors?" Logan asked when he walked into the big hotel ballroom that was hosting their walk-through.

"Yep, I'm good, I'm playing," Kenyon said, and they fist-bumped.

"Nobody I'd rather see out there," Logan said, and Kenyon ignored the pulse of guilt he felt.

Soon, everyone was going to know the truth.

He'd checked in with Coach yesterday, right after their first practice in California and told him he intended for this season to be his last. And that, more than anything, what he wanted was to retire in Piranhas blue and yellow.

"That means a lot to me," Coach had said, his gaze understanding. "Will mean a lot to the team, too."

Like, just as Julian had predicted, he'd known maybe before Kenyon was even sure, and he'd had time to get used to the idea.

They'd agreed he'd announce his decision to the team tonight, after the walk-through.

Kenyon was expecting it to be tough.

Still, he wasn't expecting when he took his seat for the walk-through to feel the gravity and emotion already begin to creep up on him, when Coach picked up the microphone and began to talk.

At first, it was routine enough things. A few additional play wrinkles he wanted to show. Reminders of everyone's assignments. Micah was going to *attempt* to cover Chase Riley, and this time, Sebastian was going to assist him, because no one corner could truly cover Chase Riley. His record-setting numbers in the last few years had proven that.

But then, Coach sighed, and set a hip on the edge of the table up front.

"I've been asking myself," he said, "all week, how we got here."

There was a rumble through the audience. Of comprehension, because how *had* they gotten here? They certainly hadn't begun the year like a playoff contender. They'd been a mess. But then they'd circled the wagons and been a mess *together*, and somehow just having each other's backs had changed everything—until they weren't a mess anymore.

"There's a lot of answers, aren't there?" Coach continued, smiling. "More than I really thought I'd have when I first started asking the question. But here's what it comes down to for me. I took a chance, the coaching staff took a chance, we had goals, we had plans, we had ideas on how to make things work, how to make the puzzle pieces fit together—but the real responsibility for why we're here, tonight, ready to step onto that field tomorrow, is *you*. You not just bought into what I and the other coaches were selling, you gave an extraordinary effort. You changed an entire franchise around. No matter what happens tomorrow, that's what I want you to take from this. That you showed up, every single day of practice. Every game day. You made each and every one count."

A cheer went up through the audience. Kenyon felt the emotional fire flame to life inside him, and watched as it lit up the whole room.

"That's another question I can't stop asking," Coach said, "*why not us?* So we haven't put our time in. Sure, we haven't done more than put together a single great season. Maybe there isn't anyone in Miami left from that great Super Bowl–winning team a few years back. But I'm still asking myself, *why not us?* And *that*, more than anything else, is what I want you to ask yourself tomorrow. Before you take the field. Before you touch the ball. Before you move it. Before you defend it. Ask yourself, *why not us?* The only people saying we shouldn't be here, shouldn't make it past the Riptide, aren't here. None of those people are here, in this room. But you know who is here? *We are.* And we get to dictate, ultimately, how we play tomorrow. It's us holding the ball. It's all in your hands."

This time Kenyon couldn't help but join in the yell that went up through the assembled players. *Why not us?* they echoed back at their coach and leader.

"That's all I got," Coach said, standing straight up again. "But I want you to be rested tomorrow. Fresh. Rested. Ready to give it your all. Because don't get me wrong. The Riptide are a formidable team. They know what it feels like to hold the trophy, and they want to do it again. And I don't doubt they're going to give us all we can handle and more. But first . . . I do have one of your teammates who has something he wants to say. Short and sweet, since I know he's not big on sharing parts of himself, but I know this was something he wanted to have come from him, not from anyone else. Kenyon?" Coach held out the microphone as Kenyon stood and headed to the front, feeling every pair of eyes in the room latch on to him.

He'd thought he knew what he wanted to say, but with the microphone in his hand and everyone looking at him, like they knew what he was about to say, his mouth went dry. He tried to clear it, the dryness exacerbated by the sudden emotion rolling through him.

It would be the last time he addressed these guys.

The very last fucking time.

Julian had told him there wasn't a way to do it with dignity. He hadn't understood then what that meant. How this would feel.

Coach set a reassuring hand on his shoulder. "You're good, take your time," he said in a low voice.

He coughed once. Then twice. And then latched on to the back of the room. Where Beau was sitting, and Julian next to him.

"Hey, guys," he finally managed to get out. "I thought this would be easier. Not easy, 'cause it's not ever easy, but easier because I knew this was the right call for me, but it turns out it doesn't matter how right it is, it still sucks. Turns out there's no way to do this with real dignity. And maybe that's right. Because you guys are my brothers, and we don't say goodbye to brothers easily."

"Or at all!" Logan called out.

"You're right," Kenyon said, realizing the interruption—and the realization—had actually made him steadier. "Maybe this is my last season, but I know it's not goodbye. It's me standing in front of you saying I'm seeing my life going a different direction, but that doesn't mean it's goodbye. I'm still going to be around, but after I retire, it's not going to be the same. Change isn't always easy, but it's necessary. Either way . . ." The emotion hit him again, square in the chest, undeniable. He hoped the front row of guys was too far away to see the tears in his eyes—or maybe he hoped that they could. Maybe his own belief in this team would somehow motivate theirs. "Either way, it's been an honor and a privilege to play with you, and it's going to be one of the best days of my life, when we take the field tomorrow. Go Piranhas!"

The moment he set down the microphone, a sense of rightness swept over him.

Or maybe that was Tristan, launching himself into his arms, tears flowing like he didn't care who saw. "Oh my God," he cried, "I can't believe you're *retiring*. You're not old! You're kicking ass right now. Wade, *tell him*."

Kenyon patted Tristan's back hesitantly. "It's gonna be okay. You're gonna be just fine, Flounder. You know that."

"But ugh, we're gonna miss playing with you," Tristan said, finally stepping back. "Both of us." He gestured to where Wade was standing, a small, understanding smile on his face.

"*All* of us," Logan said, approaching with Dylan by his side.

"But," Pax added as he joined the group, a poignant smile on his face, "but also really, really happy for you. You're going to do amazing things."

"He's already doing amazing things," Dylan chimed in. "It's so brave to choose others instead of yourself."

"The funny thing . . ." Kenyon said, clearing his throat again. He'd expected something like this, but he hadn't expected *this*. ". . . is that I feel like I'm finally choosing *me*."

"Then it's the right call," Sebastian said. He'd wandered over, Beau and Julian trailing behind him.

"I won't be too far away," Kenyon promised. "After all . . ."

"Yeah, what is up with your boyfriend working for Beau now?" Tristan asked.

"He's gonna teach you how to *really* watch film," Beau spoke up.

Tristan made a face.

"And like it," Beau added. He shot their rookie receiver a lopsided smile.

Kenyon was a little thankful to settle into the background again, as Tristan made a comment about how Beau couldn't judge by Kenyon enjoying Julian's tutoring sessions, because didn't he know, they were *fucking*.

He was so busy being amused by Beau and Tristan's debate he didn't notice Julian sliding up behind him.

"For the record," Julian said, murmuring into his ear. "I'm real proud of you, too."

"Wait, that's supposed to be *my* line," Kenyon said.

"I told you, there is no dignity, only your own certainty that you're making the right call," Julian said.

"Hey, I didn't actually cry," Kenyon said.

Next to them, Dylan tilted his head, considering this. "Actually . . ." he said hesitantly.

"Hey, we're already demolishing so many other temples to toxic masculinity," Julian pointed out. "Why not that one too?"

"Just like Coach said," Dylan said with a grin. "Why not us?"

When Beau had first suggested he spend the game on the sideline, Julian had thought he was crazy.

The good kind of crazy, but still crazy.

"It's not crazy," Beau argued. "It makes perfect fucking sense. You're brilliant. You're gonna see something, I know it, and you'll be right there, ready to pass it on. Besides," he added with a wry grin, "I have an ulterior motive."

"Kenyon isn't gonna play any better or worse 'cause I'm there," Julian objected.

"I might be new to NFL, but I'm not new to the idea of a last game," Beau pointed out. "I coached plenty of guys in their senior year who knew it was their last game. They weren't going to be drafted, and they knew it, and that last game . . . it can be emotional. Distractingly emotional."

"You want me to keep Kenyon focused."

"You're so prosaic. You're not going to let him get carried away."

"Fine, I'll do it," Julian agreed.

So that was why he was standing here on the sideline, watching the Riptide begin their first offensive drive of the game.

It was a different kind of matchup than the Piranhas versus the Condors, from last week, in that there was not one ounce of animosity. There'd been plenty of friendly ribbing during warmups, and the Riptide were painfully confident as they took the field, but the nasty, cruel streak of anger was missing.

But that didn't mean the outcome was any different.

Julian shifted his weight from foot to foot, peering past the players milling around on the sideline, and watched as, despite a valiant effort by the Piranhas' defense, the Riptide went right down the field, first down after first down.

The defense came back to the sideline, slumping onto the benches after Sam Crawford, the Riptide's quarterback, threw a beautiful slant pass to Chase Riley in the end zone, putting them up seven to zero.

It wasn't that they were forcibly overwhelming them, the way the Condors had, they were picking them apart with flawless coaching, laser-sharp focus and an embarrassing abundance of incredible skill, perfectly applied to the situation.

In his playoff preview, when he'd still been pretending that what he wanted most was to be a reporter, he'd picked the Riptide as his hands down favorite to win the Super Bowl, because from where he stood then, they didn't have any major flaws in their game. They were well-balanced, healthy, and had an insane number of playmakers on both sides of the ball.

But it was one thing to dispassionately write about this—back when he was also still pretending that the Piranhas hadn't won him over, body and soul, right alongside the Piranhas' running back—but it was another to watch it, to stand here on the sideline as every advantage Julian had written about gave the Riptide the edge over the Piranhas.

It wasn't that they weren't as well coached, they *were*. But Martinez had been doing this for ages, had won a Super Bowl and lost another. He was sharp and knowledgeable in a way that Dawson couldn't be yet. From the way his face had settled into hard lines, from the whispered consultations with his husband, the defensive guru Scott Callaway, Julian had a feeling that wouldn't be the case after this year. But it was the case right now.

And it wasn't like the Piranhas didn't have skill. They did. But they were beat up, almost nobody functioning at one hundred percent, and almost nobody with a full week of practice.

Maybe, against another team, slightly less well coached, with marginally less skill, it wouldn't have been such a glaring difference.

But it was.

The Piranhas' offense took the field, Julian's heart racing as Kenyon took the first handoff and went around Rob's left side, as he barely managed to hold back Spencer Evans, one of the best defensive ends in football, gaining a few yards, before Spencer changed angles, Rob losing his block, and tackled him to the ground.

"Damn," Coach exhaled with a grunt. He glanced over at Julian, who was standing with Beau. "Either of you got any brilliant ideas on how to contain him?"

Beau shook his head, mutely.

First of all, Julian was shocked Coach was asking *him*, though he supposed he needed to get used to that, because next season that was probably going to be happening frequently, but second, he never knew when to keep his fucking mouth shut.

"The Stars tried," Julian said. "And if they couldn't do it, nobody could."

Coach nodded his head slowly. The Hollywood Stars, Spencer's old team, had drafted him despite his out-and-proud status, and then proceeded to diminish and bully and harass him for his queerness. He'd proven them wrong by becoming one of the best defensive ends to ever play the game, but finally, when he'd gotten sick of their attitude, he'd demanded they trade him to the Riptide.

Where he was now currently wreaking havoc as the centerpiece of their new defensive scheme.

It was a great story, or it would've been, if both Logan and Rob together weren't struggling to hold him back.

"I knew," Beau huffed under his breath, "when they traded him, it was gonna be trouble. That was the last piece they needed to just *dominate*."

And dominating was what the Riptide were doing.

Davis was pacing back and forth nearby, shouting into his headset as he and Randy, the offensive coordinator, tried to figure out a better scheme to contain the defense, which wasn't giving Pax any time at all to throw.

Then, finally, after only twenty-five hard-won yards, Spencer sacked Pax on a third down, ending the drive.

"Shit," Julian said.

Any confidence the Piranhas had when the game started was beginning to seep away, Julian could see it as they returned to the sideline.

Pax and Davis huddled up with Logan and Rob and Wade, trying to figure out how to block better.

Kenyon sat to the side, and Julian hesitantly went over, not sure of his place. They'd never discussed this, if Kenyon would want to talk to him during the game.

But Kenyon glanced up the moment he hit his field of vision, and smiled. "Jesus," he said. "Spencer Evans is a one-man wrecking ball."

"It's kind of hard to hate him for that, though," Julian said.

"Tell yourself that when he's got you pinned to the turf," Kenyon said dryly. "The man's huge."

"Your ribs . . ."

"They hurt. But they're fine." Kenyon's response was perfunctory, and Julian knew that those two times Evans had tackled him had probably hurt more than he wanted to admit. "You got anything for me?"

"Run away from Evans?"

Kenyon chuckled. "No shit. Anything else?"

"They're . . ." Julian hesitated. Nikki had always told him his blunt honesty would get him in trouble, and it certainly had earlier this year, and he wasn't sure it was the right place for it now.

"Just lay it on me," Kenyon said, clearly sensing his indecision.

"They're good. You're just going to have to push harder." *Somehow.*

"If we didn't have the Condors last week . . ." Kenyon trailed off.

It was the truth; they'd have come in a bit sharper, certainly less injured.

"I'm just glad you're here," Kenyon said. *For my last game.* Kenyon didn't have to say the words. They both knew there was very little chance, if the first two drives were any indication, of the Piranhas being able to beat the Riptide at their own game.

It was just too solid, too impenetrable.

"They're not invincible," Julian reminded him. Reminding him not to just give up.

"No, we'll give them all they can handle," Kenyon said, and there was a little flash of that smug cockiness Julian had first been attracted to.

It was so much more than that now, but it was a good reminder. He didn't need to convince Kenyon to focus. The man was dialed in. Julian wouldn't have expected anything less. It was why they understood each other, it was why they had connected in the first place.

It wasn't *exactly* why they'd fallen in love but it hadn't hurt either.

"You'd better," Julian said.

"Have I ever let you down?" Kenyon challenged.

And as Julian walked away, to check in with Beau, he realized that *no*, he hadn't. Not once. He'd been there for him, even when Julian had pissed him off, even when Julian was being unreasonable, Kenyon had never been anything but rock steady.

Kenyon gave the Piranhas credit for one thing: they didn't roll over and play dead, even when it became apparent to everyone that they weren't going to be winning this championship game and heading to the Super Bowl.

They still pushed. Pax still made some fucking incredible throws, one downfield fifty-yard pass to Tristan that would probably show up in some yearly recap reels as one of the best catches of the year.

He ground more than ran, one yard at a fucking time, his ribs screaming, his ankle aching, but never giving up.

He'd promised Julian he wouldn't.

He'd promised himself.

And he'd promised his teammates, his brothers.

He wouldn't give up, even when it seemed impossible, even when they never led, even when they were behind the whole game by at least two touchdowns.

He hadn't been sure they'd be able to win this game, not as beat up as they were after the Condors, but he'd hoped, at least, to be able to hang tighter.

But the Riptide were so talented, and so *focused*. Something didn't go quite right, and they came right back at it again, like they'd already forgotten about the failure. It was remarkable. Kenyon would've been impressed by it, if he hadn't been currently being ground underneath its heel.

"Shit," Pax said, flopping down on the bench. He looked exhausted, face pale, but still determined.

That was Pax for you. The man didn't give up, even when he probably should.

It was no doubt why he'd ended up fighting so hard for Davis.

Speaking of Davis, he was on Pax's other side, grinding his teeth as he flipped through plays on the tablet he was holding.

"They're covering all my outlets," Pax said, pointing at the screen. "See? There and there."

"I saw." Davis' voice was dark and promised retribution.

"You know," Pax said lightly, "you could've been on the other side of this."

"Yeah," Davis ground out, "holding a fucking clipboard while Crawford tears you apart, one pass at a time. Sounds like a great time."

"Could've been a ring for you, though," Pax said softly.

Kenyon wasn't sure he was supposed to have heard that. But it was hard *not* to hear it.

"I have plenty. More than enough. More than any man needs," Davis said gruffly. "Now, let's talk about running some more outs. Kenyon, you here for that?"

Kenyon heard the words he wasn't saying: *can you do that, still?*

He glanced up at the clock. There was ten minutes left in the fourth quarter. On the last drive, Dylan had come and kicked a long field goal to cut the Riptide's lead to eleven.

If they could score again, and even more miraculously, if the defense could *stop* the Riptide from scoring yet another touchdown, they might be in this, still.

He nodded.

It wasn't like he didn't hurt. He did.

But this was the last time he was going to hurt like this, and he almost didn't want it to end.

Davis sketched out some screen passes on the tablet, with Tristan, Wade and Carter looking in, taking note of their blocking assignments.

Logan glanced out at the field. "If they don't stop them . . ."

He didn't have to finish the sentence. If the Riptide scored again, none of this would matter. Well, they could always still run it, of course, there was still clock to eat, but there would be no chance of winning left. There was still barely any hope as it was.

"They will," Beau said. He'd joined the group now. "Sebastian knows how important this is."

They watched as Sebastian did what only Sebastian could do, making a herculean effort, tackling Chase Riley three yards short of the first down.

"See?" Beau said lightly, but there was that undercurrent in his voice, too. The same undercurrent they all felt, that they hadn't felt since the very beginning of the season, when they'd been fifty-two individuals, and not one team, with one mind, and one goal and one *soul*.

It's not going to be enough. It's just not enough.

But that didn't mean they wouldn't go out on the field now and try their hardest to ignite that miniscule, wavering flame of hope.

Kenyon looked around him, and thought: *if anyone can do it, we can.*

But if we don't, it's okay. We accomplished so many things nobody thought we could. Even more, we accomplished more than we thought we could. That's what I'm gonna take from this. Extraordinary effort and sportsmanship in the face of predicted failure.

He glanced back at the last second, found Julian's eyes, and nodded. And added, *and I found Julian. Or Julian found me. Doesn't matter which way you dice it, he's it.*

"Come on," Pax called out, rallying them, and they jogged onto the field as one unit, ready to make their last stand.

It might not be enough, but they were together.

They started out with one of Davis' new screen pass plays, Pax grabbing the ball from Logan, and tossing it to Carter, who then doubled back, and tossed it to Kenyon.

The second he felt the ball hit his hands, he hit the empty hole in the line, finding a new gear, churning his legs hard, squirting through the first line of defense, and finally getting tackled into the turf by the Riptide's safety.

He was breathing hard, tired to his bones, when he came back to the huddle.

But Pax had a light in his eyes now that he hadn't had before.

Maybe we can score one last touchdown, together, he thought.

One last touchdown, to say goodbye.

Pax must've taken note of his exhaustion, because the next play he called was one he altered, dropping back to pass, tossing a beautiful ball to Wade, who muscled around two defenders, hitting another first down.

Five minutes left now.

There wasn't going to be time for another drive, there would just be this one.

They would need to make this one count.

Kenyon saw it in Pax's face in the huddle. Saw it reflected around him, over and over, in everyone's eyes.

"You good?" Pax asked, and Kenyon nodded.

If the guys around him could give their last effort for him, then he could dig down, and find a reserve of energy for them.

Pax called the play, and they lined up. Logan snapped the ball, and Kenyon took the handoff, his ankle screaming as he took a sharp cut, away from where Rob had his hands full with Spencer Evans.

He took another, then spun, and got another first down.

The minutes kept ticking by as they moved, methodically, inevitably down the field.

Every time Kenyon touched the ball, it felt like a blessing and also like a goodbye.

This is the last time you're going to do this; make it count.

He did.

Pax kept feeding him the ball, interspersed with a pass or two. A few balls fell to the turf, uncaught, but the line held Evans back, and the offense, through sheer strength of will, came together to make this one last drive happen.

When they reached the five-yard line, at the two-minute warning, Pax turned to Kenyon. "You ready for this?" he asked.

Like Kenyon could answer any other way.

"Yes," he said. "Give it to me."

He was stopped short the first time, hitting the Riptide's defense like it was a wall, not a group of men.

They were determined too, Kenyon knew.

But nobody was more determined than him in that moment.

He would give his team this.

He would give *himself* this.

"Give it to me again," he demanded as soon as they huddled up.

Pax shot him a look. "You sure?"

"I'm sure." On the last play, he'd seen a sliver of an opening to the right. An opening he might not have seen—might've not even *looked* for, if not for all of Julian's film study over the last few weeks—and he thought he could squeak right through it and into the end zone.

"Okay," Pax said, and there was the thing he would miss more than anything, the thing that nothing, not a single goddamn thing, could ever replace: the wordless, everlasting trust of one player to another.

Pax knew he was going to get it done.

It was that belief that powered him through the sliver he'd seen, and when he hit the ground, ball secure in his hands, he knew he'd left it all on the field.

Maybe he didn't have anything left.

But they'd hung hard, not made anything easy for the Riptide.

Even more than that, he'd lived up to all the potential he'd believed he had.

His teammates surrounded him, lifting him to the sky, and Kenyon realized he was at peace.

You can't retire with dignity, Julian had told him. And maybe it wasn't dignity, like this, as Dylan lined up to kick the extra point, but it was enough.

He could live with himself, every day going forward.

He could face himself in the mirror.

And face Julian over early-morning coffee.

That was all that mattered.

Everywhere Kenyon turned when he jogged back to the sideline was excitement for him. Not excitement for the team, but happiness for him personally. Underneath it ran the desolate acknowledgement they were going to lose this game, but Kenyon knew it was enough, still.

They'd come back harder and stronger and smarter next year.

He wouldn't be with them, but he'd be there in spirit.

"Damn you."

Kenyon looked up from wiping his face. Julian was standing there, and he had tears in his eyes.

He grinned. "I guess I could retire with dignity, huh?"

Julian rolled his eyes, but they were still full of love and affection. Pride, too.

"You're the worst." He paused, reached out and gripped Kenyon's hand in its glove for one endless second. "And also the best. But then you knew that."

"Don't know anything," Kenyon admitted. "Just know I'm trying, that's all I can do."

"Well, damn you, but it was great. I'll . . ." Kenyon watched as his breath hitched. He was beautiful like this, his emotion finally showing on his face, so much warmer than the cold wall he'd tried to present to the world when they'd first met. "I'll never forget it."

"Me either," Kenyon said softly.

"I love you. I love watching you play, but I'm going to love you lying in our bed on a Sunday morning too," Julian murmured, and tucked himself under Kenyon's arm.

"You know what? Me too," Kenyon agreed. "Lazy Sunday mornings in bed sound pretty fucking great."

They watched, together, as the last minute ticked off the clock, and the Riptide took a victory formation, Crawford taking a knee.

They watched as the Riptide celebrated.

Kenyon was about to turn away, to head back to the locker room, because he was resigned, he had accepted the loss, but it still hurt more than he'd anticipated. But instead, Pax approached, catching his arm before he could. "No," he said in a hard voice. He'd been crying too, Kenyon could see it in his eyes. "No, you come see this."

There was a loose circle of them on the field. Wade and Tristan, Logan, Dylan, Davis, even Beau was there, unabashedly holding Sebastian's hand. "This is what I want you to see. All of you," Paxton said, gesturing to the other side of the field where the Riptide were celebrating a third trip to the Super Bowl in four years.

Pax pointed to where Spencer was still kneeling, still crying. Alec Mitchell, his boyfriend, and a famous sports agent, had joined him on the field, and was holding him while he was overcome by emotion.

What a change he'd gone through, from a team who hadn't done a thing to support him, to the Riptide, who celebrated what made each and every one of their players unique and different.

Heath and Sam were still embracing near where the stage was being set up, and it wouldn't take a rocket scientist to figure out they might even reenact their infamous Super Bowl kiss from three years back.

Maybe they'd even do it again, two weeks from now, right over the Vince Lombardi Trophy.

Kenyon didn't think there was a single team that was capable of beating the Riptide when they were playing as well as they were right now.

"Look at Evans. Look at Harris and Crawford. Look at Chase. Jamie Wright and Neal Fisher. They changed everything. But I want you to look, because this isn't a loss, not in the way you think." Pax took a deep breath.

"It takes more than one team to change an entire culture. It started with Colin O'Connor, who played for the Piranhas, first. It took him to be the first, and then it takes another, and another, and another. Maybe we weren't the first, but we're an important piece. A necessary piece. None of this continues if we didn't come here and play the Riptide today. It hurts, it really hurts like fucking hell, that we lost. I'm not gonna lie about that, but we came here bruised—not beaten, but *beaten*—and we still gave it our all. When people talk about this game, that's what they're gonna talk about. That we went toe-to-toe with the NFL's best team. And hey, guess what, it was one queer guy versus another queer guy, playing some of the best football they've ever seen. Maybe it changes one person's mind. Maybe it changes a hundred. But those people matter. Every single goddamn one matters. It might be a cold comfort tonight, but it's something I'm gonna remember for a long time. What we accomplished by coming here. By hanging tight with the heroes of our sport."

Nobody said anything for a long moment.

Logan cleared his throat. "It's not a cold comfort, Pax. It's an important reminder. We're not just what we do out here, on the field. We're more than that."

"So much more," Kenyon said, speaking up, because he'd spent the entire season realizing just that.

It was a truth that would make retiring both harder, *and* easier.

Kenyon also realized that the Pax of last year never could've faced this loss and come out the other side, even more determined than ever. It would've destroyed him.

But this Pax didn't look destroyed.

He looked invigorated.

He looked *determined*.

It was how Kenyon knew the Piranhas would bounce back from this, better and stronger than ever, and come back here, and the score the next time would be different.

"This is just the beginning," Beau said.

And even though it might be the end for Kenyon, somehow it did feel just like a beginning.

EPILOGUE

Julian had seen so many versions of Kenyon over the last year.

Kenyon, the football player.

Kenyon, the benefactor.

Kenyon, the lover.

Kenyon, *his* lover.

But he'd never seen this Kenyon before.

Light and free and happy, no longer pledged to too many causes, just sitting on the couch, with his friends and his brothers, enjoying life.

"You're grinning, and it's weird for me," Tristan said, leaning over and whispering this underneath his breath. "It almost makes you look . . . *normal.*"

Julian laughed. "I guess, I'm . . . happy? That shouldn't be weird, should it?"

Tristan stared at him for a long second, then switched his attention back to the gigantic screen in front of them, where the Riptide were currently battling the New Orleans Saints for the Vince Lombardi Trophy.

The Riptide were currently up by seven, with five minutes before halftime, when Rihanna would take the stage.

"I wanted to play in this game just to meet her," Wade said mournfully as the screen showed a preview of the halftime entertainment.

"I didn't realize you were such a Rihanna fan," Tristan said.

"Is there anyone who *isn't* a Rihanna fan?" Wade pointed out.

Most of the Piranhas had gathered here, in Sebastian's enormous penthouse apartment in Miami, to watch the game.

Several of them, Julian knew, had gotten invites to the game itself, but almost the entire team had turned them down.

"It was too soon," Kenyon had told him when he'd gotten his and sent back his regrets. "Maybe next year when it doesn't . . . well, it doesn't feel like we could've gone as players. Of course it wouldn't be an option for me next year, but I think . . . in time, maybe it won't feel like this."

Julian had hugged him tightly after he'd made this particular confession. "I love you, you know, no matter what. No matter what games you play in. What rings you wear. It doesn't matter to me."

"Character development," Kenyon had teased him.

It would've stung once, maybe, but it had been true.

Julian had never been in a relationship before, but even the meager connections he'd formed prior to this had always been about what he could do for the other guy, or what the other guy could do for him.

It wasn't like that with Kenyon.

It was them, against the world.

So when Sebastian's offer to gather for the game had come in, it had seemed like a no-brainer to go.

To his surprise, Coach and Scott were there too, a few days off from returning to Tennessee for a *very brief*, according to Coach, vacation before they got back to work.

"Maybe less brief than you're imaginin'," Scott drawled, exchanging heated glances with his husband.

"*La la la la,* I didn't hear any of that," Beau interrupted. "Remember what I asked? No more sexual innuendo within hearing distance."

Coach flushed. "It wasn't me! Blame Scott."

Beau's gaze narrowed. "Believe me, I do. I blame *both* of you."

But Julian could tell Beau wasn't truly angry, because then a few minutes later, he'd been deep in conversation with both his father and his surrogate dad, and he'd barely blinked when Scott put his arm around Asa and gave him a big smacking kiss.

Sebastian's apartment was packed with Piranhas players, and miraculously, they were all cheering when Jamie Wright drilled a fifty-five-yard field goal to give the Riptide a ten-point lead going into halftime.

"I wouldn't think you'd be rooting for them," Julian said to Pax as they filled their plates with the delectable-looking buffet Sebastian had arranged for the big game.

"For the Riptide? Hell yes we are," Pax said. "They . . . they started it all? Well, I can't say they *started* it, because O'Connor started it, but they sure continued it, didn't they? Yeah, they beat us, but damn they played a great game. I want to see them win the Super Bowl just for that. Next year?" Pax grinned. "Different story."

"You just want to see Heath and Sam make out next to the Lombardi Trophy again," Davis muttered as they settled back down in the living room.

Pax brightened. "I sure do. Every time we make a homophobe squirm, I'm here for it."

Davis laughed then, pressed a kiss to his cheek, and then they all sat back to watch Rihanna give an absolutely killer halftime performance.

When they were still clearing the confetti away from the field, Coach got up, gesturing to Sebastian to mute the TV, which he did.

"I have a few words I want to say," Coach said. "Frankly, Paxton said most of them, right after the AFC Championship, but I want to reiterate, this season is *not a loss*. Look at what you accomplished. Look at the changes you enacted in the NFL. Like Pax said, it doesn't just take one. The first paves the way, but that road is gravel. It's pitted. It's hard to drive over. But the more of us who follow, the smoother, the cleaner, the *easier* that road becomes. The more able we are to live our lives, and to play football. The Riptide made it possible for us. And think of what you're going to make possible for that next generation. So this is *not* a loss. I asked you, *why not us?* before the game, and I stand by that. Give us another year of development, and we can go toe-to-toe with any team in this league, I guarantee it. Your passion and your commitment mirrors my own, and I think with that dedication, the sky's the limit."

"Yeah," Logan called out, "you gonna kiss Coach Scott over the Lombardi next year, Coach?"

Asa blushed. "I can't guarantee that won't happen," he said carefully.

Everyone laughed.

Especially Scott, who looked smug as hell.

Julian couldn't really blame him, because loving and being loved in the kind of way he knew Scott and Asa did, the way he and Kenyon did, it was easy to be smug.

Because you were that fucking happy.

Happier than you'd ever imagined.

He glanced over at Kenyon, felt the warmth and the love in his gaze, and realized without even meaning to, he believed in him, he trusted him, he knew he'd be around forever.

The first one to ever stick, and the only one he'd ever cared would stick around.

It was miraculous it had happened with the same exact person.

"I've got one last thing to say, something that I've been asked to start to spread, quietly, throughout my team. There will be a lot of big revelations coming out, some really uncomfortable facts about a team that I know y'all are suspicious of. I was suspicious of them, too, from the beginning, because of how they treated one of our own. But now I have final confirmation from the NFL head office. The Condors are going to be forcibly sold."

Everyone's gaze immediately swung to Davis, who had a sheepish smile on his face. "What?" he asked, throwing up his hands. "Y'all think I didn't know this already? I was probably the first one they told."

"Tom Taylor is gone. Permanently suspended. There will be a new owner. New management. New coaching staff. A lot of new players. Rebuilt, from the ground up, with NFL supervision."

"Wow," Julian said.

"It's a long time coming," Coach agreed. "And hopefully, when they do rebuild, they rebuild in a better way."

"The Piranhas way!" Logan called out. "*Equality. Perseverance. Loyalty.*"

"I've been asked to consult, so that is extremely likely," Coach allowed. "But I'm just glad that the NFL finally decided to root out the problems. I have to tell you—that begins and ends with you guys. You set an example for the rest of the league to follow. And that means something. To me, as a coach. To me, personally. And I think to everyone else on this team." His gaze fell on Kenyon. "Even players who won't be with us, necessarily, it's something that I want to spread. To grow. To bring change. You were the first steps of that. So thank you, for your dedication, and your loyalty and your sacrifice. It's been an honor being your coach this year."

"Piranhas!" Logan yelled.

Kenyon glanced over at Julian. "Piranhas for life," he said softly.

And Julian knew what else he was saying.

Me and you, for life.

I couldn't dream of ending this series without one more dose of Coach, telling us how it is. (But this time, with the added bonus of Scott!). Download the bonus scene here.

For more of the irrepressible Banks brothers, you can also check out the first book in my new Charleston Condors series, *The Star*.

But before you do, I wrote a fun, quick bonus scene bridging the Piranhas and the Condors series – you can read it here.

INTERESTED IN READING MORE OF
BETH'S BOOKS?

CHECK OUT A FULL LIST OF TILES
BY SCANNING THE QR CODE
OR VISITING HER WEBSITE

WWW.BETHBOLDEN.COM/BOOKLIST

WANT TO FOLLOW BETH?

MAKE SURE YOU NEVER
MISS A RELEASE?

SCAN THE QR CODE BELOW
OR VISIT HER WEBSITE
FOR A SOCIAL MEDIA LIST,
NEWSLETTER SIGNUP,
AND SO MUCH MORE!

WWW.BETHBOLDEN.COM/ABOUT